Risky Restoration

A Novel

E.F. Dodd

Copyright © 2021 by E.F. Dodd

All rights reserved. This book may not be reproduced or stored in whole or in part by any means without the written permission of the author except for brief quotations for the purpose of review.

This is a work of fiction. Names, characters, places, and incidents either are the product of the author's imagination or are used fictitiously. Any resemblance to actual persons, living or dead, events, or locales is entirely coincidental.

ISBN: 978-1-954614-65-9 (hard cover)
       978-1-954614-66-6 (soft cover)

Edited by: Karli Jackson

Published by Warren Publishing
Charlotte, NC
www.warrenpublishing.net
Printed in the United States

To all the boys who gave me so many reasons to run, without whom I wouldn't truly appreciate the man who finally gave me so many not to. Love you, babe.

Chapter 1

"I have news," I said to Rae. She'd beaten me to Elizabeth's, a small Italian place conveniently located between my law office and her PR firm. As usual, we skipped a table, opting for the red-topped stools that lined a scarred wooden bar by the door. I slid onto the one next to her.

The worn leather seat molded comfortably under me, and I hung my purse on a hook beneath the bar. Scooching back, I took off my suit jacket and draped it on the back of the stool. The late summer heat of Charlotte had wilted my blouse, and I plucked it away from my skin.

"Let me guess," Rae said as she sipped her vodka soda with lemon and lime, keeping an eye on a group of twenty-somethings at the other end of the bar. "This has something to do with that clodhopper Roger you've been seeing." When she deigned to look at me, her long, brown hair tumbled over her shoulders. Despite the humidity, it remained sleek and straight, its rich chocolate color gleaming even in the dim light. The lines of her immaculately cut dress showcased the trim figure beneath it. Red heels accented the trendy black-and-red color block dress. Her outfit was on point, feminine, and powerful, much like the woman wearing it.

Her eyes narrowed on me. "I told you when you showed me his profile he wasn't right for you. The man practically had 'bland' written on his forehead." She shook the ice in her glass and curled her upper lip. "Plus, if he's six feet tall, my ass is a banjo."

Regan Murphy, Rae to her friends, was never one to pull any punches. It came easily in her line of work as a PR executive. She was a fixer of the highest order. The joke about lawyers was to bring us your problems and watch them expand. Her motto was Bring Me Your Problems and Watch Them Disappear. Whether it was an ex with illicit photos you wanted back or a less-than-carefully-thought-out tweet you needed eradicated from your social media history, Rae could get it done. At thirty-one, she was three years older than me, but she looked maybe twenty-five. Her youthful good looks led some people to underestimate her. Which then led to their ultimate professional demise when she used that to her advantage and outfoxed them before they even saw it coming.

As usual, she had not a hair out of place, and her makeup was flawless. I envied her olive complexion and her ability to endure humid temperatures that soared into the nineties without sweating like a wildebeest. I, on the other hand, had skin so fair it could be called translucent, and on a real Southern summer day, like today, had to apply deodorant at least twice and not just to my armpits. The walk from the car into the restaurant caused a remake of *A River Runs Through It* in my cleavage.

I separated a napkin from the stack in front of me. Lifting my auburn locks off the back of my neck, I dabbed at the dampness there. "You know, 'I told you so' isn't a very endearing sentiment. Some of us want more than ogling college boys like the ones at the end of the bar."

She sniffed. "Ogling is such a dirty word, Kesler. I prefer admiring discreetly."

I grinned at her schoolmarm snippy tone. "More like timing your strike. Those poor boys don't even realize they're on the menu."

Rae smirked, her green eyes twinkling. "By the time they do, it'll be too late."

"For all of them, or just one?"

"Remains to be seen." With one last look down the bar, she signaled the bartender. When he arrived, she said, "Hopefully, Kez is here to tell me she's finally wised up and broken the news to her latest mistake that they won't be choosing china patterns. Or, she's going to tell me she's still clinging to the remote possibility the man will become interesting. Either way it goes, we'll need booze."

"Of course," the bartender replied with an easy grin, used to Rae's unfiltered speech. "I'm assuming the third musketeer is on her way?"

I smiled. "Yeah, V should be here any minute." I'd met Vivian Walters, the third member of our little friendship trio, in kindergarten back in our hometown of Sawgrass, North Carolina. Our teacher had assigned seats alphabetically. With my last name being Walsh, we were thrown together without much choice. The two of us were as opposite as you could be: she was a petite, proper blonde from the stiff-upper-lip country-club set, and I was a gangly, loudmouthed redhead from a middle class, fun-loving home. Nevertheless, we'd become fast friends that year. Vivian and Kesler were a little too formal for five-year-olds, so we gifted each other with the nicknames Kez and V. The friendship, with nicknames intact, followed us into adulthood.

After Rae and I met at a creative writing class a few years ago, I introduced her to V, and the three of us formed a tight-knit group. Over the years, Elizabeth's had become our spot for midweek get-togethers. V's pediatric clinic was in the same office complex as my firm, and we normally rode together. But she'd had a late patient, so we'd taken separate cars tonight.

Jeremy, the bartender Rae flirted with on a regular basis, smiled back at me. "All right, a pitcher for three it is. You all want salt, right?"

At our nod, he turned to prepare what I knew would be an amazing pitcher of margaritas. Convenience wasn't the only reason we came to Elizabeth's. The booze was good and, by Charlotte standards, reasonably priced. Plus, the bartenders, especially Jeremy, were cute.

"So, what happened with Stodgy Rodgy?" Rae asked.

Before I could answer, a hand clamped onto the back of my barstool. "Hey, Red. Can I buy you a drink?"

Cringing at the unwelcome and wholly unoriginal nickname, I turned. The hand belonged to a guy in his late twenties who was not bad looking, until you got to the top of his head. Situated there was a baseball cap, with the unmistakable logo of the Buffalo Bills. Rae noticed it at the same time I did and coughed to cover her giggle. The smile on my face was more of a sneer. "Thanks, but I don't think so."

His toothy grin faltered, but his hand remained on my chair. "C'mon, don't be shy."

"Oh, I'm not shy, I'm just not interested." I pointed at his cap. "If you're a Bills fan, you're either an idiot or an asshole. I already know enough of both, so thanks, but no thanks."

His mouth dropped open and his brows lowered, giving him a dazed expression. "What the ..." He looked rather like he'd been poleaxed.

"Oh, honey, don't mind her," Rae cooed soothingly. "I can accommodate your interest just fine." Reenergized, Buffalo gave me his back and turned completely toward Rae. Now that there was a gorgeous brunette showing a modicum of interest, I was a bitchy footnote in his pickup-line history.

"Yeah?" he asked, with no clue about what he was stepping in.

Sitting forward, Rae walked her fingertips up his forearm. "Absolutely." Her voice dripped like honey, and she gave him her most alluring smile.

With one hand on the bar and the other on the back of her seat, he said, "Tell me more, beautiful."

"Well, first, I'd take you back to my place," Rae continued, making little circles on his bicep. She dropped her eyes and looked up at him through her lashes, the embodiment of seduction.

He swallowed, his throat moving quickly. "Uh-huh," he said. The man was a poet.

"Oh yes," she breathed. "Then, once we were there, I'd let you pick."

He was practically drooling by this point. "Let me pick what?"

I bit the inside of my cheek to keep from laughing at his eagerness. The guy was like a horny lap dog, desperate for a little pat from Rae. This was almost too easy. Easy, but nonetheless enjoyable to watch. I knew the punchline was coming in 3, 2, …

Rae licked her lips, drawing him in even closer. "Which jersey, silly."

Her words pierced the haze of sex she'd cast around them. Buffalo blinked in confusion. "Jersey?" he asked.

Rae gave him a bright smile, her hand on his arm. "Sure, I've got them all. Brady, Edelman, Sweet Feet …"

He ripped his arm away from her and shuffled back, confusion morphing to anger at being played. Rae wouldn't let it go. "Oh, you prefer someone from the defense? I've got McCourty's and Hightower's too. C'mon," she goaded gleefully, "tell me which one you like the best."

"You bitch," he mumbled and slunk off. Rae called after him, "Oh all right. I can wear the Gronk jersey! I know he's everyone's favorite! I'll even break out some old Super Bowl highlights!"

He flipped us off over his shoulder, and we collapsed into a fit of laughter.

"Three minutes! That might be a new record for you, although tag teaming the poor guy was hardly fair," V said from behind me. She had arrived at some point during our talk with the shallow end of the football gene pool. Her dark, tapered slacks and houndstooth shell complimented her honey blonde hair and creamy skin. She'd ditched the flats she wore for work in favor of black spectator pumps. Claiming the vacant stool to Rae's right, V's pretty face scrunched into a disapproving frown. With her hair twisted into an elegant braid and her big blue eyes, she looked like an angry Swiss Miss doll.

"C'mon," I implored her, "don't be a killjoy. Reminding Bills fans of their misery is often the highlight of my day."

Before V could reply, Rae said, "Never mind all that. Kez has news."

The two of them exchanged wry smiles and lifted brows. Simultaneously they said, "Roger," right as Jeremy delivered a pitcher and three glasses. I was at once irritated and relieved by how well they knew me. It came with the territory of being friends for years.

Rae looked at me. "Now that V and our drinks are both here, spill it, sister."

After we'd clinked glasses and taken our first sips, I launched into my tale. "Well, you're right," I said.

Rae grinned. "My three favorite words."

V shushed her. "You can gloat later. I want to hear this. Living vicariously through Kez's dating life helps keep me sane." Between a thriving practice and her uptight family's constant interference, V's sex life was almost non-existent. She rolled a hand in the air. "Go on, Kez. We're listening."

"Thank you," I said. "As I was saying, Rae, you were right. Roger, no matter how well-intentioned and polite, was a resounding dud." Roger Martin was an architect I'd matched with on a dating site V convinced me to sign up for. He was thirty-two and unmarried and had a kind smile and warm brown eyes. There were no sparks when we met for coffee, but he seemed nice. So coffee led to drinks, which progressed to dinner and somehow resulted in our seeing each other casually over the last few months. I'd finally gotten the nerve to break things off with him last Saturday. As with everything else, he'd been ridiculously nice and understanding. Which left me feeling like a bit of a heel.

"Girl," Rae said, "how did it take you all summer to come to that conclusion? I knew it the first time we met him for drinks."

"He was *nice*," I protested weakly.

"Nice is just another word for boring," Rae insisted.

I looked to V, who was usually the peacekeeper of our trio. She took a large swallow of her drink and averted her eyes, which was V-speak for "I agree with Rae, but I'm too polite to say it."

I sighed balefully. "I know, but I just thought things could …"

"Could what?" Rae asked. "Magically turn into something different?" She shook her head. "No, what you were doing was playing it safe, because the last time you didn't …" Her voice tapered off, and V pinched her arm.

"Rae," she hissed. "We don't talk about that."

"Ouch," Rae said, swatting at V's hand. "I know we don't talk about it, but it doesn't make it any less true."

"Funny you should bring up the thing we don't talk about," I said, and their attention snapped back to me. I produced a folder from my purse. Rifling through it, I pulled out an invitation. "See for yourselves, girls," I said, handing it over.

Rae took the piece of paper and scanned it. "Why am I looking at an invitation to a high school reunion for St. Pius Jesuit?"

V leaned over Rae's shoulder to read. "In Rochester?" she asked.

Smiling bitterly, I asked, "Who do we know that went to high school in Rochester? And also a huge Bills fan."

V's forehead crinkled as she mulled it over. "Well, I can only think of one person who …" Her brows shot up under her fringed bangs as realization dawned. "You're kidding!" she exclaimed. "You can't mean Miller!" Her drink sloshed over the beveled rim of her glass when she put it down with a loud clunk. Ever the lady, she dabbed at the spill with a napkin.

"Oh yes," I replied. Miller Thompson, my ex from law school. On paper, he was the perfect guy—a handsome Ivy League graduate with a crooked smile and a wicked sense of humor. His intellect was a close second to his good looks, and he seemed poised for a bright future. A future I'd thought would include me as Mrs. Thompson. News flash—it didn't. Instead, our lives diverged after graduation in a painful and drawn-out breakup four years ago.

But since then, I had a dirty little secret, really more of a guilty pleasure. One not even my two best friends knew about. I had developed a habit, a sort of ritual I'd undergo after each crappy date. After ditching my bra and changing out of tight but alluringly sexy to oversize and comfy, I'd pour a nice glass of wine and ... boot up my laptop. Into the search engine would go a name: Miller Evan Thompson.

It wasn't something I was particularly proud of, nor was it something I did every day, or even every week. But on those nights when a date hadn't gone well, or I'd spent time with guys like Roger—who'd never be anything more than a set of kind eyes—the need to see what was going on with Miller would be there. It was like a tickle in the back of my mind that would work its way forward until I had no choice but to put warm fingers to keyboard and see what I could discover. He had minimal social-media presence, so I rarely found much. He'd participated in the ice bucket challenge and a few other things, but for the most part there was nothing. This past Saturday, though, had been a different story. One that left me reeling in disbelief, followed quickly by the desire to break something. Each stroke of the keys and click of the mouse led me further down the rabbit hole, determined to uncover everything I could.

"How did you even get this?" asked Rae, flapping the invitation at me.

"I have my sources," I answered vaguely.

Tossing down the card, Rae crossed her arms and waited for me to elaborate. When I didn't, she smacked my forearm. "*How* did you get this?" she repeated.

"Ouch," I said, rubbing my arm. "Fine. His last post tagged a venue that piqued my interest, because it was so out of the norm for him. So ... I might have called in the PI firm I use to track down people who don't want to be served." I braced for impact as she digested what I'd said.

Rae's full lips flattened out into a thin line. I could see the wheels turning in her mind. Her career in PR made it necessary for her to always try to think three steps ahead. "You hired a PI to investigate your ex? Why?"

"Don't you mean stalk her ex?" V asked.

"That sounds so criminal, V," I said. "Plus, it's only called stalking if you get arrested or if you're following them around yourself. I hired a professional."

Rae said, "Let's not get tangled up in semantics, here. An ex's high school reunion isn't newsworthy. You wouldn't have tracked this down if there weren't something else out there. You've only given us half a loaf. Where's the rest?"

"Rae's right," V said. "What aren't you telling us?"

I opened the folder again and pulled out what had started me down the trail on Saturday, placing it on top of the invitation.

V picked up the printout, skimming it quickly. "Oh crap."

Rae snatched it out of her hand. "What? What does it say?" She read it as quickly as V had, her mouth dipping into a worried curve. Putting the page down, she said, "Oh, Kez, this is …"

Swiping my tongue over the flecks of salt on my glass, I took a big swallow. In the photo centered on the paper at Rae's elbow, my ex stood with his arm around a blonde woman, and the two of them smiled up at me from their engagement announcement. "Yep, it is. Right there in black, white, and what I imagine would be a tacky gold leaf on the actual announcement."

Looking between the newspaper clipping and the reunion invitation, V frowned suspiciously. "There's something else. I can smell it. What else did you find?" she asked.

This was the downside of being friends with a doctor and a business savant. They knew when you were holding out on them. Nervously, I ran my finger around the rim of my margarita, dislodging the remainder of the salt. I knew I had to come clean to them about my late-night, wine-fueled internet searches. Both that they happened and the reason behind them. "You know how sometimes in a spare moment, you'll Google an ex? Not expecting to find anything but just tempting fate a little to see what's out there?"

Rae's chin bobbed slowly. "A little internet roulette."

A weak smile lifted my lips. "Precisely. So, even before I got all of this stuff from the PI ..."

"You took a drive on the information highway that is the World Wide Web," V confirmed with a disappointed sigh.

My mouth went dry at the memory of the litany of information I pulled online. "The lady wins a prize!" I said with little humor.

"What did you find?" Rae asked, curiosity trumping her disapproval.

"The engagement was the mere tip of the iceberg," I said, taking a long swallow of my drink. The bite of the tequila was smoothed by the sweetness of the triple sec. The tart liquid eased the lump in my throat.

"The same one that sank the Titanic?" Rae asked sarcastically.

"That venue he tagged in his post? Well, their page linked me to HappilyEverAfter.com." I paused, gut churning at the memory. "I found their wedding web page." There'd been pictures of Miller and his future bride doing everything from hiking to cooking classes. Each image slashed at my insides like a razor blade, leaving me tattered and weak.

Rae's sculpted brows slashed down in a harsh V shape. "You're kidding me. Never took him as the type for that."

"Oh, I think *he* had very little to do with it." Irritation and hurt sharpened my voice. Taking a few slow breaths to relax my nerves, I pushed the folder down the bar to the two of them. "How about a little show and tell?" Unable to help myself, I'd printed out the "Photos" section from their website. I'd treated it like evidence I was gathering for a case. Evidence to prove what, I wasn't sure, but I'd compiled quite the little dossier.

Both of them went for the stack at the same time, but Rae was quicker.

"You girls see the story of how he proposed?" I asked, trying to sound light and unbothered despite the churning in my gut. There was one more piece to the puzzle I needed to give them.

Rae sorted through the pictures. "Not yet."

I signaled for the stack, and she slid it to me. I shuffled through the pile, quickly finding what I was looking for and passed it back. "Anything look familiar?"

V glanced down at the photo and sucked in a breath. "Well, that's a straight punch to the vagina."

I raised my empty glass in a mock toast. "You're telling me."

Rae looked at the page but didn't get the significance. "What am I looking at here?"

"My dear, you are looking at a picture from the costume party Miller and his dewy young bride attended the night he proposed. As you can see from the picture, they went with a group of friends as the characters from Gilligan's Island."

My captioning the picture was all she needed to understand. Rae's eyebrows shot up. "Didn't you ... ?"

A strong pulse of hurt throbbed through me, but I answered calmly, "We certainly did go as Ginger and the Professor for our first Halloween as a couple." It had been sort of an inside joke between us, given his reputation for scholarly answers in class. I'd jokingly called him the professor, to which he'd said, "Does that make you Ginger?" Apparently, the memory didn't hold as fond a place in his heart as it did in mine.

"Is that a red wig?" V asked as she glanced at the picture.

I topped off my glass. "Yes, yes it is. The young lady is a blonde."

Holding the picture between her thumb and forefinger like it was contaminated, she said, "So, he proposed to her while wearing costumes identical to the ones you wore while you were together."

"I'm pretty sure he's even wearing the same shirt," I said, ending the last word with a sharp *t* imagining the point of that *t* slicing into his heart like the pictures of him cavorting around with his fiancée had cut into mine.

V gulped. "Damn, girl." She dropped the photo back on top of the stack.

"Oh, it gets worse," I said darkly.

"How?" asked V.

"Remember right before he and I finally broke up?"

"Well, yeah. He moved back up north, and y'all lasted, what three or four months after that?" V squinted as she tried to remember.

Remembering the agony of that time wasn't difficult for me. Miller and I started dating the fall semester of our second year, and by spring I was hopelessly in love with the guy. Which was a new experience for me. Sure, I'd dated different guys here and there through high school and college, but nothing that had ever made my world stop and spin the other way like it did with Miller. He'd been it for me, and for a while, things had been wonderful. Foolishly, I'd assumed it would stay that way. I had visions of him in a tux and me in a flowing, white gown, followed by our welcoming beautiful, cherubic babies into the world who had his dimples and at least one with my red hair. All while we both excelled in our legal careers. Looking back on it, I see that multiple parts of that were pure, unadulterated fantasy, with the part where we stayed together being the biggest fallacy of all.

You see, we came from two very different worlds. I was born and raised in the South, happy to live out my life there and be buried in the family plot at St. John's Lutheran Church. Both college and law school had been a car ride away from my hometown. Charlotte had been an easy choice after law school because it was an hour away from the family homestead. That meant it was close enough to see my parents but far enough away that they had to call before coming to visit. V had made the same call for similar reasons.

Miller was the polar opposite, emphasis on the word *polar*. He was from upstate New York—Rochester to be precise. The only reason he'd come south was for law school. Had he not been waitlisted at Michigan, we never would've met. His residence in the Tar Heel State had an expiration date that coincided with graduation. A fact I studiously ignored during our time together. Surely, the two of us could work something out! We were smart people who were totally in love! How could we *not* stay together? The question I should've asked, but was too blinded by the stupid hearts in my eyes to even consider, was how *could* we stay together? He was diametrically opposed to moving south, as he'd told me on our third date. I was equally opposed to living my life in a place where sunshine was a rare gift nine months out of the year and it snowed every other Tuesday through June.

Despite all evidence to the contrary, I just knew he'd see the light eventually and decide to stay. Why wouldn't he? I was here and so was the sun the majority of the year. Job opportunities were more plentiful, and the economy was in a much better place. Every reason he needed to stay was there. Except, he didn't. May of our third year came, caps were tossed in the air, diplomas were bestowed, and he hopped the first flight back to New York. We made it six months before things imploded.

Miller was one of many in our class who hadn't received a job offer prior to graduation. The economy had soured our last year in law school, and the big firms were no longer tossing out associate positions like confetti at New Year's. So, he'd gone back to New York to take the bar and find a job. Never once did he ask me to go back with him. I had a job in Charlotte lined up after graduation, so maybe that was why. Maybe he was scared I'd say no, or maybe he never wanted me to come with him in the first place. I hadn't confronted him about it because I was too afraid of what he'd say.

The job market in Rochester had been as depressed as reported. Even with his impressive educational pedigree and after passing the New York bar on the first try, a true rarity, Miller couldn't land a job. Firms glossed over his undergrad and gave short shrift to his legal alma mater. A degree from our law school came with connections that opened doors down here, but that wasn't the case in New York. Each rejection hardened him a little bit more, the bitterness in his voice growing every time he told me. He found some contract legal work in document review but nothing steady. That type of work is drudgery of the highest order; hours spent reviewing monotonous documents another lawyer would use to either complete a transaction or litigate. With no prospects and a waning enthusiasm for his fledgling legal career, Miller turned to other pursuits, like rugby and booze.

Meanwhile, I was caught up in my own life with a medium-size civil litigation firm in Charlotte. It was a good job that let me use my degree instead of just a highlighter. I'm sure that sparked feelings of jealousy or maybe even inadequacy on Miller's part. The few times we saw each other after he moved never went well. I begged him to try and find a job down here, but he refused. He didn't understand why I took that refusal so personally, and I couldn't take it any other way. I wouldn't have cared if he'd moved down here without a job because at least then we'd be together. Miller had scoffed at the idea of being a kept man, despite knowing his prospects down here had to be better than there. Our fights got worse until finally, we broke up.

"Just over six months," I corrected V.

"But it wasn't like you severed all contact," said Rae.

"How could I forget?" V grumbled. "He would get absolutely wasted and call you at like two in the morning. Such a freaking loser."

"That shit went on *forever*," emphasized Rae. "He'd call, and you'd *always* answer. It was like you could only see the guy he'd been in school instead of the complete screwup he became once he moved back."

I couldn't deny it. I'd let the memories of what we had together cloud over the toxicity of what we'd become. I refused to believe something so good had become so awful. Which kept me trapped in the constant undertow of his late night calls and bullshit promises.

Unabashedly, I acknowledged they were right. "All true," I said. But you probably don't remember that he was on a rugby team," I reminded them.

"Ugh, yes I do," V responded with a shudder. "You dragged me to one of his stupid intramural matches when you were in law school." She'd shown up in all her preppy glory, cute plaid shorts and a white tank with low-top Converse. After the match was over, Miller and his teammates,—bruised, muddy, and bloody—had come up to the two of us. V's appalled reaction to the violent sport wasn't easily forgotten.

"Yeah, but that was here. I'm talking about after he moved back to New York," I pointed in the general direction of north.

"I sort of remember that," Rae said. She refilled her glass and did the same for V, returning the nearly empty pitcher to its place on the bar between us.

"His rugby team would always go to the same bar, McConnell's Pub, because it was one of the sponsors of the team." I tried to keep the anger from seeping into my voice as I thought about what had gone on there while I was down here.

"Okay," said V, her brows dipping in confusion.

"After a match, he would call me, usually drunk but not always. But he *always* called from McConnell's."

"So?" asked Rae, urging me to get to the point.

I jabbed at the folder, knocking a few papers askew. "Look at where they met."

Again, the two of them pawed through the sheaf of papers on the bar. I knew they found the answer at the same time because they froze for a second, then two sets of eyes met mine.

"She worked there?" V squeaked out.

I swirled the remnants of my drink. "Right behind the bar."

"So, she knew about you …" Rae's words faded.

This was the key, the final straw and harshest blow to my ego. Thinking about it ignited a slow burn in my chest that threatened to engulf me in searing flames of either anger, jealousy, or both. I was still too raw from my discovery to parse through exactly what I was feeling, only that I felt something and it was awful. "There's no way she didn't unless she was deaf, dumb, and blind. And what's worse," I slugged down more margarita, "*I* knew her too."

"You what?" V asked, aghast.

I nodded. "Well, I didn't *know* her, but I knew who she was. When I first saw the engagement thing, I felt like her name was familiar, but I couldn't place it, you know? Like, I knew I'd heard it somewhere or something but couldn't put my finger on where."

"Right," Rae said. "So, how are you so sure now?"

I slapped the papers on the bar. "It all clicked when I saw where she worked. I knew her name because I'd heard Miller say it before. He was always having people over at his apartment, and *she* was one of them. I never questioned it, but now … now I see what happened. That little tramp had her sights set on him the whole time! *She's* the reason things went to crap once he moved back."

"I don't think you can put all the blame on this girl," Rae said. At my venomous look, she held up a hand. "I'm not saying you're wrong about what she was doing. I'm just saying Miller played an equal part in it, that's all. If he'd gotten his shit together and his head out of his ass, maybe things would've been different. But he was too much of a punk to do either of those things."

"Maybe so," I said. "But this cowbird certainly didn't waste any time making herself comfortable in *my* nest!" Rejection and hurt burned hotly in my chest, choking off my words. I took a second to compose myself before I continued. "Miller was … God, y'all, he was everything to me back then. I fell so hard and so fast that when it was over, the hole was so deep, there was no way for me to climb out. And I didn't even want to try for a long time. Which worked for him because it meant when he'd get hammered and call me at two thirty in the morning, I'd answer the phone. When he'd tell me he missed me and still loved me, I'd listen and believe it. He'd say he could see himself playing in the backyard with our son while I watched from the kitchen window. All of that bullshit went on for months, and it just tightened the noose he had around my heart and pulled me deeper into that pit of misery. He would hold out these hopes of our being together when he knew there was no possibility of that."

"Kez," Rae began, wanting to deny what we all knew was the truth.

I wouldn't let her. "You know it's true, Rae. He was the first guy I ever loved. Even as things changed between us, as he changed, there were enough glimpses of the real him behind the anger and bitterness that it made me hold out hope. Hope that he'd snap out of it and come back to me. That we could build the life I'd envisioned for us. And when that didn't happen, when he didn't choose me, it broke me. There's no other way to describe what happened."

"Don't say that," said V, worry showing in the downturn of her lips. "You're in a much better place now."

I poured the rest of the pitcher into my glass as I thought about the *then* V hadn't mentioned in her praise of my progress. I'd not just blocked Miller's number, I eradicated all lines of communication between us. I even had the IT department at my firm figure out a way to divert his emails without my ever having to see them. I went cold turkey. It sucked, but then my life hadn't been a sparkling example of happiness before that either. For the first few months after I shut him out, I languished on the couch watching Netflix and comforting myself with Häagen-Dazs ice cream. I left the indentation of the cushion only to go to work and come home. It did wonders for my career. I billed the most hours of any first-year associate in the history of the firm. It wasn't as impressive a feat as it sounded. I used work to escape the devastating loneliness I felt without Miller. I filled the void he left in my life with work.

Rae and V finally had enough and dragged me out. I resisted at first, but then, I finally accepted the solace their friendship offered. I remerged into the land of the living, at least somewhat.

Finally, after a year or so, I tried dating. That experiment was still ongoing and less than successful; see Exhibit A—Roger. I'd met some nice guys, some cute guys, and some road trash that made me question the future of the human race. The common denominator between all of them was my tendency to keep things at arm's length, never allowing even the best of the bunch get too close. The idea of letting my guard down and giving someone a chance paralyzed me with fear. The walls I'd built to protect myself from heartache were equipped with booby traps that made them practically insurmountable. The possibility of being hurt again was too great, so I rarely had more than a few dates with the same guy. At twenty-eight, I was an emotional zombie, my soul shut down and vacant.

I sighed. "Just because I'm no longer in the break-up uniform of sweatpants and a hoodie doesn't mean I'm in a better place. I don't even think I'm *in* a place, just in limbo, unable to get on with my life. Which makes me wonder," I tapped the photos on the bar, "if Miller isn't feeling somewhat the same way."

"Uh, by getting engaged?" Rae asked skeptically.

I shook my head. "No, I mean, yes." I blew out a breath, trying to unscramble my thoughts and vocalize them in a way that both made sense and didn't make me sound completely nuts. "What I mean is, if this chick was in the picture when we broke up … if she's part of the *reason* we broke up, then why has it taken this long for them to get engaged? Is he doing this because he's moved on or because it's the next logical step? Is this really the decision he wants to make?"

"Okay," said V. "Say you're right. He's not wholly committed and just going through the motions. So what?"

This was the moment I'd been working up to all night. My brain whirred through the best way to drop the other shoe. To tell them the idea that had taken root in my brain Saturday night and continued to grow into a full-fledged, if somewhat unique, plan. This was going to be the most difficult part of the discussion. Neither one of them was going to sign on willingly to what I wanted to do. V had been there for the entirety of my relationship with Miller, and Rae had experienced the end and the havoc it wreaked in my life. I knew they'd have concerns about what I wanted to do, but I hoped they'd understand *why* I needed to do it.

I worked my finger across a divot on the worn bar and avoided looking at them. "I think I want to go up there." My voice was low and soft.

Rae choked out a laugh. "I'm sorry, what?" she sputtered.

Straightening my spine, I looked at my two friends. Their faces told me I'd been right about their reaction to what I wanted to do. And that I needed to come across much more certain. If I was going to convince them this was a good idea, they first had to see that *I* thought it was a good idea. "I said, I want to go up there," I repeated with as much confidence as I could muster.

Disbelief oozed from Rae's every pore. "To Rochester?" At my nod, she unloaded. "Why in the hell would you want to go to Rochester—it's an absolute dump! I mean their claim to fame is the freaking Erie Canal, also known as a giant ditch with water in it." With her crazed gesticulations, she bumped her drink, spilling some of it.

I picked up the now slightly soggy reunion invitation. "Because that's where the reunion is."

"How do you even know he's going?" asked Rae.

"I had the PI get a list of confirmed attendees," I said.

"Let me get this straight," V interjected, "next month, you want to fly to New York and crash your now engaged ex-boyfriend's high school reunion?"

"Not exactly," I said hesitantly.

"Then what *exactly*?" Rae asked. She drummed her fingers, waiting on my answer. The rat-a-tat-tat of her nails stood out against the background noise of the restaurant. It made me think of machine gun fire shredding my big idea.

Here was the big ask. I took a deep breath. "I was kind of hoping y'all would come with me." The request came out in a rush on my exhale.

Rae's fingers stilled instantly. She and V each bore horrified expressions. V looked like she could puke, and I sensed Rae was ready to strangle me. This was not going well. I had to make them see why I wanted to go.

I made my final pitch. "I'm tired of just shuffling around the shards of my heart. It's time for me to try to put it back together. And a key part of that effort is to see for myself that he's moved on. That this thing with her is real, not just checking a box in his personal life. If it is ... if he's one-hundred-percent with her, then maybe it will give me the closure I need. No more peeks into Miller's life through the internet, no more playing it safe with the Rogers of the world. I don't want to feel stuck anymore, hanging on to a memory instead of living. I want to move on. If I do this, then maybe I can finally close the door on that part of my life and get on with the rest of it. But I can't do it alone. I need you two with me." I held my breath, waiting to see what they'd say. I felt like it had been a pretty convincing plea, but I wasn't above throwing in a few well-placed tears to push them over the finish line.

Rae and V looked at each other, their faces inscrutable. With a sigh, Rae said, "I've always wanted to see upstate New York in early fall."

"Really?" asked V, blatant skepticism dripping from that single word.

"No, not in the least," griped Rae. "I remain convinced it's a shithole covered in snow eleven months out of the year. But there's no way we can let her go by herself."

V hesitated, her pretty blue eyes dark with concern. "I can't say I'm not worried about the fallout for you, Kez."

Rae clapped a hand on her shoulder. "All the more reason for you to be there to mop up after us. Just like always."

V vacillated for a few more seconds then gave in. "I guess that means I'm coming."

I smiled. "So, you're both in?"

Rae raised her glass. "Did you really even have to ask?"

Chapter 2

A month later, bright and early on a sunny September Wednesday, I left my car with the business valet at the airport. I wheeled my suitcase, saddled with an additional garment bag, behind me into the terminal. Packing for this trip had been impossible, so I brought essentially my entire wardrobe. The last thing I needed was to be without the one single item of clothing that would bring Miller to his knees, sobbing about the collapse of our relationship and begging for forgiveness. Okay, so I'd indulged in a few revenge fantasies, and glasses of wine, while packing. Sue me. Glancing around the ticket counter, I didn't see V or Rae, so I headed to the gate after checking my luggage. They were already seated at our gate, Starbucks coffee in hand.

"How am I the last to arrive?" I said, dropping my carry-on in the seat next to V.

Rae cut her eyes at V as she sipped her coffee. "Well, you were smart enough *not* to ride with this one." She elbowed V in the ribs. "Do you know what time she picked me up this morning?" Brown hair streamed out the back of Rae's baseball cap. She was in her typical traveling attire of Lululemon leggings and a fitted top. V was dressed similarly, minus the hat. Her blonde curls were pulled into a stylish low ponytail.

V rubbed her side where Rae had jabbed her. "You know I like to get to the airport early."

"Early is one thing. What you do is a whole other level. We've been here for *hours* ..." Rae whined. "Like, before they even started serving mimosas."

Her whining made me remember the night we'd met roughly four years ago when I moved to Charlotte after graduating law school. As a creative outlet, I'd joined a local writers' group that gathered a few times a month to exchange story ideas and critique each other's work. At my first meeting, Rae had strutted in like she owned the place. She snapped out a pithy response to a question the professor leading the meeting asked. Then she dropped into the chair next to mine and said, "I would legit cut off my left boob for a drink right now." We'd gotten that drink and many more over the years.

"You could have driven yourself, you know. Or called an Uber. No one forced you to ride with me," V said snidely.

I sipped the coffee V handed me and let the two of them bicker—my own female version of *The Odd Couple*. V was the good girl to Rae's bad. Whereas Rae unapologetically chewed through men like bubblegum, V was much more hesitant to get physical with a guy. She'd dated here and there, but nothing that really stuck. A lot of that probably had to do with her parents. They were the quintessential small-town Southern blue bloods. Unless he had either family money or some well-heeled profession that would provide an income well into, or over, six figures, no man was good enough to date their daughter. Ever the dutiful offspring, V always caved to her family when it came to the men she dated. The latest, Something Somebody the Third, was a complete ass, and she'd had the good sense to break it off. Her family didn't see it that way and weren't the kind of people to let it go. So while this trip wasn't a jaunt to the Caribbean, it would still be good for her to get away.

We'd all juggled our schedules to take a few days off. Our return flight was set for Sunday, but I'd set my out-of-office through the following Wednesday. If there was no emotional meltdown from this trip, I'd go into the office on Monday. If there was, I had the option of curling up on my couch with a case of wine and reruns of *Friends*.

Opening my own firm a year ago gave me a little more flexibility. It was a big decision to make so early in my career, but leaving behind the lifestyle of long hours for little glory had been the best choice I'd ever made. I still put in the hours, but they were my hours, billed by me for me, not some fat-cat partners up the food chain. It also freed me up to take the time I needed without having to justify it by billing triple the following week. With laptops and cell phones, I could work from anywhere if I had no court appearances. As long as I was responsive to my clients, I was in good shape. I wasn't footloose and fancy-free, but I didn't need to be in the office for the next week.

While Rae had an office, most of her work in PR was done outside of it anyway, so travel wasn't a problem. She'd made it abundantly clear the hardship was in the destination rather than the time away. A trip to a city whose culinary claim to fame was something known as a Garbage Plate was not on her bucket list. But she'd sucked it up and come along, even using her zillions of frequent flyer miles to bump us up to first class. Because beneath her tough-girl exterior was the heart of a true friend. Rae cared; she just didn't want anyone to know.

V's practice was the most regimented because virtual patient appointments were a little more difficult in her field of behavioral health pediatrics. While most people shy away from troubled kids, she gravitated toward them. During her residency her work with a kid who had a rare form of Tourette's had been the subject of an article published in multiple medical journals. I didn't understand half of what was in it, but I was still so proud of her. Given her cold and distant parents, V becoming a kind-hearted doctor determined to help even the most problematic child was miraculous. A lot of her patients required in-person visits, but since I'd dropped my plan on the two of them a month in advance, she'd had time to shift her schedule around.

I was an hour away from boarding a plane to Rochester, New York. The concept both thrilled and terrified me. I hadn't seen Miller in years. In moving thousands of miles away, he'd eliminated the possibility of any chance meeting around town. I couldn't run into him at the grocery store or the gym. By blocking his number and email address, there was no way for him to reach me other than showing up in person. There was a time it would've been easy to picture him outside my window with a boom box over his head, begging for another chance. But that was before his pride had taken over his heart and made the idea of him making any type of grand gesture almost laughable.

As with any heartbreak, the passage of time soothed the ache, but it was still there. The pain of Miller leaving me behind always lurked just under the surface—simmering and ready to scald me. I wasn't sure if I was still pining over him or pissed that *he* left *me*. And now, here I was, getting ready to jet off to Rochester. While I couldn't know what would happen when we saw each other, I knew I wasn't the only one carrying battle scars from our relationship. He might think I was crazy for just showing up after all this time, so I knew I needed to come up with a plan to handle our first encounter. No lightening bolts of insight had struck yet, but I was confident I'd figure something out. Nothing like a little pressure to make the creative juices start flowing.

My phone rang from the depths of my purse, the sound of my older sister Hudson's ringtone blaring loudly. In true Southern fashion, our mom had named us using our grandmother's maiden names. I debated declining the call, but that would just lead to a longer conversation later.

"Hey, sis," I said.

"Imagine my surprise when I called to ask you to lunch today and heard an out-of-office message on your work phone. Why is that?" she asked instead of saying hello. Hudson was a successful interior designer in Charlotte, having moved there shortly after college. Her presence was one of the plethora of reasons I'd chosen to live there.

"Because I'm out of the office," I answered. I walked away from the row of seats we'd claimed, seeking some privacy.

Her irritated sigh resonated in my ear. "Don't be a smart-ass, Kez. Where are you?"

"The airport," I said.

"Am I really going to have to drag this out of you?" she asked. I had avoided telling my family about this trip. If there was anyone who disliked Miller more than Rae and V, it was my mom and sister. Mama hadn't liked him from the start, convinced he'd find some way to get me to move up north and away from our tight knit clan. Hudson hadn't rolled out the welcome wagon for him either, telling me after meeting him she thought his arms were too long and his accent was moronic.

"I'm going up to New York with the girls," I said. "I'll be home Sunday."

There was a pause, then she said, "New York?"

I swallowed "Yep. V has a conference in the city and asked us to come with her." Looked like I was right about pressure sparking inspiration. Maybe this could be our cover story. I'd have to talk to the girls about it later.

"I see," she said. Suspicion crackled from her side of the phone. My sister always knew when I was lying. I crossed my fingers and prayed she would let this go. That her sister ESP wouldn't work well over the phone. Resisting the urge to fill the silence, I kept quiet. Finally, she said, "Well, have fun and tell the girls I said hey. Let's plan on lunch when you get back to town."

"Sounds great," I said. "Talk to you Sunday." I hated lying to her, but there was no way I was opening that can of worms. Hudson and I were close, but she was still my big sister, and I knew she'd flip out on me for going through with this. In her mind, Miller was permanently in my rearview mirror, so why tempt fate at all?

It would be easier to come clean once I got back home than endure a lecture about how this was a stupid idea.

"You good, Kez?" Rae asked.

Guilt for being less than truthful with my sister put another layer onto the complicated pile of emotions I had about this trip. "I guess we'll see in a few days, right?" I responded breezily. I didn't want them to see how freaked out I was. They might try and talk me out of going, and in that moment, I may have let them.

V opened her mouth, ready to unleash all her misgivings, but I held up a hand.

"I'm fine, V. I swear. Don't waste the mothering while we're still in North Carolina; save it for when I'll really need it." She closed her mouth but still looked worried.

After takeoff, V turned to me but said nothing. When she continued staring, I sighed. "What is it, V?"

"How exactly is this going to work?" she asked.

"Well, now that we're airborne, the captain will climb to cruising altitude, then ..."

"Stop it, Kez," she said, rolling her eyes, but the worry was still there.

"I'm just trying to answer your question," I said, adjusting my carry-on to avoid eye contact.

"No," she corrected, "you deflected and made a joke. You didn't answer the question."

Arguing with someone trained to spot the classic signs of avoidance was a real pain in the ass. Making it worse was that I couldn't deny she had valid reasons to worry. This plan was crazy at best and asinine at worst.

"Look, I wish I could tell you I've mapped this whole thing out in my mind, and I know precisely how things are going to unfold. But I can't, because I haven't, and I don't. All I know is that when I saw that engagement announcement, it was like my mind shut down, except for one thought."

"Which was ..." Her face made it clear she wouldn't find any thought I'd had on this subject to be rational.

"What do you think it was, V? Best wishes for your life together?" I said sarcastically.

"Of course, I know it wasn't that, Kez. But I'm nervous because you're going into this thing with no vision of the endgame."

"I can't guarantee how things are going to turn out—I know that. But that doesn't change the fact I need to do this. If he sees me and has the reaction of a cardboard box, then we get on the next plane home. If he sees me and realizes I was the best thing that ever happened to him …" I paused, then lifted one shoulder in a shrug. "Well, I'll cross that bridge if and when I come to it."

"More like nuke it," she muttered.

I laughed. "Maybe so. It's been years since I've seen him, so who knows what's going to happen?"

"I don't want you to crawl back into that hole, Kez. That was a tough time for all of us," she said somberly.

Even though she echoed my own second thoughts, I brushed her off. "I won't. I promise. Regardless of how this trip ends up, I'll still be standing at the end of it."

"I hope that's true," Rae chimed in from across the aisle.

I sent her a look, but she just jingled the ice in her glass because apparently it was five o'clock somewhere. We were barely airborne, and she'd already had a drink. How was that possible? I hadn't even seen the flight attendant. It wouldn't surprise me if Rae traveled with her own minibar.

Rae set her glass down, her face serious. "I didn't know you when you started dating Miller. I was only there for the end and the aftermath." She pointed at V, then back to herself. "We saw what that breakup did to you, what *he* did to you. The thought of you even dipping a toe back into that cesspool of dysfunction makes me anxious you'll get sucked right back under."

I refused to admit their concerns mirrored my own. "I've got you two with me to make sure that doesn't happen." I knew they weren't buying my attempt at reassurance, but before they could call bullshit on my false confidence, I hit the call button for the flight attendant. Rae wasn't the only one in need of refreshments, or, at this point, a numbing agent.

Once I had my drink, I let my mind sift through thoughts about the man who broke my heart. The first time we met popped into my head. It had been anything but romantic, but there'd been enough sparks to start a four-alarm fire.

*

Fall semester of my second year of law school, I'd gotten roped into serving beer at a charity auction. The public interest law association sponsored the event, so it was held at school. From the student lot where I parked, the lower entrance was the quickest way inside the building. Passing through the outer door, you entered a long, windowless hallway that led to a second set of solid, double doors, so you couldn't tell if someone were on the other side.

Since I was running late for my tenure as a glorified beer wench, I hustled down the corridor. Checking the time on my phone, I reached for the door handle. Just before my hand closed around it, the door flew open. With a scream, I jumped back, the edge of the door missing my face by inches. Standing in the doorway was a tall, good-looking guy holding a red plastic cup. One of his legs was still partially raised from where he'd kicked the door open. He was flanked by two other guys, and together they looked like a preppy gang clad in khaki shorts and pastel button-downs, each wearing the same bewildered expression. As though they couldn't fathom why someone else was on the other side of the door.

Even my rage didn't blind me to the shoulders filling out the lead moron's shirt. Those could only be the product of some serious hours in the gym. A glance at his face confirmed I'd seen him around campus, so I knew he was a student. Our class was small, only about 150 people who were then divided into smaller sections. This idiot wasn't in my section, so I didn't know his name.

Recovering from almost receiving an impromptu nose job, I caught the door before it could close. I yelled, "What is wrong with you?!!" His two friends edged away, but he had no qualms about squaring off with me.

"Uh, sorry?" he said. The low rumble of his voice held more of a question than a true apology. Lifting his cup to his lips, he took a quick sip of what I assumed was the beer I'd soon be serving.

My chest flushed with anger, an unfortunate side effect of being a redhead. I wasn't sure if the buzzing sound I heard was the fluorescent lights above us or my blood sizzling from being so pissed. Who the hell kicks open a door when you can't see who or what is on the other side? If I'd been just a little closer … "You do know you almost broke my face, right?" I asked. If I gritted my teeth any harder, I'd dislocate my jaw.

"That'd have been a shame with a face like that," he responded, giving me a teasing half smile. His blasé attitude only made me angrier. The nerve of this jackass!

My grip on the door tightened, nails digging into the wood to keep from smacking him. "What exactly are you saying? Because it sure doesn't sound like, 'Oh my God, I'm sorry I'm such an asshole!' "

Humor lit up his blue eyes as he grinned. He put his free hand above mine on the door and bent down so we were eye level. Then he winked at me. He freaking winked at me! This guy was unbelievable!

Even though he was crowding into my personal space, I didn't back up. Wishing I'd worn heels so he wasn't towering over me, I stood taller and threw my shoulders back. The movement made his eyes dip to my chest, then move back up to meet mine. Wanting to take him down a notch, I said, "I notice you didn't deny the asshole part."

Again with the shrug. "Don't think I have a great defense to that one." He let go of the door and held out his hand. "Miller Thompson."

Ignoring it, I pushed past him, my shoes slapping against the floor. "I'll be sure and let my insurance carrier know."

"So it's like that, huh?" he called to my back, refusing to let me just walk away.

Without slowing my pace, I said, "As if you really want it to be any other way."

With a laugh, he replied, "See you around, sweetness."

I gave him the finger over my shoulder and kept walking. The door clanged shut, signaling his exit. I hurried to the auditorium where the auction was being held. My interaction with Miller the Moron had made me even later.

I rushed over to the beer tables lining the far wall, making my apologies. The auction was in full swing, so they were busy. Once I'd reached my designated station, it was easy to fall into the monotonous rhythm of pumping the keg, pulling the tap, and serving. After topping off what seemed like my hundredth cup of cheap beer, I saw Miller one line over. His height made him easy to spot, and the crooked grin that sparked a dimple in his left cheek made him easy to watch. His smile showcased a small chip in one of his front teeth. That imperfection somehow made him more attractive. With a sigh, I thought, *"Too bad he's a cocky asshole."*

That was a common theme among guys in law school. It takes a special breed of type A personality to choose a profession where you are constantly at odds with someone, always trying to find a way to beat them. It requires a lot of self-confidence to deal with the fact that every day you go to work, there is someone out there who not only wants you to fail but also actively tries to make that happen because it means they win. It was no surprise the profession attracted guys who weren't just confident but entitled, egotistical asshats.

I glanced back to where he'd been standing, but he was gone. I felt annoyingly disappointed. Ugh, why did I care? He was a total ass, unworthy of a second thought. I squashed the feeling and reached below the folding table to get more cups. Popping back up, I found Miller as my next customer. He tilted his cup toward me.

"You can't be serious," I said, my hand frozen on the tap handle.

The dimple appeared. "What?"

"You expect me to serve you a beer?" I asked incredulously. Like I would be his barmaid after he didn't even apologize!

He looked around in fake confusion. "This is the beer tent, right?"

I nodded to the other lines. "You might have better luck elsewhere, but this keg is all tapped out."

Jerking a thumb over his shoulder, he said, "I just saw you pour that guy a beer."

Unmoved, I replied, "That guy didn't hit me in the face with a door."

"Neither did I!" He had the balls to sound indignant about it.

"Close enough," I snapped.

"Hey man," said the guy next in line, "either get a beer or get out of the way."

With a salesman's smile, Miller turned around. "She says the keg's tapped, bro." A collective groan went up from the people in my line. Shit.

I reached past Miller and took the guy's cup. "Oh, would you look at that? Looks like it's still good." I handed the guy his beer and smirked at Miller.

Undaunted, he slid between the tables to join me on the other side.

"Hey," I yelped, "you can't be back here." I tried to shoo him back around the table, but he refused. Instead, he sat down on the corner and crossed his arms.

"Scared you'll lose your liquor license or something?" His eyes seemed to always hold just a hint of humor, normally something I'd find attractive, but at that moment it was beyond irritating.

I shoved at his arm, but it was no use. He was ensconced, and there was no way I was getting him to move. "Get on the other side of the table," I growled at him.

The table protested as he shifted his weight. "There's another way to solve this, you know?"

My line was queuing up and people were starting to stare. The last thing I wanted to be was the subject of the school rumor mill.

Determined to keep my cool in front of all the prying eyes, I asked, "Oh yeah, what's that?"

He bent closer to me, mischief glimmering in his light blue eyes. "Well, if you won't serve me a beer here, how about you let me buy you a drink tonight?"

With another fruitless shove, I snorted. "Yeah, right." Like that was going to freaking happen.

Hopping off the table, he said, "Great, I'll pick you up at eight," and sauntered off.

I stood slack-jawed for a moment then recovered. "Wait, what? That wasn't me agreeing to go out with you," I yelled after his retreating back.

He turned and kept walking backward dimple flashing. "Eight o'clock, sweetheart."

"Ladies and gentlemen, we are beginning our descent into Rochester. Flight attendants, please prepare for landing."

I jerked awake.

"Welcome back, sleeping beauty," said Rae.

I smoothed my hair away from my face. "Guess I must have been a little tired. I didn't sleep much last night."

"Gee, got something on your mind?" V asked.

"Har, har," I replied, doing my best to dispel the memory of that damn dimple.

Chapter 3

We pulled up to the curb at the Hyatt Regency, the hotel hosting the reunion. Rae got out of the car and looked around cautiously, as though Miller were going to jump out from behind a streetlight and yell "Gotcha!"

"You know he doesn't know we're here, right?" I asked as I popped the hatch of the rental.

She continued her furtive examination of our surroundings. "I wouldn't be so sure. He had to feel the shift in the atmosphere once you landed in his hometown."

I started hauling out the luggage and placing it on the curb. A bellhop sprinted out of the hotel. "Let me get those, miss. I assume you ladies are checking in?"

I gestured to the bags overflowing from the back of the SUV. "Either that, or we're invading."

He smiled. "Staying with us for a while?"

"Through Sunday."

His eyes darted back to the SUV, and he reached for the mic clipped to his jacket when he saw how many bags there were. "You ladies go ahead and get checked in. I'll valet the vehicle and make sure all of this gets up to your room. Can I have a last name?"

"Walsh," I replied, passing him a twenty.

He touched his cap. "Thank you!"

V pulled her jacket tighter around her, shivering, while Rae rubbed her hands together then shoved them in the pockets of her pullover. Linking my arms with theirs, I pulled them toward the front doors. "Let's get you two delicate flowers warmed up."

"It's September," grumbled Rae. "How is it already this cold?"

"It's fifty-seven degrees, Rae. I think this is considered a heat wave." The few times I'd come up to visit Miller, the warmest it had ever been was seventy-five degrees. Our school schedule coupled with a lack of disposable income didn't allow for that many jaunts to upstate New York. After graduation, my job kept me busy enough that I couldn't get away but for a few weekends here and there, and we hadn't stayed together through the winter. Even so, I was pretty sure they considered the high fifties balmy.

She shuddered. "They're crazy."

Our shoes squeaked on the marble floor of the spacious lobby. At the reception desk, a young blonde attendant whose nametag read Kristi smiled. "Welcome to the Hyatt Regency, ladies. Checking in?"

"Yes, Kesler Walsh. I reserved a two-bedroom suite with a river view."

Inputting a few keystrokes, she said, "Yes, Ms. Walsh, I have you staying with us through Sunday, right?"

"That's correct."

"What brings you ladies to Rochester?" she asked, still looking at her screen.

Before I could answer, V blurted out, "Research." I arched a brow at her as I handed Kristi my ID and credit card.

"Yes," Rae agreed from my other side. "We're interested in the local rugby scene. We're in the process of determining whether or not to spearhead the effort to create some youth leagues back home."

"Mm-hmm," V nodded, warming to the topic, "depending on what we find out while we are here, we may even encourage some adult leagues as well."

I glanced back and forth between them, wondering when they had hatched this ridiculous cover and, more importantly, why we hadn't discussed it. I regretted not suggesting my conference cover story on the plane. But Kristi's eyes brightened. "Oh wow! That's cool! And, you're in luck!"

"We are?" I asked warily.

She handed me back my ID and card. "Yes, normally rugby doesn't get started until springtime," she said. Rae and V winced. "But with the reunion this weekend, they've arranged a special fall match. My baby brother plays on the team, so I'd be happy to give you all the details for it, if you want to go."

V asked, "Reunion? Like for the rugby team?" I pinched her under the counter, and she stepped on my toe in retaliation.

Kristi laughed. "No. It's for St. Pius, a local high school. They're holding it here."

"You don't say," said Rae. She sidestepped out of my reach and asked Kristi, "When does that start?"

Kristi's baby-pink nails flew over the keyboard. "Well, I think the first event here isn't until Friday night." She squinted at her screen. "Yes, here it is. There's a cocktail welcome mixer on Friday, with the main reunion lunch on Saturday." She looked up at us. "But the match is two o'clock tomorrow afternoon at St. Pius."

"How great is it, Kez, that there will be some events here to keep us entertained?" asked V with a saccharine smile.

"Peachy," I replied flatly.

"I'm going to the match with my mom and dad, so maybe I'll see you there." Kristi pulled a card from behind the desk, scribbled something down, and handed it to Rae. "That's my cell number, just in case."

Rae took the card. "Kristi, you've been such a big help. Thanks so much!"

"No problem, ladies," she said as she handed over our keycards. "We've got information boards over there." She pointed across the lobby to a tall pillar. "So, if you have any questions about where anything is or what events are going on this weekend, you should be able to find it there. But if you don't, let me know, and I'll do what I can to help you out."

"You'll be our first call, Kristi," V said.

Once the elevator doors closed and we were safely sequestered from the oh-so-helpful Kristi, I rounded on my two friends. "Rugby, really?"

"What? It got us the inside scoop, didn't it?" countered Rae.

I pinched the bridge of my nose, feeling a headache developing. "Rae, you told her we were coming up here to research whether to start a youth league back home—when it's not even rugby season!"

"What a lucky break about that fall game, huh?" asked V.

"I know, right!" Rae concurred. She looked over at me. "Kez, you pinch any harder and your nose is going to snap off."

Lowering my hand, I looked at the two of them grinning like cats who got the cream. "Ladies, other than the pictures from the wedding website, how much of that information on Miller did you actually read?" The elevator opened on our floor, and we filed into the hallway.

Rae answered for the both of them. "I guess you'd say we skimmed it, why?"

"Did you happen to *skim* over the part where it said Miller is the *rugby coach* for St. Pius?" That detail had been in the later part of the report. It wasn't as salacious a read as the wedding web page, but it was still important. Even more so now that they'd painted a picture of us as part of the rugby world.

V swallowed guiltily. "Um, no, I missed that part. I just assumed he was still doing that hourly contract work from before."

"No," I said, exasperation propelling me quickly down the hall. "He hasn't done that for a while now. He got this job last year, along with some administrative position in the athletic department."

Rae ambled along behind me. "So now we know where he'll be at two o'clock tomorrow."

I looked back over my shoulder at her. "Yeah, coaching your new best friend Kristi's little brother. What if she mentions something to her brother about us?"

"Why in the world would she do that?" asked V.

Reaching our room, I slapped the key against the electronic lock and yanked on the door handle. While I appreciated their enthusiasm, I was pissed at their lack of forethought. "I don't know, but if she does …"

Rae traipsed into the suite behind me. "You're being paranoid, Kez. Why would that come up?"

I dropped my purse on the table in the small entryway, her flippant attitude fueling my frustration. "In passing, Rae." I mimicked Kristi's bubbly cadence " 'Oh by the way, Bobby, at work today I met these three women who are looking into starting a rugby league where they're from. They might even be at your game tomorrow.' 'Gee, that's great, sis! Remember their names? I'll pass them along to Coach, so he can reach out.' And guess whose name she knows because it's the one on the reservation?" My voice climbed an octave as I finished my rant.

Immune to my hysterics, Rae moved farther into our suite. "Like I said, paranoid. No way that happens." She opened the drapes across from the main door, looking at the river in the distance. "Not bad. It's not white sand and blue water, but I expected much worse."

A couch flanked by two chairs surrounded a coffee table in the center of the main living area. To the right was a small counter with two stools, separating the kitchen from the living room. Rae stood in the dining area, which offered a table for four in front of the floor-to-ceiling windows. To the left were two doors, each leading to a bedroom.

I flopped onto the couch. "Rae, what if he finds out we're here?"

"Well, he's going to, right? Otherwise, this is kind of a wasted trip," said V from across the room. She began sorting through the suitcases the bellman had left against the wall separating the bedrooms.

My head fell back against the couch. "I know that! But him finding out I'm here with my two best friends posing as some sort of rugby ambassadors is not part of the plan."

V wheeled one of the suitcases into the bedroom farthest from the front door. "He'll never know," she said. "Plus, now we have an opportunity for some recon."

"Recon?" I asked.

V poked her head back out of the bedroom, snagging a carry-on bag. "At the rugby match, dummy." The impish smile on her lips made me worry what she had planned.

Pushing off the couch, I grabbed my luggage and followed her into the bedroom. Given Rae snored like a lumberjack, V and I would be sharing a room. Heaving my largest bag onto the remaining luggage rack, I asked, "What are you talking about?"

Rae came into the room, holding a vodka soda she'd mixed up from the minibar in the living room. I looked pointedly at her drink.

"I'm on vacation in *Rochester*." Disdain coated her words, and she tilted the glass toward me. "Alcohol is going to be my coping mechanism for this trip. Get used to it." After sitting gingerly on the queen bed closest to the door, she plumped up the pillows and leaned back.

V emerged from the adjoining bath and started hanging her clothes in the closet. "What I'm talking about, Kez, is the opportunity for you to spy on Miller while he's busy coaching."

"There's no way we can go. He'll see us," I protested. Following her lead, I unzipped my bag and started lifting out clothes.

"No, he won't," she argued.

"It's not like this match is in Gillette Stadium, V. It's a high school rugby field. There won't be tens of thousands of screaming fans to hide behind," I cautioned her.

"So, we hide in plain sight," she responded.

The stab of pain I'd felt behind my eyes in the elevator intensified. Ignoring my aching head for the moment, I focused on unpacking. "And how do we do that, Mata Hari?"

"With these," she replied. I looked up and choked out a laugh. V held up three wigs of varying lengths and colors. One was a chic blonde bob; the other two were longer and in differing shades of brown, one curlier than the other.

"You can't be serious?" But even as I asked the question, I knew she was.

She frowned and propped her hands on her hips, making the wigs hang from her waist in a bizarre-looking hair skirt. "Just because I don't support this plan one hundred percent doesn't mean I didn't come prepared."

"What about something a little simpler? Maybe just a hat and sunglasses?" I suggested.

She snorted derisively. "You really think that's all it takes to hide you? Please!"

I looked in the mirror above the dresser by the door. At five feet eight, I was taller than most women. My Irish coloring was unique, although something told me there would be a lot of other pale people in a place where it started snowing in October. What would stand out though, was my hair. Long, wavy, and red, it was a dead giveaway.

When my shoulders slumped, she knew she had me. "Brunette or blonde?" She twitched her hands, making the wigs shake disturbingly.

I took the straight-haired brunette wig with bangs. "I'm still not sold on this idea."

"Um, Kez," said Rae from behind me. "Speaking of not the best ideas ..." I turned and saw that while I was busy choosing fake hair, she had been going through my suitcase. She held up a red teddy and a matching robe. Jiggling the slinky fabric, she asked, "Exactly what part of your plan involves wearing this?"

I snatched the lingerie out of her hands and tossed it back into my suitcase. "V's not the only one who came prepared."

"Prepared to do what, exactly?" Rae asked sharply.

I shifted on my feet like a guilty child. "I'm not sure."

Rae pointed accusingly at the now-discarded lingerie. "*That* says you are."

"No, what that says is that I'm prepared for anything," I parried, but my heart wasn't in the denial.

"You're not planning on sleeping with him, are you?" V was horrified at the thought.

Instead of answering, I walked to the window on the far side of the room and looked down at the city below us. I didn't know why I'd included lingerie. Miller was engaged to someone else. Was I so twisted that I'd sleep with him knowing that? No matter what I thought she had done with him while he'd been mine, was I willing to go that far for payback? Had he kicked my moral compass that far off-kilter? I hoped not. Things had seemed much clearer before I got here. I'd believed my mantra of closure and moving on, but then … why had I included the lingerie?

V came up beside me. "You're starting to see you don't quite have a handle on this whole thing, right?"

Rae appeared on my other side and gently nudged me with her elbow. "But you know that regardless, V and I will be here. Whether it's hooking your garters or burying his body, we're in this with you."

V wrinkled her nose. "I'll leave the garters to you, Rae."

"That means you're stuck with the shovel," she replied.

I put my face in my hands and groaned. "What am I doing here? How in God's name is this a good idea?"

"I don't think anyone ever said this was a good idea," V reminded me.

"Look, if you don't want to go to the game tomorrow, we won't," Rae conceded. "We've got a day and a half to figure out a way into that cocktail party on Friday night. Or we can chuck the whole thing and head to the airport right now. I've got enough miles to get us to Aruba and back and still have some left over."

While I appreciated the offer, I knew running away wouldn't accomplish anything. The decision to come up here and face the fact that maybe he'd moved on was the right one. It might hurt, but it might also free me from the shackles of our past. I needed to go through with this. *Fully clothed.* "No, I'm not taking the coward's way out. I just need to get my shit together before two o'clock tomorrow," I said.

"So?" V questioned.

"So tonight, we drink!" said Rae, as she spun toward her room. "I get first shower!"

Chapter 4

The three of us headed across the lobby to the hotel bar. A whistle tweeted, and we saw Kristi walking toward us. "Don't you ladies look nice!"

V's hand glided down the side of her white bandage dress. "We do our best."

"Well, your best is pretty amazing," Kristi said.

"Thanks, Kristi." Rae cocked a thumb toward the restaurant. "Any suggestions for us?"

She tapped her chin with a finger as she considered the question. "The parmesan fries are delicious!"

Rae twisted the gold bangles on her wrist. "That does sound tempting, but I was thinking more along the lines of a drink order."

Kristi laughed. "In my book, you can never go wrong with tequila."

"You wrote my favorite book," Rae replied.

Kristi grinned at Rae but put a hand on my arm. "I'm glad I ran in to you though. I talked to my brother about the match tomorrow."

I felt the color drain from my face. "You did?" I squeaked. My heart thudded in my ears as I waited to hear whether the cat was out of the bag less than four hours after we'd landed.

She nodded. "Just to make sure there wouldn't be any issue with you getting in, since it's sort of a special event, and you're not alumni or family."

"How thoughtful of you," I said in a strangled voice. "And what did he have to say?" *Please, please, please don't say he mentioned us to his coach*, I begged silently.

"He said it was no problem. He even offered up a tour of the facility afterward, if you're interested." I thought my knees would give out, but Kristi giggled. "Not that the three of you would be interested in being led around a high school stadium and field house by a sweaty teenage guy."

Her pert nose crinkled at what was probably the thought of the smell of the field house after a game. "I mentioned you were really pretty, and he got superexcited. High school boys are disgusting," she said. Then she clapped a hand over her mouth. "Sorry, I shouldn't have said that."

V laughed and shook her head. "No need to put on airs for us, Kristi. We're all friends here." She winked. "Plus, I'm never going to be mad at someone calling me pretty."

Kristi visibly relaxed. "Thanks," she said. "His friends and their hormones are one of the reasons I moved out of Mom and Dad's place as soon as I could. Don't worry, though. I told him there would be no Mrs. Robinson fantasy in the locker room tomorrow."

"As much as it warms my old-lady heart to hear that we've still got it," Rae said, "we don't want anyone to go to that much trouble for us. We'll just keep a low profile tomorrow, if we even get to the match. No need for a tour."

Kristi's smile dimmed a little. "Oh, I'm sorry. I didn't think I needed to keep your visit under wraps."

V rubbed her arm. "Oh, sweetie, don't worry about it. You didn't do anything wrong. We just have other things on our agenda tomorrow that we'll have to rearrange to get to the match. But you didn't know that—no harm, no foul. It's not like we're on some secret mission or anything."

I tried to contain the hysterical cackle that threatened to pop out but could only mask it with a cough. "Sorry, I had a little tickle in my throat." Good Lord, if I was this disturbed by the mere thought of Miller finding out we were here, it did not bode well for when I finally saw him. I had to get myself under control. Otherwise, I'd dissolve into a puddle of nerves at the first sighting.

"Well, I know just the thing for that!" said Rae as she moved us toward the bar. "Thanks so much for the recommendations, Kristi, and all your help. We'll be sure to cheer extra hard for your brother tomorrow."

Kristi's smile regained its earlier wattage. "That's so nice. He's number twenty-four, Reid Pierce."

"We'll keep an eye out for him," said V.

"Okay, ladies, have a great night," she said, leaving us with a wave.

I exhaled a whoosh of air, my body trembling from the adrenaline release. "What was it you two were saying earlier? Oh yeah, 'How could that possibly come up?'"

"So I underestimated Kristi's helpfulness. My bad," said Rae as we entered the bar.

"And it's not like she told him our names," added V.

"You hope!" I replied shrilly. Forcing my voice lower, I said, "You don't know what she told baby brother."

"Just that we're hot." Rae grinned and did a triumphant little hip wiggle.

"Of course, that would be the thing you focused on," I said. We slid onto bar stools, and I signaled the bartender. "Three shots of Herradura tequila, please."

"Getting straight to it tonight, huh, ladies?" he asked with a smile. "I like your style."

"Most men do," purred Rae. With her elbows on the bar, she gave him a great view of her cleavage. His smile widened, and he backed away, keeping his eyes on her.

I poked her in the side. "Give it a rest." I couldn't blame Rae for her interest in the guy though. He was tall and dark haired, with wide shoulders and a slim waist. Dressed all in black, he was sexy.

"What? We're here to have a good time, right?" She watched the bartender as he made our drinks. Rae licked her lips. "Well, I'm going to call him Good Time, because he's what I'm having."

Once the shots were in front of us, I wasted no time taking mine, accepting the cold burn as it slid down my throat. To pull Rae from her lusty thoughts about the bartender, I said, "Can you please focus?"

With one last look, she said, "Fine, but you owe me."

"I'll get you two just like him when we're back home. How's that?" I said.

Tipping back her own shot, she smiled. "I'll hold you to that, Kez." Rae upended her empty glass and placed it on the bar. Rubbing her hands together, she surveyed the room. "Let's get a table and cut out the distractions." V's glass remained on the bar, still full of tequila. "Aren't you going to take that?" Rae asked.

V nudged it away from her. "Must I? Why can't I just get a glass of wine?"

"Wimp." Rae tossed back the last remaining shot and followed it quickly with a squeeze of lemon.

V shuddered. "I don't see how you do that."

"Years of practice," she replied, hopping off her stool. "Let's grab that table in the corner."

Once we were seated, a waitress appeared. "Hi, ladies, I'm Erica. I'll be your server this evening. Did you need some menus?"

V smiled at her. "Yes, please."

"Just drinks or dinner?"

"We'll start with drinks and go from there," I said.

She slid three single-page menus from her apron. "Here you go. I'll be back to take your order."

Rae turned to me. "So, what *is* the plan for tomorrow?"

"What do you mean?" I asked.

"I mean, what if you totally freak out and become a blubbering mess?"

"You're such a comfort, Rae ..." I said dryly.

As she lifted her shoulders in an elegant shrug, her dark hair fell forward over one of the lapels of her tuxedo-style jumpsuit. Impatiently, she flicked it back behind her. "You want comfort, get a dog. You want honesty, hang out with me. To manage a situation, I need to know what I'm working with."

I nervously played with a lock of my own hair, looping it over and over between my fingers. "I think I'll be fine, but we have to make sure he doesn't see us."

"Are you forgetting V's fabulous disguises?" laughed Rae.

"Yuk it up, smart-ass," V said, tossing her hair. Her gesture resembled Glinda from the play *Wicked*. It was easy to imagine V as the good witch and Rae as Elphaba, the wicked.

Rae held her hands up. "Don't get me wrong, V. I'm thrilled that we may be nominated for Best Costume after this little adventure, but why do the two of *us* need to wear one? It's not like Miller would recognize us from that far away."

Exasperated, V explained, "He's going to see us with Kez later at all this reunion stuff, Rae. Don't you think it'll be weird if he sees us at the game ..."

"Match," Rae said.

V grunted in irritation at Rae's correction. "At the *match* and then with her? Plus, even if he doesn't remember us then, he will once he sees us with her. My idea eliminates that possibility and allows us to observe without *being* observed."

Rae sat back in her chair and grinned at V. "You're like a tiny, blonde sleeper agent right now. It's kind of freaking me out. Admit it—you've been in deep cover this whole time and have just been activated."

The waitress reappeared with a bottle of wine and three glasses, only we had yet to order. "This is from the gentleman at the bar," she said. Intrigued, I tried to see around her shoulder but couldn't. She rotated the label of the bottle toward us, and I was shocked.

Rae noticed the label as well, and she, too, tried to see past Erica to the bar. "Who's sitting there, Bill Gates?"

Giggling, Erica said, "No, I think this guy is in town for that reunion here this weekend."

I shot out of my seat so fast, my chair slammed against the wall behind us, and I almost fell out of my heels. My lungs constricted as I searched the bar. When I didn't see Miller, I dissolved weakly back into my seat. Not the most inconspicuous effort on my part. I was going to have to do much better tomorrow.

Rae lifted a questioning brow at me, and I shook my head, letting her know the wine connoisseur wasn't Miller.

As though I were one of her clients who'd just made a public spectacle of themselves, Rae went into spin mode with our waitress. "Sorry about that. It's her first day out of the home, and she's a little nervous. You should see her when a car backfires," Rae made a diving motion with her hands, "shoots right under the table."

The young waitress took a cautious step back, but Rae winked at her. "Kidding! I'm kidding! Kez is just nervous because she's trying to avoid an ex. We've all been there, right?"

Erica exhaled. "Of course."

"Now, to keep from giving Kez here another heart attack, why don't you clue us in on who sent this over?" Rae instructed.

Without looking, Erica said, "Tall dark-haired guy in a white button-down, left end of the bar." All three of us leaned in unison, the epitome of smooth.

"Oh my," breathed V.

"Oh my, indeed," added Rae.

I said nothing, opting instead to just stare at him. A white dress shirt stretched across broad shoulders, its sleeves fitting snugly over impressive, but not steroid-induced, biceps. Beneath his cuffed shirtsleeves, tattoos wound around his forearms. Dark jeans sheathed long legs and covered the tops of scuffed boots. Even though he was sitting on a barstool, his feet were flat on the floor. I took in his dark beard, barely sprinkled with white. It wasn't made up of mismatched patches of scraggly hipster whiskers, nor was it pretty-boy stubble that never materialized into anything other than a slight shadow of scruff. It was an honest-to-God *beard*, thick and lavish—what a fully evolved man, not a boy, grew. Unruly dark hair curled over his collar. He stared back at me over cheekbones that could cut glass. This guy was sex on legs.

"I think you have something on your face, Kez," Rae said.

I snapped out of my stupor. "What?"

V giggled. "I'm pretty sure it's drool."

They high-fived across the table.

Amused, Erica asked, "Should I go ahead and pour then?"

Suddenly, it was like I'd walked a thousand miles across a desert my throat was so dry. Clearing it, I said, "Yes, please."

When she poured just enough for a taste, Rae said, "Unless you're in the habit of putting boxes of Franzia into bottles with that label, there's no need for a tasting."

Chuckling, she poured us each a glass and set the bottle on the table. "I'll bring some snacks over for you ladies, if you want."

"Is he one of them?" Rae asked as she nodded toward the bar.

"Please, Rae," said V. "That man is not a snack. He's an entrée, although the hair and the beard are a bit much for my taste."

"I'd settle for having him for dessert," I said.

Two sets of eyes focused on me. "Well, well," said Rae. "Look whose ovaries are showing!"

I raised my glass toward the bar and smiled at him in thanks. He returned the toast and drank from his own glass. A bourbon, I noticed, neat with no ice.

Tossing a few bills on the bar, he stood up and made his way over to us. My belly gave a little flip as I watched him walk over. It was more of a prowl than a walk. There was no strutting, just a languid movement of limbs that caught a woman's attention—this woman in particular. His long legs made short work of the space between us, and within moments, he was standing across the table from me.

"Ladies," he said. The deep bass of his voice thrummed in my ears and warmed my skin. It had been a long time since a guy had such an instant impact on me.

Rae looked around. "Where?"

He laughed and put his drink on the table, the tips of his long fingers resting on the rim of the tumbler. Inclining his head in the direction of the wine, he said, "I hope you didn't mind my sending that over." He lacked the blunted accent I expected of someone from the area, which made me wonder if he was from somewhere else.

"Not at all," said V politely. The slight wrinkle of her nose signaled she'd noticed the tattoos.

"Please, sit," I invited, indicating the chair in front of him. He folded down into it.

Looking around the table, he asked, "So, what brings three Southern belles this far north?"

"Awful quick assumption you made there," I said. Heat sizzled between us when he looked at me, sparking a low burn in my chest and other points due south. This close, I could see his eyes were a vibrant shade of blue. The amber liquid in his glass swirled as he spun it, his smile showcasing even, white teeth. My pulse ticked up as he regarded me from across the table. I needed to get a grip. He was just a guy. *A really, really attractive guy*, my lady parts pointed out helpfully.

"There's no way that voice, or either one of yours," he included Rae and V, "comes from around here."

"Guilty as charged," responded Rae. "We're visiting from North Carolina."

"That was going to be my guess," he said.

"Why is that?" asked V.

He crossed one leg over the other, resting an ankle on his knee. "It's where I live now."

Well, hot damn, I thought, then stopped myself. I wasn't up here to meet a new guy, but to get closure with an old guy. My mojo whispered, *No reason you can't do both*. Squashing that thought, I tuned back into the conversation.

"What part of North Carolina?" V was asking.

"Near Charlotte," he said.

Okay, universe, what game are you playing with me? I wondered to myself. In my out loud voice, I asked, "If you live there, what are you doing here?"

"It's my high school reunion this weekend." Oh, sweet Jesus—this was too much. What if he knew Miller? What if they were friends? Panic rose inside me as all the ways this could explode in my face flashed through my mind.

"Is it now?" asked Rae. Her green eyes practically glowed as she absorbed that little tidbit. "How interesting."

He sipped his drink. "Why is that?"

"We've just been surrounded by talk of this reunion since we got here," I said hurriedly. "I guess it must be a pretty big deal."

He fixed those glacier blue eyes on me, and my stomach flipped again. "I suppose."

"Did you come alone?" asked V. I kicked her under the table, but she ignored me.

"I did," he confirmed. "Although I'm meeting up with some friends that I haven't seen in a while."

"Your wife didn't want to come?" Rae pried with no shame. She must have left her Captain Obvious costume at home.

His teeth gleamed against the darkness of his beard when he laughed at her lack of subtlety. "Now, what kind of man would I be if I were married and sending a bottle of wine to a table of beautiful women?"

Rae tapped a manicured nail to the hollow of her cheek. "Hm, let's see. Oh, I know," she snapped her fingers, "just your everyday, average jackass. That's not you, is it Mr. ... ?"

He reached a hand across the table. "Jackson Jenkins, but my friends call me Triple. And I can assure you, I'm not average."

"Oh, well, just what any woman dreams of—an above-average jackass," she replied as she shook his hand. "I'm Rae, this is Kez, and that's V." She attached our names to each of us with a tip of her wine glass.

"A pleasure." He eased back in his seat in a way that wasn't a slouch but an indication of how comfortable he was with himself. Relaxed confidence rolled off him in waves, as did a raw crackle of energy that did funny things to my insides. To me, he said, "You never did answer my question about what brings you all the way up here."

I answered his question with one of my own. "Why do they call you Triple?"

He grinned. "Playing it close to the vest, I see. Well, if you're looking for something to do tonight, I'm going to Tonic with a few friends of mine. Should be a good time." His gaze was so intense, I felt the heat of it along my skin. "If you come, I might even tell you how I got that nickname."

"Tonic?" asked V.

Without looking away from me, he answered, "Yeah, it's a little speakeasy, nothing fancy, but it has good drinks and a decent band. You should come check it out."

"That sounds—" Rae began.

"We'll see. You never know what could happen between now and then." I said, trying to ignore flips and dips of my stomach.

"I think you'll show," he said bluntly, fingers teasing down the sides of his glass as he watched me.

"Oh, you do, huh?" I concentrated on keeping my breathing even and not showing any reaction to the challenge he'd thrown down. He might think he was God's gift, but I'd be damned if I'd feed into that by fawning over the man.

"Yeah, I do," he said arrogantly.

Even as I tried to resist it, I had to admit his confidence was sexy as hell. I felt the pull of attraction between us. This guy could be a player of the highest order, but I was sorely tempted to suit up for the game.

I propped my elbows on the table and tipped forward in my seat. "And why is that?" I asked, daring to maintain eye contact even though his were mesmerizing.

He mirrored my posture, narrowing the distance between us. "Because the promise of amazing is much better than the chance of average," he said and then drained his drink. Levering out of his chair, he tapped his forehead in a two-fingered salute. "Enjoy the wine, ladies." Giving me a last, sultry look, he added, "See you tonight, Kez." And with that, he walked off.

"Wow!" exclaimed Rae, fanning herself with a napkin.

V made a face. "Ugh, those tattoos and that beard." She looked at me. "Let me guess, those were the two things you liked best?"

V's observation was snooty yet accurate. Jackson had the look of a bad boy and the swagger to match, both of which piqued my interest. Again, I tried to bank the simmering coals left from the heat of his gaze, but resistance was futile. Jackson had stirred up a long-dormant part of me, and she wasn't going back to sleep without finding out if Mr. Jenkins was more than just a smooth talker with a pretty smile. We were going to Tonic. No doubt about it.

Chapter 5

"Are you sure this is the place?" V asked the Uber driver. She peered out the rear window, taking in the sketchy surroundings.

"You said Tonic, right?" he asked.

"Yes," I answered.

"Well, then this is the place," he confirmed, jerking a thumb at a building to the right.

In the back seat, the three of us exchanged a look. We were parked in front of a nondescript multistory building, with no signage or marquee to indicate anything about what it housed. The tinted glass front obscured the inside. A streetlight on the corner flickered anemically. It was a scene straight out of a horror movie, right before the three female leads made a really bad decision.

When we didn't get out, the driver angled back to look at us. "It's not a ritzy spot, but if you like live music and good booze, it's the place you want."

I opened the door. "What the hell ... you only live once, right?"

"Yeah, but I'd like my life to extend past tonight," V grumbled as she followed me out of the car. Leaning into the passenger side window, she said primly to the driver, "Don't go too far. You might be hearing from us shortly."

The driver chuckled and nodded, passing her a card with his information on it. "If you need a ride, give me a call."

"I was sold at good booze," Rae said as she joined us on the sidewalk.

"Of course, you were," retorted V.

Our reflections were wavy and distorted in the smudged plate-glass window. The smooth lines and crisp colors of the dresses V and I wore, together with Rae's elegant jumpsuit, contrasted sharply with the gritty area around us. Slowly, we skirted the larger cracks in the sidewalk and walked under the dark awning of the front door.

Inside, the ceiling of the lobby arched far above our heads with a large crystal chandelier adding a dose of unexpected elegance. Light from the multitude of candelabra bulbs sparkled across the plaster of the vaulted ceiling, illuminating the expanse of the room. Black-and-white tile flooring stretched over to double mahogany doors. A large man in a dark suit stood in front of them. Above his head a vintage neon sign spelled out Tonic.

The clickety-clack of our stilettos echoed throughout the room.

"Come here often?" Rae asked him when we reached the doors.

His rich laugh bounced around the lobby. "Ladies, first time here at Tonic?"

"Yes," I responded. "Someone suggested we check it out."

"That someone wouldn't happen to be Triple, would it?" he asked with a knowing grin.

Surprised, I said, "Um, yeah, as a matter of fact it is."

"So, that makes you Kez, I'm guessing." He eyed me up and down.

His blatant perusal and the fact he knew my name had me taking a hesitant step back. I asked, "And how would you know that? Not that I am either confirming or denying it."

Again, his laughter pealed out. "Well, if you are Kez, I have a table reserved. If you're not, then I'll need a cover, and you'll be fending for yourself." Looking down at my shoes, he said, "Something tells me you'll want the table."

Never one to turn down the opportunity to sit rather than stand, Rae inclined her head toward me and said, "She's Kez," then pointed a thumb to her chest, "I'm Rae," and with one more head nod she finished, "and that's V. Which makes you …?" It was his turn to be assessed as Rae looked him over.

"Rodney," he answered, his wide smile revealing a gold bicuspid. "Right this way." He opened the door and led us past a hostess station. "Guests of Triple," he said to the girl at the desk. She smiled as we passed, then returned her attention to the door.

The space was intimate. Well-placed, dimmed chandeliers hung from a tin ceiling above a wide-planked dark wood floor. There was a dance floor between us and the stage, around the perimeter of which was a smattering of tables. A few deep purple, velvet-lined booths hugged the wall to the right of the stage. On the left was a bar with four large upholstered squares evenly spaced in the wire-brushed wood front. The squares were the same purple velvet of the booths. Metal barstools offered additional seating for those not interested in a table or booth. Strings of Edison bulbs looped above the shelves of liquor. The antique lighting, coupled with the decor, provided a sexy, art-deco vibe. It was where you could linger over that last martini with your date's arm draped across the back of your chair. His fingers would tease along your collarbone, heightening the anticipation of what would happen when the two of you got home.

Rodney led us to a table in front of the bar near the stage. "Enjoy yourselves," he said and then headed back to his post.

The bartender, who was roughly our age, came to the table. He was cute, in a guy-next-door kind of way, with wavy blonde hair, dark eyes and a welcoming smile. "I'm guessing you're Kez?"

Rather than confirm it, I asked, "How does everyone here seem to know who I am?"

The smile on his face widened, revealing dimples in each cheek. "Triple hoped you three would be coming by. I'd about given up on you. But I guess what they say is true."

"And what is that?" asked V.

He squatted down next to her chair. "That good things come to those who wait."

V giggled and blushed, while Rae snorted. "They teach that line in Bartending 101?"

He clutched his chest. "You wound me, madam. I speak nothing but the truth and only from the heart."

"In my experience, that's not the organ bartenders use the most," Rae said.

"Maybe you just need a few new experiences," he said good-naturedly.

"How about you help me experience a vodka soda?"

"Absolutely," he said, his laid-back manner never wavering in the face of Rae's sarcasm. "And for you ladies?"

"I'll have a glass of prosecco, please," requested V.

"Should have pegged you as the bubbly one," he said, and she gave him a sweet smile. Looking to me, he asked, "What about you, Kez?"

"Tequila—make it a Herradura—rocks, with a twist of lime," I answered.

"Coming right up." He walked back to the bar, and V fidgeted with her necklace, trying not to get busted checking out his ass.

"He's cute," I said to her.

"Hm?" was her only response, and she focused on a spot past my right shoulder. It was a dead giveaway she was interested. Looks wise, the clean-cut blonde was just her type.

Letting her play dumb, I said, "The bartender. He's cute."

"Really? I, uh, hadn't noticed. Well, I mean, yeah, maybe just a little," she stammered in an adorable stream of word vomit. Oh yeah. My blue-blooded friend was hot for the blue-collar bartender—and had no idea what to do about it.

Rae scanned the room. "This does look like a pretty cool place."

It was an eclectic crowd, some folks dressed more casually than we were. But we weren't overdressed either. Most of the booths were filled, as were the tables. For a Wednesday night, the place was packed. Based on the exterior, I'd expected something seedy, but the clientele would've fit in at any of the upscale bars back home.

A door opened to the side of the stage, and the band began to drift onto the elevated platform. I glanced back at the bar, but a sharp jab from Rae made me turn around. "Ouch, what was that for?" Her eyes didn't leave the stage, so I followed her line of vision.

Another person had joined the other band members. A worn navy T-shirt had replaced the white button-down, displaying more of his tattoos. Picking up a guitar, Jackson strummed a few chords, making small adjustments. Hooking the strap over his shoulder, he threw a quick glance at our table, as if he'd looked a few times before and expected it to be empty. He whipped back once he saw it was now occupied, and a huge grin broke out on his face. He had a great smile.

The bartender reappeared beside Rae with our drinks. "Here you go, ladies. I'm Dave. If you need anything, just ask." Instead of going back to the bar, he tucked his tray under his arm and vaulted onto the stage. He gave Jackson the standard one-arm bro hug around his guitar.

Dave took the microphone. "Good evening, ladies and gentlemen. Thank you for joining us at our humble establishment." His intro was met with a round of applause and catcalls from the audience. Once everyone quieted down, he continued. "We've got a special treat for you tonight. One of our favorite sons is back in town this weekend and, for old times' sake, has agreed to dust off his guitar and serenade you good people." Behind him, Jackson shook his head, but a half smile pulled at one corner of his mouth. "Without further ado, please give a warm Tonic welcome to Jackson Jenkins, or as those of us privileged enough to call him a friend know him, Triple!" Again, the crowd erupted into applause, interspersed with whistling.

Jackson stepped to the mic. "Thank you. That was a lot to live up to, Dave. I'm just a hometown guy with an old guitar, so please, be kind." Laughter rippled through the bar. The drummer counted off, and Jackson began to play.

After a little while, V said over the music, "He's good!"

"I'll say," Rae added as she swayed with the beat.

I nursed my drink and watched Jackson sing, his fingers sliding effortlessly over the chords as he played. His voice rasped through the speakers and flowed around me. He wasn't just good, he was captivating. I found myself leaning forward, drawn to him and the raw quality of his voice. When he looked at me during the chorus of the song, a tingle danced down my spine.

Rae bent close to me. "You look like you're about three seconds from throwing your panties on stage."

I shot her a glare and stood up, moving toward the bar and away from Jackson. I *wasn't* here to meet a guy. Even if that guy was sinfully hot, could sing and play the guitar, and had excellent taste in wine. After ordering another drink, I leaned back against the bar and took a long swallow. The tequila coursed through my veins, threading warmth down all my limbs. My plan to put distance between me and Jackson by leaving the table failed spectacularly because his voice followed me over the sound system. It was rough and masculine while simultaneously soothing. The melody and the words he sang enveloped me. I could feel the pull of his stare, forcing me to meet it. That same potent energy from earlier hummed between us. I was the first to look away.

I stayed at the bar for the rest of his set. There was no question he was talented. The confidence I'd seen at the hotel was in full effect as he played and sang—an aura of self-awareness with a healthy dose of charisma. It no longer mattered that I hadn't come up here looking to meet a guy because the truth was I had. Now I had to decide what to do about it.

When the last song wrapped, the bar exploded into cheers, my friends included. With a smile and wave to the crowd, Jackson placed his guitar on a stand and hopped off stage. He moved through the room, stopping here and there to shake hands and speak to certain people. At our table, he leaned down to talk to my friends, both of them laughing. Soon, he headed my way like a heat-seeking missile. I slurped the last of my drink, spun around, and set my glass down with a thunk. I wanted to gather my thoughts before he reached me but didn't have time. I sensed his presence at my back just as two tattooed forearms appeared in my peripheral vision. Jackson's large hands gripped the edge of the bar on either side of me.

"You came," he whispered, his lips next to my ear. I faced him, bracing backward to put a little more space between us. Light from the overhead vintage bulbs let me see the sheen of sweat on his face. Long, sooty eyelashes any woman would kill for rimmed his eyes, and flecks of light blue shone from within the darker pools of his irises. Being this close to him was almost as intoxicating as the tequila. My palms were clammy, and my breath caught while my heart beat out an erratic rhythm. The hard edge of the bar bit into my back.

I ducked under his arm and signaled for another drink, all the while knowing that might not be the best plan. We probably should've had more than just the paltry bar snacks back at the hotel. "I heard there was a decent band tonight," I said.

He grinned, accepting the bottle of water Dave offered, and twisted off the cap. The plastic crunched as he drank half of it in two gulps. Placing the bottle next to my elbow, he said, "You look gorgeous, by the way."

I looked down at my royal blue dress. I'd chosen the halter style specifically for the way it highlighted all the right curves. "This old thing? I'm pretty sure you saw me in it a few hours ago."

Broad, calloused fingers flexed when he picked up his water, and I wondered what they would feel like on my skin. After another generous gulp, he said, "You looked gorgeous then too."

The compliment, coupled with his proximity, made my skin flush warmly. Trying to cool down, I avoided his gaze and looked back to my table. Rae and V were staring at us. Rae waved cheekily, so I flipped her off. She laughed and went back to talking to V.

Jackson touched my arm. "I'm glad you came tonight." His hand was so large where it rested on my bicep, his fingers wrapped almost all the way around my arm. He gave a gentle squeeze, making me look at him. I'd never met someone whose blue eyes could be called warm, but that was the only way to describe his. They weren't piercing or probing, but kind and caring.

I teased him. "I thought you knew I'd come."

He grinned. "I might've been a little more concerned than I let on."

"So, all that bravado back at the hotel was a bluff?" I picked up my drink.

Releasing me, he leaned against the bar. His forearm lay right behind me. The slightest movement on his part or mine made his arm graze the bare skin of my back.

"Not a bluff, exactly," he said.

Fighting the impulse to lean into him, I played with the lime in my glass. "If not a bluff, then what would you call it?"

"Offering Eve an apple?" His fingers brushed my side.

"Does that make you the devil," I smiled, "or just a snake?"

He chuckled, skimming his fingers up the back of my arm. "It makes me a man, Kez. A man who knows that getting a beautiful woman's attention requires something more than asking if you come here often."

"So, you think you have my attention?" I asked.

"The goosebumps on your arm say there's a pretty good chance I do, yeah."

"Maybe it's cold in here."

"The flush in your cheeks says otherwise."

"You've got an answer for everything, don't you?" I laughed, sipping my drink.

"Except what brings you up to Rochester," he said.

Well, shit, talk about a mood killer. How could I tell Jackson why we were here without sounding pathetic?

Deciding to just cannonball into the deep end, I huffed out a breath. "You know that reunion that brought you back to town?"

"Yeah." His one-word response was drawn out, encouraging me to go on.

This was going to be so awkward. "Well, we're here for the same one."

He snorted, obviously thinking I was joking. "Even if it hadn't been an all-boys school, I'm sure I would have remembered you in high school."

Ugh, this sucked. "My ex went to your high school," I clarified. His eyebrows knit together in a puzzled expression, so I babbled on. "We dated all through law school but broke up after he moved back here. Now, he's engaged to someone else."

He tilted his head, making a dark swath of hair fall across his forehead. Reflexively, he swiped at it and said, "How does that end up with you coming to the reunion?"

After a quick taste of tequila, I said, "Good question." He settled back on his heels and crossed his arms, content to wait me out. I couldn't help but notice the way the lines of his tattoos rippled with the flex of his arms. I wondered how far up they went, if the thick black streaks ended at his shoulder or stretched across his torso. *Not the time, Kez!* I berated myself silently.

Shaking my head to blot out thoughts of strong arms with dark ink, I tried to explain. "He was the guy I planned to spend the rest of my life with. That plan went to shit when, instead of staying with me, he moved back here, saying we could make things work long distance."

"I'm guessing that's not what happened." Jackson's arms dropped, and he tucked his hands in his pockets.

Clutching my glass, I said, "No, not so much."

He said nothing. The lights of the bar reflected in his eyes, giving them a haunting glimmer. I felt myself being pulled into them, my body unconsciously moving toward his.

A server set down a rack of glasses behind us with a loud thump. The noise jolted me out of the moment, and I looked away from him. My words tumbled out. "The whole time he was up here and we were together, he and his buddies would go to McConnell's Pub. He would call me drunk from the bar or drunk from the bathroom or drunk from anywhere in that place, moaning about how he still loved me and missed me and all this other crap."

"Okay, so ..." he said, still unsure what any of this had to do with how I wound up in Rochester. I was taking too long to get to the point.

"So guess who he's marrying?" I said, jumping to the conclusion. Jackson looked blankly at me. I tossed back the rest of my drink and choked on tequila and emotion. "The bartender from McConnell's."

"Wait, what?" He took my empty glass from my hand, placing it at the back of the bar.

"Yep." I shook a finger in the air. "That same bartender who poured him the beers he cried into about me is going to be his awful, uh, *lawful*, wedded wife." I swayed a bit, and Jackson steadied me.

"And you think his fiancée had something to do with the two of you breaking up?" Now he was getting it. Only to my inebriated ears, it sounded like he didn't agree that it was her fault.

"You're saying she didn't?" I asked belligerently, my hands fisting at my hips.

He put his hands up, fending off my pending attack. "I'm not saying anything. I'm trying to figure out how all that culminates in you being here for the reunion."

"I had to see for myself," I said, or quite possibly slurred, at this point. I regretted my decision to dive into this discussion without any preparation.

There was a pause, filled by noises from the crowd around us, then he said, "See what, Kez?" His voice was tender. He'd sidled closer to me, resting one forearm on the bar next to mine. We were close but not quite within each other's personal space. Hesitantly, he touched my shoulder. It was a light dusting of his fingertips but held the promise of more.

I swallowed nervously, still not looking at him. "See if he looks at her like he used to look at me."

"And if he does?" The rough pad of his thumb stroked gently against my arm, warm and comforting. At my lack of response, he asked, "So, you're still in love with him?" His hand dropped, and his voice lost its smoky undertone.

And just like that, the spell was broken. Angrily, I poked him in the chest. "Don't look at me like that."

"Ow! Like what?" he asked as he rubbed his sternum.

"Like you think I'm pathetic," I smacked a hand on the bar.

"I wasn't …"

I cut through his denial. "And to answer your question—no, I am not still in love with him. The whole point of this isn't to get him back." I thought of the lingerie Rae had pulled from my suitcase earlier. Well, so what? Even if things got to that point, I *wasn't* here to get him back. I was here for me—so *I* could move on. I wasn't here to revisit the past, lingerie notwithstanding.

"Then what is it?" Jackson asked.

I felt my cheeks heat with embarrassment. I really should have thought this through. "I … I want to get on with my life, but I don't know that I can until I see the two of them together and I know that it's real. If it is, then I … well, then I can finally close the door on it, on him, and on us." I looked at him. "That probably sounds stupid to you, huh?"

"Stupid? No." He let his eyes roam over me, leaving a trail of heat in their wake. My body hummed in response to the hunger in those blue eyes. "Actually, I'm wondering how his dumbass let you go in the first place."

Lacking a great response to that, I headed back to our table and Jackson followed. V and Rae were asking Dave for another round. After pulling out my chair, Jackson took the one next to it. He asked, "Having fun, ladies?"

Rae grinned. "Absolutely! Thanks for daring Kez to come out tonight."

He returned her smile. "I'd almost given up hope you were going to show."

She leaned forward conspiratorially. "Well, one thing you'll learn about Kez is that she doesn't make *anything* easy."

"You do know that I'm sitting here, right?" I asked Rae.

"And your point would be ..." she retorted, taking her drink from Dave. Lifting it to her lips, she said to him, "You're proving to be quite useful."

He gave a deep bow and set my drink in front of me. Saving V's for last, he slid her flute of bubbles across with a flourish.

Her coquettish giggle at his antics didn't escape Rae's notice and she said, "Maybe even more so than I thought."

V shoved at her arm but didn't deny it.

Jackson steepled his fingers in front of him and asked, "So did either of you try and talk her out of this plan? Or are you here as willing accomplices?"

Stunned by his question, V almost spit out her first sip. "You told him?"

I didn't answer, just squeezed the lime into my glass and stirred.

Rae sent Jackson a flinty look across the table. "What is it that you think you know about why we're here?"

"The three of you came to crash the reunion," he said simply.

Rae's smile was tight. "Jackson, you seem like a pretty decent guy or at least by your own admission, an above-average jackass, so I'm going to level with you. Yes, we came up here because Kez found out that her ex was engaged, but that's not the whole story."

Jackson slung his arm over my chair, grasping the slatted back and pulling it closer to his. He left his hand on the top rail, between my shoulder blades. Every breath I took made the ridge of his knuckles touch my back. I leaned into it, enjoying his hand on my skin.

Rae kept talking. "The three of us," her hand moved in a circle that encompassed herself, me, and V, "are are referred to in the wild as *independent women*. Strong-willed, take-no-shit women who don't apologize for knowing what they want and going after it with everything they have. As such women, it's hard to fall in love because it's a weakness. You're showing your soft underbelly to someone and giving them the opportunity to slit it open like a ripe piece of fruit. It's not something to take lightly or jump into quickly, but when you do admit those feelings and give into all that lovey-dovey crap, you go all in, just like in every other part of your life. You're committed for the long haul, to the vision of your future with this person and how it will look in twenty or thirty years. Because you are as driven to succeed in that relationship as you are in anything else. And you expect your partner, the love of your life, to be right there with you, investing as much sweat equity as you are in building a life together. So if you're down in the trenches, putting in the hard work required to make a relationship last, and then, out of the blue, the other person climbs out and kicks dirt in your face in the process ..." She stopped, leveling a meaningful look at Jackson. "That's a straight donkey punch to your pride, not to mention what it does to your heart. It hurts like a bitch and leaves a deep scar. And then, when that scar starts to fade, you find out he's engaged to some nitwit whose greatest talent is changing out a keg, well ..." she spread her hands, "that's how you end up in a bar in Rochester hanging out with the band. And what kind of best friends would we be if we hadn't come with her?"

Rae's story tracked mine, but it also sounded personal. In all the years of our friendship, she'd never delved into her romantic past. Any woman who avoided all discussion, good or bad, about their exes had to have one hell of a story. I'd always wondered what hers was, but she stonewalled every attempt to find out. She'd always been very anti-Miller, even though she'd only met him once or twice. I'd assumed it was just sisterly solidarity. He'd hurt her friend, so she hated him. But now, I wondered if it didn't run a little deeper. If Miller wasn't a stand-in for someone who'd failed to be the man she'd needed them to be.

"I can handle that," Jackson said calmly. He traced a finger along the top of my spine, right at the base of my neck. It was the barest of touches, but it sent shockwaves through my system. Letting that lone digit slide across my shoulder and down my arm, he shifted his chair so we were facing each other. The table fell silent. He took my forgotten drink from my hand and put it on the table. With a hand on either side of my chair, he pulled me toward him. My seat scraped across the floor, and my closed knees slid between his spread ones, the rough denim of his jeans chafing along my outer thighs. His large frame surrounded me. Everyone waited on him to speak.

When he did, his voice was low and rough. "I don't know what happened with your ex, but he sounds like a complete dick. I don't know anything about you either, Kez, other than you look *amazing* in blue. I can't say you don't have a good reason for the walls you've put up, but," his stare blazed a searing path over me, "don't expect them to scare me off or keep me out. You ladies aren't the only ones willing to go after what they want."

Well, hot damn. This guy was direct, which threw me off guard. My brain screamed, "Say something!" but my mind had gone blank. For once in my life, I was without words.

From the corner of my eye, I saw Dave motion toward the stage. Jackson waved in acknowledgment. "Looks like I need to get back to work." He stroked the back of my hand. "Stick around for the next set?"

Before I could answer, V said, "Oh, trust me—there's no way we're letting her leave now."

Jackson laughed all the way back to his guitar.

Once he was out of earshot, I blew out a long breath. "Holy shit."

"I'll say. He wasn't even talking to me, and I'm turned on," said Rae.

With trembling hands, I picked up my drink and chugged it in a few gulps. Fanning myself at the burn from the alcohol and the enduring heat left by Jackson's declaration, I said, "Interesting little synopsis you gave there, Rae."

"What?" she asked unflappably. "The man needed to know what he was dealing with."

"*I* don't even have a tight grasp on what he's dealing with!" I said hotly.

"Then I guess you'd better figure it out, real quick. Plus," her grin turned evil, "I didn't think you were up here to meet a guy."

I risked a look at the stage. Jackson caught me and winked. The magnetic pull that had started at the hotel was only getting stronger the longer I was around him.

Rattling the ice in her glass, Rae asked, "So, does this mean things have changed?"

I broke the staring contest with Jackson and looked back at her. "No, it doesn't change the main event, but it just might sweeten the after-party."

Chapter 6

"Ugh, V, where did you get these?" I asked, clawing at the nape of my neck. I flipped the visor down and peered into the small mirror, trying to get a look at what was scratching me. Without eyes in the back of my head, it was impossible.

"Are you sure you want to know?" In the passenger seat, Rae rubbed along her hairline, just under the front of the platinum blonde wig she had on. Against her olive skin and emerald eyes, the look was less incognito and more "Here I am." She'd apparently decided to forget the part of the plan that called for our going unnoticed.

"I'll have you know these wigs are made of real human hair, and they weren't cheap!" V smacked the back of Rae's seat. Her denials didn't keep her from running a metal nail file she'd pulled out of her purse around the edge of her scalp.

"So they threw in the scabies for free?" I asked.

From the back seat, V knocked my hand away as I tried to pull off the wig. "Stop! We finally got your ridiculous red mane out of sight. If you take that wig off now, there's no way we're getting it all back under there."

Sighing, I straightened the blunted brown bangs across my forehead and slapped the visor back against the headliner. "This better be worth it."

"Oh, I think it will be," said Rae. She'd given up monkeying with her wig and was looking out the windshield. Waggling her fingers at V, she said, "Hand me those binoculars!"

The three of us, dressed in jeans and casual sweaters, had parked on a hill overlooking the high school athletic fields. The residential street offered an unobstructed view of where the rugby match would start in about a half hour. Jitters careened around in my stomach like pinballs.

After scrounging through her oversize bag, V tossed the binoculars to Rae. "What? What did you see?" she asked, craning forward, squeezing her petite frame between our seats.

"More like *who* I saw," Rae replied, focusing the binoculars. "I think Miller just walked out of the field house."

"*What?*" I howled. The flutter in my belly turned into a roiling vortex. I grabbed for the binoculars. "Let me see!"

She handed them over, and I zoomed in where she directed. She was right. Miller Thompson was making his way to the sideline.

Thanks to V's spy-grade binoculars, I could tell he was in *excellent* shape. Wearing khaki shorts and what I assumed was a school-issued polo, he could've passed for a graduate assistant rather than the coach. He walked with the grace of an athlete, greeting people I assumed were the parents of some of his players. I waited for the familiar twinge from the summersaults my stomach used to turn at the sight of him. The burbling in my gut was still there, but it wasn't the same, and I wondered if it were more nerves rather than need. It certainly wasn't the zap of high-voltage electricity that sparked between Jackson and me the night before. But I wasn't naïve enough to completely discount the flutter in my belly, and I couldn't deny Miller was still hot.

"The least the sonofabitch could do is get fat," I mumbled under my breath. Was it too much to ask for even a hint of a paunch or a double chin? The man lived where Buffalo wings were a staple and blue cheese was a sacred condiment. Fat and grease were food groups up here, but he remained as fit as ever. Life wasn't fair.

Miller gathered his team and knelt in the middle of them. When he disappeared within the circle of high school boys, I lowered the binoculars to my lap. A loud buzzing sound next to my ear had me looking around the car. "What was that?"

"What was what?" asked V.

"That buzzing noise," I said.

"I didn't hear anything," said Rae.

Staying quiet for a second, I listened, but the noise had stopped. Dismissing it, I reached for the binoculars, only to discover a gigantic, disgusting bug with a zillion legs and twelve antennae crawling across them. "*Aaaaahhhhh!*" I knocked the binoculars to the floorboard.

"Jesus Christ, Kez," Rae said, clutching at her chest. "What is wrong with you?"

"There's a freaking prehistoric insect in here!" I said, my voice cracking sharply as abject fear took over my body. By hurling the binoculars to the floor in front of me, I'd given the creature an opportunity to crawl up my leg. My lungs seized, and black spots dotted my vision when I saw the rhythmic ripple of its scaly legs moving across my knee.

"Holy shit, what is that thing?" Rae shrank against her door, fumbling for the handle while keeping one eye on the beast.

I screamed bloody murder and knocked the monster onto the console. I groped frantically at my door, legs churning as I tried to run away while still in the car. In the midst of my panic, my foot slammed onto the gas pedal, revving the engine. V and Rae screamed. My foot slipped and got wedged under the edge of the pedal. Horror gripped me at the thought of being trapped in here with the king of the centipede underworld. Trying to wrench my foot loose only succeeded in jamming it further between the pedals. The engine roared with each jerk of my foot, and the buzzing increased. My terror level hit crisis proportions.

"Oh my God, you made it mad!" yelled Rae. We screamed again and tried to get out of the car. Pure fear overrode any ability I had to grasp the door handle and pull. My elbow connected with the horn and the loud *honk* almost made me wet my pants.

"OHMYGOD, OHMYGOD, OHMYGOD," V chanted from the back seat as she struggled to get out. She'd finally spotted the thing as it attempted to maneuver around the gearshift. "Do you have the child locks on?" she asked as she jerked on the door handle to no avail.

Miraculously, Rae got her door open and hurled herself out of the car, landing on her hands and knees. She scrambled to her feet and ran around the hood, opening both mine and V's doors at the same time. In my haste to get out, I forgot to undo my shoulder harness, and it choked me back into place. For a horrifying second, I thought the creature had me in its clutches.

"Seat belt!" Rae shouted, pointing at the nylon restraint. I slapped at the buckle, releasing it, and I tumbled onto the asphalt, leaving my shoe behind to fend for itself. I crawled away from the car.

V ran behind Rae, peeking over her shoulder. "Is it still in there?" she asked.

"Of course, it's still in there. There was no shadow blocking the sun as it flew away!" I yelled. The three of us stood there panting, waiting on the bug to hook its seat belt and drive away. I hated to lose that shoe, but I damn sure wasn't risking my life to go back and get it.

"What was that thing?" Rae asked again.

"The source of my nightmares for the next six months," quipped V. "God, it was disgusting!"

Our collective gaze stayed locked on the car to make sure we knew the moment the monster crawled or flew out to return to the primordial ooze from which it had spawned. My heart pounded, and I may have peed a little. I caught a glimpse of our reflection in the side mirror. Dirt smudged my knees, and my wig had been knocked askew. A sock hung halfway off my shoeless foot. Streaks of mud marred the sleeve of Rae's shirt, and gravel was caught in the stylish tears of V's jeans. We were a hot mess.

The Goliath of the insect world emerged onto the driver's side mirror. Mesmerized, we watched it spread its wings, which were only slightly narrower than a 747's, and lift off. I half expected it to seize the mirror with its talons and take our rented SUV back to its creepy lair. I swear to God the car shifted when the thing pushed off. It flew toward us kamikaze-style. Rae and I screeched and dove to the ground, while V dashed behind the car.

Pushing myself off the asphalt for the second time in a span of five minutes, I helped Rae stand. V popped up from behind the trunk. "Is it gone?" she asked tremulously.

Looking around to make certain, I said, "I think so."

"Good, then let's get the hell out of here before it comes back," said Rae. She walked over to the passenger side door and yanked it open.

After a deep breathing exercise to get our heart rates below three hundred, we drove to the stadium, finding a parking space a few rows away from the entrance.

Rae asked, "So, are we getting tickets and going in, or have we had enough excitement for one day?"

I killed the engine. "It's going to take more than a throwback from the Paleolithic era to stop me."

"What about a bearded guitar player?" asked V.

I shot her a glare in the rearview mirror. "What about him?"

She lifted a shoulder. "Seems to me he's a much better way to move on from Miller than staking out high school sporting events."

Rae adjusted her wig. "I tend to side with V on this, Kez."

I shifted in my seat to look at the two of them. I knew if I denied any interest in Jackson, they'd immediately see through that. I hedged a little. "Hooking up with a new guy isn't the reason I came up here."

"Even if the new guy is ..." V started.

"Amazing," Rae finished. "Time spent with Jackson has to be better than any more wasted on Miller."

It was a good point. After last night, I couldn't ignore the chemistry I had with Jackson. The night before, the three of us stayed through his second set, and when they'd finished, he and I got to know each other a little more. He'd moved to Charlotte to take a job as a CPA with a firm downtown. Finding that less than satisfying, he'd opened his own business. It could have been the noise in the bar or the endless stream of tequila I'd consumed, but the details of that business were a little fuzzy. It involved him working with his hands, that much I did remember. There was also some mention of his moving outside town, but again the details were murky.

He'd insisted on giving us a lift back to the hotel, saying he wouldn't feel right putting us into an Uber in a strange city. When we walked into the lobby, Rae and V headed to the elevator, but before I could follow, Jackson stopped me. He touched my elbow tentatively, almost as though he was worried I'd make a break for it. "Kez," he said.

"Yes?"

He moved closer, his arm stealing around my waist. On its own accord, my hand drifted to his shoulder. Under my fingertips, the soft cotton of his T-shirt stretched taut over toned muscle.

"I had a lot of fun tonight," he said.

I squeezed his shoulder, his amazingly *firm* shoulder. "So did we. Thanks for inviting us."

"Kez, I ..." His words drifted off.

"You what?" I asked, the question coming out as a whisper.

We stood inches apart, our bodies almost touching. With one gentle press of his hand, I'd be flush against him, a not-altogether-unpleasant possibility.

"I think you know that I'm attracted to you." He hesitated.

"Believe it or not, I *have* picked up on that."

Muscles flexed beneath my hand as he rolled his shoulders, as if readying himself for the next part of the conversation. "I know you've got your own reasons for being up here that have nothing to do with me. And I'm sorry that you went through all that with your ex."

And with that, just like the Holy Ghost at a Catholic high school dance, Miller Thompson wedged himself between us. I cleared my throat. "Yeah, well, I ..."

Jackson didn't let me finish. "What I'm trying to say is that while I'm sorry that happened to you, I'm also glad it did because it brought you here. And without that happening, I wouldn't be here ..." There was a heavy pause, then he said, "with you."

Now, normally I'm not a woman prone to swooning. Largely because it's not 1862, and I don't wear corsets, well, at least not out in public. However, between his words and his touch, I was dangerously close to needing a fainting couch.

"Jackson, I ..."

He smiled and brushed a kiss across my cheekbone. "Good night, Kez." Dropping his hands to his sides, he stepped back. "I think your friends are waiting for you."

Rae and V stood at the elevators, making no attempt to disguise the fact they were watching us. "Er, yes, right, well then, good night." I stepped away but looked back. "I'll see you, later?"

Still smiling, he said, "Oh, you can count on it." He walked away, and I stared after him because any guy whose ass filled out jeans that well had to be watched and appreciated. I hated to see him go, but I couldn't help enjoying the view as he did.

Pulling myself out of the memory of Jackson's lips skating across my cheek, I said, "Nothing's changed about why we're here, Rae. I need to get resolution with Miller—real, final resolution—before I can even think about anything else." Like how soft Jackson's lips felt. Or what they'd feel like on places other than my cheek ...

She raised her hands. "Fair enough, but be forewarned that over the next few days V and I are going to point out continuously there are over six feet worth of deliciously muscled reasons for you to turn this weekend into that next phase you keep saying you want to move toward. It can be a beginning not just an ending."

"Duly noted." I shoved open my door.

The field was circled by an asphalt track surrounded by chain-link fencing. The home side had stadium seating with concrete stairs and a brick concession stand at the top. A grassy knoll next to it allowed people to spread out blankets and watch the games. Across the field on the visiting side was a simple metal bleacher. Students and adults, probably some of the alumni in town for the reunion, milled around us.

We found seats on the home side with a good view of the sideline. Miller was talking to someone who looked like his assistant coach. There was a hint of salt and pepper in his hair, and a few more lines around his face since I'd last seen him. He was going gray prematurely. But instead of making him look old, it gave him an added sense of maturity, which was totally and completely unfair. He was clean-shaven, and even from this distance, I could see the muscles in his back shift under the shirt he wore.

Asshole.

Rae relaxed back, draping her arms over the bleacher behind her. She pulled a flask from her purse.

"Seriously?" asked V with a disapproving frown. While I might have had my share of nips from a brown bag when we were teenagers, V never indulged. She was as straightlaced as they came. She'd party but never partake. I think her parents had a breathalyzer at the door of her childhood home. It made sense for her to take a dim view of our imbibing at a high school, even if we were now of legal age.

"What?" Rae snapped. "If I'm going to be forced into multiple hours of staring at Miller Thompson, I'll need this. Plus, I'm pretty sure they don't sell beer here." She took a healthy swig and offered it to me.

I took a pull and choked on the fiery liquid. "Jesus, Rae, what's in there?" My eyes watered, and I fought to draw in a full breath.

"Whiskey. Jameson," she grinned.

V slapped me on the back to help my coughing fit. "Do we have to sit through this whole thing? I mean, you've seen him and haven't had a stroke, so now what?"

Wheezing, I gasped, "We still need to see if *she's* here." Once I could breathe normally, I studied the seats below us. A blonde woman sat in the front row. I nudged V. "Could that be her?" I asked, jutting my chin at the blonde.

She looked where I indicated. "Hm, maybe. It's hard to tell from this angle."

I craned my neck to get a closer look, stretching my upper body across V's lap.

"Gee, Kez, way to be cool about it," said Rae sardonically.

The woman was shorter than me, with shoulder-length hair. In a simple outfit of a white hoodie and light-washed jeans, she sat with her elbows on her knees. She was looking at Miller. When he turned toward the bleachers, their eyes met, and he smiled, lifting his hand. She waved back, and the light glinted off her diamond.

"Well, I guess that mystery is solved," said V.

"So it would seem," I replied. I didn't have time to react because when I shifted my eyes back to Miller, he was staring right at us. My heart leapt into my throat. Out of the side of my mouth, I asked Rae, "Um, is he staring at us?"

Her hand froze with the flask halfway to her mouth. Slowly, she looked sideways toward the field. "Certainly looks that way." She took a swig and capped the small bottle. "What do you think, V?" she asked.

V leaned close as though she were asking me a question, but side-eyed Miller. "Yeah, unless Charlize Theron is doing some sort of striptease behind us, I'd say he is."

I took another peek. Miller was now shading his eyes for a better look. His assistant tapped his arm and then, when Miller failed to respond, shoved his shoulder. Miller flinched and looked away from us.

"I'd say that's our cue to leave, wouldn't you?" I lifted my bag off the seat beside me, looping its strap over my shoulder.

V's hand on my knee kept me from standing. "Slow down, Kez. Wait until they're done with this time-out or whatever is going on right now. We want to make sure his attention is on the field, not us."

Seconds ticked by. I was sure he was going to lunge up the bleachers, but he remained in the huddle with his team. Once it broke, we gathered our stuff and, at the sound of the ref's whistle, hightailed it out of there. Walking quickly across the concourse, we were almost to the upper exit from the stadium when I heard "Ms. Walsh!"

Grimacing at my name being yelled across the stands, I saw Kristi making her way toward us. "So much for not being recognized," I muttered under my breath.

"You made it!" she said happily. She was decked out in full St. Pius regalia—a blue-and-white jersey with number 24 on it with the same number painted on her cheek. Blue-and-white ribbons tied the ends of her braided pigtails.

"We sure did," said Rae. She took in Kristi's outfit. "Don't you look … enthusiastic."

Kristi said, "I know it's a little much, but we're all really proud of Reid." She took in our own getups. "You look a little different today, too."

There was no way to explain our outfits that wouldn't make us seem even more ridiculous, so I kept my mouth shut. God must have been making up for the bug incident because Rae and V did too.

Noticing we were headed to the parking lot, she asked, "You're not leaving already, are you?"

"Um …" started V, looking longingly at the gate in front of us.

"You can't go yet! They've only just started," Kristi pleaded. "C'mon and sit with us." She gestured back to the area of the bleachers she'd bounded across. Seated there was your average all-American family, each wearing T-shirts emblazoned with the number 24.

"Oh, we wouldn't want to intrude," Rae said.

"Don't be silly! My dad will be thrilled to have more people in our cheering section. He probably has spare t-shirts in the car." She spun around, her braids arcing around her head, but Rae stopped her.

"That's so sweet of you, Kristi," she said kindly. "But we can't. I just got a call from my office about a situation that needs my immediate attention, so we have to get back to the hotel." Rae was the queen of spin, so Kristi bought the line of bullshit and let us off the hook.

We hustled to the car. As I unlocked the doors, V asked, "Now that you've laid eyes on the fiancée, what do you think?"

In the driver's seat, I reached up to run my hand through my hair, only to hit hair that wasn't mine. I tugged the wig off and tossed it and the skullcap we'd had to use to flatten my hair into the back seat. Bobby pins flew around me as I finger combed my hair. It looked like I'd stuck my finger in a light socket, but at least I was free from that god-awful wig. I twisted the long strands into a topknot and secured it with a clip from my purse.

"So?" V probed impatiently.

I said, "I thought I'd feel a lot more ... hollow when I saw the two of them, you know? Like I'd feel the loss of Miller all over again." I'd expected to feel some type of envy at seeing the two of them together—like she was the understudy who'd stolen my starring role as Mrs. Miller Thompson.

"You didn't?" asked Rae, shoving her sunglasses on top of her head.

I considered her question and how it felt to see the two of them. It hadn't been the gut punch I'd expected, but then, I hadn't had much time to react before Miller had looked dead at us. So I wasn't wholly convinced by my reaction, or lack thereof. I shook my head, drumming my fingers on the steering wheel. "In the moment, I was more worried about him recognizing us than I was upset about seeing them together."

"That's a good thing, right?" asked V.

"I guess," I said neutrally. I accelerated onto the street in front of the high school, anxious to put distance between us and the game. Realistically, I knew there was little chance Miller had recognized us, but I wanted to get the hell out of there anyway. I may have jumped headlong into a discussion about our past with Jackson, but there was no way I was going to do the same with Miller. I had to be prepared when I talked to him, so I wasn't taking any chances on him appearing in the parking lot.

"Well, I think it's great," said Rae. "We now know seeing the two of them together isn't going to make you curl into the fetal position and sob uncontrollably."

"Thanks for the vote of confidence." I merged onto the freeway that would take us back downtown.

"Tell me you weren't at least somewhat worried that could happen," she pressed.

Unwilling to concede her point, I said, "I'll agree that it's a good thing I didn't feel any truly murderous or suicidal tendencies when I saw them."

"I think we can all call that progress," V chimed in. "So next step is the cocktail party tomorrow night, right?" Her face poked between the seats like a kid. She held on to each headrest to keep her position and participate in the conversation.

"You know," Rae said, tapping a finger on her chin. "It might be a good thing if he thinks you were here today."

"How so?" I asked.

Her eyes glinted with excitement. "Well, it plants the seed, right? Gets him thinking about you. Then, you show up at that party tomorrow night all va-va-voom, and he's going to be reeling."

"Like he conjured you up or something!" added V.

Rae snapped her fingers. "Exactly!"

"Right out of his fiancée's worst nightmare," V said.

"Or his best wet dream," countered Rae.

V laughed. "You just had to go there, didn't you?"

"I have a special set of skills," Rae responded.

"Settle down, Liam Neeson," I said as I took our exit. "You may be onto something though."

"You know what would be even better?" asked V.

"I'm scared to ask," I replied, but I already had a sense of where this was going.

"If you showed up at this party with Jackson." V was getting sucked into Rae's plot. I could tell by the way they began to twitch excitedly in their seats.

"V ..." I huffed.

V put up a hand. "Hear me out before you say no. You wanted to know if he's really moved on, right? If this engagement thing is the real deal. Well, what better way to do that than see what happens after he sees you with another guy? Right now, he thinks he caught a glimpse of a brunette version of you. Then tomorrow he sees you at the party, but when he's on his way to approach you ... *bam*!" She clapped her hands together and slid backward. "He sees Jackson beside you."

"You, Jackson, and his eight-pack abs," Rae said and smacked her lips. I wasn't sure if she was salivating over the thought of Jackson's abs or Miller getting pissed. Knowing Rae, it was a combo of the two.

V continued, "Miller sees you, not just in all your gorgeousness, but with another guy ... *that he went to high school with*. It's like a double whammy. If that doesn't get you the answer to whether he's totally into the fiancée, nothing will. Plus, if she's really the reason behind the two of you breaking up, what's the harm in tossing a little payback into the mix?"

This idea was starting to make sense, which meant I was as delusional as the two of them, or it truly had merit. "You're saying play on his alpha attitude to get a true response?" I asked.

"Now you're getting it," she squealed, heaving herself back up between the seats. "If Miller's still hung up on you, it will make him insane to see you with someone else, especially in front of all his high school buddies. If he's not, then you're still at a fun party with a hot guy. There's literally no downside!"

"Unless Kez has some sort of weird fit after she has a real chance to see Miller and his fiancée without the distraction of getting caught," Rae said helpfully.

"Gee, thanks," I said.

"You have a better plan?" V asked.

Rae opened her mouth, but I jumped in. "A plan that doesn't involve skipping the reunion in favor of sexy time with Jackson?" I asked her.

"Spoilsport," Rae said with a pout.

"V's plan it is," I said.

Chapter 7

A purple envelope was in my study carrel with *Sweetness* scrawled across it in Miller's handwriting. Even after eight months of dating, I got butterflies when I saw it sitting there. There was steak in the shape of a heart on the front of the card. "Valentine, you're the sizzle to my steak." Inside were more food references: "PB to my J," "Mac to my Cheese," and the like. At the bottom he'd written, "Dinner's at 7, my lil' lamb chop. Don't be late."

The rest of the day I was giddy with excitement. Hell, I even smiled through Con Law and *no one* does that. At 6:59 p.m., I arrived at his house exfoliated and tweezed with a blowout to the nines, wrapped in a fire-engine-red dress with shoes to match. In keeping with the theme of his Valentine, I planned on being the main course. Opening the door, I caught the delicious scent of whatever he was cooking.

"Miller?" I called, closing the heavy, paneled door behind me.

He came around the corner of the family room wearing a Kiss the Cook apron over a dress shirt and slacks. Letting out a wolf whistle, he entered the foyer. "Hot damn, sweetness. You look good enough to eat."

I met him halfway and followed the advice of the apron. "Something smells amazing."

Grinning, he leaned down to kiss me again. "I'm pretty sure that's you."

Pushing him away, I laughed. "Cut it out. I was promised dinner and I'm here to collect."

He offered his arm. "Right this way, milady."

We walked into the family room. Miller shared a house with three other guys who were also in law school. They each had girlfriends, and I had it on good authority from the gossip queens at school all three would be out of the house this evening. The small house was the quintessential bachelor pad, which meant there was no dining in the dining room. There wasn't even a table in there, just piles of various sports equipment, gym bags, and other athletic detritus. Valentine's Day dinner would be served in the family room on a folding table topped with a red tablecloth and flanked by two mismatched lawn chairs. A single rosebud in a jelly jar sat in the center of the table. Taking my hand from his arm, he pulled out my chair and guided me into it. With a flourish, he snapped open my napkin and laid it across my lap.

"Such service," I praised.

"Only the best for my beautiful date," he said. Straightening, he pretended to read off a pad in a horrible French accent. "Tonight, we are serving grilled lamb chops with roasted fingerling potatoes and broccolini. Would the lady care for wine with dinner?"

Giggling, I nodded, and he plucked a bottle from beside the couch, brandishing it on his arm like a sommelier. "Does this vintage suit the lady?"

I examined the label in a pretense of evaluating the wine. "I think this will do nicely."

"Very good, miss." He uncorked it and poured some in my glass. "If you'll excuse me, I'll bring out the salad."

Before he made it out of the room, I said, "I need to know what's for dessert so I can save room."

Miller raked his eyes over me. I leaned back and stretched languidly, looking up at him from beneath my lashes. Striding back to me, he pulled me out of the chair and held me against his body. He ran a finger along the neckline of my dress. "I was thinking a strawberry covered in whipped cream."

I gulped. "Just one?"

His eyes darkened as his finger dipped inside the fabric. "Oh yes, my one single strawberry with nothing on her but whipped cream."

I startled awake and sat up in bed, looking around the dim room to get my bearings. It seemed I wasn't as impervious to Miller as I'd thought, given that vivid half dream, half memory. My subconscious added a few elements, but the dream was close to real life, especially the whipped cream part. That detail was seared into my brain.

V shifted in her sleep, and I glanced at the clock. It was just after seven on Friday morning. I knew I wasn't going back to sleep. After the rugby match, we'd come back to the hotel, all needing to catch up on emails and touch base with our offices. None of us were in a field where you could leave for days at a time without at least checking in. We'd opted to order in dinner and crash early, which explained why I was up with the sun today.

I slipped from underneath the sheets and ducked into the bathroom, grabbing my running gear on the way. I dressed and brushed my hair into a high ponytail. The door clicked softly behind me when I eased out of the bedroom, sneakers in hand. I hoped a good run would help me shake that dream without stirring up any more memories.

After getting directions on what route to take from the concierge, I stepped out into the sunshine. As I stretched, I thought about yesterday's conversation with the girls. I had to admit they were right. What better way to suss out the intentions of an alpha than to introduce more testosterone into the equation? Based on what I had seen of Jackson, with his confident swagger and self-assured belief that I'd show up at Tonic, he was definitely an alpha. An alpha I'd given my number but had yet to hear from. I remembered vaguely him saying he hadn't been able to get a room at our hotel, but I didn't know where he was staying while he was in town.

Even after our sexy little goodbye in the lobby, I wasn't sure how I felt about his cocky attitude. I didn't like being seen as a sure thing, especially when a guy had only known me a matter of hours. In the abstract, it was sexy for him to say he wasn't afraid to go after something he wanted, but part of me wondered if he wanted me because he saw something he needed to fix or a problem he needed to solve. But all that aside, I couldn't deny the burn of attraction between us, nor did I honestly want to. The heat between us was a palpable thing, obvious to anyone looking. There was no doubt in my mind *if* he accompanied me to the reunion, Miller would notice.

A long time ago, while we were still in school, Miller had *freaked* when I told him I'd been riding motorcycles with boys I knew from high school. He saw as competition guys I had known since we were in diapers, which begged the question, would that sense of competition still be there? Would he even care that I had a new boyfriend since he was engaged? And even better, would Jackson be up for filling the role? Hell, was I up to asking him?

I worked my way along the jogging loop recommended by the hotel—over a bridge, through a small park, then doubled back and continued down a marked running trail. To my left, benches lined the wide concrete pathway, while the river coursed choppily to my right. The turbidity of the water mirrored the tumult in my brain.

Lost in my own thoughts, I barely avoided crashing into someone. At the last minute, I saw a guy in front of me kneeling to tie his shoe. It was too late to stop, so I dodged off the trail and stepped right into a mud puddle. I slipped in the soft soil, my arms flailing, in a failed attempt to stop myself from falling. My downward progress stopped abruptly when the guy I'd almost run over caught my arms to keep me upright.

"Oh my God, I'm so sorry!" I said, taking out my earbuds while I took in the man I'd almost plowed into. Strong fingers held me, but the hands they belonged to were not those of a stranger.

Blue eyes sparked in recognition, and his grip tightened. "Kez?"

Shock trapped the breath in my lungs as I looked up at my rescuer. On an unsteady exhale, I asked, "Miller?"

He kept his hold on me. "Kez?" he repeated. The sound of the river rushing by mimicked the blood roaring in my ears. Miller and I stood there, transfixed by the happenstance of practically colliding with each other. My hands lay on his forearms, and we stood without speaking.

Miller was the first to break. "Jesus Christ, Kez, you look ..." He drifted off as his hands slid down my arms, and he gripped my fingers in his. "What are you doing here?"

"I'm, uh ..." I stammered, my brain struggling to catch up and give him any valid reason as to what on earth I was doing in Rochester.

When I didn't answer right away, he looked down at my mud-splattered legs. "Are you okay?" Bending down, he tried to run a hand over my calf. I moved back ... and stepped in the puddle once again. My soaked sneaker came out of the brackish water with a sucking sound.

"I'm fine," I said side-stepping his hands. I was so not ready for this. Our first meeting was supposed to be after I'd spent all afternoon getting glam, not when I had one foot in a mud puddle and my bedraggled ponytail was knotted with sweat. I probably looked like I belonged under the damn bridge, not running next to it. Dammit, dammit, dammit!

"What are you doing here?" Miller asked again.

"I'm in town with friends," I equivocated.

"Friends?" he asked dubiously.

I nodded like a bobblehead. "Yep." I took a step, and my shoe squished with dirty water. This was just freaking great.

Miller crossed his arms and blocked the path. "Where are you staying?"

"A hotel," I said, denying him any specifics.

His nostrils thinned as he took in an annoyed breath. Then his lips twitched into a grin and he said, "Knowing you, I'm guessing it's the Hyatt." Irritation flashed on my face, and his grin widened, showcasing his dimples and making my heart lurch a little. "Thought so," he said. "I'll walk you back."

"I know where the hotel is," I said testily. "And I don't need an escort."

"I insist. After all, I did almost make you bite it back there. It's the least I can do." He stood there, smelling like a mix of man, sweat, and aftershave. It brought back unwanted memories of him hugging me after rugby practice. The determined set of his jaw meant I wasn't leaving without him.

Resigned to his company, I let him lead the way. For a while the only sound was the squelch of my shoe. Perspiration darkened his gray T-shirt, and his athletic shorts hung low on his waist—the picture of masculine virility. There was a time not long ago when I would've dragged him behind a tree for some privacy. Now, though, there was no surge of need for his touch, only a dull pang in my heart. It was akin to when your foot falls asleep. It wasn't painful, but it was enough of a sensation to let you know something wasn't quite right. I'd expected more of the old feelings to resurface, the ones that I'd been so convinced were still there. The ones that had driven me to late-night internet searches. But again, this wasn't the most auspicious of circumstances, so it could've been my own self-consciousness that muted my real response to him. Or, it could've been my surprise in seeing him put me on edge. There were a myriad of reasons his presence didn't have my libido tap-dancing toward the nearest horizontal surface. I wasn't ready to pass on a diagnosis of immunity where Miller was concerned. That would take further exposure to confirm whether the little flutters I felt could be fanned into something more.

As we walked, Miller said, "You know, I could've sworn I saw you yesterday."

Fear clogged my throat. "Is that so?" I asked. "Where?"

"I coach rugby now," he said, sneaking a glance at me. Our arms brushed against one another as he allowed a man to pass by. I shivered at the contact. See, further evidence was needed!

"Is that right?" I asked, glad we weren't looking right at each other because I knew my face would give me away.

He nodded, shepherding me around a break in the sidewalk. I could tell he wanted to touch me, but he didn't. His hand hovered at my side until we passed the small hazard. My skin buzzed with a sensation similar to static electricity at his proximity. It wasn't the gravitational pull I'd felt with Jackson, but it was definitely something. Exactly what, I wasn't sure.

"We had a game yesterday, and there was a woman in the stands I could've sworn was you. I mean, she had brown hair, but there was something about her that made me think of you."

We reached the center of the bridge, and I could see the hotel up ahead. It took everything I had not to sprint away and end this conversation. I might have given in and tried, but with my luck, my wet shoe would have sailed off my foot and landed on someone's car. Giving up thoughts of fleeing, I said lamely, "Well, you know they say we all have a twin out there somewhere."

Miller rubbed the back of his neck before he answered. "Yeah, I guess that's true. But there was something ..." His voice trailed off, and he made a humming sound, searching for how to end the sentence. "Familiar, I guess," he finished. With the tips of his fingers, Miller touched my arm, as if he were checking to see if I were really there. Satisfied I wasn't an apparition, he said, "It's like I summoned you from thin air."

My laugh sounded more like a dying sea gull than anything resembling real amusement. Miller's words tracked V's thoughts from yesterday almost precisely. "Weird, huh?" I croaked.

"No doubt," he replied. Hopefully, he would chalk up my odd reaction to the randomness of our encounter. We stopped on the sidewalk in front of the hotel. An awkward moment passed, then he said, "I saw in the school newsletter you started your own firm. Congratulations."

Muscular arms came around me from behind, locking me into an embrace. "There you are, gorgeous! I should have known you'd start without me," said Jackson.

I jumped at the unexpected contact and slammed back into his solid frame. What the hell was he doing here? Wearing a moisture-wicking shirt and shorts, he was dressed like he was on the way to work out. Maybe he'd been on the way to the gym and stopped by?

Miller's eyes widened as he glanced behind me. "Jackson?"

"Holy shit," Jackson replied. "Miller? Long time no see, man!" One hand left my waist and reached toward Miller. *Wait a second, they* knew *each other?* The thousands of ways this could now blow up in my face flashed before my eyes.

Miller's smile didn't reach his eyes, but he shook Jackson's hand. "You in town for the reunion?"

Jackson's grip on my hip tightened, pulling me closer as he nuzzled my neck. "Yeah, it took some begging, but I convinced my girl here it'd be worth it for her to come with me and make me look good." Shock rocketed through me. *His girl?*

Miller's expression darkened as he looked from me then back to Jackson. "Your girl?"

Sheepishly, Jackson raised his head from my neck. "Sorry, I didn't mean to be rude. Kez, this is Miller Thompson. He and I went to high school together. Miller, this is Kesler Walsh, known affectionately to her friends as Kez."

Miller made a growling noise low in his throat. "We've met," he said stonily.

I turned to Jackson, with a look of disbelief. He grinned, and I was torn between being irritated and grateful for his appearance. To Miller, Jackson said, "Oh, sorry, man. I guess you met up on the running loop, huh?"

Rather than look at Jackson when he answered, Miller directed his gaze toward me. "Something like that."

Content to continue cuddling me, Jackson asked, "Did I hear you'd gotten engaged?"

Miller paled but kept his eyes on me. I steeled my reaction into one of indifference, waiting for him to respond. It was a little easier feigning nonchalance when I could lean back into Jackson. When I did, he adjusted his arms to encircle me completely.

Miller didn't miss the two of us melding into one another, and he moved his gaze to Jackson. "How'd you hear that?"

I felt Jackson's shoulders lift in a shrug. "Good news travels fast."

"That's funny. I haven't heard anything about you and Kez," Miller said snidely. His voice was frosty and laced with bitterness, nothing like the casual, relaxed tone he'd had as we walked toward the hotel. It was like he'd gotten a personality transplant when Jackson appeared.

"Well, like Jax said, my being his date for the reunion is a recent development," I said, finding my voice.

"Is it so recent that *Jax* doesn't know about us?" Miller asked. I didn't miss the way he said Jackson's name, as though it were some sort of communicable disease.

Not missing a beat, Jackson gave Miller a rueful smile. "Wait, you're the ex she mentioned when I said I went to St. Pius?"

Following his lead, I said, "Really though, what's there to tell, Miller? We dated about a hundred years ago, and then we broke up. Not much of a story, if you ask me. I'm much more focused on my future," I turned and curved my hand around Jackson's jaw, smiling, "than my past." I could almost hear Miller's molars grinding together. I added, "But I'm sure it's the same for you, right?"

He didn't respond, just kept staring at me. Finally, his lips cracked open into a pained smile. "It's good to see you, Kez. You look as beautiful as ever."

Self-consciously, I tamped down the stray wisps of hair that came loose from my ponytail. As I considered how or even whether to respond to Miller, Jackson pressed a light kiss to my neck. The feel of his lips sent tiny tremors over my skin. He grinned at Miller. "I can't understand how you ever let this one go, man. But I sure am glad you did."

Miller's smile flattened, and his hands flexed, as if he were deciding between grabbing me or punching Jackson in the face. Before either could happen, I spun around and put my hands on his chest, surreptitiously moving him backward. "C'mon, babe," I said with a not-so-gentle shove, "let's not hold Miller up any longer. Plus, I need a shower."

Jackson's eyes glittered. "Now there's an idea I can get behind." His hand slid from my waist to just above the swell of my ass. He looked over my head at Miller. "Good to see you, man."

Rolling my eyes, I pushed him, not so subtly this time, toward the hotel. He ambled away with a flirty wink.

Miller stood rooted to the spot, staring after us. "Kez," he called out.

I turned and waited.

In a low voice, he asked, "Who says I ever let you go?"

Before I could even wrap my brain around that little bombshell, a large hand closed over mine. I turned and found Jackson behind me. He smiled and pulled me against him. "Do you trust me?" he whispered.

"What?"

He tilted my head back and lowered his so we were less than a breath apart. His hands framed my face, thumbs stroking my cheekbones. "I said, do you trust me?" he repeated softly. The way our bodies were positioned, anyone standing behind me, including Miller, would think Jackson and I were kissing.

I didn't trust him because I didn't know him, but I was reluctant to break the spell of his touch. Rational thought was momentarily suspended while I looked into those cerulean eyes. His full lips were inches from mine, and I wanted to close the distance. Public displays of affection have never been my thing, but with my body pressed against his from chest to hip, I was warming to the idea. "Did you know you have little flecks of gold in your eyes?" he asked.

"What are you doing right now?" I whispered.

He angled his head, his lips next to my ear. The tickle of his breath was warm on my skin, and his beard scraped gently against my cheek when he whispered back, "Making sure Miller knows you're taken." Something inside me shifted with the low timbre of his voice and the feel of his palms against my face. In that moment,

I wanted to know what it felt like to be taken by Jackson Jenkins. Not as a part of a ruse or revenge ploy but in real life. To be *his*.

My hands reached toward him, right as he dropped his from my face and stepped back. He grinned down at me. "Guess Miller didn't want to stick around for the show."

Rattled from the almost kiss and thrown by the insta-lust his touch produced, I blinked up at him in confusion. "Huh?"

He pointed to the spot on the sidewalk where Miller had stood. He was nowhere to be seen. "Can't blame the guy. I guess I should be glad he didn't come over here and try to kick my ass."

Surfacing from the hormonal fog and quashing the tickle in my brain that wanted to explore the whole "wanting to be his thing," I pushed away from him. "What in the ever-loving hell was that?" I asked indignantly. The question might as well have been directed at me too. What was I thinking? I didn't even know this guy. *But you want to*, the annoying little voice in my brain pointed out.

He dragged me back to him. "That was me kissing my girlfriend in front of her ex to mark my territory and make him jealous as hell."

"Girlfriend? I'm not your girlfriend!" I denied, even as my inner voice cheered.

"That's not what Miller thinks," Jackson teased.

I rubbed my temples. "What are you even doing here?"

"I decided to take a chance this morning and come by to see if I could take you to breakfast. I figured I'd call you later if I missed you. Rae told me you went running. When I walked out the door, I saw you and Miller. It wasn't hard to figure out he was your ex."

"So you decided to pretend to be my boyfriend?" Crossing my arms, I gave him my most effective cross-examination stare. It was one thing for me to approach him with a plan, but he'd more than overstepped by charging in to rescue me. Even if it had proven useful and insightful, given Miller's response, that was beside the point. I'd been in control of the situation. Sort of.

His grin was cheeky. "Rae might have mentioned you girls added me to the plan."

Humiliated, I covered my face. "This is so embarrassing."

With a low chuckle, Jackson pulled my hands down. "Why are you embarrassed?" When my only answer was a groan, he tipped my head back, making me look at him. His eyes twinkled. "Weren't you going to ask me to be your boyfriend this weekend?"

"I had *considered* asking you to be my fake boyfriend, yes," I admitted begrudgingly.

He shook his head, determination shining in his baby blues. "Oh no, Kez. We're not faking this."

"What?" That little witch who'd been whispering in my brain also perked up, eager to hear more.

His expression turned mulish as he explained, "This isn't some dumb rom-com. I told you the other night—I'm attracted to you, which means I don't want to be your 'fake' boyfriend." He made air quotes with his hands. "If we're doing this, it's the real thing. A fortunate byproduct is it makes your ex, a guy I happen to dislike immensely, insane with jealousy. But you said you weren't interested in getting him back, right? And unless I've completely lost my ability to read people, it would seem that you *are* interested in me."

Again, his personality simultaneously grated on my nerves and made me want to kiss him. True confidence was sexy, but it was too soon to know if it was that or an inflated sense of self-importance fueling his repartee. I didn't want to feed a man's bloated ego, but I would also be lying if I said I wasn't attracted to him. *Very* attracted to him.

Jackson cocked a brow and waited for me to admit it.

Scuffing my shoe against the concrete, I relented. "Fine. I guess I'm ... interested." My inner voice broke out the pom-poms and the megaphone.

"*Interested*? Don't hurt yourself with all that enthusiasm!" He leaned down, his lips tickling the shell of my ear. "Let me see if I can convince you to give this a shot."

Another round of goosebumps rose on my skin, and my inner witch fainted from excitement. His mouth touched the delicate skin behind my earlobe, and my knees wobbled. As his lips moved, my body responded on autopilot. My neck curved, and my chin tilted, granting him better access. I felt his smile against my skin and the prickle of his beard.

"As much as I'd like to continue this," he murmured, "I'm not sure the sidewalk is the best place."

His words hurtled me back to reality. I scuttled out of his arms, getting some much-needed distance from the sexual tsunami that was Jackson Jenkins. My inner witch stirred from her sex coma and screamed in frustration. Hands on hips, I glared at Jackson, but I was more irritated with myself than him, even though the self-satisfied grin on his face *was* annoying. I had to stay focused on what brought me up here. Miller, not Jackson. *You need to focus on your future, not your past*, inner witch chided me. I mentally shoved a sock in her mouth and told her to pipe down.

"Pretty convincing, right?" he asked with a sexy smirk.

"Are you always this cocky?" I asked crossly.

Jackson spread his hands wide in front of him. "I'm pretty irresistible."

I scoffed and walked around him, heading into the lobby. "What you are is full of yourself."

He jogged to catch up to me. "Right now, Kez, I'd rather get you full of me."

"Do you even hear yourself right now? Plus, *I* don't recall asking you for any help with this weekend," I said. Even inner witch was starting to question whether she'd misjudged the situation.

His grin wavered. "Kez, I'm just joking around."

"Yeah, well, it's enough to make me rethink the whole idea of a *fake* boyfriend. Especially who I'd cast in the role," I snapped. Stopping in the middle of the lobby, I faced him. There was no smirk or arrogant smile, just concern in his blue eyes. "Sprinkling a little humility and respect into all that bravado would go a long way for you," I told him.

"Hey, now, hold on a second," he tried to defend himself, but I was good and worked up, so he was going to get an earful. Inner witch had her arms crossed and was tapping her foot and nodding along with me.

"No, you hold on." My index finger stabbed his chest. "I didn't ask you to come riding to the rescue today. You took that upon yourself, without even considering if I'd be cool with it. Regardless of what Rae or V told you, the person you needed to consult with is standing in front of you, and that consultation should've happened before, not after, that little scene with Miller. If you're actually interested in anything other than a little flirting at a bar, you need more than smoldering looks and thinly veiled innuendos. Right now, I'm not sure what else you have to offer."

His brilliant blue eyes were somber, and he took my hand. "Kez, look. I think we've gotten off on the wrong foot here. I can't rewind the past few minutes, but let me take you to lunch. Give me a chance to show you I'm more than just a pretty face with a smart mouth."

"Give me a reason to," I countered.

"You don't give a single inch, do you?" he asked with a chuckle.

"Give me a reason to," I repeated.

Jackson threw his head back and laughed loudly, drawing the attention of several hotel guests. Looking down at me he said, "I'll prove it to you."

"Prove *what* to me?"

"That taking a chance on me will be the best decision you've ever made."

"I still think you're pretty full of yourself," I said, but my reservations were waning. Inner witch was already planning an outfit to wear on a date.

"That's not a no," he said.

After our earlier performance on the sidewalk, I knew going to the reunion without Jackson wasn't an option. No matter what I'd just said to Jackson, there was no way I could go with anyone but him. And, if I went, I had to at least know enough about him to make our appearance together plausible. And there was that tiny little part of me that *wanted* to see if there was more to this guy. If the attraction I felt for him could extend past wanting to feel his lips against my skin again. I sighed. "Fine, I'll have lunch with you."

His lips curled up. "Perfect. Now about that shower …"

Chapter 8

"So tell me all there is to know about Kez Walsh," Jackson said.

After sending my filthy shoes to get cleaned and taking a quick shower, *alone*, I met Jackson for lunch at the Blu Wolf Bistro. He kicked back in his chair, in what I was beginning to recognize as his signature slouch.

Those enjoying the weather I'm sure they saw as mild filled the tables on the patio. Given that I didn't share their sentiments, Jackson had gotten us a table inside. Wide windows under blue awnings provided a view of the busy street. Televisions blared everything from soccer to a basketball game from the 1970s.

I lifted a frosty mug of beer to my lips, looking at Jackson over the rim. "Not until you tell me why they call you Triple."

He grinned. "Easy—Jackson James Jenkins. Three *J*'s, so Triple. Your turn—give me the rundown on Kez Walsh."

I gave him the basics—small-town girl who'd gone to law school and started her legal career with a firm in Charlotte. Disillusioned with the politics and bullshit, I struck out on my own. With a lot of hustle and several boxes of antacids, I'd made a go of it. I now had a stable client base who valued the personal attention I provided.

"What about your personal life?" he asked. "It can't be all work and no play."

"You must not know many lawyers," I joked.

"Normally, I try to avoid them," Jackson said. "After meeting you, that's no longer the case."

I ignored his steamy look. "Good to know. You've already met my social life. Rae and V are the two people I spend the most time with. We do the usual girl things—wine, travel, spa days. Nothing scandalous."

"What about your family?" He sat forward.

"My parents still live in my hometown, maybe an hour from Charlotte. As my mom likes to say, they've been fighting happily for the last forty years. I try and get up to see them as much as I can. My older sister lives in Charlotte, so I see her more often." I turned the tables on him. "What about you?"

"My family lives here," he said. "Mom and Dad live in the city but will probably move south once he retires. I was only at the hotel the other night to get checked in for the reunion and to grab a drink before my show at Tonic."

"Wait … are you bunking with your mom and dad during your reunion?" I snickered at the thought of him in his old bedroom, surrounded by trophies from high school and posters of girls in bikinis.

"Nah, I've got a hotel room. I waited too late to book at the Hyatt, so it's more of a no-tell motel. Although," he gave me a naughty look, "if I'd known meeting you was a possibility, I would've booked a room at the Hyatt two months ago."

His words were like catnip to me, but I played it cool. "Easy, there, chief. Let's not get ahead of ourselves."

He held his glass loosely in his hands. "I wouldn't dream of it, gorgeous. So where was I? Oh yes, family. My grandmother, my dad's mom, lives outside of town in the house my dad grew up in. It would be easier to move Mt. Rushmore than to pry her out of there. Sometimes she'll stay in town with my parents, but she loves that house. We all do, really."

I nodded, commiserating with him on stubborn elderly relatives. "I know you told me already, but remind me what it is you do."

His blue eyes twinkled. "Tequila making things a little blurry?" At my dejected nod, he said, "It's a restoration business. If it's old and needs to be renovated, repaired, or restored, I'm your man. That includes anything from classic cars to old soda machines."

"So that's where the man hands come from, huh?" I asked.

"I'm sorry, 'man hands'?" He looked at his hands and flexed his fingers. "I need a definition of that one."

I pulled one of his hands across the table and flipped it palm up, tracing its rough surface and the blunt lines of his fingers. "Yeah, man hands. Hands that do real work, not just type on a keyboard or punch the speakerphone a thousand times a day."

His hand closed over mine, infusing my cold fingers with warmth. "I hate the speakerphone."

"Oooohhh, talk dirty to me, why don't you?"

"Is that what you're looking for, Kez? Someone with man hands or just someone to manhandle you?" He waggled his eyebrows.

I pushed his hand away as a laugh bubbled up. "You are such a dork."

"All part of the package, baby. Seriously though, I figured you'd go for some corporate guy." He pushed up the sleeves of his faded Henley, letting more of his tattoos show. Seeing me looking at them, Jackson said, "But maybe I'm wrong."

My hair swung into my eyes, and I pushed it back. "Just shows how little you know."

Jackson watched me for a few seconds. The way he looked at me gave me the sense I was his singular focus and the rest of the room had faded away. "So fill me in," he said. "What does Kesler Walsh look for in a man?"

I considered how best to answer his question. "I don't need a corporate guy, as you call them, or any of the fancy trappings that go along with that. All of that stuff I can get for myself. I meet enough men through work who associate their manhood a little too closely with their salary. A big paycheck doesn't make you a man. Most of the time, it makes you a pretentious asshole. What I want or *need* from a man has little or nothing to do with how much money he makes or what type of job he has. What a guy does matters a lot less to me than who he is."

"And who is the man you want, Kez?" Jackson asked.

It was a question I'd given a lot of thought to and debated endlessly with my sister and my friends, so it was easy to give him an honest answer. "The man I want is someone who checks the oil in my car before a long road trip. He doesn't want me rolling the trash can to the road by myself after dark. Someone who'll step outside to check the weather for me, not just look it up on his phone. If he's going by the store, he calls to check and see if I need anything. Even if he hates tomatoes, he learns how to pick out the best ones because I love them." Everything I listed were things that showed me a guy cared. Sure, they were small things that most may see as insignificant, but in the long run, it was the little things that mattered.

Jackson asked, "So you're looking for a mechanic willing to take out the trash and do some grocery shopping?" Laughter creased the corners of his eyes as he teased me.

"No, dumbass." I slid to the edge of my seat, flicking a coaster at him. He caught it one-handed. "I'm looking for someone who wants to handle the little stuff that I don't think about. A guy who knows money isn't what he needs to take care of his girl."

Placing the coaster I'd thrown under his glass, he asked, "So you're looking for a poor mechanic?"

"Oh my God, just forget it!" My chair scuffed against the floor as I pushed back and crossed my arms.

Jackson tried to placate me. "I'm kidding, Kez. I get it, and I think it's cool you're not hung up on what a guy does or how much money he makes. I like that you're looking for something different. Most girls would be into the corporate guy and his requisite BMW."

"Oh, don't get me wrong," I corrected quickly. "I don't want some unemployed schmo who expects me to do everything. My man still needs to have drive. He just doesn't have to be on the corporate track." It was my turn to smirk. "He also needs to understand that I'm perfectly capable of fighting my own battles and that if I need his help, *I'll ask.*"

Rubbing a hand over his chin, Jackson replied, "Hm, seems like I might just know a guy who fits that bill."

"Do you now?" I played along, scooting my chair back to the table and resting my chin in my hand. "Tell me more."

He nodded sagely, then said in a stage whisper, "I have it on good authority he's got a thing for redheads."

"Sounds like a guy I should get to know," I said and meant it. I was seeing a different side of the cocky guitarist, and I liked this one. It had been a while since I'd enjoyed this type of comfortable, silly conversation with a guy. Jackson was funny and laid-back, his relaxed manner making it easy to talk and tease.

"Yeah, it's too bad you're stuck with me this weekend." He blew out an overly theatrical sigh and lifted a shoulder in fake regret.

I chuckled at his hammy performance. "Guess it's his loss then."

"It'd be anyone's loss, Kez." His demeanor went from bantering to sincere.

"Do you practice these lines, or do they just come naturally?" My ingrained skepticism of the male species bled through in the question.

Refusing to take the bait, he picked up his beer. "I'm just being honest."

I scoffed. "Yeah, yeah, that's what they all say." But inside I preened like a peacock.

"Why do you think Miller's still in love with you then?" He'd lobbed the L-word so casually it took a second for me to process what he said.

Once I had, my denial was swift. "If he were," I said, "he wouldn't be engaged to someone else."

He snorted and shook his head. "That little confession he made this morning says otherwise."

"You heard that?"

He nodded. "Oh yeah. I heard it. And I know that tonight could be one shade shy of a total shit show. So, I hope you're ready when he tries to talk to you." He offered a bemused smile. "I know I am."

Warning bells sounded in my brain as I remembered his comment from earlier about not liking Miller. I frowned. "Something tells me that should concern me."

One side of his lips lifted higher, transforming his smile into a naughty half grin. "Nothing for you to worry about, gorgeous. It's not the first time Miller and I have butted heads, and it probably won't be the last."

"There's a story there," I said and waited for him to tell it.

He shrugged, but I pressed for more information. "Oh no. You can't dangle that little tidbit in front of me and then not give me the details. You've already said you don't like him, so I know *something* happened. All you have to do is tell me what."

Looking at his beer instead of me he said, "There was a girl."

"Isn't there always?"

Wry laughter signaled his agreement. "That's true. But this girl was my girl, or at least I thought she was until I caught her with Miller at homecoming."

"Oh damn," I said, then a thought occurred. "Wait a minute. Does that mean this," I flapped a hand between us, "is all just some revenge plot against Miller? You're getting him back for something that happened in high school?"

He grabbed my hand. "No, Kez. My attraction to you has nothing to do with that ancient history. Plus, I didn't even know about Miller when we met, so how could it be?"

I wanted to believe him but remained wary. For all I knew, he'd planned on marrying his high school sweetheart only to have Miller steal her away. I could see how bringing Miller's ex as his date to the reunion would give Jackson a little poetic justice.

Sensing my hesitation, he said, "It's the truth, Kez." His eyes flashed. "But finding out Miller Thompson was your ex *was* icing on the cake."

"Should I be worried about this little harpy scratching my eyes out at the reunion?"

Jackson laughed. "No, you've got nothing to worry about there. All boys school, remember? Plus, she was a grade behind us. She won't be coming."

I mopped my brow in a show of feigned relief. "One problem solved."

The waitress slid a plate of Irish nachos on the table between us—crispy fries with gooey cheese and sauce topped with sour cream and dotted with scallions. My mouth watered, and I wanted to dive in, but the waitress hung around. With a long look at Jackson, she asked, "Will there be anything else?" Her breathy voice made it clear what she wanted the *else* to be.

As I hid my laugh behind my beer, he reached across the table and took my free hand, nibbling on my fingertips. Without looking at her, he said, "No, thank you. I have all I need right here."

Taking the hint, she hastened away from the table. He released my hand and I laughed. "You're something else, Jackson." I unfurled my napkin in my lap. Ever the Southern hostess, I placed an appetizer plate in front of him.

"Call me Jax," he said in a low voice.

"Huh?" I asked, pausing in my quest for a fry.

Jackson circled the rim of his glass with his middle finger. "You called me Jax this morning. I liked it."

We stared at each other over a mountain of french fries dripping with sauce and cheese. Not the most romantic setting, but there was a snap in the air just from his presence. I had a need to know more about the guy sitting across from me. More than where he was from and what he did for a living. I wanted to *know* him— what made him laugh the hardest or mourn the longest. My fear of opening up to someone again fought against my growing interest in Jackson. I had no idea which side would come out on top.

He smiled. "You're staring, Kez."

We each took 3,000-calorie portions worth of fried potatoes, grease, and cheese. His fork looked tiny in his large hand. Several white scars crisscrossed the backs of each of his hands, but his fingers were long and almost elegant. It was easy to imagine him piecing something together or sketching a design. I could also picture those skilled fingers doing dirty things to me. I tried to chase away the rising heat in my cheeks with a slug of my beer.

After swallowing his first bite, he said, "Let's get down to business. With any lie, it's always best to stick as close to the truth as possible."

"Is this something with which you have a wide array of experience?" I asked.

"God, even your grammar is sexy." As our waitress passed by, he signaled for two more beers.

"What do you mean?" I asked, reaching for another napkin.

He touched my hand, caressing the tender skin between my knuckles. "Your accent is hot enough, but couple that with the *way* you talk." He bit his lip and grunted. "Damn, it's sexy."

"You are so full of shit," I said but didn't move my hand.

The waitress was lightening quick with our second round and didn't bother flirting with Jackson this time. Lifting his mug, he took a drink. "No, ma'am, just honest."

I rolled my eyes. "Well, if we're sticking close to the truth, then I guess we met in a bar when you sent over a bottle of wine."

"Sounds good. How long ago?"

"Hmm." I thought for a moment. "It shouldn't be too long, since no one has heard anything about me. But we can't say it was a few weeks because then why would you be bringing me to a reunion?"

"Have you looked in a mirror?" he asked.

"Shut up. This is serious!" I pulled my hand away from his and picked up my beer.

"So am I," Jackson insisted. "Trust me, Kez, any guy would gladly bring you home and say, 'Hey fellas, look what I got!' We're a simple breed, you know."

"I'm painfully aware," I said.

We ate in silence for a few minutes, then Jackson asked, "So, how *are* you feeling about all this, Kez?"

I took my time chewing and swallowing before I answered. "I don't regret coming up here, at least not yet. Running into Miller this morning was unexpected, but it didn't overwhelm me. His declaration on the sidewalk was ... I don't know how to describe it."

A fry hovered in the air, halfway to Jackson's lips. "Having second thoughts?"

I shrugged. The truth was I was having second, third, and fourth thoughts, largely about why I hadn't felt more of ... *anything* when I'd run into Miller. Other than that slight buzz of awareness, there hadn't been any sense of longing or regret. His saying he hadn't let me go was more confusing than affirming. What, if anything, were the two of us even still holding onto at this point? That was becoming more and more difficult to see. To Jackson, I said, "I don't know."

"You don't?" he asked, then swiped at the dripping sauce and licked his finger.

"Honestly? No," I told him. "I mean, when I planned this trip my whole focus was him, you know? But now ..." I shook my head and scraped a glob of cheese off my plate.

"Now?" Jackson pushed for more.

"Now I'm thinking Rae might be right," I said after I swallowed the cheesy ecstasy.

His voice had a gravelly quality when he said, "Not sure what she's right about, but I like the direction this is going."

I laughed. "She mentioned something about there being better ways to spend the weekend."

Jackson's lips quirked up into a rakish grin. "Oh baby, let me count the ways ..."

Jackson dropped me off at the hotel with a promise to be back at seven for the cocktail party. I let myself into our suite and tossed my purse on the table by the door.

"That you, Kez?" Rae called as I walked into the living room. She poked her head out of her bedroom, checking to make sure no one was with me. Her hair was wrapped in a towel, and she was swaddled in a hotel robe.

I noticed she was wearing two different earrings. I zigged a finger back and forth at her earlobes. "What's with the jewelry?"

She frowned at me. "A better question is what's with the face?"

"What face?" I asked innocently, trying to dodge around her.

Rae stepped in front of me. "Nah, ah, ah, not so fast. Why do you look like you're about to take a midterm you didn't study for?"

I groaned. "Because none of this is going according to plan!"

Rae was puzzled by my reaction. "What's not going according to plan? Did Jackson back out of going with you to the reunion?"

"No, he's all in," I said. "But ..."

"But what? I thought that was exactly what you wanted to happen." Her features changed from baffled to suspicious. "What aren't you telling me?"

"This is all Jackson's fault!" I said, resting a hip on the small table.

"*What* is all Jackson's fault?" She released the towel wrapped around her head and scrubbed at her scalp. Water droplets flew from the ends of her long hair and pelted my jeans.

"Because everything's moving so fast! I came up here thinking I was still pining away for my ex. That *he* was the reason my love life was crap. Then I meet Jackson, and I'm all like Miller who? Only it shouldn't be that way, should it? Because I've spent the last few years of my life thinking I wasn't over Miller. But now, I'm going to jump into something with Jackson? Does that mean I'm over Miller? That I have been this whole time and have just been in denial? I'm so freaking confused!"

Rae paused in her drying efforts, the towel still pressed against her damp hair. "Lunch must have gone pretty well because last I heard, Jackson was just a means to an end."

I shifted uncomfortably. "He sort of kissed me this morning. In front of Miller."

The towel fell from her hands and hit the floor with a wet plop. Her eyes bugged out. "What?" Grabbing my shoulders, she gave me a little shake. "Why am I only hearing this now?"

When I'd come back to the room after my morning adventure, Rae'd been on a call about some budding crisis. Her call had run long, and then I'd left to meet Jackson, so we hadn't had a chance to talk.

Her fingers dug into me as her grip tightened in agitation. "I need details, Kesler. And when I say that, I mean *all* the details. Don't skimp."

Breaking away, I slumped onto the couch and spilled my guts.

When I was finished, Rae brayed with laughter. "I would've paid to have seen that! I bet Miller was about to shit himself he was so mad."

"I wouldn't know because he didn't stick around for an encore."

"Was there an encore?" she asked, greedy to hear more.

"No, but Jackson said he didn't want to be my fake boyfriend."

"Huh? So, he's not going to help? Then what was that scene this this morning all ab—oh my God, he wants to be your real boyfriend!" she shouted excitedly.

"Wanna say it louder?" I hissed. "I don't know if the people on the next three floors heard you."

"Heard what?" V asked as she emerged from our room with a towel around her hair and another one around her body.

"Kez literally ran into Miller this morning. Then she kissed Jackson in front of him. And Jackson wants to be her real boyfriend."

"We did *not* kiss," I corrected Rae, but she ignored me, too caught up in her version of the story.

V's eyes bulged. "You do telehealth appointments for a single morning, and you miss all the fun!" Her enthusiasm echoed Rae's, but I was hesitant to join the celebration.

"I know. Yay me." I pressed a pillow over my face.

"Maybe I missed more than I thought," V said. "What's the trouble?"

I dropped the pillow and her heart-shaped face appeared upside down above me. I struggled to put my tangled feelings into words.

"Why am I not more attracted to Miller? If the whole reason I came up here was because I was concerned about whether I was over him and ready to move on, why does it now feel like that door has been shut for a long time? Is that true or just wishful thinking on my part? Stimulated in large part by how well Jackson Jenkins fills out a pair of jeans. Will I regret it if I leap into something with Jackson instead of giving myself more time to see if the feelings I have for Miller are still there? And, if they aren't, why have I spent so much time spinning what-if stories about us? What is wrong with me?"

"Why can't you do both?" V asked, tilting her head carefully so as not to dislodge her towel turban.

"Both?" I lifted my head.

She pushed against my shoulder, and I scooched over so she could sit beside me. Adjusting her towel, she balanced on the edge of the cushion. "Sure. Why not? There's no reason you can't have a great time with Jackson tonight while still sorting out any leftover feelings for Miller. Seems like a win-win to me."

"But I ..." I tried to say.

"But what, Kez?" she asked, aggravation seeping into her question. "Obviously coming up here and seeing Miller didn't throw you for a loop like we all thought it would."

"Well ..." I hesitated.

Sensing I was holding back, she poked my arm. "What aren't you telling us?"

"I may have had a dream about Miller last night," I mumbled, burrowing down into the sofa and waiting for the inevitable scolding.

"You *may* have?" V's tone left no room for half-truths. It was her naughty patient voice she used with unruly children and sometimes their parents.

"All right, fine, I dreamed about Miller last night," I admitted.

She asked, "What about?" After I gave her the gist of it, she said, "Perfectly natural."

"Not the response I was expecting," I said.

"What, you thought this is where I'd start harping on how this was a bad idea and all that?"

"Well ... yeah," I confessed.

She scooted back into the corner of the couch, drawing her legs under her but taking care that her towel didn't gape. "That dream about Miller didn't keep you from wanting to kiss Jackson, did it?"

"Um, no?" That dream hadn't made me push him away or turn down his invitation to lunch. In fact, that dream had not even crossed my mind since this morning. My thoughts had been devoted to Jackson, not Miller. Well, except for when Jackson and I were working through how to deal with him at the reunion, but even then, Jackson was the center of that conversation, not Miller.

I sat up straighter. "No, it didn't."

She continued her Socratic inquisition. "And did you enjoy it when you almost kissed?"

The blush that flamed over my face was answer enough. Sometimes it sucked to be a redhead.

"That good, huh?" V gave her diagnosis. "Well, that right there shows your dream was a visceral reaction to seeing Miller. A simple physical reaction triggered by a memory of hot sex you had with the guy a million years ago."

I hugged the pillow to my chest, cautiously hopeful. "Maybe you're right, V."

She patted my arm and got off the couch. "Of course, I am. There's no reason to let your concerns about Miller ruin your chance with Jackson. Tattoos and all, he seems like he could be a great guy for you. Just be honest with him. If those feelings you seem convinced you still have for Miller ever do surface, all you have to do is tell Jackson that. Honesty is all anyone deserves, Kez. Including you. So be honest with yourself *and* Jackson about how you're feeling through all this. If you do that, everything else will sort itself out."

I glanced over at Rae, who'd been uncharacteristically quiet during my exchange with V. She was comparing necklaces in the mirror—holding one up to her throat, then switching to the one in her other hand.

I asked V, "What's with her?"

"She's got a date," V said.

"What? When did that happen?"

"While you were lunching with your new man candy, we went downstairs to get a bite ourselves. Same bartender was working the lunch service." V lifted her hands, palms up. "And you know Rae …"

I met Rae's eyes in the mirror.

"What?" she asked. "I'm bored and he's bearded, perfect match."

"Couldn't help yourself, huh?" I asked as I pried myself out of the plush depths of the sofa.

She gave a sly grin. "Oh, I plan on helping myself to a …"

"Oh for Pete's sake," V said. "Is there anything you can't make into some type of sexual innuendo?"

"Do you even have to ask that?" Rae said. "Plus, I'm not the only one who's having the house drinks tonight …"

V froze. Her cheeks turned pink, and she fingered the knot in her towel. She dug a toe into the thick carpet, twisting her foot nervously.

"Vivian …" I said. "Have something you need to confess?"

She gave it up. "Dave called this morning and asked me out."

"Dave from Tonic?" I hadn't known she'd given him her number. Given their flirting, though, it wasn't a surprise.

She nodded. "I figured if you were going out with Jackson tonight, I could make my own plans, so …"

"She decided to sample the local talent," Rae said.

V's blush deepened, and she glared at Rae. "God, you're vulgar."

Rae shrugged and continued her jewelry carousel in the mirror. I simplified her choice by plucking one of the necklaces from her hand. "Hey!"

I spun away from her and headed to the bedroom. "I'm pretty sure you pinched this from my jewelry bag while I was out."

"It's your own fault," she called after me. "You know I can't be trusted around sparkly objects or open bottles of liquor."

Chapter 9

I opted for a bath, rather than a shower, trying for a little relaxation prior to getting ready. Soaking in the generous hotel tub, I wondered if V was right about my dream. My relationship with Miller hadn't always been wreathed in bitterness and regret. For a long time, we'd been so happy together. One night in particular came to mind because it had been the night I knew I loved him.

⚘

Canned goods, random bananas, and an ice cream carton littered the sidewalk leading up to the front porch of my friend Kya's house, where she slumped sadly against the newel post. I groaned and shook my head at the sight. Miller threw the car in park. He hustled around to open my door. "I'm so sorry," I said, taking his offered hand.

He grinned. "Nothing to be sorry for, sweetheart. Shit happens."

"But does it have to happen on our anniversary?"

He kissed my forehead. "Sure, the timing sucks, but she needs you."

Risky Restoration

Kya had notoriously shitty taste in men. Case in point, her latest boyfriend had broken up with her in the middle of the grocery store and made her Uber home. He'd either forgotten or didn't care that her house keys were in his car and wasn't answering his phone, leaving her, and her groceries, locked out and miserable. Since I had a spare key, she'd called me, right in the middle of my one-year anniversary dinner with Miller.

He'd managed to get us reservations at the Reynolds Club, a fancy, members-only club that was black tie. Miller looked good in workout gear, but he was irresistible in a tux. I'd pulled out all the stops myself, and we made quite an elegant pair. Kya called right as our appetizers arrived. Miller didn't bat an eye and asked for our meal to be packaged to go so we could ride to the rescue.

He gathered up the assorted cans and shredded paper bags from the sidewalk and out of the yard, putting everything in a canvas bag he'd gotten from his car. As I consoled Kya, he unlocked the door and ushered us inside. While she bemoaned her latest relationship tragedy, Miller put away what could be salvaged and tossed what couldn't. When her sobs turned to hiccups, I handed her the remote and the semi-melted ice cream, and we made our escape.

Back in the car, I apologized again. "I am so sorry tonight got ruined."

His brows drew down in confusion. "How was anything ruined?"

I stared at him. "Were you not with me for the past hour? How else would you describe it?"

Miller pulled away from Kya's house. "Dinner's right back there in containers, you still look amazing in that dress, and I've spent all evening with my girl. Explain to me how that counts as ruined."

My insides turned to goo at the sweet sentiment, and I kissed his cheek. He gave me a leer worthy of a movie villain and twirled an imaginary moustache. "That's not to say there aren't ways you can show your appreciation …"

"With the way you look in that tux, I'm sure we can work something out."

I popped a soap bubble and sighed. Without any plan for how things would work long distance, playful and loving times like that one faded quickly after graduation. Once the bar exam no longer consumed our every waking moment, the strain of being apart began to unravel the fabric of our relationship. The failure to find a permanent position changed Miller. He would put off seeing me, claiming it was too expensive for him to fly down or that he didn't want me to come up and stay in his shitty apartment. I knew he was embarrassed by his lack of success and probably envious of mine.

The months apart didn't just wear on, they wore me down. His unwillingness to move cut me to the bone since he had nothing tying him to upstate New York. His parents were there, but his siblings were scattered throughout the northeast. Even without any prospect of a job, or a future, he'd stayed. I had a career I'd worked for my whole life, friends I loved, and my family surrounding me, and yet I was miserable because he wasn't there and made no effort to be there. Misery hardened to anger and then morphed into resentment the longer we were apart without a solution. His drunken calls at two thirty in the morning didn't help.

He'd say he loved me, wanted to marry me and have kids, yet did nothing to make any of those things happen. I'd loved him so much, or at least I'd loved the guy he'd been. The person he became once he moved away, not so much. Thinking back on it, I wasn't only hoping Miller would come back to me. I also wanted him to come back to himself, back to the guy that I fell in love with.

The one who wouldn't take no for an answer when I first refused to go out with him. The guy who debated against me in class in the morning then made love to me that night. I could've made long distance work with that guy. He was who I missed sharing my life (and bed) with, not the jackass content to waste his life and blame the world for his failings. Miller had been my first true love. When memories like our anniversary surfaced, so did those old feelings, which again made me question whether I was right to rush headlong into something with Jackson.

The bathroom door cracked open, and Rae stuck her head in. "You need to get out of that tub and out of your own head, Kez." Her heels clicked as she walked over to the counter. With a slight hop, she landed on the counter next to the sink, legs swinging. She threw me a towel.

Her outfit was a study in casual sex appeal. A fitted charcoal gray tank with a dangerously low neckline served as the backdrop for layers of glimmering, diamond-cut silver necklaces. Dark jeans molded to her legs, stopping right at the ankle. A belt cinched her tiny waist.

After getting out of the tub, I shook out the towel and snuggled into the terrycloth. "You look good," I said.

"Thanks." After primping in the mirror for a second, she said, "You're still doing laps inside that big brain of yours. The question is, who's making you do all that running—Miller or Jackson?"

Slipping into a hotel robe, I dropped the towel and unclipped my makeshift bun. "Who says I'm thinking about either one of them?"

"Um, how about your face?"

I left the bathroom, and Rae followed me into the bedroom. "Just let yourself be happy, Kez. You deserve it."

I gave her a side hug. "Thanks, girl. I wish I knew what would make me happy in this situation."

I opened the closet with a dress already in mind. It was sleeveless and black, simple at the front but totally backless. The fitted bodice emphasized my waist, while the skirt dropped straight down my legs. Black panels were connected by sheer nude fabric, creating the illusion that the skirt was just multiple black strips swishing around my legs.

When she saw it, Rae let out a low whistle. "Now we're talking! V!" she called.

V hobbled into the room, a different shoe on each foot. "You bellowed?"

I said, "That's an interesting look."

Standing in front of the mirror on the back of the closet door, she tilted each foot one way then the other. "I'm trying to figure out which one looks best with these pants."

In black-coated skinny jeans with a metallic shine and a fitted red top, V was dressed to kill. On her left foot was a black patent stiletto with a spike heel; the shoe on her right, also black, was a peep-toe sling back with a dramatic front bow.

"Peep-toe," Rae and I said in unison. Several assorted wristlets and other small purses were scattered across the foot of the bed. I pitched the red snakeskin clutch to her. She held it at her hip while looking in the full-length mirror. She turned to the side and lifted her left foot up.

Nodding at her reflection, she said, "Yep, I think you're right." Kicking off both shoes, she shrunk back to her real height of five feet four. "Sorry, I know that's not why you called me in here."

Rae pointed to the dress in my hand. "Don't you have that reverse necklace you got that year after watching Jennifer Lawrence at the Oscars?"

"Oh yeah," she said and walked to her jewelry case on top of the dresser. After a little scavenging, she pulled out a multistrand necklace. "Here it is." Looking deeper into the case, she located the matching earrings. When I dangled the necklace over the top of the hanger, the bottom of the longest strand came down in line with the zipper at the waist.

"Girl, you are going to slay in this," said Rae approvingly. As I held the dress aloft, she reached under the hem and fluffed the skirt, showcasing the see-through panes. "Hot damn, that's sexy."

V found the mate to the discarded patent leather heel and tossed both onto the bed. "Add these to it, and you'll have Jackson on his knees."

This was the type of outfit I'd imagined wearing the first time Miller saw me, not a sweat-soaked tank top and muddy running tights. It was sexy yet elegant. The heels put me right at six feet tall, making my legs look a mile long. The illusion pieces gave the impression that you could see almost the entire length of that mile, but the final destination remained a mystery. It was perfect.

Rae lifted a chunk of my hair and said, "You know we're gonna have to put this up, right? That necklace is pointless unless you can see it."

"Who wants that honor?" I asked.

"Oh, honey, I think you know that mop requires the whole village," answered V. She shoved me, gently, toward the bathroom. "Let's get to work."

A bazillion bobby pins later, my hair was piled on top of my head in a stylish maze of curls, loops, and twists. V artfully arranged a few strands around my face to soften the look. I was putting the finishing touches on my makeup when three sharp raps sounded on the main door of the suite. My heart beat out a matching staccato rhythm, and I wasn't sure if it was nerves, excitement, or a mixture of both. I ran a nail under my bottom lip after a final coat of F-Bomb Red gloss, sealing the line. I pouted at the mirror. My smoky eye was on point, a sharp winged liner and inky dark lashes completing the seductive look. The dress hugged my figure in all the right places, and the open back accented by the drape of sparkling ropes provided equal parts sexy and classy, like a naughty Audrey Hepburn. Chandelier earrings swung from my lobes, dancing along my jawline. I looked *good*. Matching clutch in hand, I headed into the living room.

Jackson's back was to me as he chatted with Rae by the window. In a black suit with a subtle pinstripe, he was more corporate CPA than restoration expert. I soaked in the sight of him, letting my eyes wander across the broad slope of his shoulder and the way the fabric stretched over the bulge of his biceps. There was no question his suit was tailored. A man his size couldn't have bought something that fit him so well off the rack. Jackson Jenkins in a suit was the height of fashion porn.

"Hey there," I said huskily.

He turned, and I saw the rest of his ensemble. His dress shirt was a soft white, and his brilliant peacock-blue tie was pulled into a perfect Windsor knot at his throat. The line of his beard was cleaner than it had been at lunch, so I knew he'd gotten a shave. While the slightly shaggy guitarist had been sexy, this boardroom version of the man made my insides go squishy.

"Hey yourself, gorgeous," he replied. He took a few seconds to drink me in, a huge grin splitting his face. "You look ... wow."

The way he looked at me made all of the bobby pins currently working their way into my brain totally worth it. "I'll take *wow*, I suppose," I said as I crossed to him.

When I reached his side, he dropped a kiss on my cheek. "You look amazing, Kez." His cologne was earthy and masculine, without being overpowering. *It suited him,* I thought briefly.

"I always wondered how the Big Bad Wolf looked when he saw Little Red Riding Hood," Rae said sassily. "Now I know."

Jackson laughed. "Surely, you can't blame me?"

"Yeah, yeah, Kez is beautiful, we all know that," she said. Her eyes narrowed, and she crossed her arms, her face grimly serious. "She was happy when you dropped her off this afternoon, so that makes me happy. So long as she stays that way, then you and I will most likely become friends. If she doesn't ..." Her smile was sharp and menacing. "Just remember what happened to that wolf in the end *and* that I look especially ravishing in fur."

"Understood," Jackson said, equally serious.

Rae nodded, the sparkle of humor returning to her green gaze. "Glad to see we're speaking the same language." She held up one of the bottles assembled on the table by the window. The lack of selection in our minibar had resulted in a late-afternoon trip to a package store. "Care for a drink before you head down to run the gauntlet?"

"No thank you, Sister Grimm," I declined, trying to avoid any further threats of scalping or other dismemberment.

"Suit yourselves," she said as she assembled the ingredients for an old-fashioned.

V wandered out of Rae's bedroom, fastening a bracelet. "Rae, have you seen my diamond ..." she trailed off when she saw Jackson. "Oh, hello."

He smiled debonairly. "V, you're looking lovely this evening. Dave won't know what to do with himself."

"Just as long as he knows what to do with her," Rae said as she poured her drink from the shaker. She gave V an exaggerated eyebrow waggle.

"Jesus, Rae," said V in embarrassment, "show a little couth."

"Oh, relax," Rae replied flippantly, adding an orange slice to her drink. "Jackson knows I'm kidding. I'm confident Dave won't have *any* trouble figuring out how to put tab D in to slot V."

"Rae!" said V, her cheeks crimson.

"And on that note," I said, grabbing Jackson by the arm and dragging him to the door, "you ladies have a wonderful evening."

"Don't do anything I wouldn't do," Rae called cheerfully.

"Well, that leaves just about everything but nude midget wrestling still on the table," sniped V.

Jackson laughed as I shut the door on their verbal sparring. "You'd think they were sisters."

I smoothed down the front of my dress and sighed. "You have no idea. But as with any family, only the two of them have the right to say anything snarky about each other."

We started down the hall, but my stiletto caught on a loop of carpet and made me stop short. Putting my clutch against his arm for balance, I raised my foot and repositioned the back of my shoe. The fabric of his suit may have been soft and supple, but the arm supporting me was strong and unyielding.

"Should I be worried?" He kept a hand at my shoulder to make sure I didn't topple from my flamingo-esque pose.

I put my foot down, rising to my full height but leaving my hand on his sleeve. Even in these heels, I still had to look up at Jackson. My wardrobe adjustment brought me closer to him, and the air seemed to shift, becoming heavy around us. Feeling the force of it, I asked, "About Rae? Why, are you planning on dicking me over?"

Putting his lips next to my ear, he said, "No, but I can see myself trying to eat you up." With a gentle pinch, his teeth closed around my earlobe. His beard brushed against my cheek, his freshly trimmed whiskers scraping my skin.

My fingers dug into his arm. "Is that so?" His answering chuckle told me he'd heard the slight tremor in my voice.

He drew back, his face inches from mine. "Absolutely." The rasp of his speech was as telling as the tremble of mine. Attraction sparked between us so hotly it could've ignited the hall. His hand went to my rib cage, bringing his fingertips into contact with my naked back. He ran the bridge of his nose under my jaw, inhaling deeply. "You even smell delicious." His voice was dark and decadent, like the tastiest piece of chocolate. I swayed toward him, thoroughly entranced by his words and his touch.

Jackson lifted his head and moved backward, keeping a hand at my waist. "Shall we?"

I blinked stupidly for a second before my brain finally restarted and the hallway came back into focus. "Oh, um, yes, right. Let's go."

Smiling, he tucked my hand into the crook of his arm, as if he'd been doing it for years, and covered it with his own.

As I walked beside him, he finally noticed the jewels dripping down my back. He stopped, tilting his head for a better view and said gruffly, "Turn around." It was a command, not a request.

"What?"

Heat shone like blue flames in his eyes when he twirled his finger in the air. "Turn around, gorgeous. I need a good look."

I gave my best runway spin, putting an extra twitch in my hips. The skirt of my dress floated up around my thighs. Halting midspin, I peeked over my shoulder, the necklace swaying rhythmically against my bare back.

In a single stride, he was behind me. I tried to turn around, but his hand on my lower back stopped me. He ran his fingers down the longest strand of the glittering necklace and mumbled something under his breath.

"What?" I asked.

"I said, this is the first time I've been jealous of jewelry."

It took every ounce of willpower I had to keep going to the elevator instead of wrapping myself around his body like a kudzu vine right there.

Once we were downstairs, Jackson led me across the lobby. Kristi was at the front desk helping an older couple. Her ever-present smile brightened when she recognized me, then, upon seeing Jackson, she did a double take. Slowly, her hands rose in front of her, and she gave me a double thumbs-up. I lifted my chin in acknowledgment.

Plush carpet muted the clack of my heels when we exited the lobby to a long hall leading to the ballroom that was set up for the cocktail party. A folding table in front of multiple sets of double doors was manned by a diminutive guy in thick black glasses. Jackson approached with his hand extended. "Todd! Hey man, long time!"

"Hey, Triple, good to see you, buddy." He half rose from his seat and shook Jackson's hand, pumping it up and down a few times. Noticing me, he glanced down to the array of name tags spread in front of him on the table. A worried wrinkle creased his pale brow. "I didn't have you down as bringing anyone …"

I smiled at him. "I'm sort of a late development. I hope it's not a problem."

The tips of his ears went rosy. "Uh, no, no, it's no problem. I just don't have a name tag for you." He looked so crestfallen, you'd think the lack of a name tag shortened my lifespan by three years.

Jackson snaked his arm around me. "Don't worry, Todd. I'll make sure she gets introduced to everyone."

Todd beamed and said, "In that case, here are two free drink tickets and *your* name tag. You guys have fun. I'm sure I'll see you later."

"Count on it," Jackson said. He shifted his stance, allowing me to move in front of him. "Kez, shall we?"

My palms dampened with anticipation. I flashed back to Miller's earlier words. Had it really just happened this morning? It felt like days, rather than just hours, had passed. He'd been livid to see me with Jackson, who I knew had been right in trying to prepare me for Miller making a scene. I inhaled a few slow breaths to steady myself for what lay on the other side of the doors, but my hands shook slightly.

With his hand at my back, Jackson steered me into the ballroom. The warmth of his palm against my skin was soothing, helping me swallow the nerves that threatened to take over. It was easy to tell the colors of St. Pius were navy and white because every imaginable surface was covered in one of the two colors. Large, round tables were draped in alternating cloths of blue and white, each topped with a bundle of balloons in the opposite color. Next to a parquet dance floor, a DJ played the best of the nineties. The room was crowded, and the hum of conversation competed with the music. Each corner of the room held a bar.

Jackson put the drink tickets in the inner pocket of his jacket and attached his name tag. The white card bearing his name was surrounded by so many colored ribbons, he looked a bit like an admiral.

"What are all these things?" I strummed the colored strips adorning the otherwise plain white square.

"Just a list of some stuff I did in high school."

I brought his lapel closer and read off the first few accolades. "Varsity track, varsity football, all-American ..." I stopped reading and looked up at him with a raised brow. "Just some stuff you did in high school, huh?" I plucked the laminated card with a *thwack*. "Seems like it would have been easier to list the stuff you *didn't* do."

A ruddy color stained his cheeks and he bowed his head. "It's no big deal."

"Why, Jackson Jenkins, are you blushing?" I laughed and smacked his arm. "I didn't know I'd come to the reunion with the big man on campus." I fanned myself theatrically with one hand. "It's enough to give a small-town girl like me the vapors," I joked.

He snorted. "Hardly, but being here with you certainly makes me feel like that."

The reluctant hometown hero seemed much more like the real Jackson Jenkins than the cocky show-off who made an appearance from time to time. I got the feeling that guy was a façade he used when it was convenient. This version of Jackson, the humble, unassuming guy with the comforting touch, was even harder to resist.

His hands clasped behind me. Mine moved up his chest and over his shoulders. I brushed through his hair, and my nails scraped the back of his neck. As I stretched up on my toes, he lowered his head. "I don't want to mess up your lipstick." He spoke the words quietly, but the need in them was loud.

His deference was what pushed me over the edge I'd been teetering on since that morning. I wanted, no, needed, his kiss. I pressed on the back of his head, urging him closer. "I've got more in my purse."

"Thank God," he whispered as his lips hit mine and I felt it—that unmistakable *zing* you get when you kiss a boy you really, really like. It's more than that first rush of physical attraction, it's a clenching sensation around your heart. Like something latched on and wouldn't let go.

After what was much too long of a kiss to be appropriate in public, he raised his head. "Wow," he said, caressing my bottom lip with his thumb.

"Wow, indeed," I responded breathlessly. "I think you're wearing more of my lipstick than I am."

"Totally worth it," he said and picked up a napkin from the table beside us. After he scrubbed it across his face, the white linen was stained crimson. "Better?" he asked.

I tilted his head one way, then the other, inspecting for any traces of red. Finding none, I said, "Much. It wasn't your shade. But," I pointed to my lips, "I'm afraid I need to do a little more work to fix my own. I'll be right back."

I wove my way to the restrooms. Placing my clutch next to the sink on the granite counter, I surveyed the damage in the oversize mirror and sighed. My face looked like I'd made out with an overzealous rodeo clown. As I took out the necessary war paint, a toilet flushed in the stall behind me. I had started to outline my lips when the stall door opened, and Miller's fiancée appeared. My lip pencil fell from my grasp and clattered into the sink.

"Oh," she giggled. "I'm sorry. I didn't mean to startle you." She was pretty, with light blue eyes—not the unique darker shade of Jackson's but still nice. Her shoulder-length blonde hair had been pinned to the side for the evening. I was at least three inches taller, but her frame was trim, and the dress she wore accentuated all the positives. She didn't look like the evil succubus I'd made her into, but I was still wary.

Accepting her apology, I said, "Er, that's okay. Just clumsy of me." I fumbled slightly as I picked the pencil out of the sink.

She was in no hurry to leave the bathroom and leaned against the counter as she dried her hands. "Looks like someone got a little carried away."

My hand froze, rattled by her choice of words. "What?" The question echoed loudly around the small space. Miller wouldn't have told her I was here, would he? He certainly wouldn't have told her about what happened this morning, right? My mind raced as I tried to work through what she could be talking about.

She gestured to my lips. "We go to all that trouble and then one kiss later, it's back to square one."

My lipstick. I'd almost had a meltdown, and she was talking about my lipstick. I forced a smile. "Oh yes, right." My eyes drifted to the engagement ring winking at me under the fluorescent lights. It was a nice ring—not large enough to be gaudy but big enough to notice. An oval center stone was flanked by smaller diamonds down the gold band.

She held her hand out in front of her, turning it back and forth. "Isn't it gorgeous? I know that's obnoxious, but I'm newly engaged, so I can't help myself." Her excitement was palpable, like she could jump up and down and clap her hands with glee at any moment. Her bridal glow could've powered the entire hotel.

"Congratulations." I turned back to the mirror.

"Thank you!" she chirped merrily. "Well, I'll leave you to it." She checked her hair one last time and left.

Once the door shut behind her, I slumped against the sink. "Well, damn," I said to the empty room. She'd been so ... nice! Not at all the rancid, Yankee bitch I'd imagined. And she was so *happy*! Happiness radiated off her like sunshine. All it took was one sidelong glance at her ring from a complete stranger, and she lit up like a freaking Christmas tree. All that bubbly, happy goodness only made me question my coming up here that much more.

Jackson was waiting for me outside the restroom. At the sight of him, warmth flooded through the cracked pieces of my psyche. His presence alone sanded down the sharpest edges, which managed to freak me out at the same time it calmed me. He pushed off the wall, and I was once again struck by the grace with which he moved. He was a big guy, but he carried himself elegantly. His litany of athletic accomplishments in high school made sense. It wasn't hard to picture him as the starting quarterback, standing calm and collected in the pocket then tossing the game-winning touchdown.

"Feel like a drink?" He offered his elbow.

I took it and said, "More than you know."

We headed back over to the bar, sidestepping waiters hoisting trays of hors d'oeuvres.

Concern wrinkled his forehead. "Problem?"

"I ran into Miller's fiancée in the ladies' room. She showed me her engagement ring and complimented my lipstick."

Changing direction, he took me to the side of the room, away from the other attendees in line at the bar. "What?" he asked.

I put my hands up in a *what-can-you-do* gesture. "Apparently, we share a lot of the same tastes."

Jackson laughed at that. "Ha! Well, did you introduce yourself?"

"No, we were just two ladies chatting."

"Isn't she in for a treat when she finds out that the nice lady whose lipstick she coveted is her fiancée's ex-girlfriend."

Offering a wan smile, I said, "The thing is, she was so ..."

"So, what?"

I struggled to put my thoughts into words that made any sense. "So ... sweet, I guess is the word. Naïve, maybe? Like, how could there be anyone who wasn't over the moon for her that she was engaged?"

"Little did she know ..." he said, but I interrupted.

"That's just it, Jax," I explained. "I didn't feel anything when she told me or when I saw the ring. It was as if she told me about the weather or some other totally mundane detail that has no impact whatsoever on my life."

"Well, that's good, right? At least," he tugged on his earlobe, "from my perspective that's a very positive development."

I took his hand, linking my fingers with his. "No, you're right. It's great. I guess I expected a rush of, I don't know, like hatred or jealousy. I mean, I've spent all this time building her up in my mind as some sort of home-wrecker. It was *her* fault we broke up. *She* was the one who lured him into her evil clutches."

"Evil clutches?" he asked with a snort. "What is this, a Marvel comic?"

I slapped his arm with my free hand. "You know what I mean! I made her into this horrible, man-stealing whore. Only, I don't think she is."

"So, what now?" he asked.

"Now?" I reached into the breast pocket of his jacket and pulled out the drink tickets. "We use these, eat rubbery hors d'oeuvres, and enjoy ourselves."

We made our way to the bar, stopping here and there to speak to people Jackson knew. As we meandered slowly, he was in constant physical contact with me. His hands were either holding mine or touching the small of my back. In line, I stood in front of him and leaned back into his embrace. His hands were at my hips, broad fingers spanning up my rib cage. It was sexy and comfortable all at the same time.

"Well, this must be the culprit."

I turned gradually, hoping I was wrong, but one look confirmed I wasn't. Miller's fiancée was smiling up at Jax. His height made her look even more diminutive. Even in heels, she barely cracked five feet eight.

"I'm sorry?" I asked.

She gave me a conspiratorial look. "I'm guessing he's the one responsible for your lipstick smudge from earlier."

"You got me," Jax replied. "And I plan to be a repeat offender."

I rolled my eyes, and she laughed. "I didn't introduce myself earlier. I'm Callie Peterson."

Jackson shook her hand. "Nice to meet you. I'm Jackson Jenkins, and this is my girlfriend, Kez Walsh."

The smile that had looked so easy on Callie's face a moment ago turned to confusion as she tried to work through why she knew my name. Her hand was soft and cool as she shook mine. "Kez Walsh? Why does that name sound familiar?"

"Probably because you've heard me say it, sweetheart," said Miller as he appeared next to her. Dressed in a dark suit with a navy tie, he was handsome with a charming smile. He slid an arm around Callie's shoulders in a move that was more perfunctory than anything else. Giving her a little squeeze, he said, "Kez Walsh, as in Kesler Walsh—my ex-girlfriend from law school." His laugh was flippant, like "Hey, what are the odds? Isn't this hilarious." But I wasn't buying into his casual act. His eyes gave him away, just like they used to. There was no humor in them whatsoever.

Jax's fingers tightened on my waist, but he kept a polite smile on his face. "Miller," he said good-naturedly. "I'm guessing this is your fiancée?"

"Yes," Miller said, oozing civility. To Callie, he said, "Sweetheart, would you mind going to check on Davis' wife? I don't think she's feeling well."

I didn't know who Davis or his wife were, nor did I trust in Miller's sudden solicitous nature.

Callie was equally hesitant, her eyes flitting from me to Miller and then to Jackson. Miller upped the wattage on his smile. "I'll be right over," he promised her. "I just need to ask Jackson here a few questions about the picnic tomorrow."

Callie's hand went to her throat, her diamond sparkling in the ballroom lights. "Well, okay. It was nice to meet you," she said, more to Jackson than to me.

Once she was out of earshot, Miller dropped his smile and any pretense of politeness. The atmosphere among the remaining three of us was so frosty that if the sprinklers had come one, ice pellets would've rained down.

"No need to make this awkward, Miller," Jackson said.

"Says the guy who brings my ex-girlfriend to our reunion," Miller retorted. "What's your angle here, Jenkins?"

"Same one you have, Miller. I'm just here to show off my girl. So far," his eyes gleamed in triumph, "it's going really well." He held Miller's glare for a tense few seconds, then glanced ahead of us. "Well, it looks like we're holding up the line. You enjoy your night. I hope Davis' wife gets to feeling better." With a dazzling smile, he guided me up to the bar.

For a moment, I thought Miller's head was going to explode after Jackson's jab about showing off his girl. Now I knew what a filet placed between two dogs felt like, with Callie as a forgotten scrap. Again, that niggling little doubt that maybe I was nothing but a pawn in Jackson's game of revenge with Miller appeared in the back of my mind. I tried to downplay the feeling, but couldn't quell it completely.

Jackson looked down at me. "You look a little pale, Kez. You okay?"

I took the drink he'd ordered for me and downed half of it in a swallow. "That was some pissing contest."

He glanced behind me, but Miller was gone. "Will you respect me less if I said he started it?"

Part of me wanted to ask if he was including what had happened between the two of them in high school. But I refrained, not wanting to ruin the night with my garden-variety paranoia. So instead I laughed and said, "No, not at all, since it's the truth."

Jackson grew serious. "He was an idiot, Kez. He didn't value what he had when he had it. Even so, I can't blame the guy, you know?"

I blinked in surprise. "What?"

He adjusted my necklace, letting his hand loiter at my throat. "If I saw you with someone else, I'd be pissed too."

"You barely know me," I said.

He shrugged. "I know enough to know I don't want to think about you with another guy."

We walked to a high-top table. "Yeah, well, would you still feel that way if you were engaged to another girl?" I challenged him.

His elbow on the table, Jackson turned his body toward me. The tips of his fingers skimmed over my wrist, sending sizzles of heat dancing up my forearm. His hand continued its slow, upward route, his thumb grazing my bicep. Blue eyes lured me closer to him. Endorphins left over from the confrontation with Miller stampeded through my system, stoking the edgy hum coursing through me from his light caresses. "That wouldn't happen because I wouldn't be dumb enough to lose you in the first place."

He was so smooth, he could've charmed the panties right off my body. An image of him as the pied piper of panties popped in my brain, and I suppressed a giggle. "Next thing I know, you'll conk me over the head and drag me back to your cave by my hair."

Jackson palmed my shoulder, his thumb stroking my neck. He lowered his head to whisper, "We'll save the hair pulling for behind closed doors." A quick, firm tug on the hair at the base of my skull made my insides quiver at the possibilities. I leaned into his hand while he massaged the subtle sting from my scalp.

"That feels good," I mumbled as my eyes drifted closed. Yeah, self-control was highly overrated. Giving into the sensations rioting through my body was a much better idea. Inner witch was already stripped naked and panting.

He gathered me impossibly closer to him. "You know, we don't have to stay." His beard dragged gently against my chin as he peppered kisses along my cheek and down my jawline.

"Is that right?" The kisses were making it hard to think, much less argue. Hell, I was only minimally conscious of where we were or why we were here in the first place. All I wanted was for him to keep doing what he was doing and then do even more. Jackson shifted on his feet, and I moved with him.

His mouth continued south while his fingers laced through my necklace. "Mm-hmm." His response hummed along the sensitive skin of my throat, and I barely contained a moan as he sucked lightly at my collarbone. Mesmerized by the feel of his lips on my skin, the last shred of my control evaporated, along with any thoughts of Miller and Callie. I caved to the reckless need raging within me. My head tipped back in pleasure, and I seized handfuls of his hair.

Jackson paused, his lips parted and ready to plant another kiss on my shoulder. Looking up at me with lust-clouded eyes, he asked, "Should we get out of here?"

Inner witch chanted, *Yes, yes, yes!* But I took a breath and looked over his shoulder, trying to escape the quicksand of desire that threatened to pull us both under. He'd maneuvered us into a darkened alcove of the ballroom. Even with people all around us, we were obscured from view.

My fingers were still in his hair, their fair, freckled appearance standing out against his dark locks. I pulled on the thick strands and silently weighed our options. Sure, we could dash out of here and up to my room to tear each other's clothes off. Or, we could each get our libidos in check and stay awhile, postponing the inevitable tearing off of clothes. One led to instant satisfaction, but the other provided an ability to continue getting to know this man outside of the bedroom.

At the delay in my answer, Jackson straightened, making my fingers slip from his hair. He asked, "We're not leaving, are we?"

I traced his jaw, rubbing my palm against the coarseness of his beard. "If we leave, where are we headed?"

"I think both of us know where this has been headed since the other night, Kez. But tonight, the ball's in your court." I bit my bottom lip, and he zeroed in on my mouth, emitting a small grunt. His eyes were stormy as he stared at me. "Keep doing that, though, and you're gonna make it much … harder for me to do anything but toss you over my shoulder and head out of here."

I gave him a brief kiss. When he tried to prolong it, I pushed back. "A few days ago, you'd come up here to go to your reunion, which I assume means you wanted to *attend* these events."

He brushed his hands down my back. "That was before I met you."

"I know, Jax, but I'm not…" I looked away, gathering the right words. "You said earlier you wanted to see where this goes, right?"

"Yeah, but …"

I put a finger against his lips. "So let's not jump to the hot, steamy finish just yet. Let's enjoy the beginning."

He kissed the tip of my finger. "So, that means …"

"That means we drink, we dance, you introduce me to your old friends, and then, at the end of the night …" I tweaked the knot of his tie, letting my fingers glide down the length of it.

"Yeah?" There was a dark edge to his question.

I whispered in his ear. "I get to find out if you look as good out of this suit as you look in it."

He groaned. "I'd be happy to answer that question now."

I gave a pointed look down. "I can tell." I'd felt how *happy* he was at the thought.

Jackson laughed, but stepped back. "Have it your way, Kez."

"Oh, I plan to have it *every* way, Jax."

His pupils dilated, and he exhaled through his nose. Grabbing my hand, he pulled me out of the shadows and toward a table of people. "Then let's get all this socializing over with so I can get you upstairs. Or at least to the elevator."

Chapter 10

I leaned against the bar, waiting on my drink. I had the right amount of alcohol to feel that oh-so-pleasant hum in my system without being drunk. I hadn't seen Miller since our earlier skirmish. Jackson was holding court at a table on the other side of the ballroom, surrounded by a group of six or seven guys. This was like going to a reunion with the prom king and quarterback who'd won the state championship and saved a dozen puppies from a burning building. Of course, those things might be on the ribbons decorating his name tag. The thought made me grin, and I started back to the table with a fresh drink, but the sound of my name stopped me in my tracks.

I looked around but didn't see anyone. I was about to keep going, but then I heard voices coming from around the side of the bar. Intrigued, I saw a corridor to the right. Probably a passageway for the staff to get from the ballroom to the kitchen or other parts of the hotel without having to go through the main hallways. I peeked around the corner, through two large, potted ferns camouflaging the entrance. A couple stood halfway down the hallway. Feeling guilty for spying on what looked like an intimate moment, I backed away. The bare walls and linoleum floor operated as an amplifier, projecting their argument and allowing me to overhear another snippet of their conversation.

"Tell me I'm wrong, Miller," Callie pleaded tearfully. The hurt in her voice was palpable, and I froze.

From my hiding spot, I watched as he avoided eye contact with her, his posture stiff and unforgiving. He was completely detached from the conversation. "Wrong about what?" he asked irritably.

"You know about what." Her voice broke.

"I'm not in the mood to play guessing games with you, Cal," he said harshly.

"Fine," she sniffled. "Tell me there aren't always going to be three people in this relationship."

I waited for him to deny it and offer some level of comfort. He didn't. With his arms folded, he shook his head. "I'm not going to have this conversation again, Callie. It doesn't do anyone any good."

I was dying to know what conversation they'd had so many times.

Callie wiped at her eyes. "Do you still love her?"

My eyes widened. Was I the *her* in question?

"Callie," Miller said his voice weary. He rubbed a hand over his face and sighed loud enough for me to hear it.

"Do you?" she persisted.

He looked down the hallway, and I ducked back around the corner. Not that he could see me, but I wasn't taking any chances. Especially not before I heard his answer.

"Callie, I loved Kez for a long time. You know that because I was still with her when I met you. I can't help that after all these years, her showing up with Jackson," he spat out the name like a curse, "is gonna screw with my head."

She reached for him, placing her small hand on his arm. "I understand that, but I don't want it to mess up what *we* have," she said plaintively.

God, I was a total piece of shit for listening to this, but I was riveted.

Callie continued her plea. "I love you, Miller."

He shoved his hands in his pockets and looked away from her. "I can't have this conversation right now, Cal. I need some time to get my head sorted out." He headed in my direction, the soles of his dress shoes smacking angrily against the floor.

Quickly, I darted from my hiding place. In my haste, my trendy yet hazardous necklace caught on the back of a stack of chairs and almost garroted me. "Gack!" I yelped as I windmilled my arms to keep from falling. Regaining my footing, I floundered to loosen the chain enough to turn around and see what had ensnared me. Somehow, the necklace had wrapped itself between the backs of two of the chairs. "C'mon, c'mon," I wheedled frantically while picking at the strands. Finally, they popped loose, and I beat a fast path back into the ballroom. I merged into the crowd as Miller rounded the corner and disappeared toward the exit. Searching for Jackson, I saw he was still at the same table. I straightened the necklace as best I could and traversed the room, what I'd overheard tumbling through my mind.

Jackson smiled when I reached his side. "Hey, gorgeous. I thought you'd gotten lost."

I smiled back, trying to slow my thundering heart rate. "No, just got a little waylaid." Before he could ask, I clarified, "Nothing to worry about." Inner witch shouted, *Are you kidding me?* but I ignored her.

The lines in his forehead relaxed, and he introduced me to a guy who'd joined the group after I'd gone to get a drink. "This is Corbin. Don't listen to any of the stories he tells you."

"It's a pleasure to meet you," I said to the dark-haired guy standing beside Jackson.

Corbin smiled. "You too, Kez. It's nice to put a face to a name I've heard so much about."

"Jackson's been gossiping, huh?" I asked, wondering what in the world he could have told this guy. Sure, we'd had a great conversation at lunch, but it wasn't like we had some long history.

The easy banter in the group ground to a halt, and Corbin looked sheepishly at Jackson. "Oh shit, man, my bad."

"It's cool," Jackson replied. At my quizzical look, he added, "Corbin and Miller were good friends in high school and were still close when Miller was in law school. So I'm sure he's heard about you, just not from me."

Trying to assuage Corbin's guilt, I said, "Oh, well, I promise I'm not really the wicked witch of the south."

All the guys laughed, and the awkward moment passed.

Corbin said, "Seriously though, you two look good together. Seems like everything worked out as it should, you know?"

I took Jackson's hand. "Can't argue with that."

Raising our linked hands to his lips, he kissed my knuckles. "Well, fellas, I think we're gonna call it a night." This was met with a chorus of boos and pleas for "just one more round!" Jackson laughed it all off. "Thanks, but no thanks, guys."

"Fine, fine, but you'll be at the picnic tomorrow, right?" Corbin asked.

"Wouldn't miss it," Jackson confirmed.

Corbin nodded. "All right, man. See you then. Kez, great meeting you."

"Likewise," I replied. It took a few more minutes for us to exit the room. With a final promise to see yet one more person tomorrow, we made it out the door and headed to the elevators. Rae had texted earlier that she and V wouldn't be back until later tonight and that V planned on bunking with her. Jackson and I would have the suite to ourselves for a while, so we didn't have to go to the no-name motel where he had a room. Which worked well because I preferred my thread count a little higher than one.

Jackson was quiet as we waited on the elevator, but he held me close. Pushing the thoughts of Miller's fight with Callie from my mind, I put a hand under his suit coat and raked my nails up his back. "I had fun tonight."

He kissed the top of my head. "So did I, gorgeous."

"You really were the big man on campus," I teased.

Bashfully, he tried to downplay it. "Not so much."

Eyeing his name tag, I said, "The evidence is otherwise."

Jackson laughed and unpinned it from his jacket. "Guess I don't need this anymore." The elevator dinged and he stood back, allowing me to go in first. I hit the button for my floor and stepped into his arms. When the doors began to close, he said, "Alone at last," and lightly nipped my ear.

An arm snuck between the doors, and a voice slurred, "Hold the elevator!"

Jackson and I sprang apart, like teenagers caught in the act. Two guys careened inside, both swaying mightily and neither paying us any attention. One swiped the button for the floor above mine, and I cursed inwardly.

Once the doors closed, the shorter one, still wearing his name tag from the reunion, stared up at Jackson with glassy eyes. Recognition dawned. "Hey!" he mumbled, "I know you!"

Jackson surreptitiously checked the shorter man's name tag. "Norman, how are you? Long time no see."

Norman elbowed his friend, who lurched to the side. "Whaddya do that for?"

Norman pulled the guy back upright and pointed a stubby digit at Jackson. "Look who it is, Ralph! It's Triple!"

Now it was Ralph's turn to gawk at Jackson with something akin to awe. "Holy shit! It is! How ya been, Triple?"

"Oh, I can't really complain," Jackson replied.

As the two of them fawned over him, his hand skimmed along my shoulder blade and veered downward. His fingertips dipped under the fabric of my dress at the waist. Startled, I looked up at him, but he ignored me and kept smiling at his adoring fans. While the three of them talked, his hand climbed up my rib cage until it came to rest under my bare breast. I edged away, trying to discreetly dislodge his hand. He locked his elbow, keeping me clamped against him. The vee of his thumb and forefinger curved around my right breast like an underwire. So enthralled with their high school hero, the fanboys were oblivious to what he was doing to me right in front of them.

His thumb stroked the side of my breast, and I struggled to breathe normally. The tantalizing feel of his hands on my bare skin made the inane babble of the two morons with us fade to white noise. Each sweep of his thumb rose a little higher and drove me a little crazier. I wasn't sure if I wanted to kiss him or kill him, but as his thumbnail scraped right below my nipple, I was leaning more toward the latter. An ache throbbed low in my stomach, and I bit back a moan. He was now using his whole hand. Those long fingers glided over my breast, circling but never quite touching my nipple. The professional, successful woman in me couldn't believe I was letting him feel me up in an elevator, while the inner witch wanted his fingers to climb higher and pinch harder.

"Well, guys," said Jackson. "It seems we've reached our floor." I blinked. I'd been so focused on his touch that I hadn't heard the ding of the elevator. Jackson's hand slid discreetly out of my dress so that when we walked forward it rested innocently at the curve of my hip.

Once the elevator doors closed behind us, I shoved him. "What the hell was that?" Lust fought with anger as my dominant response to what had just happened.

"What was what?" he asked, the picture of innocence.

I flicked a fingertip between my breasts, their nipples hard and straining toward him. "Seriously?"

He turned me to face the mirror that hung opposite the elevators. "Look at you. How could I resist touching you when it's all I've been thinking about tonight?"

I watched our reflection as his hands disappeared from view. My sense of touch took over from sight as he teased the fabric away from my back and pressed forward, more boldly than he had in the elevator. The ridge of his knuckles appeared beneath my bodice and climbed steadily upward. My eyes darted up to Jackson's and held them as his fingers moved over my stomach and higher along my torso. Finally, he held my breasts in his palms. The moan I'd stifled in the elevator broke free. My head fell back against his shoulder.

"You are so beautiful, Kez." He kissed my throat as his agile fingers continued to work their magic, tugging, pulling, and pinching. His lips parted, and he dropped open-mouth kisses along the column of my neck. My hands came together behind his neck, the natural curve of my body thrusting my chest farther into his hands. He met my stare in the mirror. Our reflection was like an erotic painting—flushed cheeks, pupils dilated, the outline of his huge hands stretching my dress. It was one of the hottest things I'd ever seen.

"Bedroom," I gasped. Jackson grunted in what I assumed was agreement, and he pulled his hands out of my dress. Grabbing my hand, he strode purposefully down the hall. My dress flapped around my legs as I hurried along with him. When we reached the door of my suite, I rummaged in my clutch for the key card. His body vibrated with need behind me, his hands roaming over my back and down my hips. Finally, I found the thin strip of plastic and flapped it furiously in front of the lock.

When it clicked, I twisted the handle, and Jackson shouldered the door open, lifting me into the room with an arm around my waist. Once it closed, he wasted no time in pushing me against it, groaning into my mouth as he kissed me. I threw my purse at the nearest flat surface and met his kiss, hanging onto his shoulders. His mouth moved over mine, taking and dominating. My lips parted willingly. His tongue invaded and lashed against my own. My scalp tingled when he gripped my hair and tilted my head back, sucking my lower lip into his mouth. Releasing it with a pop, he rested his forehead against mine, our ragged breathing the only sound in the room. Blood hummed in my veins, and I was two seconds away from spontaneous combustion.

"Holy shit, Kez," he said hoarsely.

A laugh fizzed out of my throat, and I stopped him from moving in for another kiss. "As much as I enjoyed the elevator ride and that little show in the mirror, I'm not sure we need to give V and Rae a front-row seat to your next moves. The bedroom will give us a little more privacy." I knew the girls were still out and would be for some time to come; however, I wasn't going to chance their coming back early.

"Does this mean I don't get to bend you over that couch?"

Pressing myself into him, I said, "There's a bench in my room that will work just fine." His eyes glazed over, and he practically dragged me across the room as I laughed. Once we were behind closed doors, he sat on the edge of the bed and guided me to stand between his knees. He slid his hands under my skirt, drawing circles on the backs of my thighs as he looked up at me.

"Are you sure about this, Kez?" Raw desire roughened his voice, but I had no doubt that if I gave anything other than a total green light, he would pull back, completely willing to let things proceed at whatever pace I set.

My fingers tunneled through his thick hair. "Very sure, Jax."

"Then you're wearing way too many clothes."

I remembered that red lingerie set Rae found in my luggage. His fingers skimmed the sides of my thighs when I backed up. I said, "You're exactly right." Capitalizing on his confusion, I gave his shoulders a tiny shove, and he fell back, his upper body landing on the bed. "Make yourself comfortable, Jax. I'll be out in a second."

Before he could pull me down with him, I skipped off to the bathroom. On the way, I plucked the teddy and robe from my bag. When I was safely behind the locked door, I held the red lace to my chest. For once I didn't regret my tendency to overpack. I stripped off my dress and shimmied into the lingerie.

Glancing in the mirror, I realized that while my chic updo was perfect for the party, it didn't go with the take-me-now vibe of the lingerie. I worked most of the pins loose from my hair and let it tumble around my shoulders in deep red waves.

I switched my spike heels for a pair of strappy stilettos (possibly Rae's) and draped myself in the short, sheer robe that completed the outfit. With a swipe of F-Bomb, I was ready. After a quick prayer to the female god responsible for orgasms, I opened the door.

In my absence, Jackson had turned on the floor lamp in the corner, bathing the room in a soft glow. He'd tossed his suit coat and tie over the back of the wing chair beside the bed with his shoes beneath it. His back was to me as he unfastened his watch and placed it on the bedside table. He took off his cuff links. Small *plinks* sounded when they hit the marble top of the nightstand.

Channeling my inner Rita Hayworth, I took a deep breath, which just *happened* to enhance my cleavage. "Hey there, handsome. Miss me?"

He glanced over his shoulder, then his head swiveled back in a slow double take. The rest of his body followed. His gaze moved gradually up my body, like he was memorizing each curve. I tried my damnedest not to fidget or think about my cellulite. Nope, tonight, I was sex incarnate. I'd have plenty of time tomorrow for all my neuroses.

His Adam's apple bobbed jaggedly when those sizzling blue eyes met mine. With a yank, he pulled his shirttails free of his dress pants. "I guess you came prepared for everything this weekend."

"Once a Girl Scout, always a Girl Scout."

"You don't happen to have that outfit around here somewhere, do you?" he asked.

"One fantasy at a time, hot stuff," I replied saucily.

Holding out a hand, palm up, he wiggled his fingers. "Come here, gorgeous." With his other hand, he undid the buttons of his shirt, revealing my kryptonite—a wifebeater. A finely made dress shirt with a working man's shirt hidden away underneath was a lethal combination. It was like stripping away the polished veneer to reveal a man's inner animal. The thin, ribbed shirt molded to his body, taunting me with the outline of his honed chest and defined abs. Tattoos spread out from the square neckline and disappeared under his dress shirt.

I pushed off the doorjamb and sauntered across the room, reaching him as the last button came undone. His pulse throbbed faintly at his throat, a slow, steady rhythm that seemed to move in time with the seconds ticking by. Jackson grasped the tie of my robe and leisurely wound one end around his finger. With the slightest tug, the knot came loose, and the robe opened. As the lace whispered across my skin, the tie unspooled from his hand and dropped to the floor at my feet. Jackson placed his hands flat against my collarbone, nudging the robe off my shoulders. The filmy fabric fell to the crook of my elbows.

His hands burned down my sides and curved over my hips. Palming my ass, he lifted me into his arms. I shed the robe the rest of the way, letting it pool at his feet. I wrapped my legs around his waist and laid my hands on his shoulders, my fingers stealing under the neckline of his shirt.

"You're gorgeous, Kez," he said reverently. Jackson sank onto the bed, kneading the globes of my ass.

I pushed against his shirt collar, wanting to see more of him. "Take this off," I demanded.

He released my ass to pull his arms free of his sleeves, wadding up the shirt and tossing it onto the chair next to the bed. I traced the inked swirls covering his collarbone and winding down both his arms in an intricate design. The lines twined together, then separated before ending right above his wrists. I moved my hands down his arms, over the bulge of his biceps and the wiry hair on his forearms. "These are beautiful," I said.

"Thank you," he murmured, nuzzling my neck. The spice of his cologne mixed with the clean scent of his shampoo and invaded my senses. His scruff tickled as he kissed my pulse point, then his lips glided farther down my neck. My nails dug into his arms as my body reacted hungrily to his touch. He drew his hands up my spine and over my shoulders. In a languid motion, his fingers worked underneath the tiny straps of my teddy. The juxtaposition of his huge hands with the delicate fabric made him seem so much more masculine. He pulled one strap down, following it with his mouth. His repetition of that dizzying treatment with the other strap made me writhe wantonly in his lap. He kissed my collar bone, the scratch of his beard soothed simultaneously by his soft lips.

With the straps off my shoulders, I teased out first one arm, then the other. One deep breath and the lace would fall away completely, baring me to Jackson's gaze. A single, broad finger slid down my cleavage until it hooked into the vee of the teddy and nestled between my breasts. His eyes flitted up to mine, then back down to my chest. Teasingly, he flexed his finger back and forth. I gulped at the sensation, and he smiled. Curling that finger in a decisive yank, he had me naked from the waist up. A low sound of appreciation came from Jackson, and he let his hands fall to my legs. His thumbs stroked the soft flesh of my inner thighs.

A dangerous craving to feel all of him raced through me, threatening to consume both of us in a fiery inferno of need. I wanted this man so badly that if I tried to dial things down, my lady parts would've gone on strike.

"Now who's wearing too many clothes?" I said.

He gave my legs a light squeeze. "I still think it's you."

My legs spread wider on his lap. His eyes darkened, and he tried to move his hands higher up my thighs. I held them in place, rocking forward against him. His fingers clenched, and he twisted his arms in my grasp, straining to touch me.

"Before this goes any further," I said, sucking his earlobe, "I need to see the goods, Jax."

Lifting his eyes from my bare chest, a naughty grin played on his lips. "Whatever the lady wants." Reaching one hand over his shoulders, he pulled off his undershirt, and I shit you not, that OMG song by Usher started playing in my head. The man was carved from freaking marble. I'm talking abs, on abs, on top of more abs. Then my eyeballs made it all the way up to his chest—and *Holy. Shit.*

I could do nothing but blatantly gape at the male perfection in front of me. I shut my mouth before I serenaded him with Usher, or drooled on him—either was a definite possibility. I traced the cut lines of his stomach. "I think it's safe to say that I can work with this," I squeaked out.

I shrieked when, with one fluid move, he flipped me onto my back and ranged over me, bracketing my face with his hands. He supported himself on his elbows. "I'm so glad I passed inspection."

Turning my head, I kissed his palm. "Well, at least above the waist, though it remains to be seen about certain other parts. Although unless V left her curling iron in this bed and it's currently jammed against my thigh, I expect … *big* things await me."

Slowly, Jackson lowered himself until we were skin to skin, and there was no question about what he had going on below the waist. Sweet Baby Jesus, maybe it was true about the correlation between the size of a man's hands and the size of his …

I pulled him in for a kiss. Once I did, oh honey, it was on! He took control, weaving his hands in my hair and tilting my head back to kiss me more deeply. He kissed me until I was breathless and then worked his way down my neck. Rather than head straight down to the promised land, he feathered kisses along my shoulders and back over my sternum.

"Jax, please!" I begged, delirious with the need for more.

He lifted his head. "Please what, Kez?" Using the flat of my hand, I tried to direct his head toward either breast, but he wouldn't budge from where he hovered above me. "Seems like you need something, gorgeous." The gleam in his eyes was wicked.

I lifted my head from the pillow. "Jax, if you don't stop talking and put that mouth to a much better use, I'm going to hurt you."

Laughing, he murmured something about me being bossy and lowered his head. I closed my eyes and dropped my head back. His lips had just landed on my skin when some deranged asshole started pounding on the door of the suite. Jackson's head snapped up. "What the …"

Refusing to believe fate could be so cruel, I stroked his face. "I'm sure it's nothing. Someone's probably got the wrong room. Now, let's get back to …"

I was interrupted by further banging on the door, now coupled with a woman yelling. The noises were muffled by both the suite door and the closed door to the bedroom but still audible.

Jackson pushed himself up, letting cool air drift across my stomach. "Don't you think you should see who that is? What if it's V or Rae?"

I grabbed his waistband to keep him from getting up. "They have keys, babe, and, if it's a true emergency, the ability to dial 9-1-1. No need for me to get involved."

He kept listening, but there was no further noise from the hallway.

"See, nothing to worry about!" I unbuttoned his pants.

"In that case," he sank back down so we were almost flush against each other, "where was I?"

I dragged a finger down my chest. "I'm thinking somewhere in this area, maybe?"

His palm followed the path of my finger until it rested in the valley between my breasts. "Here?"

I sighed. "I'd try a little to the left or the right. Although if you used both hands, it would cover all the bases."

Jackson's laughter drifted over me as he licked at the hollow of my throat. Anticipation unfurled within me as his beard tickled my hypersensitive skin. As I held my breath, his mouth worked its way lower on my body, layering gentle kisses along the curve of one breast while his hand stroked over the other ... and the banging resumed on the exterior door. My inner witch, who by this time was naked and covered in body oil, threw herself off a cliff.

I slapped both hands against the mattress. "*Son of a bitch!*" I roared. Jackson wisely moved off me, and I yanked the cups of the teddy back up, shoving my arms through the straps. I jerked my robe from the floor and swept out of the bedroom, ripping the ties into a knot as I stormed to the door. "I swear to God, Rae," I yelled, "if you haven't at least lost an arm, I'm going to kill you!" Without checking the peephole, I flung open the door. "If you're just up here to ..." Any epithet died on my lips when I saw it wasn't an inebriated Rae standing in front of me.

Chapter 11

"Callie?" I asked dumbly, my hand rigid on the knob.

She was still in her dress, but her eyes were red rimmed, and black rivulets of mascara streaked down her cheeks. Belatedly, I realized I'd answered the door practically naked. I clutched the lapels of my robe together, trying to save some sense of decency.

"What are you doing here?" I asked.

She took in my outfit, and tears welled up in her eyes. "Is … is he here?" Renewed tears splashed down her face, adding to the black stripes already cracking her makeup.

"Is who her—"

"I know he is!" She pushed past me into the suite.

"C'mon in," I muttered and let the door close.

"Miller!" she sobbed as she charged into the living room.

Miller? I thought. Why would she think Miller was here?

"Miller, I know you're in here, so you might as well come on out!" She darted about like a crazed hummingbird, flitting first one way, then the other.

Entering the living room, I tried to calm her down. "Callie, wait a second. I think there's been some sort of misunderstanding here."

She whirled on me, her tiny hands balled firmly at her sides. "Oh really? Like you misunderstanding that he's my *fiancée* and not your boyfriend?"

I was taken aback by the venom in her accusation. "What?"

Abandoning her quest to ransack the room looking for her missing fiancée, she advanced on me. "Miller and I are together, and the two of you are over!" she said pointing a finger in my face. Her voice was so raw, the words sounded like she'd torn them out.

Holding out my hands, I said, "Callie, listen, if you'll just let me explain …"

Her hands were now on her hips, her elbows flapping back and forth, enhancing the bird imagery as she continued her tirade. "I don't want any explanation from you! You need to understand …"

"Kez?" Jackson called from the bedroom door. He stood shirtless with his hands in the pockets of his unbuttoned dress pants. His dark hair was wildly tousled from where I'd run my fingers through it. He looked at me with hooded eyes. Jackson Jenkins was a living, breathing cologne ad that I had been *this close* to experiencing, only to be waylaid by my ex-boyfriend's crazed fiancée. Whatever I did in a prior life had to be seven kinds of fucked up, because this was some *serious* karma. I looked at the ceiling, willing the universe to give me a reason why this was happening. On second thought, there was no way I had ever done anything bad enough to deserve this.

Callie's head whipped in his direction. "Jackson?"

"Hey, Callie." He gave her a little wave and retreated back into the bedroom.

She swiveled back to me. "But I thought …" The fight drained out of her, and she collapsed onto the couch in a daze.

Gingerly, I sat next to her. "The only *he* who's been in here all night is Jackson, not Miller."

"So Miller's not here?" Her face contorted with emotion, and she put her head in her hands. I wasn't sure if her reaction stemmed from relief in finding out I wasn't with Miller or misery that she had no idea where he was. She drew in a heavy breath and ripped her fingers through her hair. It no longer held the elegant style from the party but was now somewhat matted to her scalp. With a claw-like grip, she separated the blonde curls into two chunks and pulled them taut. Hairspray and what I had to assume were equal parts makeup and snot she'd wiped from her face kept it from falling back to her shoulders when she released it. Uncaring, she twisted her hands in her lap, a trance-like scowl on her face.

Unsure of what to do, I said nothing but remained prepared to flee at the first sign she was going to freak out on me. I mean, sure, I could probably fend her off, but who wanted to risk a broken nose? Finally, she blinked, and I was relieved she wasn't catatonic.

Looking from me to the bedroom she said, "And you guys were …"

I nodded.

"Oh my God! I am so humiliated! I barge in here like a crazy person, accuse you of trying to steal my fiancée, and the whole time you're trying to, well, you know, with your own boyfriend."

I reached over and awkwardly rubbed her shoulder. "Er, well, it's kind of tough for me to say it's understandable without sounding like an asshole." She cried harder. "Hey, hey," I began to panic, "it's gonna be okay!" Her sobs continued, ratcheting up in volume.

"Callie," Jackson said calmly. He'd come back into the living room and was holding a robe. He was also no longer shirtless. My inner witch, who'd clawed her way back up the cliff, let go of the root she was holding onto and plummeted with despair once again.

Callie didn't respond to Jackson, but her wails were no longer at a level that would attract hotel security. "Callie, look at me," Jackson said. With a blubbering exhale, she did. He held out the robe, "Why don't you go into the bathroom there and change out of that dress? Maybe splash a little water on your face? That might make you feel a little better. Then, the three of us can talk, okay?"

While her attention was on Jackson, I vigorously shook my head. The faint upturn at the corner of his mouth was the only way I knew he saw me.

"O-o-okay," she spluttered. "But only if it's all right with Kez." Big blue eyes, brimming with what had to be her hundredth bout of tears, turned to me. Oh for Christ's sake! Tossing her out now would be like shoving a baby deer into the path of an eighteen wheeler.

I molded my mouth into less of a glower, concentrating on masking the irritation in my response. "Of course, Callie. It's fine."

With a tremulous smile, she took the robe from Jackson and went into the half bath at the front of the suite.

Once she closed the door behind her, I hissed, "What are you doing?"

Jackson sat on the coffee table in front of me, elbows on his knees. He tucked a random strand of hair behind my ear, trailing his fingers down my jaw. "Well, unfortunately not you. At least not tonight."

"And whose fault is that?" I was irrationally angry that he'd put his shirt back on.

He snorted. "Seems like Miller's."

"Ugh!" I slumped back against the cushions. "I should have never answered the door!"

He took my hands in his. Gently, he pulled me up. "Agreed. But for now, and I can't believe I'm saying this, why don't you put on something a little less ... revealing."

I thumped my forehead on his chest. He smoothed his hand up my back as he said, "I know, babe, trust me. *I know.*" When I turned away to change, he delivered a sharp slap to my backside.

I glared at him over my shoulder. "Tease."

A lone tear trickled down the face of my inner witch at the ruination of her evening—and that Jackson was still wearing pants.

Dejectedly, I retreated to the bedroom and searched for something more suited for entertaining. I cursed Miller the entire time. When I came back, dressed in a more casual ensemble of yoga pants and a long-sleeve T-shirt, Callie had emerged from the bathroom. She'd scrubbed off her makeup and had, for the moment, stopped crying. Cocooned in the fluffy robe, she was burrowed into the corner of the couch with her arms wrapped around her knees.

Given her small frame and the overstuffed furniture, she looked like a kid who'd been put in time out. In my absence, Jackson had made her a cup of tea, which I didn't even know we had. He handed Callie a steaming mug that she cradled in both hands. He smiled at me and raised his chin toward Rae's stash on the dining table. At my nod, he nabbed two glasses and poured three fingers of bourbon into each one.

I downed half of mine after he handed it to me, coughing as it seared my throat. He rubbed my back. "It's meant to be sipped, not chugged."

"Desperate times," I wheezed. He kissed my forehead and held me to him. I rested my cheek against his hard chest and silently bemoaned my shattered plans of multiple orgasms.

"I really am sorry I barged in here," Callie said meekly.

Releasing Jackson, I offered her a wan smile. "Something tells me *Miller* should be apologizing for this situation, not you."

I dropped into the chair next to the couch, and Jackson stood behind it. I looked at Callie, her cleanly scoured face devoid of the happiness I'd seen earlier that night. Guilt pressed down hard on my heart. Trying to give her some comfort, I said, "I know I'm not exactly the person you'd want to talk to about all this, but I've been where you are."

She wiped the back of her hand under her nose and looked down into her mug. "I thought when he asked me to marry him, he was finally over you. Guess I was wrong."

Her words hit me with an unexpected force. When I got on the plane to come up here, a part of me had been hoping to hear precisely that. Closure or not, the selfish part of me had wanted to know Miller was still pining away for me. That if he was given the choice, he'd toss Callie out on her ass for another chance with me. But now, I was ashamed that any part of me had felt that way. Seeing her so miserable in much the same way I had been made me hate myself for being a partial cause of it.

"Callie, I'm sorry ..."

She held up a hand. "Don't apologize. I mean, it's not like you planned this or anything."

"Right, of course not." My half-hearted denial was pathetic, hollow words from an empty heart.

"All you did was come home with your boyfriend to his reunion and walk into this shitstorm." She gestured vaguely around herself, but the movement encompassed so much more.

"Uh, well, that's not …" I couldn't finish the sentence.

Ignoring my weak attempt to interrupt her, Callie continued. "The thing is, I always knew if you'd moved up here, I never would have stood a chance. And sadly, I was okay with that. I thought I loved him enough for both of us."

Determined to end this line of discussion, I said, "Callie, look, there's something you need to know about this weekend."

Jackson pointed to the bedroom. "I'll just be …"

Once the door shut behind him, I motioned to the mug beside Callie. "I don't know about you, but I need something a little stronger than that. Care to join me?"

"Sure." She sniffled.

After refilling my glass and getting Callie her own, I sat next to her on the couch and curled my legs underneath me. "I can honestly say, this is not a position in which I ever thought I'd find myself."

With a mirthless laugh, she agreed. "Same here."

"How did you even know what room I was in?"

She lowered her eyes in a guilty tell. "One of my friends works in room service here. She told me after I promised I wouldn't do anything stupid." Her lips tipped up. "We see how that turned out."

"You're not the only one who's made a few rash decisions lately," I said amenably.

Callie looked at me questioningly, and I knew I had to come clean. I ran my fingers over the designs cut into the heavy crystal glass. After a bracing sip, I told her the whole story of why I'd come to the reunion. I didn't leave out any of the snarky bits or the ugly thoughts I had about her or how her relationship with Miller had started. When I finished, she looked a little shell-shocked. She was clearly a heartbroken girl in love with a man I doubted would ever be able to give her the happily ever after she so coveted. The knowledge I was responsible for a portion of her pain weighed heavily on me.

Stewing in my regret, I put my glass down on the table and said, "So, that's the long and the short of it, I guess. But Callie, I want you to know that while I can't say I never wanted this to happen, I can say now that I'm sorry it did."

Her glass shook in her hand as she glared at me. For a second, I thought she might chuck it at my head, but she banged it on the coffee table instead. "You're sorry? You come up here to wreck my engagement, and *you're sorry?*"

I flinched as she screamed the last two words at me.

A flush spread over her cheeks as she continued, "He never cheated on you, Kez. Not one single time. I had to wait forever for him to get over you and move on, to see I was more than just his buddy at the bar who listened to him worshipping you from thousands of miles away. Then, when he's *finally* seen me as the one who can make him happy, who can give him a great life and a beautiful family, you swoop in here," Callie jabbed her finger at me, "and ruin everything!" She hunched forward and pulled in a big gulp of air.

"Callie, I ..." But in that moment, I found I had little to say. The revelation that Miller had never cheated was big. Despite how bad things had gotten between us, he hadn't crossed that line. A sense of relief washed over me at the news.

Staring at the table in front of her, she said, "I don't know if I'm more pissed at you or at the fact I've been deluding myself for so long." She looked at me. "You really are a selfish bitch."

"I deserve that," I admitted. "But in my defense, I only did all this because I'd convinced myself that you were a conniving shrew."

We sat in silence, each digesting what had transpired, then she asked, "What made you finally block his number?"

"You knew about that?" I was surprised Miller said anything about that to her, or anyone for that matter. He'd never liked for anyone to be in his business, especially if it made him look bad, or in his mind, weak. So the idea that he would tell someone I'd blocked him came as a shock.

She pulled her knees up to her chin. "Yeah, he'd worked himself into a real lather over that by the time he got to the bar that night. He was so mad about it that he got thrown out for punching a guy."

Trying to keep the emotion out of my voice, I said, "One day it finally dawned on me that he was never going to pick me. We were just going to be stuck in this miserable limbo of broken promises that would never lead to anything but more heartache. And I knew as long as he kept calling, I'd keep answering. So I did the only thing I could to save my sanity and what was left of my heart."

"You blocked him," she confirmed.

"Yep."

"You say he didn't pick you?" Callie plucked at a string on her robe.

"Right," I said, not knowing where she was going with this.

She hesitated. "Well, you didn't pick him either, did you?"

The question resonated loudly in my brain. She'd brought up a difficult truth, one none of my friends who rallied to my side in the great Miller-Kez battle royal would ever have mentioned. "I suppose that's true," I said. "But it would've been nice to have at least been asked to come with him." I stood up. "I think that's enough introspection for tonight, don't you?"

Callie rose off the sofa. "Yeah, probably so." She checked her phone.

"Still nothing from Miller?"

Sadly, she shook her head. "I guess I'll call an Uber."

Tentatively, I said, "You're welcome to crash here, if you want."

I could hear her reluctance as she asked, "Are you sure?"

The clock on the wall behind her told me the night was already shot. There was no harm in letting her stay until morning. Plus, making her change back into her dress and stand on the curb alone awaiting an Uber driver would only add to my guilt load. "I am," I said and walked to the closet to grab the extra blanket and pillow I'd seen in there when we checked in.

Accepting them from me, she said, "Kez?"

"Yeah?" I asked, hoping she wasn't looking for further discussion of Miller.

"Jackson seems like a good guy. Maybe he's the silver lining in all this for you."

Her kind words warmed me, and I caught myself smiling. "I hope so."

Chapter 12

I pushed open the bedroom door as quietly as possible, in case Jackson had dozed off while I was talking to Callie. He'd switched off the floor lamp, but the bedside lamp was on, supplementing the ambient light coming in through the sheer curtains. Jackson's suit pants were folded neatly over the back of the wingback chair with his jacket on top of them. The man himself was stretched out across the duvet, sleeping peacefully. When the door clicked shut behind me, he didn't stir, so I did what any other woman would do—loitered in the doorway and stared at him like a total creeper. Yeah, if I'd been a guy, it would've been pervy, but I was a girl, so it was perfectly fine to salivate over an unsuspecting man while he slept. Trust me—I'm a lawyer and I know things like this.

Moving closer, I marveled at the landscape of his body. He'd stripped down to navy boxer briefs, and I thanked Calvin Klein for his craftsmanship. A light smattering of hair dusted his chest, narrowing to a thin strip that bisected his abs and disappeared beneath his waistband. His face had softened in sleep, and he'd thrown one arm above his head. Dark lashes rested on his cheeks, his full lips pursed slightly as he breathed evenly. His hair was messy, some of it falling forward to lie against his forehead. A line from Disney's *The Jungle Book* popped into my head: "a delicious man cub." Jackson looked amazing clothed, but seeing him half-naked it was hard to believe he was real.

"Jackson," I said softly. He twitched but didn't wake up. "Jax," I said a bit louder.

His eyelids fluttered open, and he blinked, focusing on me with a sleepy grin. "Hey."

Standing there awkwardly, I toed the carpet. "Hey," I said. I was nothing if not a dazzling conversationalist.

Shifting into a sitting position, he patted the space beside him. I came closer to the bed but didn't join him. The interruption from Callie had reset the night, and I was no longer sure of what to do. I wondered what he was thinking but didn't have the courage to ask. Should we just pick up where we left off, or should we talk about anything? Insecurity swelled within me and kept me from crawling in bed next to him.

Jackson didn't have any patience for my indecision. "Seriously, Kez? You're shy now?" With one arm, he hauled me over his lap and propped me against the headboard. Thankful for his direct approach, I curled into his warmth, laying my head on his shoulder. His hand floated over my thigh and came to rest on my hip. "You girls get it all sorted?"

I blew out a breath. "I don't know. I mean, I came clean about everything and so did she, to an extent. I can't call it sorted, but we came to a sort of … understanding, I guess."

"Well, that's good, right?" He began leisurely rubbing my hip bone.

Trying to focus on the conversation rather than the tingle of his touch, I said, "Probably. A lot of what she said mirrored a feeling I'd had but wasn't ready to admit to."

"What's that?" His hand stilled as he awaited my answer. I could feel the tension spreading throughout his body. Not that I could blame him. The night had taken a definitive turn in an uncomfortable direction. But I had to give him credit for stepping up to have this conversation.

"After Miller and I broke up, it's like I put my life on hold. Rae says I was keeping a seat warm for him in case he decided to come back."

"Given what he said this morning and how he reacted tonight, it seems like that's something he's interested in," Jackson said. The reference to Miller brought a tightness to his voice that I wanted to drive out as quickly as I could.

I debated whether to mention the conversation I'd overheard at the reunion. Remembering V's advice that at a minimum, Jackson deserved honesty, I said, "The thing is, I think he could be."

"Are you?" Jackson asked as he shifted away from me.

"What? No!" I said, grabbing his arm to stop him from getting out of bed. His blue eyes were clouded with suspicion. Pushing myself upright, I held his wrist and said, "I overheard a conversation between Miller and Callie earlier tonight, so I know my coming up here knocked him right on his ass. But whatever turmoil he's going through, the same isn't true for me anymore. I need to leave Miller in the past where he belongs and concentrate on my future, which doesn't involve him at all. His whole life was and still is here, just like mine was and still is back home. Both of us were too stubborn to make a change for the other. He didn't ask me to come and wasn't willing to stay. But I never volunteered to come here either. Neither of us were willing to upend our lives and take a leap of faith for the other, and that should have been a sign to both of us that things weren't right. That *we* weren't right. Time hasn't changed that fact, Jackson. Miller's not the guy for me."

He considered my summation, and I couldn't remember ever being this nervous while waiting on a verdict. "You're sure about that?" he asked.

I linked our fingers and squeezed his hand. "Positive." His fingers tightened reassuringly around mine, and a sense of relief flooded me.

With his free hand, Jackson stroked his beard and grinned. "Of course, it also helps that you finally met the guy who *is* right for you."

Grinning up at him, I said, "Oh yeah, Dave's great. Too bad he's interested in V."

"Oh, you think you're funny, huh?" Jackson flipped me underneath him and dug his fingers into my rib cage, tickling me until I gasped for breath. "Do you take it back?" he asked sternly.

"Yes." I panted for air between giggles. "Yes! Just please stop doing that!"

He stopped the tickle torture. "Not exactly the words I'd planned on making you say in this position."

My laugh morphed into a yawn.

"You look exhausted, Kez."

I tried to deny it, but another huge yawn followed on the heels of the first.

"C'mere, gorgeous," he signaled for me to get under the covers, "let's get some sleep."

"No, I'm fine, really." My protest was weak, and Jackson wasn't buying it.

"You're dead on your feet, and you know it," he scolded.

All the drama of the last few hours came crashing down on me, and I was too tired to argue. "Okay, let me wash my makeup off."

After my evening beauty ritual, I changed into some shortie pajamas. Clicking off the light in the bathroom, I rejoined Jackson. He took in my pj's, or more accurately my bare legs, and licked his lips.

"Those are ... nice," he said carefully, his hands fisted in the sheets.

Hooking my thumbs into the waistband, I tugged it below my hip bone. "Well, I normally sleep naked, so if that would make you more comfortable ..." I let the bottoms dip a little farther, and he growled.

"Bed. Now."

Like a good girl, I slid between the cool sheets. Jackson's body curled behind me, and his arm draped over my stomach. Succumbing to exhaustion and the desire to be next to him, I cuddled back into his chest. "Good night, Jax."

He kissed my shoulder. "Good night, Kez."

Saturday morning, I woke up exactly where I'd known I would—sprawled out like a starfish in the middle of the mattress, not touching Jackson in any way, shape, or form. I sat up and snickered when I saw him folded into an origami-like pose in the uppermost corner of the bed. And yet somehow, he was fast asleep.

Needing to pee, I got up. A glance in the bathroom mirror confirmed yes, I did look like Death with a hangover. I ran a comb through my hair and brushed my teeth. Anything more and it would look like I'd ducked in here to primp for him. Which I had, but there was no reason to let him know that.

In my absence, Jackson had moved closer to the middle of the bed. The sheet draped over his waist, leaving his chest and the tapered lines of his stomach exposed. There was no question he was a gorgeous guy that any woman would fawn over. At least any woman who liked brawny, bearded guys covered in intricate ink. What I'd learned about him over the past couple days made me think the pretty package he came in was a reflection of the person he was on the inside. Maybe Callie was right—I'd come out of this with not simply what I wanted in the beginning but also what I needed in the end.

"You know, it's weird to stand in the shadows and watch someone while they sleep," Jackson said in a scratchy voice.

"Busted," I replied without any shame.

He opened his eyes. "Come back to bed, Kez."

I snuggled in next to him and let my hand drift down his stomach. Trapping it with his larger palm, he brought my fingers to his lips, kissing the tips of them. Stroking his beard, I tried to angle his head toward me.

He gripped my wrist. "Not a good idea until I at least use that free mouthwash in the bathroom," he said. When he stood and stretched, I watched the muscles in his back ripple.

I plumped the pillows and arranged myself against the headboard in a pose I hoped was more come hither than desperate. "Hurry back."

The look he shot my way made me confident I'd nailed come hither, or he *really* liked desperate women. Either way, I did want him to hurry up so we could finish what we'd started last night. While he was in the bathroom, I straightened the sheets and fluffed my hair. With a quick breath check, I settled back against the pillows, ready for my close up.

Jackson appeared in the doorway, backlit by the vanity light. He held on to the top of the door frame and stretched languidly, giving me a good look at the hard planes of his body. If he were any sexier, my panties would've disappeared into thin air. His predatory smile had my nether regions all aflutter with anticipation as he came to stand at the foot of the bed. With a flick of his wrist, the covers flew back. Kneeling between my feet, he started at my ankles and took a slow path up my calves and over my knees. His lips followed his fingers, and shivers ran through me with each kiss. His splayed fingers roamed up my legs, thumbs skating along the insides of my thighs. *Oh, sweet Lord, keep going*, was the only thought going through my mind.

"Jax," I said on a sigh when he brushed the elastic of my panties. Finally, we were going to …

The door flew open, and Rae came in, trailed closely by V. "Hey, Kez, what happened last night? Have you seen this?" A sheet of hotel stationary was in her hand, and her attention was on it, rather than the two of us.

"Seriously, Rae!" I yelled in frustration.

She looked up, and for a second, her face was blank. Then her lips hooked into a smile at the sight of Jackson, in nothing but his boxer briefs, nestled between my legs with his hands scant millimeters from where I'd wanted them for what seemed like years.

"I didn't know the room came with a complimentary pelvic exam," Rae said.

Aghast, V covered her eyes. "Rae, I told you to knock! C'mon!" With an apologetic peek at me, she shoved a still-grinning Rae out of the room. "Sorry, Kez."

When the door shut behind them, Jackson rested his forehead on my stomach. "Why did I book a room at such a shithole? And why don't your friends have any boundaries?"

I slumped against the pillows, toying with his hair. "Your first one is an excellent question. As to the second, Rae never met a boundary she didn't plow right through, usually with V hanging onto her shirttail."

He plucked at the waistband of my tiny sleep shorts. "Am I ever going to find out what's under here?"

Sighing, I said, "We should've stayed in the hall last night, or maybe the elevator. I think there were fewer people."

He pushed himself up. "I'll remember that tonight. But I'm not taking any chances. We'll have our own room." When my nose wrinkled, he added, "At a nice hotel, not the fleabag down the street."

Moving from between my knees, he held out a hand. I let him help me to my feet. Without heels, my head came to his shoulder. My arms looped around his trim midsection, and he rested his chin on my hair. "We could stay in here until they leave," he said.

Pointing at the varied assortment of heels, flats, and sneakers scattered near the window, I said, "V wouldn't leave without her shoes, which, as you can see, are all in this room with us."

With a regretful grumble, he agreed. "I guess we have no choice then."

I placed a kiss at his throat. "I'll make it up to you, Jax."

His hands stole under my shorts and cupped my ass. "I'll hold you to that."

Resigned to a sexless morning, I stepped out of his embrace and took a robe off the back of the bathroom door. He dressed in his dress pants and wifebeater. I have never hated anyone as much as Rae in that moment. I played with the hem of his shirt. "Maybe we could stay in here for just a while longer."

"Easy, tiger, you'll get your shot at me. Don't worry." A gentle shove had me moving toward the door. Opening it, I saw Rae curled in a chair looking way too pleased with herself.

"Hey there, lovebirds. Have a good night?" she asked.

"It was on the way to being a great morning until you barged in," I said resentfully.

She did have the sense to look a tad remorseful. "I was preoccupied with this." The note she'd held earlier was on the coffee table in front of her. I picked it up. It was from Callie.

Kez,

Thanks for letting me stay last night. It's weird to think that the one person I never wanted to meet turned out to be the person I needed to talk to the most.

Callie

Chapter 13

"All right, spill it," said Rae within seconds of the suite door closing behind Jackson. Like a line of ducklings, she and V followed me into the bedroom. I hung the robe up and pulled on a sweatshirt over my pj's.

"I'm too tired for a full postmortem right now," I replied, falling onto the bed.

From her position at the foot, she waggled her eyebrows. "Oh, I bet you are."

I chucked a pillow at her head. "Not for the reason you might think, perv."

V hopped onto the bed beside me. "Really? So y'all didn't …"

"Between Callie's late night visit and Rae's untimely interruption, no, we didn't."

"Why *was* Callie here?" asked V.

"Because it seems after taking one look at me with Jackson at the reunion last night, Miller flipped a shit. They had a fight. She put two and two together, came up with five, and came here."

Rae's eyes landed on something next to the bed. Retrieving it, she popped up with a flourish, the teddy pinched between her fingers. "And found you in this?"

I snatched it out of her hand. "I had on a robe."

She brought out the sheer kimono from behind her back and smirked. "Right."

I took the robe from Rae and threw both it and the teddy in the general direction of my open suitcase. "After she realized Miller wasn't here, we talked."

"Talked?" prodded Rae.

I nodded. "I told her the whole scoop."

V's mouth formed a perfect O. "Like, everything?"

"Yep, all of it."

"Why?" asked Rae.

Adjusting the pillows against the headboard, I sank back into them. "Because she deserved to know."

Rae scoffed at my sudden choice of honesty. "I'm sorry, but three days ago you thought she was a home-wrecker who deserved to die miserable and alone. When did she go from being the Antichrist to your new best buddy?"

Her characterization wasn't far off, and I knew I had to give them a better picture of Callie. "In my mind, I'd made her into this scheming witch, but the girl who showed up sobbing at my door last night was anything but that. She honestly thought Miller had thrown her over after seeing me."

"Well, turnaround's fair play, right? I mean, she did the same thing to you, didn't she?" asked V, not getting why I wasn't happy with this outcome.

"Turns out that she didn't. Miller never cheated on me with her," I said.

"For real?" Rae asked, wide-eyed.

"Yep. And even if he had. Even if the two of them had sunk to that level, why would I want to join them? I don't want to be that person, and I'm ashamed to think I ever considered it. I don't want to be so fixated on something from the past that it ruins the future, not just for me, but for everyone else."

"Well, look whose heart grew three sizes, and it's not even Christmas!" extolled Rae. I threw another pillow at her. She caught it and joined V and me on the bed. "So does this mean you and Jackson are ..."

I didn't want to get into a discussion of what Jackson and I were, or weren't, going to become. I'd barely come to grips with needing to move on from Miller. It was too early to tell what could or would happen with Jackson, and I wasn't in the mood to analyze it. "It means Jackson and I are going to this picnic today and then we," I pointed at the three of us seated on the bed, "fly back home tomorrow. Beyond that, I have no idea."

"I think he has ideas, Kez," said V. "Ones involving the two of you seeing each other after we leave. And I, for one, think those are very good ideas."

My heart fluttered at her words. "I can see myself being open to that."

"Girl, if a man who looks like that has those kinds of ideas about you, you should already be at a steady boil, not just warming up. Hell, I get hot flashes when he walks in the room." Rae fanned herself and pretended to swoon, toppling across V's legs.

V rolled her eyes. "You are such a drama queen."

Rae batted her lashes at V and made no move to get up. "And yet you love me anyway."

"Just goes to show there's no accounting for taste," V said.

"Dave will be so hurt to hear you said that" Rae grinned.

V flushed and nudged Rae with her knee. "Shut up, Rae."

I turned to V. "How was your night with Dave?"

She hopped off the bed. "I need some coffee."

"That good?" I called after her as she scampered from the room. I looked to Rae. "What gives?"

"Well, Chris and I ..."

"Wait, who's Chris?" I asked.

"That yummy bartender from the bar downstairs. Anyway, we met up with V and Dave to go dancing. Long story short, we all ended up staying at Dave's place."

Gleefully, she joined me against the headboard. "I took a water break around two this morning and met V in the kitchen of

Dave's house ..." her well-timed pause created the requisite drama, "wearing nothing but *his* T-shirt and a big ol' smile."

"Oh wow!" I was surprised at my normally reserved best friend. V didn't hop into bed with just anyone so that meant Dave had become pretty special since she'd met him Wednesday night. It was an interesting development.

I heard the pad of V's bare feet before she reappeared in the doorway. "You know I can hear you, right?" she asked crankily. Her cheeks were tinted red, maybe from our teasing, but I was betting it was from remembering her night with Dave.

I jumped up and hugged her. "Our little girl is growing up!" I said over her head to Rae.

V shrugged me off her. "You guys are a bunch of assholes. It's not like I'm a virgin or anything!"

I felt bad for embarrassing her when what I really wanted to do was celebrate the fact she was living a little. She'd let herself be governed by her prim and proper pain-in-the-ass family for way too long. "Yeah, but c'mon, V. You have to admit this is a little bit of a surprise. I mean, Rae doesn't have to buy pajamas because she has so many bartenders' T-shirts as souvenirs from her sexual journey through this great nation, but you ..."

"You're just jealous of my collection, Kez," Rae said with a touch of pride and absolutely no regret.

"I do love that black one from that bar in Kentucky," I said.

"The shirt or the bartender?" Rae teased.

"Jesus, Rae ..."

"Anyway," V interjected. "I decided to take a chance and see what happened."

"So *what* happened?" I asked.

At first, I didn't think she was going to answer. Then, with a sly grin, she held up four fingers.

"I don't get ..." Rae's voice faded as she understood what V meant. "Wait a minute!" She leapt off the bed. "Are you saying he got you off four times?"

V grinned and walked away.

"Are you kidding me? I had to settle for two!" Rae yelled at her retreating back.

I pointed at myself. "Zero right here, Rae. Thanks, in no small part, to you!"

"Four," she muttered. "Unbelievable!"

I threw an arm around Rae. "It's always the quiet ones."

We wandered into the kitchen in search of the coffee V had started. "Dave says Jackson's one of the good ones," V said from her spot at the counter.

I paused in pulling down a coffee mug. "Way to jump right to it, V. What else does Dave have to say about Jackson?"

She poured me some coffee. "He says he went to college on a football scholarship."

I told them about his name tag. "Based on it, he could've gotten a scholarship doing anything from football to basket weaving."

Laughing, V went on. "He got his master's degree and started with a huge accounting firm."

"Accounting?" Rae asked. "He looks nothing like my accountant."

Since we each used Ernest P. Sherrill as our CPA, I could confirm that the elderly man with soda-bottle-thick glasses bore no resemblance to Jackson. "Your accountant is pushing seventy, Rae," I reminded her. I edged past her to grab the cream from the small fridge.

"Makes me think I need to start looking for a new one," Rae said.

"Only *you* would use your ovaries to evaluate a CPA," V admonished her.

"We all have our methods," Rae said, undaunted.

Stopping their bickering before it could get to full squabble level, I said, "Sorry to disappoint you, but Jackson's not a CPA anymore."

"No?" Rae's face fell at the news she was stuck with Ernest.

Stirring sugar into my coffee, I said, "Nope, he left that firm and started his own restoration business."

"Yeah, Dave says he's making a killing," said V. She sat on one of the small stools at the counter. "A few of his pieces were featured in some magazine spread, and now he's like one of the most sought-after people in that field. As I hear it, he's got some huge deal brewing with a hotel chain to furnish all kinds of unique stuff for their new line of lodge resorts."

Rae gave me a naughty wink. "That means he must be good with his hands."

Ignoring her, I took the stool beside V. "Any other details Dave shared?" I sipped and waited for her to dish.

V put down her mug. "Not much else. Just wanted to make sure I knew Jackson was a good guy."

"And in doing so, make sure *I* knew he was a good guy?"

She grinned. "That's the underlying gist of it."

A knock sounded at the door, and the three of us exchanged a look. When no one else moved, I started to get up.

"Wait!" V whisper shouted, grabbing my arm to keep me seated.

"What?" I whispered back.

"It could be Miller." She perched on the edge of her own stool, throwing an anxious glance at the door.

"Why would Miller be at the door?" I asked.

"Why did Callie come here last night?" she countered.

She had a point. I waved at the locked door. "You answer it then."

V tiptoed over to check the peephole. Tension ebbed from her shoulders, and she opened the door. "Oh hi," she said.

Rae and I craned our bodies toward the door, but the conversation was muffled. At the sound of the dead bolt sliding back into place, we came around the corner. V held a huge bouquet of white roses arranged in a cut glass vase.

"Four orgasms and a dozen roses? What kinda magic vajajay you got going on down there, girl?" Rae asked.

V scowled. "As endearing as that was, Rae, these aren't for me. They're for Kez."

"For me?" The heady scent of the roses filled the room. They were long stemmed with bright white petals. The pale blooms were just starting to unfurl into fragile spirals.

"That's what the delivery guy said. There's a card." V set the vase on the coffee table and pulled the card from its holder, passing it to me.

Kez,

Since I didn't know your favorite, I thought I'd go with white. Kind of like a fresh start or a blank slate. We can fill it however you like.

Jax

"Seriously? Those arms and that ass come with a poetry option?" Rae cried from where she'd read the note behind me. "Makes me wonder what other accessories are available."

My phone chimed a text alert. A glance at the screen showed it was from a number listed as Man Hands.

MH: *Too much?*

K: *Roses are never too much, but stealing my phone and putting your number in it as Man Hands? Maybe crossing the line …*

MH: *Someone said something to me about desperate times last night. Just following her example. Card sappy enough?*

K: *Appropriate amount. Even Rae liked it and she's allergic to sappy.*

MH: *Oh well, if Rae liked it, that was all I was worried about. *eye roll emoji**

K: **laughing emoji* Seriously, though, the flowers are beautiful, thank you.*

MH: *You're welcome, gorgeous. See you soon.*

K: *Can't wait, Man Hands.*

Chapter 14

The field spread out in a blanket of verdant green, with the sun reflecting off the white yardage markers. Blue-and-white tents had been set up along the home sideline. Underneath them stood tables weighted down by enough food to feed an army. The stiff breeze made me glad I'd worn a fleece jacket over my long-sleeve T-shirt and jeans.

Adults stood talking in different groups while kids darted between the tables. Jackson passed me a beer from one of the multitude of coolers. From the back pocket of his jeans, he pulled a soft red koozie, passing it to me with a smile. "You're not the only one who's prepared."

I read the letters written on the koozie in bold script above a picture of an older model Chevy truck. "Rightful Restoration? That's you?"

He rubbed the back of his neck and grinned. "That's me."

With a quick twist, I pulled the cap off and pushed the bottle into the neoprene sheath. "Cheers," I said, clinking my beer to his. After a sip, I assessed the crowd. There were a lot of people here, way more than I thought would come to a reunion.

"Exactly how many people went to your high school?" I asked.

"Well, keep in mind St. Pius is one of the largest churches up here, so we not only went to school there but also to church. Plus, there was an all-girls school. Last night was the class reunion, but today is open to anyone associated with St. Pius. So you're getting a lot more than just classmates and their families."

Now the large gathering made more sense. This wasn't just a reunion; it was more like a homecoming.

"Should we go be social?" he asked.

Given the crush of people there, the idea that we could do anything else was laughable. "I can't imagine these folks letting their hometown hero escape unnoticed."

"Cute, real cute."

Linking his hand with mine, we began the rounds. It was like being at a political rally with the favorite candidate. He shook hands, kissed cheeks, and yes, even held babies. Jackson never rushed out of a conversation. He made time to chat with everyone who approached him. Just like the night before, though, he was either holding my hand, or his arm was draped around me—across my shoulders, around my waist, or resting against my hip. Throughout the afternoon as we sampled three thousand different kinds of wings, he always made sure to introduce me to the person with whom he was talking. It was as natural a move for him as breathing. So while he gave everyone his attention, I always had his focus. Whenever Miller and I had gone anywhere together, we usually splintered off to mingle with different groups. Jackson's desire to keep me close was a change of pace, but I liked it.

Last night had been great with the potential to be amazing, but that was based mainly on the fact that the man looked like an underwear model. Today, I saw more of what I'd seen at the cocktail party. I saw a man who was comfortable in his own skin, whether he was talking to former jocks, current millionaires, or his eighty-six-year-old calculus teacher. These glimpses of Jackson the person, rather than Jackson the potential sex god, fed the hope that the chemistry between us wasn't a fluke brought on by the lunacy of the situation I'd created. Maybe, just maybe, he and I could, as he put it "be in this for real." The idea didn't spook me as much as I thought it would. There was no overwhelming urge to bolt, but a growing one to stay and see where this thing between us would go.

I perused the desserts. While upstate New York was a far cry from my home in North Carolina, one thing was clear—neither area feared the use of butter or heavy cream. Cakes, pies, and cookies stretched across the length of the table before me. I evaluated the cavalcade of calories while Jackson finished his conversation with what had to be the fifth woman to come up and "just say hi," which consisted mainly of squeezing his bicep and rubbing their boobs on his arm. I was beginning to think the name of the girls' school had to be St. Pius Academy of the Slutty Virgin. Each time, he'd found a tactful way to dislodge them and swing me in front of him like a human shield. This last one was a little more reluctant to retreat than the others.

"Jackson," she said, her long, red fingernails clutching his arm like a hawk grasping its prey. "I can't believe you moved down south! I mean, it's so, I don't know, provincial down there." She spared me a glance. "No offense." That simpering platitude and side-eye with which it was delivered made it clear that offense had been her *only* intention.

I tried to flash a smile so sweet it should have given her diabetes. "Bless your heart, none taken."

Jackson choked on his beer at my over-the-top accent.

"I'll admit," I continued in my best Scarlett O'Hara impression. "It is a lot different up here. I mean," I gestured to her outfit that could only be described as Debbie Does the PTA, "I just love how y'all dress in a way that shows you don't care what other people think! In my little backwater, we'd never be able to do that."

I slid my arm around Jackson's waist. "Jax, honey, I'd love to sample some of those desserts." Looking back to her, I said, "If you'll excuse us, it was super nice to meet you."

She released her death grip on Jackson and stomped off in a snit.

"Why, Miss Scarlett," said Jackson. "I do believe your claws are showing. You're awful cute when you're jealous."

I wound my arms around his neck. "Jealous? Of little miss Nice 'n Easy? And, no, I'm not just talking about that dye job."

Jackson threaded his fingers in my belt loops. "So, not jealous?"

"Not in the least," I lied.

"So that was what? You marking your territory?" he teased.

"No, but this is." I pressed my lips to his. I felt him smile, then his lips softened and parted. I resisted (barely) the urge to wrap my legs around his waist. There were children—and nuns—present, after all. After a few moments, we broke apart, both a little breathless.

"Consider me bagged and tagged, gorgeous" he said, tapping a finger to my chin.

Laughing, I led him toward the buffet table. "I wasn't kidding about the desserts."

Way too many cookies later, I was stuffed and watching Jackson toss a football with some other guys. Heeding the call of nature, I signaled that I was going to head to the field house. He smiled, cheeks rosy from the cool air and the exertion of the game. With an incline of his chin, he indicated he'd come with me. I shook my head no, and he went back to his friends.

I trudged up the hill toward the restroom, shoving my hands in my pockets as I walked. Keeping an eye on the uneven ground at my feet, I didn't notice someone reaching for me until I was roughly jerked into an alcove on the side of the building. The little niche was behind a copse of trees, which meant it was obscured from the view of those at the picnic below. My back hit the wall, and a scream formed at the back of my throat. Fear tightened my lungs, then I saw who'd grabbed me.

"Hey, Kez," said Miller.

I wrested away from him. "What are you doing? Why are you hiding up here?" I was no longer afraid, but being alone up here with him didn't make me altogether comfortable either.

He paced back and forth in the small area, his gait agitated and jerky. Finally, he stopped and said, "I saw you and Jackson making the rounds. Quite the power couple."

"I don't have time for this, Miller," I said and turned to leave, but before I could, he came up behind me, locking his arms around my waist. "Kez, please wait." His breath was hot and sticky against my ear. It also smelled like beer.

I pushed against his clenched hands, but he held on. I refused to face him, so I directed my question to the space in front of us. "What are you doing, Miller?"

"I had to talk to you," he said. Memories of the times he'd called me drunk with similar slurred declarations filled my head. Talking was something he was good at. It was the whole follow-up thing he'd had trouble with. When his hands loosened a little, I knocked them away and spun around.

"What is there left to say at this point?" I said coldly.

He crowded in closer. The solid concrete of the field house pressed against my back, scraping roughly against my clothes. He loomed over me. Resting one hand on the wall beside my face, he said, "You're so beautiful, Kez, just like how I remembered." He traced the line of my cheek and pulled me to him as he lowered his head. I could not believe he was going to try and kiss me. His lips hit my cheek as I turned my head and pushed against his chest until he backed off. I wiped a hand against my cheek, trying to eliminate the feel of his lips. "What the hell was that?" *How dare he think he had any right to kiss me*! His actions poked at the rage that had festered within me for years and now threatened to burst forth and drown us both.

He extended a hand to me. When I didn't take it, he dropped it limply to his side. "That's something I've wanted to do for a long time." His voice came out husky, and I could see his pupils were dilated. Whether it was from booze, the almost kiss, or a combination of both, I wasn't sure.

"What are you talking about? I haven't seen or heard from you in years." I tried to ease my way past him, but even drunk he was still agile. Every step I took, he countered.

"Only because you blocked all my numbers *and* my email." Pain resonated in his voice, but I felt no pity for him. His decision to leave me, not my efforts to protect my heart, had brought us to this point. I was not about to let him blame me for whatever crap was running through his head right now.

"I had to for my own sanity, Miller!" I yelled. "You were making me a crazy person. Plus, *we were broken up*! I had to at least try to move on with my life."

"By cutting me out of it?"

"Yes!" I ducked under his arm, but he stumbled back in front of me. This was getting ridiculous. I wasn't scared of him, nor did I think he would hurt me. But the situation needed to end with me getting the hell out of there.

"But why?" He sounded like a petulant five-year-old who'd had his favorite toy taken from him.

I looked at him incredulously. "Are you serious? We were toxic."

"If we were that bad, then why are you here?" He leaned closer. Again, I found myself with my back against the field house.

Keeping my voice level, I said, "What do you mean? I'm here with Jax."

He scoffed, slapping the wall next to me. To my ears, it was as loud as a gunshot, but there was no way it traveled any farther than the slope we occupied. "No, you're not, Kez," he snarled.

I refused to be intimidated. "*Yes*, Miller, I am."

His sharp laugh rang with disbelief. "You might have shown up with him, but there's no way the two of you are together."

"And how would you know that?" Callie could have told him, but something about the way he was ranting convinced me that wasn't true. He was fishing to confirm a suspicion, but he didn't *know* anything. If he did, he'd have called me on it immediately, rather than shading it in innuendo.

Shoving his hands in his pockets, he looked away for a moment, then brought his eyes to mine. "Because I know you, Kez. *We* were together. Hell, even after we broke up, I still felt like your man. So don't tell me, the guy who actually *was* with you, that you're with Jackson now."

I dodged his question. "What about your fiancée?"

He winced and looked away again. I took the slight advantage and slithered past him. His shoulders sagged and he slumped despondently against the wall. "Callie," he murmured sadly.

I backed up, ready to get back around people. "She came to our room last night when she couldn't find you. For some reason, she thought you'd be there." I started back down the path.

Miller came off the wall with more speed than I gave him credit for in his inebriated state. Before I'd gone two steps, he grabbed my elbow, stopping me in my tracks. "If I'd asked, would you have come with me?" he asked.

Shocked, my mouth dropped open, and I gasped, "What? Last night?"

He shook his head, trying to bring me closer but I held my ground. "No, back then, when we were still in school and together … if I'd asked you to move to Rochester with me, would you have come?"

It was one of the questions that I'd pushed from my mind so many times since we'd broken up. I justified not answering it because he'd never asked. I'd also ignored the fact that I'd never even offered to come. What I would or wouldn't have said was irrelevant because it was in the abstract. Now, he was standing before me asking for an answer.

"What does it even matter now, Miller? You never asked me, so my hypothetical answer means nothing."

I twisted away from him, but he wouldn't let me escape. "You know if I'd asked you to move, you wouldn't have, Kez." And there it was, the truth I'd avoided for so long. It hung suspended between us, as though the words were in a cartoon bubble.

"You don't know that because you never asked." My response was trite, even to my own ears.

"I'm asking now, Kez. Would you have moved?" His eyes begged for an answer.

Regret took the place of anger. I couldn't look at him when I spoke. "Miller, that was years ago. I can't tell you … ."

"Yes, you can, you just don't want to," he insisted. "You would never have left North Carolina to come to New York. You know that but won't say it because then you'd have to share some of the blame for why things didn't work between us."

"I had a job, Miller," I reminded him. "I couldn't give up a sure thing on the hopes of finding something in New York."

"You never even looked for jobs in New York when you interviewed, so don't give me that shit!" he shouted.

"Did you look for jobs in North Carolina?" I carped back at him, descending into a childish standoff. It was easier than the discussion he wanted to have. I took stock of our surroundings. The field house reeked of adolescent male and old rubber. Nothing about this situation was good, not the isolated location or the fact he was drunk enough to be belligerent. "Miller, this is not the time nor the place for us to have this conversation."

"It's not like you gave me much of a chance to have it back then."

"You would've had to have been sober for it, so the window was pretty limited." And the childish insults continued. Before he could toss a stinging retort back, I said, "I'm not interested in playing the blame game here, Miller. We *both* made choices back then. Maybe they were wrong, maybe they were hurtful, but it doesn't change the fact the decisions we made set us on different paths."

"Yeah, but your path brought you back to me, Kez," he said with a strained urgency.

"No, Miller. It took me away from you and led me to Jackson."

The truth of what I'd said hit me squarely in the chest. This trip had started because I wanted closure with Miller so I could move on and maybe have a healthy relationship with someone else. I'd been using what happened with Miller as an excuse to shut myself off from people, mainly men. But Miller wasn't the problem, I was. *I'd* been the one holding back—not because I was stuck on Miller, but because I was afraid of going through another hard breakup. The possibility of leftover feelings for Miller had been a convenient excuse. Fear of heartbreak was what was pressing the pause button in the story of my life. My proverbial finger, not Miller's, had done that. Meeting Jackson had me eager to push play. Maybe he would be in my future, maybe he wouldn't, but I didn't want to wait any longer to find out.

Miller, on the other hand, wasn't ready to give up. "Kez, c'mon. Be honest. You're not really with him, are you?"

Wanting nothing more than to end this conversation, I said, "Honestly, I'm wondering why I'm not with him right now."

Miller tried to contradict me, but I cut him off. "Just stop, Miller. We had this same fight all those years ago and got nothing out of it but misery. Maybe I did come up here hoping to see you. Hell, maybe I came up here hoping you'd say even half of the shit you did. But now that I've heard it, all it does is drum home the fact that I've been so busy focusing on my past that I've missed out on the present. I've wasted years on this bullshit, Miller, but you know what? I'm done."

He crossed his arms. "So what now? You're going to skip back down the hill into Jackson's arms? Ride off into the sunset with him in front of all *my* friends and make me look like a jackass?"

"You don't need me to make you look like a jackass, Miller. You did a fine job of that all on your own last night when you abandoned your fiancée." I wheeled around, determined to get out of there. Once again, Miller's hand on my wrist stopped me. I was so over this shit. "Let go of me, Miller," I said.

"I'm not ready to let you go, Kez."

"That's not your call, is it?" I tried to get away, but he tightened his grip. I looked right in his eyes and said, "Think about what you're doing, Miller."

"Oh, I know what I'm doing," he said darkly.

"What it looks like you're doing," Jackson's voice came from behind me, "is harassing my girlfriend. But I know you wouldn't be that stupid, Miller, so it must be my eyes playing tricks on me, right?" Cold anger coated his words and the look in his eyes was murderous.

Miller pulled me backward. "Your girlfriend, huh?" He nuzzled my ear. "Does that mean you know how sweet she tastes? 'Cause I do."

Jackson's hands balled into fists, but before he could move, I wrenched away from Miller and slapped him hard across the face. Furious, I brought my boot heel down on his foot. His yelp of pain turned into a groan of agony when my knee connected with his balls. He fell to his knees.

Leaning down so we were face-to-face, I said, my words like chips of ice. "Look at yourself, Miller. Take a good, long look in the mirror, once you regain feeling in your testicles, and think about the man you see looking back at you. I wonder if you'll even recognize him because I sure don't." I walked away, holding out my hand to Jackson. He looked over at where Miller was still crumpled on the ground, then down to my outstretched hand. The anger in his eyes eased off a bit, and his lips tipped up into a smile. His palm engulfed mine, and he led me back down the hill, neither of us wasting another look at Miller. "And here I was going to be your knight in shining armor," he said blithely.

"That guy usually turns out to be some asshole wearing tinfoil. I like you much better in jeans."

Chapter 15

After the scene with Miller, neither of us wanted to spend any more time at the picnic. We hopped in Jackson's car and, after a brief bathroom break for me, left the city. Buildings whizzed by, and soon concrete and chain link gave way to rolling hills and split-rail fences. Exiting the freeway, we sped down a smaller two-lane road with farmland on either side. Tin-roofed barns and silos dotted the landscape, with livestock grazing in the foreground. The rural scene wasn't all that dissimilar from where I'd grown up.

"Where are we going?" I asked as we passed a sign announcing we were twenty miles from Canandaigua, wherever that was.

Jackson drove with one hand on the steering wheel and the other on my thigh. Aviators hid his eyes but couldn't disguise the twitch of his lips as he tried to hold in a smile. "Patience, gorgeous. You'll see." Visions of girls helping Ted Bundy load a fictional canoe onto his VW Bug ran through my head. I sent up a prayer he wasn't a serial killer and pushed thoughts of severed limbs from my mind.

A half hour or so later, fifty percent of which consisted of him giving me small clues when I asked repeatedly where we were going, he turned onto a wooded drive. Passing underneath the bows of large oak trees, our car bumped over a rutted lane bordered by a whitewashed fence. We wound our way through the bucolic setting, and the trees thinned to open pastures. Horses stood nose to tail in the distance. Around a bend was a huge, red barn, but the narrow drive didn't end there—it curved around out of sight. Jackson stopped in front of the barn, got out of the car, and came around to open my door. After getting a blanket from the trunk, he led me toward the far side of the barn.

I resisted a little, digging my heels into the gravel. "Jackson, where are we?"

At my reluctance, he slowed his purposeful strides but didn't let go of my hand. He gave it a subtle tug, urging me forward. "Just a place I try and come every time I get back up here." He kept walking, but I didn't budge. Raising his sunglasses, he squinted at me.

I blurted out, "You know, it'd be a shame to kill me in a place this peaceful. It'd really upset the vibe."

He blinked slowly. "What?"

"I watch a lot of true crime on Netflix. It's the first place my mind went."

He chucked a finger under my chin and laughed. "You're one special snowflake, gorgeous." Releasing my hand, he put one of his over his heart and raised the other, then vowed, "I solemnly swear that I am not going to kill you if you accompany me to the other side of the barn." Sliding his glasses back down, he asked, "Satisfied?"

"I guess so," I said dubiously but my curiosity outweighed any real fear of dismemberment.

"Good, c'mon!" Excited, he pulled me along with him. A large pond came into view, and centered on its bank was a faded red Adirondack love seat. Weeping willow trees dotted the banks of the pond, their reedy branches swaying in the breeze. In the summer, I was sure the long tendrils of leaves would dance over the surface of the water. The late-afternoon sun lingered above the horizon, streaking various shades of pink and lavender across the sky.

"Wow," I said.

"Almost takes your breath away, doesn't it?" Jackson asked.

"It's gorgeous, Jax." I sat down on the love seat, and Jackson sat next to me, spreading the blanket over our knees. The seat rocked under me, and I realized it was a glider. Scooching closer, I tossed my legs over his lap. His strong arm across my shoulders cuddled me into him. He was so warm I didn't need the blanket, but it added to the coziness.

For several minutes, neither of us said anything, content to take in the view and enjoy being next to each other. The only sounds were the creak of the wood as we swayed back and forth and an occasional whinny from one of the horses. Jackson's thumb rubbed my shoulder. With the view of the water, dotted here and there with ducks, and the solid presence of Jackson beside me, I felt a growing sense of peace. It was welcome after the scene with Miller.

"I want to say something, but I don't want to sound like an asshole," Jackson said.

"Usually conversations that begin that way don't end particularly well," I said with a nervous laugh.

Jackson rubbed a hand down his jeans. "Yeah, that's true, but I've never been one to shy away from an uncomfortable topic."

I took it as a good sign that his other hand never left my shoulder. "Well," I said gamely, "then let's dive right in. What do you need to say?"

"I didn't like finding you with Miller," he said, his mouth tightening at the corners.

I tried not to sound too defensive. "Well, it's not like I invited him to the field house."

"I know," he said. "Hence the reason I feel like an asshole for saying anything. But I can't *not* say anything because I don't want you to misunderstand how I feel about you or the situation with him. It's not that I don't believe that you're ready to move on. I want that to be true, and I want to be there while you do. It's just that …"

"It's just what?" I asked, putting a hand on his knee.

"I've been burned before when I believed what a girl told me about Miller," he said. "And I know that was a long time ago, and you're not her, but I ..." He sighed in frustration. "I'm really screwing this up."

"Jackson, I don't think there's a right way to have a discussion about your ex. Especially when your ex cheated on you with my ex. That's uncharted territory," I said. Patting his leg, I went on. "You haven't known me long enough to trust me yet, Jax. I get that. And I get that it must have been ... difficult to find me with Miller."

"That's one word for it," he said.

"But the good news is that he's back there with an ice pack on his crotch, and we're here ... together. That's got to count for something, right?"

His lips twitched, and he squeezed me tighter. "You were impressive back there, Kez."

"Well, I learned early on not to suffer fools lightly. Confrontations like that don't bother me. If they did, I'd be pretty bad at my job." I gave a small laugh. "I guess it's safe to say I'm a bit of an acquired taste and not everyone's cup of tea."

He grinned and kissed my temple. "Which is exactly the reason I brought you here."

There was my opening. "I'm still not sure where here is."

"It's a place that's very special to me, Kez."

"I've gathered that, but it doesn't answer my question." Irriatation with his evasive answers crept into my voice.

"I still want to kick his ass, you know," he said.

"Jax, he's not worth it."

Gently, he pushed me away from his side so he could face me, putting one knee on the seat as a barrier between us. Even with his sunglasses, his anger was obvious through the fierce scowl that set his mouth in a grim line. "No, he's not, but you are. When I saw him with his hands on you like that ..." Jackson paused and looked out over the pond. "I saw red, Kez. I wanted to beat the shit out of him. Then when he said what he did, I could've ... for him to talk about you like that, I ..."

I pressed my fingers against his mouth to stop the flow of his angry speech and bring him back to the here and now. "Jax, I dealt with Miller."

He kissed my fingertips and then held my hand in his. "But you shouldn't have to deal with that."

I pushed against his leg until his foot was flat on the ground again and climbed into his lap, the blanket pooling around my hips. "No woman should have to, but it doesn't mean we can't. So long as there are asshole ex-boyfriends, women will have to deal with stuff like that. And you need to learn that you don't always have to come rushing in as the white knight. I'm not looking for a savior, Jackson."

The deep furrows in his brow told me he disagreed. "That's not what I was trying to do."

I touched a small scar above his eyebrow, seeing my reflection in his opaque lenses. "Yeah, it was. You're a fixer, Jackson. Whether it's people with a problem or some broken-down antique, you see something you can fix. Life doesn't work like that. *I* don't work like that. I'm perfectly capable of fighting my own battles. Like I said the other day, I'll ask for your help if I need it. You don't need to come rushing to my rescue without an invitation."

Jackson's arms linked around me. "Is that so?"

My hand slipped into his hair, letting the silky strands sift through my fingers. I nodded. "It is."

Turning into my touch, he said, "You did say you were an independent woman."

I kneaded the base of his skull. "Very independent." He hummed in pleasure as I massaged the back of his neck.

"Does that mean I should ask before doing this?" He pulled the zipper of my jacket down, his deliberate momentum making the teeth click slowly against the slider. His hands pushed inside my coat, fingers slinking along my rib cage. Using a firm, circular motion, he rubbed my lower back.

I practically purred in response. My mind drifted back to the elevator from the night before and a low burn ignited in my belly.

He pressed harder, working out the knotted tension. "Is that a yes?"

"Sometimes it's better to ask forgiveness than permission," I said.

"I'll keep that in mind," he said and kissed me softly, moving his lips slowly over mine. He didn't deepen the kiss, allowing me to set the pace.

I shifted my weight back and dropped one knee on either side of his hips so I was straddling him. A little risqué for the setting, but the ducks could fly south if it bothered them. It seemed like we were the only two people around for miles, and I took advantage of the solitude. Pulling back, I ran my fingers over his cheekbones and across his jaw. Lifting off his glasses, I put them next to us on the seat. The brilliance of the blue in his eyes was still startling. Staring into those vibrant blue depths, I held his face with both hands. From my angled perch, I said, "Thank you for being there for me today."

He grimaced, angry at what he perceived as a failing on his part, but he didn't look away. "I wasn't there in time."

I smoothed my thumbs along his cheekbones, shaking my head. "Your timing was perfect, Jax. You let me handle it and walked away with me." He tried to respond, but I kept going. "You were there to back my play. And you would have stepped in if things had gone sideways. If he'd tried to hurt me, you'd have been there to stop him. You were there, Jax. You were there for me in all the ways that matter."

He pulled me down to him and kissed me, taking full control this time. I moaned into his mouth as his tongue tangled with mine. It was a kiss of possession, and for once in my liberated existence, I was A-okay with being possessed, so long as it was by *this* man. One of his hands moved into my hair, using his grip on it to tilt my head to his liking. Oh yeah. I could get used to this whole dominant thing. His other hand slid down my back and onto my ass, grinding me into him.

Needing oxygen, I lifted my head. "Should we go back to the hotel?"

Dipping inside the back of my jeans, he plucked the waistband of my panties. "I don't think I can make it back to the hotel. What if we …"

"Jackson?" a woman called.

My head snapped up, and I saw an older woman clad in black jeans and a buffalo checked farm coat—total farmer chic right down to her Hunter boots capped in red. She was about halfway down the large hill behind us. As she neared, I could see the puzzled look on her face. I wanted to move off Jackson's lap but couldn't get my legs to work.

He muttered, "I thought she'd still be in the city."

Prickles of unease marched up my back, causing the hair on the back of my neck to rise. "You thought *who'd* still be in the city?" I asked in a tense whisper.

He looked up at me through his lashes, like a toddler who'd smashed modeling clay into the new rug. "My grandmother."

An ice pick of terror spiked through me. "I'm sorry," I hissed. "Did you say your *grandmother*?" I could hear the tinge of mania in my tone.

He nodded, and I tried to scuttle off his lap like a crab. Unfortunately, I moved too quickly, and my feet caught in the blanket. What had been a snuggly cocoon became a tourniquet of fabric around my legs. I couldn't gain solid footing. Jackson tried to grab me, but it was too late. I was already falling. I landed in an unglorified heap in the dirt, right as his grandmother reached us.

"Oh dear! Are you all right?" she asked.

Jackson, to his credit, hid his laughter as he helped me up. "Don't worry, Nana. Kez is tougher than she looks."

I threw the blanket at him and tried to dust off flecks of what I prayed was mud and not duck poop. Wiping my hands on my jeans I said, "I apologize. I'm not usually that clumsy." Afraid what I would see if I met her gaze, I pretended to search for something on the ground.

With her hands on her knees, she, too, bent down to study the terrain. "Did you lose something?"

"Yes, my dignity," I deadpanned. "I'd like to get it back."

The skin around her eyes crinkled when she smiled. "I should be the one apologizing. I didn't mean to startle you two, but I didn't think I'd see Jackson until tomorrow, and I wasn't expecting to find him ..."

I flushed with embarrassment at the implication she didn't expect to find me dry humping her grandson by the duck pond.

Seeing my discomfort, she gave in and laughed, a full and hearty sound. "Don't be embarrassed. You two aren't the first couple to be inspired by the scenery around here." She held out a hand. "I'm Betty Jenkins. It's nice to meet you ..."

My manners kicked in, and I took her hand. "Kesler Walsh. It's nice to meet you too, Ms. Jenkins."

She waved a hand. "Please, call me Betty. Ms. Jenkins makes me feel old, and I don't need any more help in that department."

Smiling, I said, "Okay, Betty, but only if you call me Kez." Up close, Betty Jenkins was a striking woman. Her ash-blonde hair was cut bluntly at her shoulders and held back by a simple black headband. She was slim and wore little makeup, other than a bit of mascara and lip gloss. If Jackson hadn't told me she was his grandmother, I'd have guessed she was his mom. This family was blessed with amazing genes.

Betty linked her arm with mine. "I was about to have a cocktail so I could work up the energy to think about making dinner. Care to join me?"

Unsure how to respond, I glanced back at Jackson. "Oh, well, I ..."

Without waiting for an answer, Betty started walking. I had no choice but to fall in step with her. A last look at Jackson caught him staring up to the sky, as if asking why we could never find a combined ten minutes alone without interruption. With an exasperated shake of his head, he grabbed his sunglasses and followed us.

When we crested the hill, a white farmhouse appeared. The steep slope we'd climbed obscured the house from below. It was positioned to allow its occupants to see far and wide, but anyone at the barn or on the road coming in couldn't see the house. I had no doubt that the views across the landscape were gorgeous. By my guess, we were at least a mile off the main road. I started to wonder how much land Jackson's family owned out here. Had I stumbled onto the Rochester branch of the Kennedys?

The house had an expansive screened porch and was flanked by a chimney on either end. White slatted walls rose from a stone foundation circled by a lush carpet of grass. Wide slate steps extended off the porch, ending at a patio with a firepit surrounded by Adirondack chairs.

As we got closer, the back door was nosed open by what I assumed was a dog, but from a distance, he looked like nothing more than a mass of wrinkles. He waddled down the steps and ambled across the lawn. His gait resembled a seal undulating down a beach, except with jowls flapping and an impressive underbite. Skidding to a stop at Betty's feet, the dog shook his head, spreading slobber in an arc five feet into the air.

"Russ!" Betty chastised. "Is that any way to greet our guest?"

Russ snuffled my boots. At Betty's nod, I leaned down and let him sniff my hand, then ruffled the excess skin behind his ears. He leaned into my touch and let out a satisfied doggie noise, his tongue lolling out of the side of his mouth.

"Seems like a friendly fellow." I'd grown up with dogs, mainly my daddy's hunting dogs, but I'd always wanted a French bulldog, with their huge bat ears and soulful dark eyes. Russ was more English bulldog than French, but that didn't make him any less adorable.

Betty gave Russ a pat on the head. "Oh, he is. Only way he'd hurt you is if he licked you to death."

"I see you met the Walrus," Jackson said as he joined us.

"Walrus?" I asked, confused.

"You saw him run, didn't you? And those tusks coming out of his mouth? What else would you call him?" Russ rolled onto his back, and Jackson gave him several belly rubs, making one hind leg dance in response.

"So, Russ is short for …" I thought I knew, but waited for them to finish the sentence.

"Walrus," Betty and Jackson said together.

"Okay, Russ, that's enough. Let's go on up to the house," said Betty.

Jackson hurried in front of us to open with a little bow one of the French doors into the house. Betty chuckled and cuffed him lightly on the shoulder as she passed by. "Such a gentleman." Russ shouldered in front of him, and his nails clicked on the wide, wood floors.

Before I could cross the threshold into the house, Jackson pulled me back against him. "One of these days," he grumbled against my ear, "you and I are going to finish what we started."

He nipped at my earlobe, and I pushed him away. "Jackson! Your *grandmother* is three feet away from us."

He grinned wickedly while I frowned. Unrepentant, he used an arm across my shoulders to hold me close as we entered the house. I shoved him, but he didn't move. Instead, he nuzzled my hair. "I'm glad you're here, Kez."

Normally, meeting the family after knowing someone less than seventy-two hours would have sent me running for the hills. But this time, I wanted to curl up in a corner of Betty's sofa with an afghan and hear her tell stories about him as a kid. One more item on the long list of signs that things with Jackson were different.

Betty called out, "I should've asked, Kez, but I just assumed you'd be fine with an old-fashioned. If I'm wrong, I can make you something else or send Jackson out to grab a bottle of wine from the cellar."

The cellar? Who were these people? "No ma'am, that would be fine. Thank you. You really didn't have to go to any trouble."

"Nonsense. If I am making one it's no more trouble to make three instead. Just stop calling me ma'am. We aren't that formal up here."

While she was busy playing bartender, I took in the spacious and inviting family room we'd walked into off the porch. High pine ceilings were gridded by exposed, worn beams. A huge stone fireplace with a raised hearth and a live-edge mantel loomed on my right, the rough bark of the wood outlining the smooth sanded top. The room flowed into a large kitchen outfitted with spotless stainless-steel appliances. Four metal barstools sat on one side of a large island that broke up the space without separating it. It was a house made for family gatherings and holidays.

Betty came around the island carrying a tray with three drinks. Setting it down on an ottoman, she handed me a glass.

"Thank you," I said again.

She smiled in response and sat in a worn leather club chair. "Please, have a seat." Jackson and I sat together on the matching couch across from her. It was so deep, my feet barely touched the floor.

"Your house is lovely," I said.

"Thank you. Jackson's great-grandfather built it. We've modernized it here and there but tried to stay true to the family home he designed all those years ago."

I sipped my drink, enjoying the herbal bite of the bitters tempered by the opposing sweetness of the dissolved sugar.

Betty settled back into her seat, placing her glass on the small table beside her. "Jackson didn't tell me he was bringing anyone with him this weekend. In fact, he didn't tell me he was seeing anyone at all. So you are an unexpected, but very much welcome, surprise, Kez."

"Oh, I ..."

"I didn't meet Kez until this weekend, Nana," Jackson said, correcting her before I could.

Betty's eyes lit up with interest. "Is that right?"

He nodded. "Yep. I picked her up in the hotel bar Thursday night."

"Jackson!" I protested, sliding away from him on the couch.

Laughing, he sat forward, elbows on his knees, his glass hanging loosely from one hand. "I'd gone over to the hotel to get checked in for the reunion and thought I'd grab a drink before heading to play a few sets at Tonic. Right when I was going to get the check and head out, Kez walked in with her friends. She was a vision, Nana, all that gorgeous hair, that beautiful smile. Then when I saw her shoot tequila and heard her laugh, I was a goner. I had to meet her. I nursed my bourbon until they got a table, and I made my move."

"Based on what I saw by the pond, it must have been a pretty good move." Betty chuckled.

Jackson jostled the ice in his glass and smiled. "Best one I've made in a long time." He took a sip and sat back, his free hand drifting to the curve of my cheek.

I grasped his wrist and pulled his hand away from my face, slipping my palm into his. "Next time, lead with the extended version, okay?"

He touched his drink to mine. "Yes, ma'am," he agreed softly.

"Well, regardless of how or when you two met, I'm glad *I* got to meet you, Kez. It's been a long time since I've seen my grandson act like a giddy little schoolboy over a girl. Really, it's just been too long since I've seen my grandson," she finished with a sharp look at Jackson.

He grinned at her. "Sorry, Nana. Things have been so busy at the shop, I haven't had much time for anything other than work."

"Well, now that you've got Kez, I hope you make some."

Jackson replied, "Easy, Nana. I don't want to scare her off."

Betty cast a knowing glance at our interlaced fingers. "That vice grip you've got on her isn't going to let her get far," she said. "Why don't you give her some breathing room and go get some firewood? I think it'll be cool enough for a fire tonight, plus it'll make the bourbon taste that much better."

Getting up from the sofa, he snapped off a quick salute. "I live to serve, Nana." He directed an accusatory digit in her direction. "But you have to promise not to talk about me while I'm gone."

She played innocent, with a hand to her chest. "Who, me?"

He dropped a kiss on her cheek as he headed out of the room. "Yes, you, old woman. No gossiping behind my back."

"I promise I won't say anything that I wouldn't say to your face," she teased him.

"That's what I'm afraid of!"

Once she heard the door slam, her shrewd blue eyes narrowed onto me. "I don't think I need to tell you that he's as good a man as they come."

I swallowed nervously, hoping she wouldn't notice the slight tic next to my eye. "No, ma—" I stopped myself and said, "I've picked up on that."

She linked her hands at her knee and said, "Good. I know you two just met, and you're still getting to know each other. I can't ask you to be anything other than honest with him. But I can tell you I've never seen him look at a girl the way he looks you. So I guess I'm asking you not just to be honest but to be kind as well."

The side door slammed again, and Jackson shuffled into the room, his arms full of firewood. He looked between Betty and me, trying to read the room. "What'd I miss?"

We shared a knowing smile and said in unison, "Nothing."

His brows winged up. "Now I know I'm in trouble."

With a laugh, Betty shoved up out of her chair. "What's that old saying? 'You'd be paranoid, too, if everyone were talking about you.' I knew you were coming tomorrow," she said to Jackson, "so, as usual, I bought too much food. I'm going to start dinner. I hope you two will join me?"

From his position kneeling in front of the fireplace, Jackson looked at me. "I'm not sure, Nana."

"I should probably check in with my girlfriends and see what's what," I said in response.

"Invite them," Betty said.

"Oh, I wouldn't want to impose."

"Nonsense, the more the merrier," Betty insisted.

Giving in, I said, "Um ... okay, I'll give Rae a call and see."

"Tell her Nana makes a mean old-fashioned and I bet she'll hitchhike if she has to," Jackson teased.

Being totally mature, I stuck my tongue out at him and stepped onto the porch to make the call. It was just after five o'clock. I should've at least texted my friends before now, but I'd been too caught up in Jackson. After begging them to come with me, I felt bad at leaving them to fend for themselves so much on this trip. But then again, if Chris and Dave were any indication, they'd managed pretty well without me.

"Jackson finally let you up for air?" Rae said by way of greeting.

"Hello to you too," I replied, grasping the back of one of the chairs facing the backyard. The legs of the chair scraped against the stone floor as I moved it closer to the railing. When I sat down, the worn, wooden boards creaked underneath me. On the phone, I heard a rustling noise in the background. "Where are you?"

The rustling stopped, and she said, "V and I just got back from stimulating the local economy, and I'm changing clothes. A better question is where are *you*?"

She was going to love this. "I'm sitting on the porch of Jackson's grandmother's house."

The pause on her end was so long, I checked to make sure the call hadn't dropped. "Rae, are you still there?"

She said, "Sorry, it sounded like you said you were at Jackson's grandmother's house."

I heard a muffled shriek in the background and assumed V was in the room and heard Rae's comment. "You heard correctly, Rae. And tell V to calm down before she gets a noise complaint."

"Never mind her," Rae replied testily. "Explain to me how attending a reunion picnic morphed into quality time with his extended family."

"It's a long story. I'll give you all the gory details later," I said vaguely.

She persisted. "I'll settle for the condensed version. You know, slightly more than 280 characters, so I can get the gist if not the whole plot."

I propped one foot on top of the other on the railing in front of me. "He said he wanted to take me somewhere but didn't say it was his grandmother's farm. He didn't expect her to be here, but she is. So I got an introduction."

"And you didn't leave skid marks in the driveway hightailing it out of there?" Her skepticism was well deserved. Miller's parents had been my last experience with meeting the family. To say it had gone poorly was beyond an understatement. I'd met them briefly at graduation, which had been innocuous and fine given the whirlwind that accompanies those types of events. The real kicker had been when I flew up to see him after we were finished with the bar exam later that summer. His mom wasn't thrilled with her Catholic son dating a lapsed Protestant who only attended church on the odd holiday. She made it clear that if things were to continue with Miller, I would have to convert. It was a tense weekend, and I had no desire for a repeat. It was also yet another comparison between Jackson and Miller that had Jackson coming out the victor.

"Surprisingly, no," I said, absorbing the peaceful nature of my surroundings. It was beautiful out here—no smog or grit, just lush green fields and brown fertile soil, framed by neat white fences.

"We'll discuss the psychological implications of that at a later date."

"I expect nothing less, Dr. Freud."

Ignoring my jab, she asked, "If you're all cozy in the country, does that mean V and I are on our own again tonight?"

"Well," I hedged. "Not exactly." I heard the door open, and Jackson walked in front of me, signaling for me to give him the phone. I shook my head, and his hand gestures became more insistent.

"Kez," Rae asked, "what does *not exactly* mean?"

Jackson pried the phone from my hand. "Hey, Rae, it's Jackson." He leaned against the railing beside my foot and listened for a moment. As he talked, I studied him, something that was fast becoming a favorite pastime of mine. His jeans were faded and hung low on his lean hips. They weren't the ridiculous skinny jeans that every man under the age of thirty-five seemed to own. The worn denim cupped but didn't constrict all the right places. His boots were scuffed—not for fashion, I was willing to bet, but from function. As he crossed his arms, the fabric of his flannel shirt tightened at his biceps. I knew from last night that the muscles under there were chiseled and firm. Jackson was, in a word, a m-a-n.

I tuned back into what he was saying. "Yeah, I guess you could say that." I could hear the murmur of Rae's voice on the other end of the line but not what she was saying. "Uh-huh," Jackson said, "right. But listen, Kez said she was coming out here to call and let you and V know the two of you were invited to dinner with my Nana." More squawking came from the earpiece of my phone. "Oh, she hadn't gotten that far, huh? Well, good thing I came looking for her then."

I waggled my fingers to get him to hand me my phone, but he just circled his fingers around my calf and squeezed. He talked to Rae another few minutes, then rattled off his grandmother's address. "Okay, Rae, here's Kez." He tossed me my phone but didn't vacate his post at the rail.

"Sorry, I'm back," I said.

"His Nana? Are you kidding me?" She was cracking up.

"What?" I asked. Jackson arched a brow, but I ignored him.

She replied, "If you gotta ask girl, you don't deserve him."

"Thanks a lot!" I said indignantly.

"Don't get all self-righteous with me! I'm just messing with you. Listen, if V and I are gonna make it out there for dinner, I need to go get ready. I'll see you shortly." She hung up.

I dropped my phone into the seat beside me. "I hope your grandmother knows what she just invited out here."

He chuckled. "She'll love it."

"We'll see."

Releasing my leg, he crouched down in front of me. "Don't worry, Kez. And, I'm sorry."

His apology took me off guard. "Sorry? For what?"

"Ambushing you with Nana. I didn't expect her to be here. I thought she'd be at my parents' house. We were going to meet for breakfast in the morning, so I was as surprised as you were by her appearance this afternoon."

I scoffed, remembering my oh-so-graceful reaction to seeing her. "Somehow, I don't think that's possible."

He smoothed a hand over his beard and shrugged. "Well, maybe not, but I had no intention of springing part of my family on you like that."

My boots clunked against the stone floor when my feet dropped from the railing. I sat forward in the chair, opening my knees so he was between them. "You don't seem like the kind of guy who would set up a make-out scene to be crashed by his grandmother." He was close enough for me to smell the bourbon on his breath when he laughed. I toyed with the hair at his collar. "Out of curiosity …"

His hands were on my knees, and he pitched forward slightly. "Yeah?"

"Before Betty showed up this afternoon …" I gathered his hair into a tiny ponytail and tugged lightly.

He dropped to one knee for balance, his hands going a bit higher up my legs. "Yeah?"

I released his hair, and it fell in shaggy layers behind his ears. I let my hands dangle off his shoulders. "Where were you going to suggest we go?"

He gave me a boyish grin while thumbing the inside seams of my jeans. "Hayloft."

His answer was so cliché that I couldn't help but laugh. "You're kidding, right?" I asked.

His palms dove under my legs, and he easily drew me to the edge of my seat. My legs widened further into a vee with his torso at its apex. Reflexively, my arms curled around his neck. Our chests pressed together when he shook his head. "Nope."

"A roll in the hay—seriously?" I couldn't stop my smile when he wiggled his eyebrows. "You're something else, Jax." He leaned in to kiss me, and once again I felt that unmistakable zing. I hummed against his lips. "You're also really good at that."

"You haven't seen the half of it, gorgeous." He stood up, taking me along for the ride. Slowly, he released his hold on my thighs and lowered me to the ground, my body dragging the length of his until my feet reached the porch. The man had my sex drive running from zero to sixty in under three seconds with less than two moves.

Keeping my arms around his neck, I said, "At some point, I hope to see the whole of it without interruption."

With a playful pull on my hair, he nodded toward the house. "C'mon, let's head back in before I say the hell with it and head to the hayloft."

Chapter 16

When we got back inside, Betty immediately put us to work. Jackson was on steak duty. He filled and lit the charcoal chimney for the grill while I was put in charge of getting the salad together. Betty busied herself julienning potatoes, then moved on to lathering the dinner rolls with butter. It was a trick my mom also used that made the outsides nice and flaky. The entire time, Betty and Jackson bantered back and forth. Their relationship was comfortable and uncomplicated, and it was obvious she adored him. It made me miss Granny, who died right after I graduated law school. She and I had the same type of relationship, with equal parts love and teasing.

Jackson had just stepped out to see if the charcoal was ready when I heard a knock, followed by, "Yoo-hoo! Anyone home?"

"In here," Betty called back, sliding the potatoes in the oven.

Rae strolled into the kitchen, spying Betty at the stove. "You must be the famous Nana I've heard so much about."

Betty laughed. "I'm guessing you're Rae."

"Live and in color," Rae responded, extending a hand for Betty to shake.

"Can I fix you a drink?" Betty asked.

Mischievous green eyes sparkled when she said, "Why Nana, it's like you already know me!"

I'd expected V to follow Rae into the room. When she didn't, I looked questioningly at Rae. She shrugged. "V and Dave already had plans for dinner tonight, so she sends her regrets. And I hope you can tell by my tone that she now spells Dave with a heart for an *a* because she luuuuuuvvvvvs him." She selected a chunk of tomato from the salad bowl on the counter and popped it into her mouth.

"Sorry. She doesn't come with an off button," I said to Betty.

Rae slung her arm around my neck and pulled us cheek to cheek. "Ignore her, she's always been jealous of my dazzling personality. She tries to make up the difference by being insanely gorgeous, but I mean, beauty will only get you so far … am I right?"

I broke out of her forced embrace and gestured to the barstool on the other side of the island. "Sit down, show-off. I'd say you could help, but you are as culinarily challenged as they come."

Rae dropped into the seat, crossing one jean-clad leg over the other. Tossing her fishtail braid over her shoulder, she heaved a dramatic sigh. "Sadly, it's true. I could find a way to burn water. When we exchange recipes, I hand out take-out menus." I put the salad on the island and slapped Rae's hand away when she tried to grab another tomato.

"You girls act like sisters," Betty said with a laugh as she dropped a sugar cube into a glass.

Rae's eyes tracked her movements like a lion watching a gazelle, only hungrier. As Betty began muddling the sugar, Rae licked her lips. When the bourbon splashed over the ice, you'd have thought she was having a religious experience. She took the offered glass from Betty as though it were the sacrament. After a taste, her eyes drifted closed, and she made a noise that was part hum, part moan and altogether inappropriate.

"Need a moment alone, or are you okay?" I asked drily.

Cracking one eye open, Rae looked at Betty. "Ever considered adoption? I could be the daughter you never knew you always wanted."

Betty slid the bourbon back into in her liquor cabinet to the left of the stove.

"Careful," I said to Betty, "now she knows where you keep it."

Rae sniffed in pretended offense. "Please, as if I would ever steal from my Nana."

Jackson came back into the kitchen at that moment, his eyes flicking between us. Betty was trying to contain her laughter, and I resisted, barely, the instinct to smack Rae. "I've gotta quit leaving the room. What'd I miss this time?" he asked.

"Rae here has been baptized by bourbon as an honorary Jenkins." I clued him in, sliding a coaster across to her.

He grinned. "Welcome to the family, sis. Guess that means you're on dish duty."

She frowned, then took another sip. "I believe that's up to Nana, not you. And we all know I'm her favorite."

I handed Jackson the plate of seasoned steaks. "Remember, it was your idea to invite her."

He kissed my cheek. "I invited both your friends. Where's V?"

Rae batted her lashes and propped her chin on her hands. "She had plans with Dave."

Jackson arched an eyebrow. "Really?"

She nodded. "Yep, seems she's quite smitten with your buddy."

"Huh," he said. "Well, you could've brought Chris with you."

Rae blew him a raspberry to dismiss that idea and twirled on her stool. "Honey, please. If there's one thing I've learned over the years, it's that you don't let them follow you home. It gives the wrong impression."

Jackson stopped on his way toward the back door. "Um, what?" he asked.

"You've asked for it now," I muttered, wishing I hadn't turned down Betty's offer to make me another drink.

Undeterred, Rae continued. "You know how when you go on vacation, you always want to sample the local flavor? Like, when you're in Bermuda, you try the dark and stormy. It's great while you're there, but never the same if you try to make it back home.

So you enjoy the taste of it for that brief time, and when you're through, simply file it away as a pleasant memory."

"I take it Chris is now a pleasant memory?" Jackson asked.

Grinning over the rim of her glass, Rae said, "Whose taste I very much enjoyed."

I groaned and turned to Betty, who'd been sipping on her own fresh drink during this exchange. "I feel like tonight is going to be one long running apology for Rae's lack of a filter."

Betty leaned across the island and clinked her glass to Rae's. "Nothing to apologize for, Kez. Rae has quite a ... refreshing view of the male-female dynamic." She patted my shoulder reassuringly. "Besides, I lived through the sixties. My generation wrote the book on casual trysts."

Rae whooped with laughter. "Oh my God, Nana, we are going to be *best* friends!"

Betty nudged Jackson out the door as he attempted to cover his ears while simultaneously carrying the platter of steaks. "Don't be such a prude. I wasn't in a convent prior to meeting your grandfather."

"I do not need to hear this," he replied, mortified. "Please, for the love of God, be talking about something else when I get back!"

"Like I said," I called after him, "it was your idea to invite her!"

Jackson escaped to man the grill, and the three of us finished putting the rest of dinner together. Even Rae roused herself to grab plates and silverware. When Jackson returned with the steaks and *several* bottles of wine, which I assumed came from the aforementioned wine cellar, the kitchen was filled with delicious smells and raucous female laughter.

"Enjoying yourself?" he asked me.

I plucked a bottle from his hands and kissed him without thinking about it. Immediately regretting my familiarity with him in front of his grandmother, I pulled back. I glanced over at Betty, but she and Rae were setting the small table in the dining nook off the kitchen.

"Stop it, Kez," he said calmly.

"Stop what?" I asked, putting the bottle on the counter and busying myself by searching through drawers for a corkscrew.

From behind me, he set down the remaining bottles of wine. His big body crowded me against the counter, large hands gripping its edge on either side of me. Sinewy arms corralled me and cut off any avenue of retreat. He wasn't going to let me escape this conversation.

Jackson spoke to my back. "Doubting, questioning—whatever you want to call the thoughts running through your head right now."

To the cabinets, I said, "This is all a little too domestic, don't you think? I mean, I just met you, yet here we are …"

I felt his lips against the crown of my head. "Getting to know each other."

"In front of your grandmother …"

His laugh ruffled my hair. "Yeah, that's an unexpected twist, but while I had very different plans when I brought you here, I can't say I'm disappointed with how things turned out."

The confession warmed my heart. Judging by the tone of his voice, he was glad I'd met his grandmother and altogether happy we'd spent the afternoon with her. And, if I stopped being neurotic for five seconds, I could admit I was too. The last of my resistance to the homey evening drained out of me, and I sagged back against him. "Not even at missing out on a roll in the hay?"

When I looked at him over my shoulder, I saw the dark shift in his blue eyes. "The night's not over yet, gorgeous." My inner witch, who'd been surprisingly dormant, perked up and rubbed her hands together in anticipation.

"All right, lovebirds," Rae interrupted from across the room, "save it for when you're alone."

"She says that like there will come a time when that happens," Jackson muttered.

She joined us to browse through the bottles Jackson brought in. Finding one to her liking, Rae rummaged in the drawer I'd opened for a corkscrew. After pulling the cork, she slid two glasses out of the rack above the counter and splashed a generous pour in both. Handing one to each of us, she winked at Jackson. "Patience is a virtue, my friend. Now, let's eat!"

I took a sip and savored the roll of the wine over my tongue. It was a rich cabernet, thick and hearty. Perfect for a meat-and-potatoes meal. Jackson and I joined Rae and Betty at the table, and we began the ritual of passing and serving until everyone's plate was full. Rae shoveled a mountain of potatoes into her mouth and moaned. "Oh God. It's official!"

Slicing into my filet, I looked at her. "What's that?"

"I'm moving in with Nana so that the two of us and these potatoes can live happily ever after."

"Wait until you try her mac and cheese," said Jackson, encouraging her theatrics.

Rae clutched at her throat, affecting disbelief. "Nana, are you holding out on me?"

Betty harrumphed, "Hold out on my favorite adopted grandchild? Absolutely not. I'm using it as a lure to make sure you come back."

Spinning the chunk of ice in her glass, Rae took a long swallow of the decadent brown beverage. "Nana, believe me. You had me at old-fashioned."

"How are you planning on getting back to the hotel?" I asked.

"There's this cool new thing called Uber, Kez. Maybe you've heard of it?"

Betty chimed in, "I've got plenty of room here, if you want to stay, Rae."

Losing the sarcasm, Rae said, "Oh no. I don't want to put you to that trouble."

"No trouble at all, dear. In fact," she continued, with a sly look at Jackson, "there's enough room for all of you to stay tonight."

"Nana," he said in a warning tone.

"What?" she asked innocently, spooning more potatoes onto Rae's plate.

Looking between the two of them, Rae grinned. "I appreciate it Nana, but I'll call an Uber. I do think it's a great idea for Kez and Jackson to stay, though." I kicked her under the table, but she didn't even wince. She was *not* on her first old-fashioned because she was feeling no pain. "I mean, that is unless you two have *other plans* tonight?"

Jackson used me as an excuse. "Well, I mean, Kez doesn't have any of her things with her, so it'd probably be best for her if we went back to the hotel."

"Don't be silly," Betty said. "Between all of your cousins, I could run a boutique with the stuff they leave behind here."

"Betty, I don't want to impose." I tried to argue, but she refused to be derailed.

"How is it an imposition if I'm asking you to stay?"

Rae's smile widened. "So I guess it's settled then. You're having a slumber party with Nana!"

In one gulp I finished my wine. "Looks that way, doesn't it?" Jackson was quick with a refill. So now, instead of the sexy last night in Paris (so to speak) with Jackson I'd envisioned, I would be sleeping in a twin bed wearing some other woman's pj's. *Ain't life grand?* Inner witch stomped her foot and swore a blue streak.

"Oh good," Betty said. "Jackson, you and Kez can stay in your old room."

Did I just hear my sex life being resurrected by his grandmother? Please let it be so! My small-town Southern upbringing wouldn't allow me to let it go, though. "Um, are you sure you're comfortable with that, Betty?"

"Pfft," she said. "I may be old, dear, but I'm not an idiot. Especially not after Jackson's senior prom."

He cleared his throat and squirmed nervously. Color rose in his cheeks as he said, "Nana, I don't think we need to get into that."

Honing in on his distress, Rae disagreed. "Oh, I beg to differ. Please, by all means, tell us about Jackson's senior prom."

Refusing to let him off the hook, I said, "I'd love to hear that story."

I could see the details were ready to burst out of Betty, much like the giggle that did as she began to tell us. "Well, you have to understand that his mother has always been a bit of a worrier. She wanted her boys to go to college and didn't want them making any mistakes in high school that could hold them back. Those mistakes included Jackson's prom date, Amy Greene."

"Oh?" I asked. "Mama didn't approve of Amy?"

"Didn't approve?" Betty chortled. "More like wished she would disappear. Amy had it *bad* for Jackson and wasn't shy about showing it, whether it was out behind the barn or at the dinner table. And Jackson, being seventeen and full of raging hormones, didn't know any better."

"Nana!" Jackson said her name in a strangled plea. His leg began to bounce up and down next to me. It was the first time I'd seen him anything other than totally at ease. This story *had* to be good.

Enjoying the lighthearted torment, she said, "What? You didn't! You were trapped in a fog of lust and that ridiculous perfume she wore. What was it?" she tapped a finger to her chin, then snapped her fingers. "Rapture, that was it! That mess could've peeled the paint off the walls."

Jackson's neck went from pink to a deep red above his collar, and he had a death grip on his wine glass. I reached out and put my hand over his, stroking his knuckles. He turned his hand palm up to clasp mine. Betty noticed and smiled, but didn't stop her story.

"So Jackson asked Amy to prom, and Mary Beth was practically having convulsions she was so worried about prom night. She decided she needed to have 'the talk' with him."

"Oh God," said Rae, giddy with the prospect of Jackson's impending humiliation.

Betty nodded, taking a drink. "Oh yes. The Sunday before prom, we were all here having lunch, and Mary Beth starts in on Jackson about practicing safe sex and how he needs to be careful and not take chances with his future. I mean she'd worked herself into a real lather over all of it. And Jackson just sat there, taking it all in and not saying anything. So at the end of her spiel, Mary Beth looks at him and says, 'Well, don't you have anything to say?' I'll never forget the next part," she said, breathing through her laughter. "Jackson wipes his mouth, looks at his mother and says, 'Don't worry, Mom, I've got a plan.' Mary Beth says, 'A plan! Well, just what is your plan, young man?' Cool as a cucumber, Jackson says, 'I'm going to do her in the butt, Mom.' And goes right back to eating like nothing happened."

"Oh my God!" I said, laughing so hard tears ran down my cheeks.

Betty dabbed at her eyes with a napkin. "I know! I thought Mary Beth was going to have a stroke."

Rae cracked up. "I bet so!"

"Needless to say," Betty went on, "that was the last time she brought up Jackson's sex life. And I'm telling you, I'm not dumb enough to repeat her mistake. You two can share a room and do, or not do, whatever you want to in it. I don't need to hear about it either way."

I looked at Jackson. "I can't believe you said that to your mom!"

Attempting to regain his cool, he shrugged, but the remaining red splotches on his neck gave him away. "I was a seventeen-year-old dumbass, what can I say?"

"So, did you?" asked Rae.

"Did I what?" he asked in response.

"Do her in the butt?" Rae guffawed.

I threw a piece of bread at her. "Rae, seriously?"

"What! Inquiring minds want to know!" She wheezed between belly laughs.

Jackson's hand on my wrist stopped me from lobbing another bread bomb. "No, Rae, I did not. You'll be happy to know that I resisted Amy, although she found certain other people irresistible." The look he gave me made it clear Amy had been the girl he'd caught cheating with Miller. He went on, "Last I heard, she'd married a pharmacist and has three kids."

"She divorced the pharmacist because he caught her cheating on him with a stock boy from Wegman's," said Betty.

"Damn," Rae said wide-eyed. "That's harsh."

"I'll say," I added. "She could've at least gone for a cashier." Betty and Rae erupted into another round of laughter, while Jackson put his head in his hands.

"Anyway," Betty said, "what you do or don't do isn't my business. But Kez, you are welcome to your own room if you'd be more comfortable."

I was on the horns of quite the sexual dilemma. I could choose to stay with Jackson and accept that, despite what she'd said, his grandmother would be speculating on whether or not we were down the hall getting it on. *Or*, I could forgo what had the potential to be a truly glorious sexual experience, banking on the hope he and I would find some alone time in a room with a door that locked and wasn't within earshot of any of his elderly relatives. Inner witch was already preparing her argument to do the nasty a few doors down from Betty.

"I think Kez and I can control ourselves for one night, Nana," Jackson said placatingly.

My ovaries shriveled up and died just a little.

"Again, not my business," she said. "But remember, your mother gave me that sound machine for my birthday last year. Works pretty well."

"Behave yourself, Nana," Jackson scolded. "Any more comments like that and Kez may sleep alone just to prove a point."

Not likely, I thought to myself.

Betty began to gather up the dishes. Rae and I both jumped up. "Let us help."

After the washing was done, Rae checked the status of the Uber she'd ordered. "Looks like my ride's almost here." She hugged Betty goodbye. "I'll be back for the mac and cheese."

"I hope so, Rae. Be safe," Betty said sincerely.

Once the door shut behind Rae, Nana yawned. "I'm headed up to bed. If you need extra sheets, they're in the hall closet."

Jackson kissed her cheek. "Thanks, Nana. Dinner was great."
"Thank you, sweetheart. I'll see you in the morning."
"Good night, Betty," I said.
She smiled. "Good night, Kez."

Chapter 17

Instead of climbing the stairs to his room, where in my mind was a bed made up with G.I. Joe sheets, Jackson went down the hall to the back door.

"Um, isn't the bedroom that way?" I asked, pointing toward the stairs.

"I've got a better idea," he said, beckoning me over to him. Intrigued, I complied. Once outside, we walked across the lawn, finding our way in the moonlight to the door of the barn. He pushed the levered handle, and the big door opened with a rusty squeak. He stepped inside and flipped a light switch to the left of the door.

It wasn't a livestock barn with hay, feed, and dusty, old farm equipment. The concrete floor was clean, except for a little sawdust and what could have been metal shavings. Woodworking equipment and several other intricate machines I didn't recognize stood at varying intervals around the large space. On one wall a workbench was flanked by Snap-On toolboxes. A drafting table sat in the corner. Planks of wood and sheets of metal were stacked neatly on a tall rack against the opposite wall. In a slatted storage bin, live-edge slabs leaned against one another, separated by foam inserts.

Jackson came up behind me. "Is this some kind of workshop?" I asked.

"It was my grandpa's. Now it's mine. At least when I'm here, it's mine."

Spinning me to face him, he ran his hands down my arms. Talking was obviously the last thing on his mind as he took off my fleece and draped it across a nearby workbench. The weight of his stare was heavy with promise as he maneuvered me over to the front corner of the building, toward a large object under a cotton tarp. Once we got close, he reached around me and pulled the tarp off, revealing a huge wood and wrought-iron bed. The mattress was bare, but an old quilt was folded neatly at the foot of the bed. Before I could ask why there was a bed out here, he lifted me onto it and was pulling off my boots.

"I made it for my house and haven't had time to come and get it," he said, answering my unasked question. My boots landed with a thud.

From my position in the middle of the mattress, I looked at the intricate headboard. It was a wooden frame, embellished with whorls of wrought iron. The design was reminiscent of Jackson's tattoos. I touched one of the thick metal rods. "You made this?" I was impressed by detail of the craftsmanship.

He shucked off his own jacket, leaving him in a flannel and jeans. Once he'd unlaced his boots, he joined me on the bed. "Your continued amazement at my skills is humbling and flattering all at the same time."

I said, "I didn't know you were this talented."

His full lips curled up into a lopsided grin at my backhanded compliment. "Gee, thanks."

I cringed. "Sorry! I didn't mean that like it sounded."

With a smile, he kissed me. Before we could get carried away, I said, "So, that's why the bed is here, but it doesn't explain the mattress …"

"I got the mattress to make sure of the bed dimensions. The quilt is a lucky coincidence from the last late night I pulled out here."

He leaned down for another kiss, but I stopped him. "One more question." Jackson hung his head and waited. "Does that door lock?"

His chin lifted, and a broad grin unfurled across his face. With a nod, he said, "And I have the only key."

"Hallelujah!"

We crashed together in a tangle of limbs and roaming hands. Jackson swallowed my moans as he kissed me, his firm grip on my hair keeping me where he wanted. He shoved his other hand under the hem of my shirt. Ravenously, I pulled him closer. The lace cup of my bra folded in on itself when his searching fingers dipped inside. Tendrils of fire danced across my skin from his caress.

He lifted his head, his chest heaving with the need for air. "You're gonna be the death of me, Kez."

Guiding him back down for more, I replied, "Only if you stop doing what you're doing."

My eyes cracked open to moonlight filtering through the slats of the door. I was disoriented until Jackson moved beside me, and I remembered we'd come out to the barn after Betty had gone to bed. The darkness cloaking the room let me know it was still night, I was guessing a little after midnight. We must've dropped off to sleep after the second round. I shivered at the memories of Jackson's hands running over my skin. My blood sizzled as I remembered his touch, and I wanted more. I inched across the cool expanse of the mattress, feeling my way over to him. When I fit the front of my body to his side, he mumbled in his sleep and dropped an arm over me. I combed my fingers tenderly across the faint sprinkle of coarse hair on his chest.

Jackson's eyes drifted open, and he looked down at me. "Hey." His voice was thick with sleep.

"Hey, yourself," I said, continuing to stroke his chest.

He ran a hand through my hair. "You look like you need something."

I kissed his rib cage. "Maybe," I said flirtatiously. My finger outlined the defined ridges of his abdomen.

"Anything I can help you with?"

My hand disappeared beneath the sheets. "Maybe," I said again, stretching the syllables.

With a rough growl, he flipped me onto my back, wedging his hips between my thighs. Before I even knew what was happening, he'd trapped both of my wrists above my head. The move curved my back and thrust my breasts forward. I could barely make out his smiling face above me. The hand not pinning me in place moved slowly from the top of my rib cage down to the dip of my waist, raising goosebumps in its wake. "Maybe, huh?" he asked lasciviously.

When he flexed against me, I bit my lower lip to keep from admitting I was more at a solid *yes, yes, yes*. Tingles of desire bloomed through my body as he lowered his lips to mine. He devoured my mouth, in complete control as the full weight of his body plastered me to the bed. I squirmed beneath him, making the hair on his chest scrape over my skin with a sensual friction. The tingles became full-on pulses of pure lust running through me.

Breaking the kiss, he held himself above me on one corded forearm. Amusement mingled with hunger in his eyes when he dipped his head. When his lips hit my skin, my spine arched, and I begged for more. "Jackson, please."

His left hand tightened on my wrists as I struggled to move my hands, longing to touch him. While the light flicks of his tongue at my breast almost drove me out of my mind, his other hand trailed talented fingers down the back of my thigh. Reaching the bend of my knee, he pushed my leg farther out, then pulled it up over his own hip. Lifting his head, he asked, "Still just a maybe?"

"Moving closer to a definite yes," I panted. My heel jammed into the small of his back, egging him on.

A feral smile split his face. "Well, let's see what we can do to push that along." He shifted lower, raining kisses down my stomach. He looked up at me as he licked my hip bone and I moaned. "Sounds like we're making progress," he said, nibbling his way across my pelvis.

"Jackson." His name tumbled from my lips as a wild plea.

"Is this what you need, Kez?" he asked, mere inches from where I needed him.

"Please, Jax, please. I need you. I need you to … oh, God!" Fire raged through me as his beard scrubbed against my inner thigh, and then I was pretty sure I saw God. Jackson absolutely feasted on me in a ruthlessly passionate onslaught of my lady parts. I rocked against him, giving up all pretense of anything other than total surrender to him and his magical tongue. Each lick, flutter, flick, and flit drove me higher until with a starburst of sparks, I tumbled into oblivion, moaning his name. My legs went slack, and I melted into the mattress, limp and boneless.

"We're not quite through, Kez," Jackson said as he kissed his way back up my body, detouring slightly to grab a condom from his pants.

This time was much slower and more sensuous than the frenzied coupling we'd had mere hours earlier. Our bodies moved in tandem, gliding against one another. His gentle touch made me feel worshipped and desired, like I was the center of his entire world. Our breathing slowed, and we remained intimately entwined, neither ready to break apart. I rubbed his back as he caressed my cheek.

Finally, Jackson broke the silence. "That was …"

"Amazing?" I supplied helpfully, my body wrung out like a rag.

He grinned triumphantly. "Finally, she believes in my skills!"

Once he'd disposed of the condom, he pulled me against him and settled his head next to mine on the pillow, with one long arm stretched underneath it. The other crossed over my chest, holding me close. I looped my fingers over his forearm, and he kissed my shoulder. "I want to enjoy the feel of you a little longer," he said, and my heart tumbled over itself at the sentiment.

Lying there in his arms, I was totally sated and relaxed. The only thing I wanted to do was burrow deeper into his embrace and keep his skin against mine. So I did. I pulled his arm tighter around me and twined my legs with his, sighing in pleasure.

His chest shook with laughter. "Comfortable?"

"Yeah, I am," I said contentedly. I luxuriated in the comfort of his strong arms around me, enjoying the decadent sensation of his body behind me. It had been a long time since I'd enjoyed being wrapped in a man's arms. Jackson's lips nipped and sucked their way up my neck, and I stretched in pleasure as his tongue flicked against my earlobe.

"Again? Already?" I asked in amazement.

His laugh blew past my ear. "What can I say, gorgeous. Having you in my bed after waiting this long ..."

"Dude, it's been three days at most," I said.

"I've wanted to be in this position since I saw you walk into that bar, Kez,"

"Just this position?" I teased, angling my hips back. His hand connected with my rump in a stinging slap. "Ouch!" I complained half-heartedly.

He eased the sting with a few strokes of his palm. "Stop trying to use this," his fingers cupped the curve of my ass, "to change the subject."

I rubbed said ass against his groin. "Seems like it's working," I said.

With a rumbling groan, he took my chin in his hand, forcing me to look at him. "Naughty girl," he said, his voice low and rough.

Those words and their promise of dirty things had me shivering in anticipation. I flexed my hips again, and a breath hissed between his teeth.

"Kesler, unless you want to be facedown in that pillow, you need to stop," he warned, tightening his grip on my backside.

"Promises, promises," I sassed him, daring him to make good on his threat.

I should've known better. Jackson Jenkins was not a man to be teased with something he wanted. And he wasn't going to hesitate in taking what was offered.

"You asked for it, gorgeous," he said gruffly.

Once again, I wiggled my butt. "Oh, I'm asking, all right," I said. "Some might even call it begging."

His answering laugh was sinister in all the right ways. "Don't play with me, baby, unless you're really ready for it." His fingers bumped up the ridge of my spine, stopping between my shoulder blades to push me farther into the mattress. "Last chance, gorgeous. Speak now, or forever hold your peace." I heard the crinkle of foil behind me.

His dark promises and sexy teasing were driving me to the brink, and if he didn't hurry up, I was going to go insane. His yearning for me bled through his dirty words, so I knew he was as close to the breaking point as I was. His control was slipping. It wouldn't take much to make him lose it. I shot him a sultry look over my shoulder. "I'm not asking to get married, I'm asking to get laid."

His blue eyes flickered like the hottest flame. "Careful, Kez."

Fed up with waiting, I said, "Jax, I think careful went out the window a while ago. Now, if you're not up for it ..." The rest of my sassy response was reduced to garbled nonsense when Jackson took over. While before he'd been slow and reverent, he was now hard and fast. This was a man staking his claim and making sure there was no question who was in charge. His strokes were swift and drove deep.

I clawed at the sheets, feeling the swell of my impending orgasm. "Jackson, I'm ... I'm, oh, God!" Indescribable pleasure erupted deep within me, and incoherent syllables of carnal gibberish spewed from my lips. With a primitive yell, he plunged forward, and together we rode out our climax, collapsing onto the mattress, utterly spent.

"Holy shit," I wheezed from underneath him.

"My sentiments exactly," he mumbled into my hair. His weight shifted, and I let him roll my body into the crook of his arm. I was so loose and relaxed, my limbs could've been connected by rubber bands. The sheen of sweat on my skin matched Jackson's. My head lolled to the side like a rag doll, and I smiled goofily up at him. I wished I could do something sexy, but simply breathing was difficult enough at that point.

"I think you're trying to kill me," he said still breathing hard.

"You're the one with superhuman stamina. I'm just trying to keep up," I said feebly.

"I warned you to be careful," he reminded me.

I shrugged. "What can I say? I like life on the wild side sometimes."

He kissed me. "You poked the bear, gorgeous."

I kissed him back. "He can't hibernate forever. Especially now that I've seen what he can do."

Jackson flopped back against the pillow. "And here I thought I'd won you over with slow and sweet."

I draped my leg over him. "I like variety."

He held me tighter. "I like this."

I kissed him. "So do I."

Sunlight rather than moonlight greeted me the next time I opened my eyes. Jackson breathed deeply beside me, and for a second I relished the feeling of being in his arms. Then, it hit me that if the sun was shining high enough to penetrate the barn, it was well after the break of dawn. I sat up with a start and shoved him. "Jax!"

He jolted awake with a snort. "What's going on?"

"We fell asleep!" I leapt from the bed and searched for my clothes.

Jackson rubbed one eye and pushed himself into a sitting position, looking entirely too sexy to have just woken up. The hem of the quilt rested at his waist, giving me a glorious view of his chest and abs. The undulation of his muscles as he adjusted his position was hypnotizing. "Calm down, Kez."

I tore my attention from his abs and the growing need to taste them. Clutching my jeans to my chest, I said, "Calm down! How am I supposed to calm down? We're out here in your sex den while your grandmother's inside probably making breakfast."

Yawning, he asked, "Sex den? That's a little much, don't you think? Plus, did you not hear her basically tell us to get busy last night?" His stretching brought my eyes back to the lines of his body and my mind to the lithe way he had moved mere hours before.

Snatching his shirt from the floor, I threw it at him. It fluttered harmlessly through the air and landed on the bed. "That doesn't matter! What she said and what she really meant are two different things."

He scratched his beard, considering. "Nah, Nana isn't like that."

Hopping on one foot, I began to pull my jeans on.

Still making no move to get out of bed, he asked, "Don't you wanna put this on first?"

My G-string twirled in a circle around his index finger. Jerking my pants on the rest of the way, I lunged to grab my underwear, but he held them just out of my reach. He wrapped an arm around me and dragged me under him on the bed.

"On second thought, maybe I'll just hold on to them," he said with a wink.

As I struggled to shove him off, he laughed and kissed me. As his mouth took mine, I stopped trying to escape. The feel of his naked torso against me made me forget about Nana, breakfast, and anything else that might exist outside the doors of his workshop. Nimble fingers moved down my stomach and into my jeans. "What's your hurry, gorgeous?" His lips moved across my jawline, his beard tickling my throat.

"Mmmmmmm," was the only response I could form as he worked my jeans down over my ass.

"You're so sexy, baby," he said. "I can't get enough of you." My fingers dug into his shoulders, and he kissed his way down my chest.

In the back of my mind, the practical side of me was throwing a fit, but the inner witch wrestled her to the ground and broke out the duct tape. Unfortunately for the witch, my cell phone had been in the pocket of my jeans and chose that moment to ring loudly.

Jackson's greedy mouth persisted on its way south. "Ignore it," he said as he swirled his tongue into my belly button.

I gave his shoulders a half-hearted push. "I should answer it."

He looked up from between my legs, his dark hair mussed from the night before and his muscles strung taut. "Really?" Kissing the crease of my hip, he said, "I think it can wait. All I need is five minutes, gorgeous." If the Devil ever took human form, he would probably look like Jackson—all bedroom eyes and tempting, impish grins.

My phone alerted again, jarring me from my contemplation of Jackson as temptation incarnate. I questioned my own sanity when I flipped away from him and hauled my jeans back up. My cell phone tumbled onto the bedspread. V's face flashed on the screen. "Hey, V. What's up?" I said in a rush as I zipped my pants.

"Why do you sound weird?" she asked.

Jackson gripped my belt loops and pulled me back onto the bed. I tried to ward him off with one hand, but he was dogged in his pursuit. "What do you mean weird?" I asked, trying to keep my voice steady as his hands roamed freely across my torso.

"I mean out of breath and all flustered," said V.

As much as I hated to do it, I knew V needed something, so I held the phone away from my ear and shoved Jackson hard with my other hand. "Stop it!"

Reluctantly, he held up his hands and allowed me to untangle myself from the sheet and get out of bed. Bending over, I started looking for my bra and shirt. "I don't know what you're talking about," I said into the phone.

"Anyway," she said, "we are flying out today, right?"

My heart clenched, which was dumb since Jackson lived roughly half an hour from me. I guess I had some leftover PTSD from Miller's choice to stay up here. Jackson wasn't Miller though. I had to remember that. "Um, yeah, we're still flying out today."

She sounded disappointed. "Oh, okay."

Remembering why she hadn't made it last night, I was intrigued. "Why? Do you want to stay another night?"

Jackson's eyebrows shot up, letting me know he was keyed into my conversation. His foot poked around under the covers, emerging with my bra hooked on his toe. I gave him a gimme gesture, and he tossed it to me. Cradling the phone against my ear, I quickly hooked the clasp and lifted the girls into their rightful perky places. Semicovered, I resumed the hunt for my shirt but was distracted by Jackson getting out of bed. Good God, the man had an ass so perfectly shaped it would stop traffic. The lean muscles in his back were just as good as his abs. He did not have a bad side but was genetically gifted from every direction. He caught me gawking at him and flexed his ass. I flipped him off.

My shirt dangled from one corner of the headboard. "Hold on a second." I tugged on the thermal. Once my head popped through, I said, "Okay, sorry, I was … never mind. Is there an issue with leaving today?"

She sighed. "No, I guess not."

"I know you saw Dave last night, and according to Rae, we should be planning a Christmas wedding," I prodded, hoping to get her to fess up.

Her laugh bubbled across the line. "I don't know about all that. He's nothing like the guys I normally date."

I watched Jackson bend over to rescue his jeans from the blade of a circular saw. "You mean not a total douche living off his trust fund from mommy and daddy? Yeah, I picked up on that."

She hmmphed into the phone. "Whatever. I mean he's a bartender."

And here was where dear old mummy's country club criticisms would come to the surface. "So?" I challenged her.

"Well, that's not long-term material, is it?" V had been force-fed this horseshit from her parents for so long, she would regurgitate it from time to time. As her friends, Rae and I had to remind her that her own happiness was more important than a guy's social standing or earning potential.

"Does it really matter what he does, V? It's not like you need, or want, a sugar daddy."

"Yeah, but …"

"But what? The guy makes you happy, V, and you like him enough to contemplate spending more time in the land of the frozen tundra, so that must count for something. Plus, aren't you putting the cart way in front of the horse at this point?"

I stood and straightened my jeans over my boots, watching Jackson pull his shirt over his head. I cried a little inside at the loss. There should be a law somewhere that required him to be shirtless at all times. Chiseled, tattooed perfection should not be covered up. Well, except with a wifebeater on special occasions, like my birthday or Christmas.

"But, let's discuss this later because I need to go," I said abruptly.

"You need to go? What are you …? Ooooohhhhhhhhh," she said.

Rather than get into all of the glorious details, I said, "Yep, you got it."

"Okay, well, call me when you're headed back. I'm going to look at flights."

I clicked off and slipped the phone into my back pocket. Jackson straddled a bench and pulled on his boots. Coming up behind him, I laid my hands on his shoulders.

He leaned back and rested his head between my breasts. "Problem?" he asked.

"V's trying to wrap her mind around the fact she's super attracted to someone who doesn't fit her carefully crafted idea of a man."

"Dave's good people," he said a bit defensively.

"Never said he wasn't," I said smoothly. "She'll get it figured out, one way or the other. In the meantime, we should get up to the house."

Standing, he took my hands in his and pulled me around in front of him. "Kez, last night was …"

"Yeah, it was," I agreed. "And who could forget about early this morning?"

His eyes twinkled, and he kissed me. "Definitely not this guy." Growing serious, he asked, "You good with all this?"

I cuddled into him. "Starting off my day by waking up next to a hot, naked guy? Yeah, I think I can handle that."

He rubbed my back and chuckled, but there was an underlying solemnity when he said, "Not what I meant."

With one last hug, I pulled back. "I know, Jax. I can't promise that I won't have a random freak-out at some point, but that doesn't mean I regret last night at all."

He pushed a hand through his hair and sighed "I'm asking about more than just last night."

"That's a big conversation to have before I've had any coffee, and when I'm still under the influence of your intoxicating pheromones." I could see he wanted to argue, but I kept going. "I'm not saying we can't have that conversation. I just think we should do it at a point when I'm not sleep-deprived and delirious from sex endorphins."

Jackson started for the door. "Then let's get you some coffee."

Chapter 18

The two of us walked into the kitchen and caught Betty feeding Russ a piece of bacon. Strings of drool hung from his jowls as he scarfed it down, and looked for more.

"Red-handed," said Jackson.

She looked up at the sound of his voice. "There you two are! I was about to send a search party."

Trying to play it cool, I said, "Good morning, Betty. Is that coffee I smell?"

Pointing to the pot and mugs on the counter behind her, she scratched Russ' ears. "I take it you two had a good night."

My hand shook when I reached for the coffee pot. I was going commando in the same room as his grandmother after spending the majority of the prior evening naked and sweaty with her grandson. Who, by the way, still had my panties in his pocket. I decided to let the panty thief himself field that question. I poured my coffee and added cream and sugar.

Jackson said, "My grandmother taught me not to kiss and tell."

From her place at the island, Betty popped him with a dish towel. "She raised you right." He kissed her cheek as he passed by to get his own coffee. She lifted a cloth napkin off the counter in front of her to reveal a stack of golden French toast next to a plate of bacon. "Help yourselves," she said.

My mouth watered, and I took a plate, stacking up a pile of toast with a generous helping of bacon, then drowning it in syrup. When he reached around me to get a plate, Jackson's pelvis brushed my hip. My body thrummed in response and recognition. His chuckle turned cough told me he knew the effect that simple touch had on me. I sat down and ignored him, determined to tamp down my raging hormones.

"I showed Kez my workshop, Nana," Jackson said. "She was very impressed with all my ... tools."

I choked on a piece of bacon at his double entendre. Jackson whacked me on the back to dislodge it.

"Kez," Betty cried. "Are you all right?" She dropped the towel she was folding and rushed over to my side.

Tears streamed down my cheeks as I coughed. "I'm fine," I insisted, as she rubbed my shoulder.

Over her head, Jackson mouthed, "Sorry!"

Once she was certain I didn't need the Heimlich, Betty topped off her coffee. "My husband used to spend hours out there tinkering. I think Jackson was five when he started 'helping' with projects. He's been hooked ever since."

"Well, based on what I've seen, he's very talented," I said. My inadvertent insinuation played right off Jackson's earlier intentional one, which made me blush to the roots of my hair. Betty was kind enough not to comment. For a few moments, the sound of breakfast being eaten was the only noise in the room. But the silence was more companionable than uncomfortable.

When I'd finished, Jackson stacked my plate on his, rinsing both and then placing them in the dishwasher. He leaned against the farmhouse sink, coffee mug in hand. "Kez needs to head back to the hotel," he said to Betty. "One of her friends is having a bit of a crisis."

I took my cup to the sink and rinsed it out. "Did you need help cleaning up anything before I go?" I asked Betty.

She dismissed my offer. "Don't worry about it, Kez. Do you want to take any of this with you?" We'd made a dent in what she'd fixed for breakfast, but there was still plenty left over.

I pictured shoving Jackson in a piece of Tupperware. "No, I think I'm good. Thank you so much for everything."

Betty hugged me, and I stooped down a bit to return it, catching the light floral scent of her perfume. "Don't mention it, honey."

Jackson walked me out to the rental Rae left behind last night. His hair was messy and his clothes a little wrinkled, and I'd never wanted anyone more. A light wind blew my hair into my face, and he brushed it back. He curled a hand around the back of my neck and pulled me forward. I came willingly into his arms, resting my cheek against his chest. His heart beat a strong rhythm in my ear.

"I'll see you later?" It might have been phrased like he was asking, but there was an undercurrent of certainty to it. I liked it.

"Well, it sounds like V's changing her flight to at least tomorrow, so, if you want, I could do the same."

His fingers worked their way into my hair. "I'm glad to hear that," he said. "I've got a few things to do around here today, but I'd love to take you to dinner tonight." He angled back to look at me. "Unless you think you'll need to talk V off a ledge?"

I laughed. "No, we'll have her squared away by then. Dinner sounds great."

He tilted my chin up and kissed me. "I'll pick you up at seven," he said. "We can finish the conversation we started in the barn this morning." I swallowed nervously. Seeing my reluctance, he hemmed me in against the car door. "Don't think about running from this, Kez," he cautioned. He palmed my cheek, lifting my gaze to his intense blue one. "You run," he kissed my forehead, "and I'll find you." The last part was whispered in my ear in a steamy promise.

How was it possible to fear something at the same time you craved it? I longed for whatever was happening between us to grow and blossom while agonizing that he'd turn out to be just like Miller—a shiny beacon that tarnished with time, eventually leaving me in shrouded darkness. I didn't want to make another mistake. While I was with Jackson, his presence kept my doubts at bay. Each time we were apart, though, they crept back in and took root in the crevices of my bandaged heart. My defense mechanisms warred with the desire to give into the feelings I was developing for Jackson.

As if he could read my vacillating thoughts, Jackson said, "Fight for this, not against it, Kez." Then he moved back and opened the door for me to get in the car, trusting I'd take his request to heart. I buckled up and drove around the circle drive. Jackson waved and went back into the house. Pausing at the edge of Betty's driveway, I plugged the hotel address into the GPS. I'd just turned back onto the main road when my phone rang. *Shit*, I thought when I heard my sister Hudson's ringtone. It was time to face the music.

"Hey, Sunny," I answered, using the nickname our granddaddy had given her. When we were little, she'd always had a smile on her face. Grandaddy said that her happy disposition brought a little more sunshine into the world.

"Hey, baby sister," she replied. "You on your way home from the airport?"

"Um, well …" I said slowly.

"It's not a trick question, Kez. You either are, or you aren't."

I blew out a breath. "I'm not."

"I thought you were coming home today?"

"Are you at home?" I asked.

She groaned. "I wish. Somehow, I got talked into coming to Mama and Daddy's for Sunday lunch. I still don't know how that happened. I'm barreling up I-85. Why?"

I figured now was as good a time as any to break the news. "Well, I've got a little something to tell you, but you can't tell Mama and Daddy."

"Oh, Jesus," she said impatiently. "Any time you start with don't tell Mama and Daddy, I know it's a doozy. Like the time you ran over that pear tree with Grandaddy's go-cart. First words out of your mouth were 'Don't tell Mama and Daddy.' Lay it on me, baby sister. Your secret is safe with me."

In between directions from my GPS, I filled my sister in on the past few days. When I finished, she said nothing. "Hudson, you still there?"

"I can't believe you didn't tell me all this was going on!" The hurt I'd caused her resonated in the cabin of the SUV. I hated myself for it.

"I'm sorry, Sunny," I said truthfully. Obeying the computerized voice, I merged onto the freeway. "I just didn't want y'all to worry about me."

"Ugh, Kez," she said, aggravated with me. "You're family, so we're always going to worry about you. That being said, why on Earth would we worry about you going to Rochester to see the guy who broke your heart? That's totally normal and should cause us no concern whatsoever." Sarcasm dripped from the speakers.

"Can we focus on the fact that I met someone else?" I asked, trying to get her to see that while she may not have agreed with this trip, some good had come out of it. *Fight for it, not against it.* Jackson's plea repeated in my head.

"I swear you could get swallowed by a bear only to emerge smelling like a rose when you get crapped out," she grumbled. I took that as her grudging agreement my meeting Jackson was a good thing.

"I think I like him," I said gingerly. *Fight for it, not against it.*

"It certainly seems that way," she replied. "And it sounds like you're at least trying to resist your ususal plan of cut and run, so that's progress. You're one hundred percent sure he does live down here, right?"

"Yeah, right outside Charlotte," I confirmed.

"Thank the Lord," she said, relieved this wasn't Miller Part Deux. "You know Mama and Daddy are going to want to meet him, right?"

"I don't think we're quite at the meet-the-parents stage," I said. I wasn't ready to let him experience the inquisition that would be my family.

"Um, didn't you just leave his grandmother's house?" she asked.

"That was an extenuating circumstance," I clarified. "But regardless, Mama and Daddy don't need to hear about Jackson from you."

"Fine, fine," she agreed reluctantly. "But we are having a much longer discussion when you get back. Namely about why you didn't think you could talk to me about this."

"We will, I promise," I said. My GPS told me I was five miles from my destination. "Hey, I'm almost back at the hotel, so I gotta go."

"Okay, love you, bye."

"Love you, bye," I said. The phone rang again almost immediately, the caller id flashing Rae's number.

"Hey," I said, "I'm almost back at the hotel. What's up?"

"Hurry up and get back here," she said in a harried whisper. "V's freaking out."

"What do you mean? I talked to her a few hours ago, and everything was all good. She was going to look at later flights."

"Well, that's no longer the case," Rae said irritably. It was obvious she was covering the phone to keep V from hearing her. "She says she's leaving *tonight*."

"I'll be there in," I checked the GPS again, "five minutes."

"You'd better be speeding," she said and hung up.

Exactly five minutes later, I screeched up to the valet at the hotel. I tossed my keys to the nearest attendant and raced through the lobby. Darting into the elevator, I willed it to go faster. Once it hit our floor, I rushed down the hall to our suite.

Rae met me at the door, fury distorting her features. "What's going on?" I asked in a low voice.

"In between her talking to you and my getting back to the room with coffee, her mom called," Rae seethed.

"Oh crap," I said.

"She filled her head full of that elitist gobbledygook, and now she's packing up all her shit!"

This was not good. "V?" I called.

"In here," she answered. We followed the sound of her voice back to the bedroom. She paced between an open suitcase and the closet, yanking clothes out and tossing them haphazardly into her luggage.

"V, what's going on?" I asked.

At first, I thought she wasn't going to answer me, then her legs gave out, and she plopped onto the bed. Covering her face, she wailed, "I don't know!"

Rae signaled to me she was going to get a drink. I held up three fingers, and she nodded. Sitting down next to V, I asked, "What happened between this morning and now?"

With a long snuffle, she lowered her hands, twisting her fingers in her lap. "He's a bartender in Rochester!"

Bumping her shoulder with mine, I said, "That was true this morning, so I'm pretty sure that's not what changed."

"I can't date a bartender who lives thousands of miles away!"

I pulled a few tissues from the box by the bed and passed them to her. "Why, because your mom says you can't?" I asked, unable to hide my annoyance.

V sniffled. "He doesn't fit into my life plan."

"*Your* life plan, or the plan your parents have *for* you? There's a big difference, you know? Mainly because you're the one living the plan, not them. They can't dictate what happens in your life, V. You're a grown woman who deserves to live the way *she* wants."

She jumped up and resumed shoving clothes into her suitcase. "It's not that simple, Kez. You know how my parents are."

Yes, I was painfully aware that her parents were stuck-up assholes who treated her like a broodmare to continue the lineage. I shut the lid on her luggage. "V, stop. Tell me what's really going on here."

"I'm a doctor," she said. Her hands strangled the sweater she was still holding. Gently, I took it from her.

"Yes, I know. I was there when you graduated med school and took you out to get smashed once you finished your residency."

"How does a doctor date a bartender who doesn't even live in the same state?" She pulled at her hair, the tension on the strands contorting her face.

"Well, it probably involves dinner, at a minimum," I said, trying for levity.

"This isn't a joke, Kez! This is my life!"

Okay, no levity—got it. "Okay, okay, calm down," I said soothingly. "We've established your residences and respective professions. Now, explain to me how that results in a stage-five meltdown."

Slouching back onto the bed, she replied, "I think I could really like him, Kez."

"And what's wrong with that?" I asked, determined to make her say it.

"Well, for starters, he lives thousands of miles away."

"So? If you want to start something with him, you'll figure out the logistics. He can fit into your life any way you let him, V. Maybe this is a weekend fling; maybe it lasts a little longer. Who knows, but if you like him as much as I think you do, then it seems to me you need to take a little time to figure out how *you* feel. Not your mom or anyone else in your snobby-ass family, but you. That's the right choice here, not turning tail and running away."

"You don't think it's far-fetched to think it could work?" Her eyes were red rimmed but hopeful.

"I think you owe it to yourself and your own happiness to see if it can. If you don't, there's always going to be that feeling in the back of your mind of what could've been. Take it from me," I said ruefully, "that is the *worst* feeling." She cracked a smile at my lame humor. "If it turns out he was a fun chapter in a longer story, that's okay. There's not a wrong answer here, V, if he makes you feel the way you say he does. It's worth taking a chance to see where it goes."

She hunched against me, and I put an arm around her, just as Rae came back with three cups of coffee.

Rae cautioned, "They're Irish coffees."

Taking two from her, I passed one to V. "Nothing wrong with an occasional freak-out. Happens to the best of us."

V took a swallow and gagged. "I'm not sure if the two of you are who I should turn to for confirmation my feelings are normal."

"Not a chance," said Rae jovially. "But we can at least tell you if you're being an idiot. Which, by the way, you are." She shoved V's suitcase aside and sat down on the bed behind us, folding her legs beneath her.

I turned sideways so I could look at her. "You know," I said, "one day we're going to talk about *your* dysfunction and the reasons behind it."

Rae's normally bright eyes flattened. I recognized the blank stare as the barrier she put up any time she was asked her about her past relationships. It was like an impenetrable glass wall between us. I could still see her, but there was no getting through. "That's going to be a very one-sided conversation, so I hope you enjoy the sound of your own voice," she said firmly.

I asked, "What? We can talk about how messed up I am and V's ridiculous view of Mr. Right, but you're off limits?"

Her smile was tight. "You're a quick study."

"That's not exactly how friendships work, you know?" I said blandly.

"It's how mine do," she retorted, a stubborn set to her chin.

Not wanting to push her until she got pissed, I gave up. "Fine, but we're here for you, girl. You know that, right?"

She nodded. "I do and I appreciate it, but that's just not my bag. I can handle my own shit."

V piped up, "I think there's a line of guys, including Chris, who would disagree with that."

Rae's cold green gaze landed on V. "As long as I handle their dicks for the limited time we're together, I seriously doubt they care."

V frowned in distaste. "There's more to life than … dick, Rae."

"Speaking of dick," Rae said, "I want to hear about Kez's night with Jackson."

Allowing her to change the subject, I said, "Well, you were right."

"Of course, I was," she said confidently. She tilted her head, considering all the great many things she thought she'd been right about. "Which time?"

"The man is *very* good with his hands. And everything else." Heat licked at my insides as I remembered our night together.

Rae rubbed her hands together gleefully. "Now we're getting to the good stuff."

"You do know I'm not giving you a play-by-play, right?"

"I'll settle for a blow-by-blow, so to speak." Her grin was wicked.

"You're truly a disgusting human being," V said, her face scrunched in revulsion.

Rae brushed off her disapproval like an annoying fly. "No one's arguing that point. Now dish, Kez!" she wheedled.

"I'm not going to kiss and tell," I said primly.

Rae groaned and flopped backward. "Who said I wanted to hear about the kissing?"

"Even if he kissed me ... *everywhere*?" I teased.

She sprang back up into a sitting position, her coffee sloshing precariously. "Now *that* I do want to hear about."

I laughed at her excitement. "I'm not giving you the full rundown, but I will say that there is a baaaaaad boy underneath that beard."

"No way! Tell me more!" she demanded.

I threw her a crumb of detail. "He's not above a little discipline if the class gets unruly."

Rae fanned herself. "Oh my God, for real?"

"I've got the handprints on my ass to prove it."

"Holy flapjacks, Batman, that's hot." Rae swooned backward, holding her mug above her head to avoid spilling anything on the comforter.

V's phone rang, and she got up to answer it. "It's Dave," she said, chewing her cuticle.

"So answer it, and see what he's doing tonight and if he still wants it to be you," Rae responded.

V made a face, but answered the phone, leaving the room to have her conversation with Dave. I looked down at Rae. "You're such a relationship guru, you know?"

She blew on her nails and polished them against her shirt. "What can I say?"

"Makes me think you had one at one point," I said blithely.

She sat up and finished her coffee in one swig. "Seems like you've got flights to move to tomorrow." With that, she, too, left the room.

Chapter 19

Hooking my purse below the bar, I waited to get the bartender's attention.

"What can I get you?"

"Tequila, rocks, with a twist of lime."

"Coming right up."

For a Sunday night, the hotel lounge was busy. There were some leftovers from the reunion that I recognized, mixed in with other patrons. I'd come down to get a drink while I waited on Jackson. Rae was napping and had been evasive about her plans for the night, while V had gotten over her earlier breakdown and was out with Dave.

"Is this seat taken?"

The sound of Miller's voice made each of my vertebrae click into place. "I don't think that's a good idea," I said, avoiding eye contact. Maybe, if I didn't look at him, he'd just disappear.

He took the seat to my left anyway. "I come in peace, Kez. Just give me five minutes," he said beseechingly. When I didn't immediately tell him to leave, he smiled, activating the dimple in his left cheek. "I promise I'll be on my best behavior."

Resigned to his company for at least a little while, I said, "Fine. How did you even know I was still here?"

"I called the hotel and made sure you hadn't checked out, so I thought I'd swing by and try to catch you. I saw you get off the elevator."

"So, what, now you're stalking me?" I accused.

He looked pained "No, I want to apologize for yesterday. I was out of line."

Of all the things I expected, his apology wasn't one of them. "You think?" I asked, my sarcasm so thick it probably dripped into my drink.

"I'm sorry I was such an ass, Kez," he said, his eyes downcast and his smile turning contrite.

"This situation seems so familiar. It's almost like we've been here before ..." I sniped, refusing to let him charm his way out of how he'd acted yesterday.

Miller signaled the bartender for a drink. Once she'd taken his order and gone, he put his hand on my knee, touching the hem of my dress. I crossed my legs to dislodge it. We weren't going back down the touchy-feely road he'd tried at the picnic. Getting the hint, he put his hand on the bar. He said, "I deserve that. Look, I know I fucked up, Kez. I had no right to talk to you that way. I don't even know why I said the things I did."

Because you're an asshole, I thought, but aloud I said, "Yes, you do. You said it because you were pissed I showed up with Jackson. Although I can't understand why it matters who I'm here with when you're the one that's *engaged*." I emphasized his relationship status.

"I'll always care who you're with, Kez. That's never going to change," he said.

I wasn't having it. "You lost the right to care when we broke up."

The bartender reappeared with his drink and, sensing the mood, quickly scampered off. He took a swallow. "That's not true and you know it."

I felt like I was on a merry-go-round with no way off. "What do you want, Miller?"

"If I knew the answer to that question, it would've saved everyone a lot of grief."

"I'm not in the mood to participate in your existential crisis."

He laughed. "That's one way to describe this."

Glancing at my watch, I saw that Jackson could walk in at any moment. I didn't need him to happen upon my little tête-à-tête with Miller. "Look, you've apologized. That's what you wanted to do, so let's leave it at that."

"There was so much more I want to say …"

Frustrated, I spun my stool toward him. "All right then, what *do* you want to say to me? Because I think we've said all we needed to and then some."

He kept fidgeting with his drink, not speaking.

So typical, I thought, then waved to the bartender. "I'm done here."

Miller's hand shot out to stop me. "Kez, wait, please."

I glowered at his grip on my arm. "Hands off, Miller. I thought you learned that lesson yesterday."

He dropped my arm like it was on fire, his posture deflating. "I'm sorry. God, I'm just so sorry."

Seeing him so pitiful and dejected, I couldn't help but feel a little bad for him. Even after he'd been such a dick yesterday, it hadn't completely hardened my heart toward him. It seemed like I'd always have a little bit of a soft spot for him. Praying I wasn't getting suckered, I conceded, "Miller, I think that sums up how we both feel at this point. Which tells me there's nothing left for us to say to each other."

Staring morosely into his drink, he replied, "I loved you, Kez. Hell, I probably still do."

This was a direction we did *not* need to be going. I tried to steer him away from it. "Miller, that's …"

"No, wait, hear me out," he pleaded, pushing his glass aside. "I fell in love with you pretty much the first time you told me off in that hallway, I just didn't know it. You were everything I'd always wanted in a beautiful, smart-ass package. I should've asked you, begged you even, to move back up here with me after graduation, but I was afraid you'd say no. And if you'd said no, well, then where did that leave us? So I took the coward's way out and did nothing. Then later, when you told me to move down with you, I chose my pride instead of us and spent the next few months trying to find the bottom of a bottle and ruining our relationship in the process."

I felt no sense of victory from his confession. In my revenge fantasies I was always elated upon discovering he'd been miserable. Now, there was only sadness and an overwhelming sense of pity that our younger selves wasted so much time being angry and hurt rather than simply talking to each other. If we had, things could've ended so differently. The heartache would still have been there, but it wouldn't have been fueled by feelings of rejection and betrayal. His plaintive admission spurred my own regrets, and I wanted to offer some comfort. Tentatively, I touched his knee. "We were young, Miller. So young and so very focused on ourselves instead of each other."

His hand covered mine. "I should've been focused on you, Kez."

A small smile played across my lips. "It's amazing how clear things appear in hindsight."

His mouth curved into a cynical grin, but I wasn't finished.

"Which is why I think you need to be careful not to make the same mistakes again."

He cocked his head in confusion. "What do you mean?"

With an uncomfortable grunt, I said, "I cannot believe I'm about to say this, but ... what I mean is that you need to think about Callie. She was devastated when she came to my room the other night."

Miller looked sheepish. "I haven't talked to her since Friday."

I rolled my eyes. "Jesus Christ, Miller."

Owning his mistake, he said, "I know, I know! I don't know what to say to her."

I pulled my hand from under his. "Well, you need to figure that shit out," I said. "I managed to calm her down, but *you* need to talk to her. I can tell you, based on my conversation with her, that girl is head over heels for you, and if you're not, then you owe it to her to tell her. Don't let the past repeat itself, Miller. You need to talk to Callie before it's too late and she gets even more hurt. Or at least lessen the pain she's already going through."

His lips twitched. "You do realize this is an extremely weird conversation, right?"

"It hasn't escaped my notice." Giving relationship advice to my ex might rank high on the list of bizarre shit I'd done, but it also felt good. It meant my main goal in life was no longer his misery but my own happiness.

Miller scrubbed his hands down his jeans. "I don't know what to say to her," he repeated.

"The truth is always a great starting point," I advised.

"Yeah, right. First, I have to figure out what that is." He sounded lost and without a clue as to what he should do.

I gave him a warning. "Well, you wait around too long and someone's going to step up and give her what she wants. Ask yourself if you're ready to let that happen …"

"For a second time?" he interrupted.

I shrugged. "Your words, not mine." I finished my drink and stood. "I never thought I'd say this and mean it, but it was good to see you, Miller."

He rose. "Kez, I …"

"Don't, Miller. Let's not make this any more than it is. Seeing you helped me sort through and discard some particularly heavy baggage that I've dragged around for far too long. That's the extent of it."

"So, if I said we should try to keep in touch …"

The utter absurdity of his suggestion floored me. "In the history of dumb ideas, that has to be near the top. Take care of yourself, Miller."

He pulled me into a hug. "You, too, Kez."

"Am I interrupting?" Jackson asked from behind me.

Crap!

I took two large steps away from Miller. To Jackson, I said, "Not at all, babe. You ready to go to dinner?"

His face was a mask of barely controlled fury as he glared at Miller. Without answering my question, he simply held out his hand. Looping my fingers into his, I let him gather me into his embrace. Leaning down, he took his time kissing me, exploring my mouth in a total show of male ego. While my ovaries broke into the Electric Slide, I was a little put out at being marked like a fire hydrant. When he lifted his head, I whispered, "Wanna pee on my leg next?"

"Don't tempt me," he murmured. Straightening up, he said, "Miller."

Miller crossed his arms. "Jackson."

"Seems like this is the second time in a few days I've found you with your hands on my girl." Despite the casual sound of his voice, there was an undercurrent of steel in it.

With a shrug in response, Miller replied, "Just catching up."

Tension radiated from Jackson like a coiled spring, but he kept his voice even. "Is that so? Seems like the last time her knee caught up with your nuts." It was a well-placed barb, and Miller's flinch let Jackson know it hit home.

Trying to keep things from erupting into anything more than macho posturing, I pulled on his arm. "Let's just go, Jax."

"You should listen to her, Triple," said Miller condescendingly. I couldn't believe I'd felt sorry for him a few minutes ago. It was like Jackson brought out Miller's inner asshole.

Jackson's answering laugh was mirthless. "See, that's just it. I listened to her tell you yesterday she didn't want anything to do with you and yet," his hands spread wide, "here we all are. So now I'm thinking, maybe you need to hear it from *me* to drive the point home." He stepped forward so the two of them were nose-to-nose. "Stay away from her, Miller. I'm not going to tell you again." The warning was sewn with venom. Jackson's eyes were frigid blue pools of anger.

Miller dropped his arms to his sides, his hands flexed, not backing down from Jackson's challenge. "Is that right?"

Jackson's mouth peeled back into a sneer. "Back up, Miller. This doesn't end well for you."

The bartender called out, "Is there a problem here?"

Without breaking eye contact, both Miller and Jackson barked out, "No." Any hope I had she'd call someone over to separate the two of them evaporated when she backed away to the other end of the bar. Great, now I was stuck here with these two puffing at each other like a couple of bantam roosters. Where was a water hose when you needed it?

"Jax, please," I implored. He flicked his eyes to me but made no move to end his standoff with Miller.

"Well, well, what do we have here? I must have missed the announcement about the cockfight tonight. Good thing I decided to pop down for a drink before heading out for the evening." Rae moseyed up to our tense little threesome. Dressed to the nines, she was a welcome sight. Hatred lit those expressive green eyes when she said, "Miller, still acting like a giant dickhead, I see? Good to know some things never change."

"Rae?" asked Miller, his attention snapping from Jackson to her. "What the hell are you doing here?"

The two of them had never had a good relationship. It didn't help matters that Rae hadn't known Miller during the good times. They'd met right as my relationship with him was ending. So she only knew the embittered guy who turned to booze and refused to grow up instead of the flirty, charmer I knew him to be. She felt like he needed to man up and admit he'd chosen poorly by not staying in North Carolina. He felt like she needed to mind her own business. Their disagreements came to a head the weekend I had flown him down to Charlotte in an ill-fated attempt on my part to salvage things. The first night he was there ended with the two of them in a full-blown screaming match in the middle of the street. Bloodshed had been avoided, but only barely.

She plucked a nonexistent piece of lint off her fitted black dress. "I think the better question, jackass, is what are *you* doing here?"

"Still as classy as ever," he responded rudely.

"What can I say?" With a downward sweep of her lashes, she gave him a quick once-over. "I stoop to match my surroundings."

Miller fumed at her, while Jackson laughed and his shoulders relaxed. "Rae, you certainly know how to make an entrance." He backed away from Miller and put his arm around me.

Rae looked to Jackson, slightly disappointed. "Oh, please, don't refrain from kicking his ass on my account. I'm willing to wait my turn. After all, I've waited this long. What's a few more minutes?"

Jackson shook his head. "Nah, Kez is right. He's not worth it. Plus, I'd rather take her to dinner than waste any more time listening to his bullshit."

Now that Jackson wasn't about to come to blows with Miller, I breathed a sigh of relief. I had plans that didn't include bailing him out. Handcuffs, maybe, but not an actual jail.

Rae adjusted her stance so she was now squaring off with Miller. Quirking a final questioning brow at Jackson, she asked, "You're sure?"

Jackson nodded. "Yeah, I am."

She shrugged. "Okay, so long as you're sure." Then, she wound up and punched Miller right in the face. "Dammit," she said, shaking her hand. "That shit hurts!"

"What the fuck!" yelled Miller. He stumbled backward, blood dripping from his split lip.

Jackson tried to get between them, but Rae held up her uninjured palm to stop him. She scowled up at Miller. "Tell me you didn't have that coming, Miller. I dare you." He wiped a hand under his mouth and didn't respond. "That's what I thought," she said. Flexing her fingers, she asked the bartender, who, like most of the people in the bar, was now staring at us, "Any chance I could get some ice in a towel?" The young woman hurried away. I hoped it was to get the ice and not call the cops.

"What are you looking at?" Rae asked the group of spectators. "You've never seen a guy get his ass handed to him by a girl? Y'all really need to get out more." Her curt words embarrassed and then dispersed the small crowd.

A uniformed man I assumed to be hotel security appeared. "What's the problem here?"

With a straight face and what had to be bruised knuckles, Rae drawled, "Problem? There's no problem here. Right, Miller?"

She knew there was no way Miller would fess up to being punched by a girl. He pressed a napkin to his mouth to staunch the trickle of blood. "Nah," he confirmed, "there's no problem here, sir. Just old friends catching up." The explanation was muffled by the cloth against his lip.

Security looked skeptical, but without someone pointing fingers or offering a different explanation as to what happened, he didn't have many options. "Well," he said, "maybe the four of you should go catch up somewhere else, huh?"

Rae took the ice pack from the bartender. "Like I said, no problem. Jackson, Kez, enjoy dinner. Miller, fuck off and die."

Chapter 20

Jackson wiped his eyes as he laughed about Rae punching Miller. Catching his breath, he said, "I'm telling you, between you and Rae, a man could feel a little emasculated." Dressed in dark jeans and a button up under a half-zip sweater topped by a quilted navy vest, Jackson looked like he'd stepped off the pages of *Town & Country*. All he needed was an obedient Labrador lying at his feet.

He'd taken me to a very romantic Italian restaurant a few blocks away from the hotel. High-back, U-shaped leather booths curved around tables draped in starched white linens lit by flickering candlelight. The seating arrangements gave couples no choice but to sit side by side as they ate. The ambiance made it seem it was just you and your date because you couldn't see any of the other diners. You only heard the faint murmur of conversation and the clink of glasses from somewhere outside your private little sphere.

I took a sip of my wine. "You claimed to enjoy my being somewhat of an acquired taste, remember?" I reminded him. "Plus, she gave you a chance to run the night we met."

"And I told you before, running's not my style. I know it's early on and there's a lot we don't know about each other, but one thing you can trust is that I'm sticking around, Kez."

"That's a lot of certainty for someone I've only known a weekend."

He shrugged. "It's true."

"What if you find out some things you don't like?"

He touched my cheek. "I'm not looking for perfect, gorgeous, I'm looking for real."

"Oftentimes, I'm a little too real for most people. Guys start out liking the idea of me, but experiencing the reality of it is a different story. Sure, they all say they're looking for a woman who is independent and outspoken. Someone who has her own interests and doesn't rely on them for everything. In the abstract, that all sounds good, but usually, when a woman has her own opinions, her own money, and her own success … a lot of the time it's more intimidating than intoxicating. It's a threat, not a turn-on, and it turns the relationship into some type of weird competition where the guy is always afraid he's going to come up short." I added, "Or feel emasculated."

He reached over and took my hand. "I was kidding, Kez. No real man would be emasculated by a woman who can take care of herself. But that doesn't mean I enjoy finding Miller with his arms around you." I had to admit, he had a point there. "I don't like it at all," he said frowning. "And nothing would make me happier than for it to stop happening."

I stroked his knuckles. "I promise, no more walking in on me and Miller."

"I'll hold you to that," he said. "That's not my main point, though. What I'm trying to say is that I think you've consciously chosen guys who lack any potential for a real relationship. Dating guys you know don't deserve you or who won't value you gives you an out because you can keep your walls up and not risk anything." When I didn't respond, he asked, "I'm not telling you anything you haven't already thought of yourself, am I?"

I couldn't lie to him. He'd essentially summed up my entire post-Miller dating history. Except he'd left out my dating the ones who were dull as dishwater because it felt safer than giving someone a real chance. I saw no need to point that out, though. "There may be some truth to what you're saying," I admitted.

His palm pressed against the back of my hand, emphasizing his next words. "It doesn't matter whether I think you're worth the effort, Kez, if you're not willing to admit I am too. I'm not like Miller or the other guys you've been wasting time with since the two of you broke up. I'm the guy you want. I just need a chance to show you. Don't treat me like I'm already a nice memory. Let me in and open yourself up to the possibility of making even better ones."

I wasn't sure what to say. I wanted him to be *the* guy. He seemed to be willing to understand and, more importantly, value my independence, even if it conflicted with his white-knight complex. I'd seen him struggling to let me handle things with Miller instead of stepping in and beating the tar out of him. He'd wrestled with it but managed to accept that he only needed to step in when I asked him to. I knew he wanted some reassurance that our initial give-and-take wasn't all him giving and me taking. I could do that, right?

"These last three days have been a little intense," I said. "I didn't know what to expect when I got on the plane to come here, but never in a million years did I expect to meet you. A lot of things have run through my mind, and if I'm being completely honest, I'm still reeling from all of it. But the one constant in everything has been you and the way I feel around you. It started when I met you and it's only gotten stronger."

His fingers closed around my hand. "So what are you saying?"

"I'm saying I want to believe you when you say you're the guy. I want to see if you are who I want you so badly to be."

A smile started to form on his lips. "Sounds like you're willing to give me that chance?"

I nodded, feeling more vulnerable than I had in a long time. "Don't make me sorry I did."

"You won't be, Kez. I promise."

After dinner, Jackson held me in front of him as we waited for an Uber. I was snug in his embrace, a little buzzed from the wine we'd shared, and just the right amount of full from our meal. He rested his chin on the crown of my head, absently running his fingers over my upper arms.

Our ride arrived, and Jackson opened the door for me. I slid across the back seat and watched him contort over six feet of well-built man into the compact sedan. "Evening," he said to the driver, earning him a mumble in response that *could* have been a hello. Jackson asked me, "Feel up for a little adventure?"

The kind of adventure I had in mind involved Jackson naked and an imaginative use of body oils. Since I didn't want to risk ruining his Uber rating with an X-rated suggestion, I simply said, "Sure. What'd you have in mind?"

Rather than answering me, he told the driver, "Seventy Lighthouse Street, please."

"Lighthouse Street?" I asked.

His arm draped across the seat behind me. "Yep." I knew from prior experience he wouldn't give any details until he was ready, so I didn't ask, even though I wanted to.

Maybe fifteen minutes later, the car stopped in front of three concrete pillars. A brick walkway illuminated by light posts made to resemble gas lanterns extended from the end of the road to a two-story, red brick house. Its windows were bordered by black shutters, some of which were closed. The river was to our right, and there was a lighthouse directly in front of us. The gleaming white of its curved exterior rose austerely next to the small, brick home.

"Thanks, man," Jackson said as he exited the car, holding a hand back inside to help me out.

Once we were alone on the sidewalk, I asked, "Um, what are we doing?"

Tweaking the tip of my nose, he said, "If I told you, it'd ruin the surprise."

I followed him up the short pathway to the front door of the house. We passed a grouping of benches and flower beds, with some determined late-summer blooms still holding on. A lighted informational placard declared we were at the Charlotte-Genesee Lighthouse. I couldn't believe it would be open this late.

The door opened in response to Jackson's two sharp raps. A gnome-like man poked his head out, frowning, but when he saw who it was, his face split open with a smile. "Jenkins!" he cried. "What the devil are you doing here?"

"Hey, Harvey," Jackson replied. "I'm in town for the reunion and," he brought me up beside him, "I was hoping to give my girl here a private tour of the lighthouse."

Harvey's rheumy visage turned toward me. "A private tour, huh?" He waggled his shaggy brows, and I blushed. Chuckling, he adjusted the suspenders holding up his ancient trousers. "You know that's against the rules."

Jackson gave his best choir-boy grin, one I was sure had gotten him out of trouble while simultaneously making some unsuspecting girl's inhibitions vanish into thin air. "C'mon, Harvey," he cajoled. "Just this once?"

Harvey poked a gnarled finger into Jackson's abdomen. "I'm messing with you, Jenkins." Taking a key ring off a hook to the left of the door, he handed it to Jackson. "Make sure you get these back to me."

Jackson saluted. "Yes, sir." Once Harvey closed the door, we walked back down the path and over to the base of the lighthouse.

As he put the key in the lock, I said, "Wanna clue me in here?"

The key turned, and the heavy door swung open on quiet hinges. Jackson went inside and turned on the lights. I peered in through the open door. There was a worn brick floor with an old wooden bench built into the far side of the wall. Rising in front of me was a winding set of black wrought-iron stairs, with a rope bannister bolted into the curve of the wall. Jackson leaned against the pole at the base of the staircase, looking entirely too sexy. All of a sudden, it was like we were back in high school and I'd snuck off to get frisky with the captain of the football team. I stepped inside the small space. He wiggled his fingers in a come-hither move, and I obeyed. His hands came to the curve of my waist.

"I volunteered here in high school," he said by way of explanation.

"I didn't see that on your name tag the other night."

He pinched my side and I yelped. "Smart-ass," he said.

"Who's Harvey?" I asked.

Unhooking the chain from the base of the stairs, he answered, "He lives on the second story of that building. First floor is a museum, and he's the curator/caretaker. I've known him since I was a kid." His foot landed on the first riser of the stairway. In the wavering light, his smile looked a little dangerous. Rae's Big Bad Wolf analogy floated through my brain and shot a naughty little quiver all the way to my toes. I was in the wolf's den, but I liked it. I looked down at my outfit, specifically my shoes. While the strappy heels had been perfect for the romantic restaurant, they weren't designed to troop up a narrow, metal staircase.

Jackson stooped down in front of me and lifted one of my feet. My hands dropped to his shoulders for balance. He undid the straps of my shoe and slid it off. Placing it on the brick floor, he ran a fingertip over the arch of my bare foot. I had no idea why that move was so sexy, but damn if it wasn't! Putting that foot down, his long fingers curled around the heel of my other shoe and picked it up, slipping off the straps and setting it next to its mate by the stairs. The floor was cool and slightly rough under my feet. Abandoning my shoes next to the newel post, I followed him up the steps.

His booted footsteps echoed off the iron treads of the winding staircase until we emerged into the cramped lantern room. The platform that encircled the large brass beacon in the center of the room was barely wide enough for two people to stand shoulder to shoulder. Probably no more than four or five people could fit in here at a time. Windows ringed the space around us, and I saw the marina below with boats bobbing in the current of the river.

I went over to the windows facing the water. With his hands on the sill in front of me, Jackson stood at my back. Being up here with him all alone felt illicit and forbidden, which, technically, I guess it was. I melted back into him, soaking up the warmth from his body.

"What do you think?" His question feathered across the shell of my ear, stirring a few errant strands of my hair.

"I think you've got quite the seduction scene going on, Mr. Jenkins. Makes me wonder how many poor little high school girls got coaxed out of their clothes up here."

I felt as much as heard him laugh. "You're saying there's a chance for me to get you out of that dress?"

Categorizing it as a mere chance was a joke at this point. I spun in his arms, the thin material of my green wrap dress swishing against my legs. One by one, I undid the three big buttons down the front of my black coat and shimmied out of it. I draped it over Jackson's forearm. Without taking his eyes from me, he hung it over the railing behind him. Following my lead, he unzipped his vest and laid it on top of my coat.

"Know what happens if I pull this?" I asked, playing with the sash of my dress. His eyes, now glued to the small strip of fabric, burned with desire. "This little bow is the only thing holding all this," I trailed a finger down the front of my dress, "together."

"Is that right?"

I nodded, still toying with the tie at my waist. "Yep. One little tug and it all comes undone."

Jackson rocked forward on the balls of his feet. His words were a soft rumble in the small space. "It's not the only thing about to come undone."

My fingers closed around one end of the bow and pulled. The neckline of my dress dipped, then opened completely to reveal a black lace bra. Jackson's eyes sparked, and his hands flexed at his sides. As I stepped closer to him, the rest of the dress fell open. His hot blue gaze traveled down the length of my body. The matching lace G-string broke his last remaining bit of resolve, and he crushed me against him. His kisses were desperate and hungry, like my lips were his last meal. I couldn't stop the moan that sounded low in my throat.

He pulled back, sucking in several breaths. "Jesus Christ, Kez." My hands fell to the hem of his sweater and pulled it upward, but he stopped me. "I didn't bring you up here to …" He broke off when I slipped from his grasp and ran a hand under his shirt.

I felt the sharp lines of his stomach under my fingers and bit my lip. "So, you don't want to …"

"No man in his right mind looking at you right now would say they didn't want to." Glancing around the tiny room, he gave a frustrated sigh. "I don't think there's anywhere up here for that to happen."

"Oh," I said sweetly. "I don't know about that." I shimmied out of my dress, then slid the straps of my bra down and undid the hooks in the back, letting it fall to the floor in front of me. Jackson's pupils dilated as he took in the sight of me standing before him in nothing but a tiny scrap of black lace. "Seems like this spot should work just fine."

⁂

"And that ladies," I said the next morning. "is how you get it on in a lighthouse."

I'd met Rae and V for breakfast that morning. After our tryst in the lighthouse, Jackson made good on his promise from the day before and rented a room in the hotel. He and I christened every flat surface, and some vertical ones, that were available. I hadn't had this much sex, judging by quantity *or* quality, in, well, ever. It was glorious, and I was in no mood for it to stop.

Rae let loose an appreciative whistle. "Damn, girl. That is hot as hell."

I shifted in my seat as I remembered *just* how hot it had been. My little striptease unleashed something primal inside Jackson. I rubbed my abraded palm, left over from the scrape of the brick against my hands as he'd taken what he wanted and given me what I needed. I'd needed it so badly that I was quite vocal. So vocal that Jackson had put a hand over my mouth to muffle the sound. Now *that* had been hot. Not to mention the weight of him stretching over me from behind. His beard chafing against my shoulder as he'd sucked on my neck. Holy shit, it was hot all of a sudden. I took a drink, trying to cool down.

"I can't believe you did that right in front of a window," V said, scandalized. "What if someone saw you?" I couldn't tell if her awe at my sexual escapades was good or bad.

"Not what was at the forefront of my mind at the time, V."

She blushed. "Well, I guess not. And it *does* sound super sexy." Leaning more in the direction of good, then.

"There you go," said Rae proudly. "Proof that Dave is exactly what you need."

"What do you mean?" V asked.

"Pre-Dave, you would never have admitted getting bent over in the top of a lighthouse is sexy. He's good for you, girl." She gave V a congratulatory slap on the back.

"Oh, shut up," V giggled.

I topped off Rae's mimosa. "So we're all flying out after lunch, right?" I'd booked Rae and myself on a 2:00 p.m. flight, but V had said she'd book her own ticket.

V's laugh died on her lips and she frowned. "Yeah, I guess."

Rae and I exchanged a knowing look. "I'm guessing you've gotten over your geographical issues, or whatever was holding you back?" I asked.

She twisted her glass by its stem. "I don't know. I mean, I really like him, but ..." Rather than finish her sentence, she looked at us with a hopeless expression.

Rae reached out and squeezed her hand. "V, if you really like him, then don't you owe it to yourself to see where it goes? So what if he's not a Fortune 500 or even Fortune 5,000 guy? He makes you laugh, and the sex is great. That counts for a whole lot more than what's in his bank account. Plus, you're successful enough on your own that you don't need to worry about what a guy does for a living. You've got your own shit, girl. You just need someone to help you enjoy it."

V huffed. "I know that. And I don't care about the bank account. We're just so different."

"Are you, though?" asked Rae. "Seems to me if the two of you were that different, it wouldn't be so easy for you to be with him. Maybe you're more alike in the things that matter than you realize."

"I guess," V said, but she didn't look convinced. "But he lives *here*."

"Um, did you miss the part where we took this thing called a *plane* to get up here?" I asked. "You know, they have more than one of those, and I have it on good authority they come this way on a regular basis. Pretty sure they also have flights *to* North Carolina as well."

She speared a wedge of cantaloupe off my plate. "I know."

"Speaking of, is Jackson on our flight today?" Rae asked.

I'd just stuck a bite of eggs in my mouth, so I signaled for her to wait as I chewed. After a swallow of mimosa, I said, "No, he's driving back because he has to haul some furniture down to his place. He's staying up here through the end of this week and driving back Saturday morning."

"And in your bed by Saturday night?" she joked.

"From your lips to God's ears," I said, crunching into a piece of bacon. "Seriously, though, I'm sure things have been hopping in my absence, so it will be good for me to get back to the office and start on the pile of work that awaits me."

"Same here," Rae said. "I have to get back to keep an eye on my minions." When V remained quiet, Rae asked, "V?"

She sighed and said, "You sure y'all won't be mad if I stay another night? I cleared my schedule through tomorrow, so ..."

"Mad?" I asked. "Why in the world would we be anything other than happy for you, honey? Stay up here as long as you're able if that's what you want to do." Rae and I each grabbed one of her hands in reassurance.

V brightened and said, "Okay, then I'll take you girls to the airport today and fly out tomorrow."

I tossed my napkin onto the table. "Well, if we're leaving this afternoon, then I need to get up to the room and somehow cram all of my crap back into my bags. I didn't even buy anything while we were here, but I swear my clothes multiplied in that closet."

V grabbed her purse. "I can come back with you and help."

Directing her back into her seat, I said, "No, don't worry about it. Finish your breakfast. I'll be fine."

Hurrying to the elevator, I let my mind wander over the events of the weekend. I'd gotten what I needed to close the door on Miller. Then, as if the universe were making up for all the bullshit I'd lived through with him, Jackson had been dropped into my lap as some sort of cosmic apology. So far, he couldn't be more perfect if I'd ordered directly from Boyfriend.com. I was so lost in my own musings, I didn't notice I was no longer alone in front of the elevator. "Hey, Kez."

Startled, I turned and saw Callie beside me. "Hey, Callie. Um, what are you doing here?"

Her blonde hair was in a tiny ponytail, and she was dressed casually in leggings and an oversize sweatshirt. She wore minimal makeup and carried a large tote bag. Her fingers twined in its straps. "I needed to get out of my house for a few days."

My scalp prickled with an uneasy feeling. "Any particular reason?"

She held up a room key with her left hand, which was now sans engagement ring. "Yes. Miller and I broke up."

Chapter 21

If nothing else, this trip had given me some of the more memorable elevator rides of my life. Callie and I stood side by side in awkward silence. The only sound was her occasional sniffle as she dabbed at her eyes with a tattered tissue. The fragility of her expression would've pierced even the coldest of hearts.

At the *ding* for my floor, I said, "Um, would you like to …" I feebly motioned to the hallway in a lame attempt to signal I was willing to lend a sympathetic ear.

Her watery smile was pitiful. "Are you sure?"

"Not in the least, but that seems to be a running theme for this weekend." With a weak laugh she followed me out of the elevator and to my suite. I dropped my purse onto the counter of the kitchenette. "Can I get you something to drink? Water? Soda? A shot of whiskey?"

She twisted the handle of her bag, seemingly unsure of whether to venture any farther into the room. I knew the pain she was going through, so I didn't rush her. Her indecision was obvious, but eventually the side telling her to stay won out, and she walked up to the counter.

"A water would be great, if it's no trouble."

I pulled two bottles from the small fridge and passed one to her. Uncapping it, she took a long drink, then crossed to the sofa. Our positions mirrored those we'd occupied Friday night, which now seemed like a lifetime ago.

"I don't want you to take this the wrong way, but wasn't there somewhere other than a hotel for you to go? Your parents or a girlfriend?" I asked, knowing how long I'd depended on my family and friends after Miller and I broke up.

Her refusal was so firm, it shook loose a few strands of hair from her ponytail. "No," she said emphatically. "I haven't told anyone about the breakup yet. I'm too humiliated and not ready to face them. But I can't stay in the house with Miller either. So, I booked a room here for a few nights. The friend I told you about got me a discounted rate."

My heart went out to the girl since she was in a place where she had no one to confide in—except, apparently, me. The absurdity of that did not escape my notice.

Callie rolled the bottle between her hands. "It feels weird, you know?"

My own bottle halted halfway to my lips. "What's that?"

She peeled the corner of the label. "That it's really over."

I put down my water and toed off my shoes. "So what happened?"

With a long sigh, she rested her head against the back of the couch and closed her eyes. "I got tired of finishing second."

It seemed like things were about to become more uncomfortable, if that were possible.

Without opening her eyes, she said, "I've been the third wheel in our relationship the entire time. Even without being *here*, you were always *there*."

I gathered my hair on top of my head, then let it fall in a nervous fidget. "Well, I ..." I stopped because I had nothing to say that would make her feel any better.

She rubbed a hand over her face. "Deep down, even when he asked me to marry him, I knew there was a part of him that would always be with you. I convinced myself it was a small part, when it was the opposite. I was the one who held a sliver of his heart and the rest still belonged to you." Her eyes opened into a vacant stare. "So I left him."

"Did he tell you that, Callie? Or are you making assumptions?"

With a humorless laugh, she said, "He's told me that every time he's looked at you this weekend."

An unsettling thought occurred to me. "Callie, does he *know* the two of you have broken up?"

She looked at her watch. "He should've found the ring and the note by now."

My eyes widened. "You just left the ring?"

"And a note," she said.

"A note," I parroted.

She nodded. "Yeah, I didn't think there was much point in having the same conversation one more time."

The bad feeling from the lobby started to grow stronger. "You didn't happen to tell him where you'd be in that note, did you?" Round three with Miller was not on my to-do list for the day. We'd said what needed to be said the night before. Plus, I wasn't anxious for him and Jackson to have yet another opportunity to get into it.

"Well, I might have mentioned that I was getting a hotel room …"

Trying to relax, I told myself the odds that he'd come look for her here were—A pounding on the door interrupted my thoughts. I mentally crossed my fingers, hoping against hope I was wrong about who was on the other side of the door. One glance through the peephole proved luck wasn't on my side. I opened the door. "Miller, what brings you by?"

He pushed past me. "Is she here?"

"By all means, please, come in," I said.

His eyes locked onto Callie. She stood up, eyes darting around for an escape route. He held up a crumpled piece of paper. "A note, Callie? Seriously?"

Callie's lips moved, but no sound came out.

I moved to stand between them. "Miller, you need to calm down. How did you know she was here?"

Ice blue eyes jumped to me, then back to her. He shook the note in my face. "I knew when she said she was getting a room it'd be here because of the friend discount. Only when I got here, she wasn't in *her* room. She'd come to you once before, so I figured she might have again. The front desk girl is the sister of one of my players, so I got your room number from her."

Kristi, you little traitor, I thought uncharitably.

He dropped the piece of paper onto the coffee table and his ass into the chair behind him.

Callie watched him without moving. "What are you doing here, Miller?" she asked.

His chin was covered in light stubble, and his eyes were slightly bloodshot. Dressed in the same clothes he'd had on last night, he looked hungover and miserable. Callie edged cautiously closer to him while I moved closer to the minibar. Moments passed as the two of them looked at each other. I prayed the floor would swallow me up so I wasn't a witness to my ex and his possibly soon-to-be-ex doing whatever it was they were about to do. He took her hand, and she smiled hopefully. He looked from her to me and then back to her. Her smile wavered, and she tried to pull her hand away, but he captured her fingers.

"I'll give you two some privacy," I said and headed toward the bedroom.

"No," said Miller, and I stopped. "You're as big a part of this discussion as either Callie or I am, so there's no need for you to leave."

Other than my own sanity? I thought but resumed my position next to the booze.

Miller spoke to Callie. "Callie, I know I haven't given you the answers you wanted every time you've asked me about Kez." She flinched like his admission physically hurt. "I couldn't give you those answers because, in all honesty, I didn't have them. When you'd ask me if I still loved her, I knew the truth would only hurt you. And I didn't want that."

Dear Lord, why was this happening, and more importantly, why did I not have a drink?

Miller went on. "How was I supposed to tell my girlfriend and then my fiancée that I loved another woman?"

Callie crossed her arms, closing herself off from the incoming heartache. Her tone was harsh when she asked, "You came over here to tell me *that*?"

He had the good sense to look abashed and said, "I talked to Kez last night …"

Callie's head whipped toward me. I would've objected, but Miller beat me to it.

"Not like that, Cal," he said tenderly. "She told me to get my head on straight before I screwed things up with you. And instead of listening to her, I almost got into a fight with Jackson." Her eyebrows shot up. I poured a generous amount of bourbon into a glass. Hell, it was close enough to noon, and it didn't look like these two were leaving any time soon.

"After her friend Rae punched me," he said, and Callie's eyes rounded so far I wondered if they might pop out of her head. "Kez left without so much as a glance in my direction. Watching her walk away, I knew it didn't matter if a part of me still loved her because there was *no* part of her that felt the same way about me."

He took both of Callie's hands in his and leaned toward her. "I also knew I wasn't being fair to you by holding on to her. Callie, you've been everything any man could ever want in a woman. You're beautiful, thoughtful, and you gave all of yourself to making our relationship work. You deserve someone who's going to do the same for you."

"But that someone isn't you, is it?" she asked, choking up.

Miller looked pained when he admitted, "I'd like it to be, Cal. I would, and maybe it can be. But right now, I can't be the man you deserve."

Tears spilled onto her cheeks. She dashed at her face with the backs of her hands. "I can't wait for you, Miller. I won't put myself through that."

"I can't ask you to, Cal. Even I'm not that big of an asshole," Miller said with a sad smile. "I know what I'm risking, and it's on me if I miss out on a life with you. But life with me won't be what you want until I've gotten my head where it should be."

"Well, I guess that's that," Callie said. On wobbly legs, she stood, grabbed her bag, and walked out the door without a backward glance. The lock clicked behind her.

I was left alone with Miller.

"How stupid are you?" I asked, taking a slug of the bourbon.

He blanched. "What?"

"I said, 'How stupid are you?' " I repeated, glaring at him. "That girl who just left is hopelessly in love with you despite the fact you are a self-absorbed jackass!" I stabbed a finger toward the door. "You need to go after her, Miller."

"But I ..."

I interrupted him, my anger at his consistent failure to own up to his mistakes coming to a head. "Or don't. Honestly, I don't give a shit what you do. You can continue to give it your all in screwing up your life, if you should so choose, but I'm done being dragged into whatever dysfunction you've got going on. What we had is over and has been for a long time. I just hate it took me this long to see it."

"Kez, I need to ..."

I cut him off, fed up with his bullshit excuses. "The only thing you need to do, Miller, is leave. What happens once you walk out of this hotel room is totally up to you, but you need to get out. Now." The finality in my voice brooked no argument, and he stood up. Trying to ensure his departure, I abandoned my drink and walked over to the door. He followed but stopped short. "Sorry," he said and walked back to the living room.

My hand was on the door, ready to usher him out. "What are you doing?" I asked as I turned the knob.

"Hang on a sec," he called back to me.

With a frustrated sigh, I wrenched open the door. Jackson stood on the other side, his hand raised to knock.

Oh crap, I thought as my stomach dropped to my shoes.

"Hey, gorgeous," Jackson said, stepping into the room. "Is something wrong?"

"Sorry, Kez, I forgot the …" Miller's voice tapered off.

A myriad of emotions flashed over Jackson's face. Shock was replaced by hurt, which quickly changed to rage as he took in Miller standing behind me. "I texted you I was stopping by. I guess you didn't get it," Jackson said. The flat calm of his voice was worse than if he'd yelled.

Of all the times for me to leave my damn phone on silent, this had to be the worst. "No, I, um, that is … it's in my purse. On silent," I said, knowing how bad that sounded and how much worse things looked.

Jackson's eyes narrowed as he looked from me, then back to Miller. "On silent," he said in the same monotone.

"Yeah," I said. "But, it's not … I mean, we weren't …"

Miller jumped in and said, "Easy man, Kez is right. Things are cool. I was just leaving."

"Cool?" Jackson's question was a low growl. "No, Miller, things are definitely not *cool*."

Miller tried again. "Look, I get how, with our history, you might take things the wrong way, but I'm telling you, this is nothing like that. Trust me."

Lightning quick, Jackson slammed Miller against the wall, jamming a forearm into his throat. "Trust you?" Jackson's laugh was a harsh rasp. "Why in the hell would I trust you with anything, Miller? You've been trying to get next to her this whole weekend." His eyes were cold when he looked back to me. "Guess you finally got what you wanted."

The sting of his accusation made my breath catch, but I was more worried about Miller's choked gurgle as he clutched Jackson's arm, struggling to breathe.

"Jackson, stop!" I shouted, rushing toward them.

He didn't loosen his hold on Miller. I grabbed at his elbow, trying to pull him off. "Jackson, please stop!"

Finally, Jackson dropped his arm, and Miller doubled over, clutching his throat and gasping for air.

"Are you all right?" I asked, temporarily ignoring Jackson's raging-bull energy a few steps away.

"I'm fine," Miller wheezed with a furtive glance at Jackson. I helped him stand up straight and walk toward the door. He paused before leaving. "Are you sure I should …"

"Just go, Miller," I said and opened the door.

When the door shut behind him, I turned back to face Jackson. Anger rolled off him. This wasn't good. "Sorry for the interruption," he said in a cold voice. "Maybe you should've put up the Do Not Disturb sign."

My heart stopped at the ice in his tone. "It wasn't what it looked like."

His laugh sliced through me. "Oh, c'mon, Kez. A smart girl like you can do better than that."

"Jax, please, let me explain," I said, clutching his forearm.

He shook me off, "I don't need you to explain what I saw with my own eyes, Kez."

"Jackson, it's not like that at all. He only came up here to …"

He cut me off. "I know what he came up here to do, Kez." His eyes were cruel when he asked, "Was it just like old times?"

It would've hurt less if he'd slapped me. But I knew there had to be a bit of déjà vu for him, so I choked back my own hurt, swallowed my pride along with it and tried to be a little understanding.

"Jax, don't. Don't take what we had and trivialize it."

"I'm not the one in a hotel room with their ex, Kez. So you tell me who's trivializing what here," he shot back.

"Do you really believe that's what happened?" I asked. "That I'm just like Amy? I'll hop from your bed into his within the span of a few hours?"

When he didn't answer or apologize, my whole body went cold and numb. Even with everything we'd talked about, everything we'd shared over the past few days, Jackson was ready to toss me into the tramp heap with the little witch who'd cheated on him in high school. There was being understanding and then there was being a doormat. In that moment, I wasn't willing to be either one. Screw him. I didn't need his hypocritical bullshit. I brushed past him and jerked open the door. "Get. The. Fuck. Out."

Jackson didn't move.

"I said get out!"

"Kez, wait a second ..." His voice lacked the spitefulness from a moment ago, and his eyes were no longer dark with anger. He may have been rethinking what he'd said, but it was too late. The damage had been done.

"For what?" I snapped. "So you can come right out and call me a whore or just throw some more veiled insults my way? I don't think so, Jackson."

He reached for me. "Kez, hold on ..."

I twisted away from him. "I'm not going to stand here and let you take a shit on my character. I haven't done anything to deserve your suspicion, Jackson. From the moment we met, I've been nothing but honest with you about everything. I didn't need to sleep with you to get to Miller. If I'd wanted him, he would've been in my bed the night of the reunion, but he wasn't." I slapped the center of his chest. "You were. You were there that night and every night since, which apparently meant a great deal more to me than you. So do us both a favor and get out!"

His jaw clenched, and he set his lips in a firm line. For a second, I didn't think he was going to leave. We glared silently at each other, which I'm sure would have seemed bizarre to anyone walking by. I had a death grip on the doorknob, and he looked like he wanted to shake me until my teeth rattled. It was a standoff that would rival the one at the O.K. Corral.

Jackson dragged a hand over his face with a disgusted sound and a few muttered curses. He walked out the open door and looked back to me. "This isn't over, Kez."

"Oh yes it is," I replied and shut the door in his face.

Chapter 22

I dialed Rae and she answered on the first ring. "What is going on?" she yelled into my ear. "Jackson just stormed out of here like a bat out of hell."

"Come up to the room, and I'll fill you in. But make sure V is with you. I'm only telling this story once," I said in a shaky voice. I hung up without waiting for a response. A few minutes later, they found me in the bedroom, packing. No one said anything. They watched me weave a frenetic path around the room, haphazardly tossing toiletries, shoes, and clothes into my suitcase.

After my third circuit around the room, Rae asked, "What changed between you getting busy in a lighthouse twelve hours ago and now?"

When I didn't answer, V stepped in my way, forcing me to stop. "What happened, Kez?" she asked delicately.

Fighting back tears, I ran them through what had happened with Callie and Miller and the altercation between Miller and Jackson, ending with what he'd said to me. While I talked, my simmering anger at Jackson bubbled over. "All his talk about relationships and him being the right guy was just that: talk."

When I sputtered to a stop, Rae asked, "So ... that's it? You're just going to bail?"

"Seems like *he's* the one that did that, not me," I snapped.

"Oh my God, Kez!" she exclaimed. "Get over yourself already. So he was an asshole in the middle of your first fight. That doesn't negate the fact the guy is crazy about you. If you'd talk to him, you two could work this out. Now is not the time to shut him out."

"I think it's exactly that time," I retorted. "He called me a whore, Rae."

With her hands on my shoulders, she said calmly, "What he said was messed up. But an even bigger screwup is casting him aside for one stupid remark we both know he didn't mean. And technically didn't make."

I wasn't interested in technicalities. I tried to get around her, but she was entrenched. "Aren't you supposed to be on my side?" I asked.

Her green eyes flashed. "I am, dummy! And that's why I'm telling you to shelve your pride and give him a real chance to apologize. Call the man and work this shit out."

"Rae," I said.

"No, Kez. Shut up and listen to me. I've watched you go from one guy to the next, never letting any of them get close because you were scared of what could happen if you did. I didn't say anything since I didn't think any of those guys could ever amount to anything other than a nice distraction and a few good screws. And who would I have been to stand in the way of that? But I'm telling you, Jackson is the real deal. Please, please, please don't turn tail and run. Give this a chance. Give him a chance. You *both* deserve it."

"Are you done?" I asked, crossing my arms.

She cocked an eyebrow. "Depends. Did you listen to what I said?"

"I heard you, Rae," I said.

"Are you going to take my advice and talk to him?" She stood in front of me, hands on her hips. The air between us was charged with tension.

"No," I shouldered her aside.

Rae threw up her hands and said to V, "You're it, I'm getting nowhere with her."

V held out my phone. "At least call him, Kez."

I shook my head, going back to the closet to get more clothes. "I've got nothing to say to him."

"You're using this as an excuse, Kez," Rae said contemptuously.

"Seems like a legitimate reason rather than an excuse," I fired back.

She groaned. "You're impossible."

My phone rang, showing Jackson's number.

V held it out to me once more. "Answer it."

"No," I said petulantly.

"For the love of God, Kez, answer the phone!" yelled V.

I took the phone, hit decline, and then turned it off. The two of them stared at me openmouthed. "What?" I snapped.

"Unbelievable," grumbled Rae. She headed to her room. "I'm going to pack."

V looked at me. "Are you sure about this, Kez?"

I didn't miss the irony that she'd asked me the same question at the beginning of this trip for totally different reasons. The truth was I wasn't sure about anything right then, other than I needed to get the hell out of New York. I flipped my suitcase closed and zipped it with a finality that I didn't feel. "I'm sure, V."

I kept my phone off the entire ride to the airport. V was quiet as she drove. Rae made a point of not speaking to me, choosing to spend the time maniacally typing out texts and muttering to herself.

V pulled over to the curb under the Departures sign. With a concerned look on her face, she said, "I still think you should talk to him before you leave."

"Not happening," I said. I leaned across to hug her and got out of the car. Rae shut her door and summoned a skycap to get our luggage.

"You know, if you don't talk to me, this is going to be a very long flight," I said to her.

Lowering her sunglasses, she asked, "Are you going to admit to being a stubborn moron and talk to Jackson?"

I hefted my carry-on. "Maybe it's best if you and I don't talk."

She swanned past me. "Fine by me," she said airily.

I mumbled a few choice words but followed her into the terminal.

At our gate, Rae plunked down into an end seat, putting her purse and carry-on in the seat next to her.

"Seriously?" I asked.

Smiling sweetly, she put in her earbuds and ignored me. Her phone rang a few minutes later, and she wandered off to take the call, leaving me no choice but to sit with our bags. I considered turning my phone on but decided against it. I wasn't ready to deal with Jackson and the smarmy things he'd implied. What was it he'd said before I left his grandmother's? Fight for this, not against it. What was there to fight for when he was so willing to believe the worst? Screw him and his stupid romantic bullshit.

My rational mind tried to horn in on my pity party to remind me that it was technically the *third* time Jackson had walked in on me with Miller. That it wasn't the first time Miller had tried to take his girl. That the last time, he'd succeeded. Maybe Jackson had a right to be upset. Yeah, he'd taken it too far, but who hadn't during an argument? I couldn't get the image of Jackson's face when he'd seen me with Miller out of my head. He'd looked … devastated. I took my phone out. Maybe I should call him or at least see if he'd left a voicemail. But then what? Deciding to rely on my old instinct of avoidance, I left my phone off and dropped it back into my purse.

Rae returned to our seats, carrying a plastic bag. From its depths, she produced a package of peanut M&M's and handed them to me.

"Thanks," I said.

With a shrug, she pulled her own candy from the bag. "You know I love you, right?"

Tearing open the chocolate, I nodded.

She went on. "I wouldn't be your best friend if I didn't tell you when I thought you were being a dumbass."

Shaking candy into my hand, I said, "I know, Rae."

"Well, for the record, counselor, I think you're being a huge dumbass and are risking losing something good because of your own stubborn pride."

Crunching on the chocolate-covered peanuts, I said nothing, so she kept going.

"Coming up here was nuts, there's no question. What's even crazier, though, is that you got the answers you were looking for from Miller." She flexed the hand she'd used to punch him, grinning widely. "I guess we all got what we wanted in that department."

I laughed, and the look she gave me was intense. "But, Kez, you have the chance at so much more with Jackson. He's a good guy, and if he didn't care about you, he wouldn't have gotten so pissed when he walked in on you with Miller." Her eyes bored into mine. "For the third time, I might add. You owe it to him, and yourself, to freaking *talk to him*! Don't just run home with your tail between your legs and chalk it up as another relationship failure."

The candy stuck in my throat, and I forced it down. "I don't know if I can."

"That's bullshit and you know it," she said fervently. "We both know it's a question of whether you will, not whether you can. Jackson gives you that same feeling that Miller did once upon a time, and it scares the ever-living shit out of you. But I'm telling you, there's no reason to let one bad experience ruin your next chance at happiness. Don't hold back because you're scared. That's not the Kez that I know and love. She's the most fearless bitch on the planet."

The entire flight home, my mind ran in circles until I was exhausted. Rae's words stuck with me. Of course, she was right. I certainly had the ability to call Jackson back and work through things. And, between the look on his face before I'd shoved him out the door and the fact he'd called before I'd even left for the airport, it seemed like he already regretted how he'd handled things. The pump was primed and ready; all I had to do was grab the handle.

I wasn't sure if it made the decision harder or easier that when I'd gotten past his initial overdose of swagger to the real man underneath it, he'd seemed so perfect. He said and did all the right things and checked every box on my list of what to look for in a man. He'd been understanding about my hang-ups and seemed committed to scale any wall designed to keep him out.

All of that made me want to see where this went, to see how we would fit together. Hell, I'd even told my sister about him and had planned to let him meet the family ... eventually. It was easy to imagine flying back up with Jackson to see Betty, meet his parents, and have more family dinners. The vision of our future was much clearer than the murky fantasy I'd had of one with Miller. No, I'd developed a clear, 4K-quality picture of Jackson in my life and loved it. At least until he'd taken a big crap on it this morning.

It wasn't that I didn't understand why he was upset. I'd have been livid if I'd walked in on him with someone else. It was that, even if only for a moment, he'd believed the worst. I couldn't make that mesh with all the flowery sentiments he'd spouted to me over the past few days. Each time I thought about it, I got mad all over again. I hadn't done anything wrong and had nothing to feel bad about, yet he'd made me feel cheap and tawdry. Which in turn made me question whether he'd meant any of what he'd said or if it was all a bunch of carefully packaged bullshit.

When the plane touched down, Rae glanced over at me and groaned. "Oh hell, I know that look."

"What look?"

"In all your quick-tempered, redheaded glory, you've decided Jackson's the bad guy in all of this and you're better off without him. When you calm down, you'll see what an asshole you're being."

I got my carry-on from underneath the seat in front of me. "Drop it, Rae."

Her reply was drowned out by the captain announcing we'd arrived in Charlotte and could now use our cell phones. I still refused to turn mine on, but Rae's lit up like Christmas the minute she had service. "Who's so desperate to get in touch with you?" I asked.

Glancing down at her phone, she lifted one shoulder. "No one." Quickly, she typed in a reply to whatever mysterious texts had landed on her phone, then shoved it into her purse.

Trying to eliminate some of the tension between us, I bumped her shoulder with mine. "Is it Chris?"

Rae gagged. "God, no. That was just V, checking to make sure we'd arrived. I figured I should text her back since you've gone incommunicado." She looked at my bag, like she could see through it to my phone. "You do know you're going to have to turn it on at some point, right?"

"That point is not right now."

"Fine," she grumbled.

People around us started to get up and move off the plane. "Rae," I said quietly. "I know it's hard for you to understand where I'm coming from …"

"That's just it," she said sadly. "I know all too well where you're coming from, so I can tell you the way to deal with it is *not* by running. He's worth the fight, Kez. You should stick around and have it. Take it from me—it's better to stay and hash it out than it is to spend the rest of your life running away." She gathered her things and stood up.

"One day, Rae," I said. "I'm going to hear the story of how you got so wise in the ways of love."

She gave me a wan smile. "I'll make it a part of my toast at your wedding."

I followed her down the aisle and off the plane to baggage claim. Once we'd gotten our bags, I asked, "Wanna share an Uber?"

Her lips thinned. "You just don't want to turn on your phone to open the app."

I held my palms up. "Guilty."

"You're insufferable, you know that?" she asked, pulling out her phone and ordering a car. A text chimed, and she glanced down, delight flitting across her face.

"What?" I asked suspiciously.

She fired off a response and blanked her face. "Nothing, just glad to be home."

I studied her, trying to figure out what was going on. "You look weird."

"Gee, thanks." She turned and called over her shoulder, "C'mon, our ride's already here."

With our bags safely stowed, we hopped into the SUV idling at the curb. Rae instructed the driver to drop her first, then take me home. Her phone chimed again.

"Seriously, Rae, what is going on? Your phone has been blowing up since before we left New York."

Sparing me a sidelong glance, she typed back a reply. "What? I'm in high demand. This is not a surprise."

"We've been home less than fifteen minutes. You can't have already scheduled a booty call."

She laughed loudly. "Not exactly."

"Fine," I said, settling back into my seat. "Don't tell me."

Twenty minutes later, we pulled up to her building. She opened her door, then turned to me, her face serious. "Don't regret this weekend, Kez."

I took her hand. "I don't, Rae. Really, I don't. At the very least, I got closure with Miller."

"Closure with him is fine—just don't close yourself off completely."

Releasing her, I said, "You could write fortune cookies."

Rather than the laugh I expected, she remained serious. "I mean it, Kez."

I felt tears prick my eyes and could only nod. Her door closed, and once I was sure she'd made it inside the building, I gave the driver my address. I'd meant it when I told her I wanted to find out what was behind that Teflon facade she showed the world. There had to be something deeper there. I pondered what it could be as waning summer colors flashed outside my window.

Leaving the highway, the car wound its way toward my town house. We drove down tree-lined streets with people out walking their dogs and enjoying the cool, late-September air. A lot of folks thought this was the ideal time of year in North Carolina, when the humidity finally broke and evening temperatures hovered in the mid-seventies. Leaves remained green, but you could feel the coming change of season in the air. The robin's-egg blue of the summer sky cooled to a paler shade, with wisps of clouds swirling above. Long shadows haunted the ground as the final days of summer faded into fall.

I watched a little girl walk her dog, or rather the dog drag her down the sidewalk. She giggled and her blonde ponytail bounced between thin shoulder blades. Her parents followed along behind them, hand in hand. I felt a little twinge of longing for that in my own life—a happy little family unit taking a late-afternoon stroll. I could see myself walking beside a tall guy with dark hair and a beard, as a little redheaded girl skipped along in front of us. Quickly, I shoved the thought away. What I needed was a good, long soak, a glass, or six, of wine, and some mindless sitcom to take my thoughts off my love life, at least for a few hours.

The car rattled over the brick pavers that made up the driveway to my corner unit. After unloading my stuff, I trudged up the walkway to my house. Keying in my code to the pedestrian gate, I swung it open with a clang and hauled all my luggage inside. Leaving it on the small terrace, I pulled the gate closed, made sure it was locked, then walked up the three steps to my front door.

I'd just put my key in the lock when I heard, "Kez."

I screamed and whirled around to find Jackson sitting in one of the chairs on the far corner of my porch. I clutched my chest, waiting for my heart to restart. "Christ on a cracker! What are you doing here? You almost gave me a heart attack." I sucked in a deep breath, trying to calm down.

My heart stuttered back to life as he stood up and came toward me. I told myself it was because he'd just scared the living daylights out of me and had nothing to do with how good he looked in worn jeans and a black T-shirt. His hair was disheveled, as if he'd been sitting there raking his fingers through it. Those deep blue eyes locked onto mine, and his hand curled around my elbow. "I told you, if you ran, I'd find you."

"Even if I run right back to Miller?" I said cattily.

"I deserve that," he agreed.

I snarled, "You *deserve* a lot worse than that."

"You're right," he said.

His admission threw me. "I am?"

He nodded.

"Well ... of course I am!"

"Kez," he said. "Can we talk?"

Crossing my arms, I asked, "What the hell are you doing here?"

"I want to talk to—"

"No," I cut him off. "I mean what the hell are you doing *here*," I circled my hand to take in my front stoop, "at my house?"

A sly smile peeked through his beard, and it suddenly dawned on me what Rae's multitude of secret text messages had been about. "Rae," I sighed.

He nodded. "She called me after you sent me to voicemail that first time, told me what flight you were taking, and helped get me an earlier one so I could be here when you got home. I wanted to come to you at the hotel, but she thought this would be better."

"Rae and her freaking grand gestures," I muttered.

Jackson laughed and came closer. When I didn't push him away, he leaned down and his lips grazed my cheek, then drifted toward my ear. "I'm so sorry, gorgeous." He kissed behind my ear. "So very sorry. As soon as said it, I knew I was wrong."

My girlie bits sparked to life like electrodes and must have overridden my brain. That's the only reasonable explanation for why instead of pushing him away I let him continue to trail kisses down my neck. "Then why didn't you take it back?"

Drawing back, he ran a fingertip down the bridge of my nose. "Just because I knew it didn't mean I was ready to admit it. I was pissed, okay?" His eyes reflected what looked like a mix of regret and irritation. "Plus, I seem to remember calling you within the hour, ready, willing, and able to grovel for your forgiveness. But *someone* refused to take my call."

"I tend to ignore calls from people who call me a whore," I retorted vengefully.

Jackson groaned and tucked my head underneath his chin. "Oh, baby," he said as his hands stroked up and down my back.

I thrust my hands against his chest, making his arms fall away from me and drop to his sides. "I still haven't forgiven you." *Yes you have*, screamed my inner witch, already tearing her clothes off. I ignored her.

Inclining his chin at my door, he asked, "Can we at least go inside and talk?"

Anxiety warred with desire. Everything south of the border pleaded for me to say yes, please, *please* come inside in more ways than one. North of my belt loops was another story. My heart, duct taped and bandaged, cowered in a corner. My brain whirred with indecision, holding on to the guy I'd started to fall for while simultaneously pushing against the one who'd been so callously cruel.

He took my hand. "Just to talk, Kez. I'll leave if you want."

The solid comfort of his hand in mine made the decision for me. I unlocked the door. "Only if you carry in all of my stuff."

He made it in one trip.

I left Jackson to his own devices in the foyer while I ducked into my room to change. I needed to get the airport funk off me and take a second to center myself. I leaned against the closed door, then pulled out my cell. I dashed off a text to Rae, *"Et tu, Brute?"*

Bubbles appeared immediately. She responded, *"You're welcome, dumbass. Now go get horizontal with the man."*

I couldn't contain a snort of amusement at her advice.

I dug through my drawers, finding a set of soft, gray cashmere pants and tank with a matching pullover. I'd brought my carry-on into the bedroom with me, so I freshened up a bit. No sense looking like the backside of a camel's ass for this conversation. A dab of gloss, a dash of powder, and a spritz of perfume combined with a quick hair flip left me refreshed.

I found Jackson in the kitchen. He'd poured two glasses of wine and taken a seat at the island, looking around my home. The floor plan was open concept. The small foyer merged into the living room, furnished with a large sectional with bright throw pillows. The island separated my kitchen from the living space. His gaze moved to me, but he said nothing. I sat next to him and swiveled in my seat. He offered me one of the wide-bowled glasses.

"I think this is the point in time you begin pleading in earnest for my forgiveness," I said.

"Didn't I just do that on the porch?" he asked.

"Oh honey, that was just the opening act. I expect much more from the headliner."

He took my glass and put it on the counter. Then, he flipped my hands over and enveloped them in his, using his thumbs to trace the blue veins in my wrists. "I was an idiot."

"Encouraging start, but I need more."

Jackson lifted his eyes to mine with a shy smile. "Kez, I'm ..." He faltered and cleared his throat nervously. "What I mean to say is that ... I'm falling for you."

My heart peeked out from its hiding place, but I kept quiet.

He went on, "I'm pretty sure you already knew that. There's no other way to describe how I feel. Thoughts of you consume me. I can't breathe when I think about my life without you in it. When that door closed this morning, it gutted me."

Inching slowly out of the corner, my heart waited optimistically for him to say more.

"But regardless of the feelings I had for you, I could also feel the push/pull thoughts you'd had about us all weekend. I knew our getting together wasn't what you'd planned for, so I was worried. I wanted to make sure we were on solid ground and that you weren't too in your head about everything."

My inner witch leaned against my heart, both of them now enthralled with this story.

Jackson paused for a sip of wine. "And it seemed like every time I turned around, there was Miller. Even if he wasn't physically there, he was there in your head. Not that I blame you for that because I don't. How could I? But that didn't make it any easier for me to deal with. He was the reason you were pulling back."

"That's not ..."

"I don't mean that you wanted to be with him," Jackson corrected. "I just mean that at the heart of everything, all your hesitation and uncertainty about taking a chance on me, all that was because of him. And there was nothing I could do to change that because I couldn't erase your past with him. So, with all that swirling around, the door opened this morning and I ..."

"Saw me with Miller," I finished for him.

His eyes darkened, and he pulled away. "Yeah. And after seeing the two of you the night before ..." He broke off, his hands curling into fists. With a visible effort, he relaxed his fingers and took any heat out of his voice. "You looked like lovers, not exes."

I tried to explain "It might have looked like that, but ..."

Jackson's grin was apologetic. "I know, gorgeous, I know. Rae told me what happened when she called." He looked sheepishly at me. "*After* she cussed me out for what I'd said to you and for even thinking you'd go back to Miller. Hell, I knew it before she told me, but in that moment, it was like all my worst fears had come true. I was so mad, so hurt, so ... I don't even know what. It was like my brain couldn't process anything but the image of the two of you. It was wallpapered inside my head, and I couldn't get it out."

"That might explain why you were so angry, but what you said to me ..." He needed to see it would take more than pretty words to make up for his scathing ones.

"I know, Kez. *I know.* I should never have said anything like that to you. There aren't words to tell you how sorry I am." My anger started to fade with the depth of his remorse. Before I could say anything, he lifted me into his arms.

"What are you doing?" I screeched, my hands scrabbling against his chest.

His only response was to kiss me so soundly, it chased away anything other than the feel of his lips against mine. His tongue plundered and took, his teeth grated against my lips. I was vaguely conscious of us moving into the living room. He twisted around and dropped onto the couch, holding me against him.

"That's what I should've done, Kez," he whispered against my lips.

My eyelids fluttered. "Huh?" I asked, my lust-addled brain failing to follow what he was saying.

"Instead of talking, instead of leaving, instead of doing anything else, I should have kissed you like that. I should've remembered how it felt to have you willing and pliant in my arms, moaning my name. I should've focused on how your hair felt wrapped around my hand or how your lips tasted. If I had, I would've known what I was seeing couldn't be what was really happening. I would've known that what we had was real and you couldn't have been pretending with me. But I let doubt creep in when I should've been certain, and I'll regret that for the rest of my life." His thumb ran over my bottom lip. "I promise that won't happen again, gorgeous."

Every cell in my body wanted to believe him. "That's an awful big promise, Jax."

He rested his forehead against mine, his fingers ghosting up and down my spine. "I know."

"You shouldn't make promises you can't keep."

His lips brushed over mine in a kiss that was every bit as gentle as the other had been passionate. Caribbean blue eyes stared into mine. "I know," he repeated.

Neither of us moved for what felt like an eternity but was probably only the span of a few heartbeats. "Let me in, Kez. Let me all the way in," he said longingly.

"If I do, how do I know you'll stay?"

Jackson caressed my collarbone. His feather-light touch moved upward until he held my jaw in his hand. "Because there's nowhere I'd rather be than exactly where you are."

Oh, he was good. The face touching, the low rasp to his voice, direct eye contact—that combination wore down the last of my resistance. "Please," I said, feeling the last of my walls tumbling down in an avalanche of hope, "don't make me regret this."

I kissed him, losing myself in the press of his lips and the slide of his tongue against mine. He groaned into my mouth and shifted me in his lap so my knees came to either side of his hips. His hands slid under my jacket, and together we worked to take it off without breaking the kiss. Once my arms were free, I clung to him. The sweep of his fingers under the hem of my tank top rivaled the feel of the cashmere against my skin. Slowly, he peeled it up over my ribs. We broke apart long enough for him to get it over my head. My hair spilled in an unruly mass down my back.

Tossing my top aside, he sat back against the cushions. He tangled his hands in my hair, then spread it out, twisting strands around his fingers. "You're so beautiful, Kez."

I basked in the heat of his steamy indigo gaze. With a gentle nudge, he brought me to him, kissing under my jawline while sliding the straps of my bra off my shoulders. His lips moved over my pulse point, his tongue darting out to taste me. His hands bridged the width of my back, and I leaned back into them. Swiftly, he unhooked my bra and stripped it from my body. The fragile fabric melded with the rougher texture of his hands as it skimmed down my arms. He rubbed the lace between his thumb and forefinger. "Red," he said, giving the single word a salacious sound.

"Red," I echoed suggestively.

His smile was wolfish. "My favorite color." His eyes dropped to my breasts. "Well," he licked his lips, "one of them at least."

Angling onto my elbows, I arched my back and displayed myself to him. My reward was a rumble from deep in his throat and his eyes narrowing to predatory slits. "See something you like?" I purred.

Casting my bra aside, his hands came up my sides but stopped just below my breasts. "I see so many things I like," he said. He kissed his way up my torso, outlining shapes on my skin with his tongue. When he raised his head, his pupils were dilated. "So many things." My hands in his hair guided him toward my breasts. He nuzzled into one, the scruff of his beard tickling my heated skin. It was like I was on fire from the inside. My body ached for his touch.

His hands slid down my back and cupped my ass. He stood, cradling me against him as my legs locked around his waist. Jackson strode toward my bedroom. When we reached the end of the hall, I pointed left. My back bumped against the door as we kissed. I groped for the doorknob, rejoicing when it finally twisted in my hand and the door swung open. Jackson wasted no time getting to the bed. He unwound my legs from his waist and laid me down on top of my soft, gray comforter. Quickly he took off his shoes and socks and joined me.

"Why are you always wearing so many clothes?" I asked as I pulled up his T-shirt.

Yanking it up over his head, he said, "I think your neighbors would've called the cops if I'd been sitting on your porch naked."

Taking in the glory that was Jackson's tattooed chest and abs, I shook my head. "You don't know my neighbors." I parted my legs so he could notch himself between them. He laid soft kisses across my cheekbones while my hands strayed over his back and down the muscles of his arms.

We were chest to chest when he stopped and looked at me. My hands stilled in their exploration of his body. "What?"

His teeth shone white when a beautiful smile spread across his face, but he didn't answer me. I tickled his ribs. "What are you smiling about?"

"That you're mine," he said and kissed me.

And in that moment, I knew he was right. I was his for the taking, and as much as that thought terrified me, the thought of being without him scared me more. With his face in my hands, I returned his smile. "I'm yours," I said.

CPSIA information can be obtained
at www.ICGtesting.com
Printed in the USA
LVHW032236111021
700176LV00004B/114/J